THE BACKWARD SHADOW

Also by
LYNNE REID BANKS

★

THE L-SHAPED ROOM
AN END TO RUNNING
CHILDREN AT THE GATE

THE
BACKWARD
SHADOW

★

LYNNE REID BANKS

THE
COMPANION BOOK CLUB
LONDON AND SYDNEY

This edition, published in 1971 by
The Hamlyn Publishing Group Ltd,
is issued by arrangement with
Chatto & Windus Ltd.

Made and printed in Great Britain
for the Companion Book Club
by Odhams (Watford) Ltd.
Standard 600771385
De Luxe 60087138X

For Pat, who helped so much,
and my menfolk, who didn't.

Chapter 1

I DON'T KNOW exactly when the restlessness began. I think it must have been round about September. That would fit in with my normal pattern, wherein autumn is always the vigorous, renaissance time. Besides, the lovely novelty of David was beginning to wear off. Not that he was any the less interesting at four months than he had been in the weeks after his early birth; he grew more fascinating daily. But very young babies do have a way of just *lying* there for a lot of the time, leaving any but the most besotted mother (and I was reasonably besotted when he was awake and reacting) with a lot of thinking time on her hands.

During the first few months of David's life, I was content just to enjoy him, and life in Addy's cottage. It was such a marvellous place, full of nooks and beams and angles and little irrelevant flights of stairs, strange-shaped rooms (though none L-shaped) with uneven floors, low ceilings and wide fireplaces. I spent hours and days happily examining it in all its enchanting detail and marvelling at my ownership of it. Strangely, there was very little sadness left over from Addy. She must have been very happy in it, and even as her intentionally lonely death approached, her own natural strength and quietness of spirit must have kept her from destroying the peaceful atmosphere of her home with an overspill of disquiet or fear.

She was still in evidence everywhere—in her books, her arrangements of furniture (always for convenience and comfort, without regard to conventional taste), in her garden, and, it sometimes seemed to me when I was sitting quietly alone, in some less tangible way. Being far too down-to-earth a person to give much credence to 'that sort of thing' generally, I hesitated to confirm this to myself, but in the end I came

around irresistibly to believing that there was something of
Addy left to keep me company. How else to explain why I was
never lonely? I am far too gregarious to take kindly to living
alone in the depths of the country.

'Aren't you nervous-like, alone here at nights?' Mrs Griffiths, my bi-weekly charlady from the village, would often
ask. 'Miles from anywere—wouldn't do me, I don't mind
admitting. Ever so brave you are, or silly, one or the other.'
Her voice dropped. 'You hear about Mrs Stubbs?'

I had, many times, heard about Mrs Stubbs, who had been
strangled (or stabbed, or beaten—it varied) to death one dark
night by a demented chalk-pit worker. Only as it happened
in 1928, and as nothing, not even the War, had since disturbed
the tranquility of this remote Surrey backwater, I didn't let
the poor lady's fate disturb me overmuch—or Mrs G's
ghoulish retelling of it.

Of course I was never alone for more than a few days at a
time. Father liked to come down at week-ends, and it was
surprising how many other people could manage to get hold
of cars and make the journey to the country when they knew
that a pretty period cottage equipped with all mod cons and
feather beds, an outstandingly attractive baby with an
intriguing 'past', and, if I do say it, some rather splendid meals
were waiting at the other end. Most of them nevertheless were
full of complaints about how difficult it was to find the way,
and how their cars had suffered from the last half-mile of
rutted track. They never failed to ask how I could bear to be
stuck such miles away from civilization, or to relate gruesome
Mrs-Stubbs-like tales, the way women delight regaling their
pregnant friends with the horrid details of their own deliveries.
Furthermore, my relations—aunts and uncles on my father's
side—actually had the nerve to tut over David's head and
mutter about what a shame it was, all right while he was a
baby of course, they don't need their fathers then, but what
about later? . . . All this, while I was laying on a huge great
meal for them, and in point of fact hadn't invited them in the
first place.

However, I shut my ears to these and similar Cassandral
prophesies regarding the future. The policy of getting through
one day at a time—or even one minute, when things were

really bad—had worked admirably while David was pending, and while he was being born. It seemed fairly fruitless to fret myself to a frazzle now about how I would cope five years ahead. Besides, worry wouldn't do my milk any good. Or so I told myself as an excuse for being happy.

He really was a most wonderful baby. He had one fundamental good quality on which all the rest were built—he didn't seem to resemble his father in any particular. He didn't resemble me either, that I could detect, which also struck me as no bad thing. He was not one of those big flabby babies, but small and neat, with very dark hair and beautifully marked eyebrows, which even the doctor said was most unusual. He was remarkably self-contained, almost from birth, seldom crying except politely to call my attention to the fact that he was wet or hungry, or that he wanted a cuddle. He never made unreasonable demands on me, such as that I should stick strictly to a schedule, something I would have found a great bore as I've always loathed routine. If we were out in the woods, which we often were during the long dappled summer days, and I was doing something interesting like making a moss garden, or reading, or watching a spider, he was content to lie on his rug and stare upwards at the leaf-filtered sky until I was ready to feed him.

It was lovely to sit under the trees in the long grass with the breeze unfamiliarly touching my secret flesh through which the warm milk was drawn into David's strong little body. Nobody ever disturbed us. The birds sang and the sun shone warm and God-like on our faces. Half-naked and close to the earth, we sat together, the scents of the woods mingling with the smell of fresh milk, my function and David's clearly and simply interlocking like the function of lovers, each to solve the need of the other. Once as we sat like that the sun went in and the sky darkened, and soon a summer rain was pattering on us through the leaves. As the first cool drops fell on my breast and on the baby's little upturned face, he drew away and sneezed, and my impulse was to cover us both up and go home. But after a puzzled moment, he seemed to accustom himself to this new prickly feeling. He made anxious goldfish faces until I restored the nipple to him, whereupon he closed his eyes again in his customary bliss and went on sucking, unaware of the rain which tapped his skin and ran down my breast and into his mouth with the milk. I sheltered him in my arms and stayed where I was until he'd finished, and then carried him slowly home as usual; he laughed briefly and then slept, with the rain still gently falling on him.

So he grew, and I seemed to grow as well. At moments I felt I was growing strong and quiet inside, like Addy. I was sure all this peace, this closeness to nature, was the way to wisdom and self-knowledge. At other times I knew, with equal certainty, that it was the way to complacent cabbagehood. Here there were no problems, no decisions, nothing to face up to—just day after day of tranquillity and pleasure. It was not real life at all, just as my stay here with Addy during my pregnancy had not been real life, just time out of time, a resting space, a period of gathering-together for the plunge back into the complex of living, facing, feeling, deciding.

Here, it was too easy to believe that nothing was more natural than to bring a child into the world, that being married or not married was the merest formality which did not in any way affect the rightness of furthering nature's cycle. My visitors from 'outside', with their reminders of the world's codes, could not really touch me here. I was armed against their strictures by the strong, primitive inner conviction, reinforced each time I looked at David's healthy body, that I had done well. It was what I had felt making love to my Toby. The word 'immoral' had no meaning whatever in the face of the essential goodness of it.

Among the innumerable books on Addy's shelves was one by Ernest Hemingway in which I found these words:

'What is moral is what you feel good after. What is immoral is what you feel bad after.'

Emerging from the dazzle of finding something which so simply and exactly expressed what I felt, I thought: Nothing that parents, or the Church, or Society can say can basically affect this fundamental truth. One can even tell one*self* that one is wicked, sinful, immoral, or whatever; if one *feels good*, one doesn't believe a word of it. Yet there must be women who sleep night after night with their husbands in perfect rectitude and feel so guilty and misused afterwards that the mere fact that Society smiles on their state cannot convince them that they are anything but the most depraved and miserable of sinners.

On the same basis, no amount of rationalization can save you from a sense of sin if you *have* done something immoral, by Hemingway's definition. I suffered cruelly from it after Terry and I had conceived David so stupidly and lovelessly. I didn't suffer from it after Toby, despite everything, despite the circumstances—it felt *right*, and I felt right about David now. The trouble with this concept was, it didn't give you any real guide to living. There was no way of knowing in advance. I had thought I loved Terry; I had no idea of loving Toby. I'd known Terry for seven years (on and off); I'd known Toby a few weeks. Why was it 'immoral' with Terry and 'moral' with Toby? Why was the conception of David immoral, and yet his birth moral? Could the whole business of morality be based on nothing more stable and predictable than hindsight? Were there no workable rules, only one's fundamental instincts to go by—and at that, instincts which were only wise after the event?

All these sincere, and sometimes comforting, reflections did not cure my periodic unease. I knew the place protected me, as the L-shaped room in which I had awaited David's birth had shielded me, as much from my own pusillanimousness as from the world's censure. I knew that, however much I might arm myself with self-confidence *here*, it was all likely to crumble into enforced guilt and ruin when the full pressure of public opinion hit me amidships on my return to 'civilization'.

The obvious answer to that, of course, was—don't return at all. Surely the sensible thing was to stay here, tucked away in my own secure little niche with David for years and years until it was time for him to go to school, by which time anything might have happened. The way moral standards were turning themselves inside out there might well have been a sort of Wolfenden Committee on Bastardy which would end by recommending that illegitimacy should become a privileged condition . . . that only illegitimate sons could inherit . . . 'Bastards of the world, unite!' . . . there'd be a tremendous campaign to win public sympathy, all the great bastards of past and present would be enlisted to support the New Doctrine, namely that you couldn't be really intelligent, creative, artistic, etc., etc., unless you were born on the wrong side of the blanket.... When I caught myself indulging in these ludicrous fantasies I always pulled up short, telling myself it was essential to be serious, to appreciate the gravity of what I'd done, and that it showed an immaturity bordering on infantilism to play games with myself like this instead of brooding on my responsibilities. I would laugh the other side of my face, I told myself severely, when the time came for David to understand his situation.

But that time was not yet. The time now was for him to lie in my arms and drink my milk and listen to me talking and singing to him while growing strong and brown in the sun. The time was for me to nurture the illusion that at long last, after twenty-eight years, I was learning how to live alone.

So the future threw back only a pale shadow. It wasn't that which got under my skin, prickling and irritating like hunger as the summer began to end. I didn't know what it was—a nagging that was more than conscience, a need that was not merely for the city and for real life. It was a sort of superstition, really, left over perhaps from my theatrical days, that nothing good lasts, that it must all be paid for, and that the longer it goes on the farther the luck-pendulum will swing back in the other direction eventually. It was better, this superstition said, to keep a balance by pushing the pendulum back before it went too far, to turn your face voluntarily away from ease and pleasure, for fear the gods would force you to it later, more fiercely the longer you had let yourself relax.

But I waited. I waited for a sign. 'Let's get you safely into the fifth month,' Addy had said while I was under her wing in January. I said the same thing now to David, with a trace of Addy's own acerbity, as if it were David who was nagging at me to leave this haven. But really I was waiting—as I've always waited—for something outside to push me, to give me my direction.

I got my signs in October. They came, as they always seem to, in a cluster—three in one day.

It was one of the first real autumn days, with that faint crisp smoky smell in the air, the smell of things dying down which, perversely, always makes the sap rise in me. I pushed open the mullioned window over the sink which commanded the front path, and noticed that I could see the postman's breath, very faintly; he left footprints in the damp grass as he left the path to pass my letters through to me.

'More visitors announcin' 'emselves?' he asked, as I took the letters with one hand and passed him his accustomed cuppa with the other.

'Shouldn't think so. Summer's over; the country's not such fun in the winter.'

'Yup, in for a cold snap all right. How's the nipper?'

'Thriving, thank you.'

He nodded to me, drained the tea, and tramped away between the hedges. The sun drifted wanly down, not even strong enough to make the dew sparkle. The dahlias and big yellow daisies were hanging their still-splendid heads, as if the strength had gone out of them overnight.

I sat on a high stool by the sink and examined my letters. There were three, or rather, two and a postcard. The postcard was typewritten; it said: 'This is a tip-off. The Michelin Man will call at your establishment after closing-time tonight, disguised as a weary traveller. Give of your best, and you, too, may have a crossed knife and fork in the next *Guide*.'

It was unsigned. The style was familiar, but elusive. Dottie? Possibly. She'd just bought a car. . . . I decided to lay on a sumptuous feast just in case, and keep David up later than usual. She hadn't seen her godchild since the christening.

The first letter had a businesslike look about it which made me distrust it. But the other had the name of my bank on the envelope, which was considerably more ominous. I'd been living very cheaply, but a capital of £123 10s. doesn't last for ever unless you're actually dead, and that was all I'd amassed at the time of David's birth and my retirement to Addy's cottage. Addy's other assets, also left to me, had consisted of a few Greek Government Bonds bought impulsively years ago after a holiday there and now down to £14 in the hundred, and the rights to a book she'd written which I had edited and typed. Not a penny of actual cash—her annuity had died with her. Father would help me if I asked him, of course, but I didn't want to ask him. And I didn't want Terry's help either, though he'd begged and begged me to let him give me an allowance. I felt a bit mean for refusing; I could see it would make his conscience infinitely easier if I let him pay something . . . but that would give him rights, would sanction his paternity, and I shrank from that. David was mine. I'd earned him all by myself—or at least, with no help from Terry—and I wasn't going to let anyone horn in on him now if I could help it. I saw my fierce independence for the stubborn, unlovely thing it was, and didn't flatter myself; but I could not deny it.

I turned from the two discouraging red figures at the bottom of my bank statement to the other typewritten envelope. It had been forwarded from Fulham. I tore it open.

Dear Miss Graham,

Sorry I've been so long getting in touch with you about your aunt's book, but I wanted to wait till I had something good and definite to tell you. Now I have. As I suspected, the English publishers, always inclined to be timorous, have all shaken their money-wise old heads (some with genuine regret, I think). So I tried across the water, and halleluia! one of the New York firms has come up with an offer. It's a very good list, and your aunt can congratulate herself on landing in it with her first book. They're very enthusiastic, as you'll see by the enclosed copy of their letter. Once it comes out there, I think it'll undoubtedly find a place here too.

Will you now ask your aunt to get in touch with me direct? I don't seem to have her address. I'm simply longing to meet her. I still think it's one of the most fascinating pieces of writing that's ever come into my hands.

Yours sincerely,
Billie Lee

I fell off the high stool, and tottered to the living-room to seek something more stable to sink into. The truth was, I'd forgotten all about the tough, hard-bitten little red-headed literary agent to whom I had taken Addy's manuscript months and months ago. I remembered her now, though, clearly— small, tightly corseted, smartly dressed and coiffured, three charm-bracelets jangling on one tiny wrist and a man's watch incongruously strapped round the other. An impression of compactness, self-assurance and determination. . . . Where had I heard of her? Oh yes, from Toby. She must be his agent. . . . I read the letter again, letting my eyes slide over the final paragraph. I would think and feel about that later. After my first outburst of grief when Father told me of Addy's death, I hadn't shed one tear for her; it seemed oddly incongruous to mourn her here, where she still seemed alive. But now I was going to have to face those realizations which are a far sadder part of death than merely missing the person—those if-only-she-could-have-been-here-for-this regrets.

But first the letter from the American publisher. I was disappointed to see it was a carbon copy on commonplace flimsy, not as I had hoped the impressive original on high-quality airmail paper. The letter itself was very dignified and restrained, quite English in fact—a far cry from the sort of uninhibited New World enthusiasm I would have expected from an American firm. But a genuine excitement was apparent between the lines. Secure in the knowledge of being alone, I read it aloud to Addy's shade. I read Billie Lee's letter aloud, too. Then I put them both in my apron pocket, went out into the autumn garden, and wept.

A lovely thing about living miles from anyone else is that you can cry out loud, luxuriously. How well I understand the Irish and other women, who wail and keen over their dead! How it helps, and how much more, instinctively, you feel you are paying tribute to your dead when you don't bottle it up, but let it all come out with a lovely, mournful, anguished sound! I could imagine how Father, and my aunts and uncles and cousins, had blinked back their tears with stiff upper lips at the funeral (I was still in hospital from David), concealing their genuine grief behind impassive British façades. I imagined Addy, somewhat improbably dressed in her voluminous canvas gardening apron, so tough she could keep shears in its pocket, and her muddy Wellingtons, looking on with disappointment and contempt. As I bent now over the drooping dahlias, scattering them with un-English tears and making a noise that would not have shamed an Arab wake, I could hear her saying: 'That's more like it! I was beginning to wonder if anyone had noticed I was missing!' Suddenly the misery of wanting her sank down another fathom inside me; my legs went weak with sorrow and I found myself sitting on the wet grass, bawling, my head between my knees. . . .

Suddenly I straightened up and listened. I had competition —David was bawling, too. I rushed in to him; even by my haphazard standards, it was hours past his feeding time. I scooped him out of the wooden cradle so swiftly I left it rocking, and in two seconds the bawling had stopped—both lots. It was difficult to be unhappy with him in my arms, quite impossible while he sucked me. He tucked his near-side arm under mine, and I could feel his hand clutching my ribs in spasms of ecstasy as he drank.

I dressed him more warmly than usual (a jacket as well as a nightgown) and put him down to sleep in his pram in the garden. He didn't feel like sleeping right away, so we had a nice long stare at each other, which was good for meditation. His eyes were not going to be blue, after all—one more unlike-Terry item which I added to his mounting score of good points. His hair, practically partable already, looked rather like Kenneth Kaunda's—it gave him a perpetually startled look, even when he was asleep. Suddenly, for no good reason, he grinned at me. It was his first recognizable smile *at me*, as distinct from indiscriminate face-experiments. I straightened up from my slouched position over the pram-handle. His eyes followed me, and he grinned again. I felt like a lioness whose offspring brings her his first kill.

If only Dottie *would* come tonight! Perhaps he would do it again for her. Her reactions to such an achievement were bound to be entirely satisfying. Only it wasn't Saturday, so how could it be her? Tantalizing. I left David asleep, climbed into Addy's aged Morris, and drove into the village, where I resolutely put the two red figures on my bank statement from my mind and laid in a pot roast with every trimming I could think of, including a bottle of Châteauneuf du Pape.

While I was in the pub I put through a call to Billie Lee. It was not very easy to say what I had to say, but she was so unexpectedly good about it—sympathetic in a terse how-*damned*-awful-I-*am*-sorry way—that I didn't start crying again as I'd feared.

'Well, m'dear,' said her deep, mannish voice, 'it all devolves

16

on you, then.' She paused, and then added, 'You know, I'm not only sorry for you, losing your aunt, I'm actually jolly sorry for myself as well. I *had* so looked forward to meeting her . . . damn. What a bitch life is. Oh well, I suppose we must just do our best for her book . . . she's left something of some importance behind, at least, which is more than most of us will.'

She went on to tell me the details of the American sale. It seemed the advance royalties were something in the neighbour-hood of four hundred pounds, and even while I was glorying in relief, I was wondering for the first time whether there wasn't something rather dreadful about spending Addy's money. I felt I should keep it for her, somehow—as if she'd be needing it.

You poor eedjit, what d'you think I left it to you for? And mind you do something exciting with it, too, and don't just let it dribble away.

I put the pot roast in the oven early, and David and I spent a restless two hours waiting for the 'Michelin Man'. Finally I couldn't keep the poor child hanging on any longer, and reluctantly gave him his supper and put him to bed. I waited another two hours, unable to settle to anything, listening attentively for a car. The oven was turned down to almost off, the living-room fire had had four replenishments of pine-logs and I was getting decidedly sleepy myself, not to say hungry and a bit cross. Perhaps the card was someone's idea of a joke? Finally I could stand it no longer. I slammed down my book, stamped to the elegantly-laid table and swept one lot of cutlery back in the drawer.

Right on cue came a double knock on the door.

I'd heard no car, and there was no question of having missed it, as you could always hear them, whoomphing and protesting in bottom gear over that last half-mile of pot-holes. Even a cycle could be heard swishing through the puddles, and any light at all on the road shone through the big bow window onto the whitewashed wall opposite. I felt a marked twinge of fear, remembering poor Mrs Stubbs and her chalk-dusted assailant ('Like a proper *gole* he must've looked, dear, face and 'ands and clothes all white—but they wasn't white for long, oh no!') But there was a chain on the door, and after all, I was expecting *someone*.

I went to the door, put the chain on it, and opened it resolutely to its full six inches. Through the gap a hand, a small, strong, familiar hand, snaked in and made a strangler's gesture that was straight out of a Danziger Brothers' B picture. I looked at it, dumbly, for a moment, until that well-remembered voice said plaintively: 'Well, come on! How can I *do* you if you don't let me in?'

'Idiot, *idiot*!' I said a moment later, my face turned down against his shoulder and our arms round each other too tightly for normal breathing.

'Who's an idiot? You don't mean to stand there and tell me you didn't know who to expect?'

'How could I?'

He drew away and looked at me, the blackbird's face that wasn't like a blackbird any more wrinkling up with astonishment. 'You mean there's somebody *else* who sends stupid cryptic messages instead of just writing a sensible letter saying "I'm coming"?' he asked on a bleat.

'I thought Dottie?'

'Dottie schmottie.' He sniffed the pot-roast-scented air. 'Ah, Bisto! Let's be 'avin' it. I've walked all the way from the village.'

'But it's miles!'

'You're telling me?'

'You're mad!'

'You're telling me?'

He kissed my cheek lingeringly, and then my lips briefly, and looked at me for a moment. His wise bright eyes seemed to take in every detail, seeing my face and what lay behind it with equal ease.

'You're all right, aren't you?' he asked, softly but with some surprise. 'I thought your letters sounded almost too cheerful, but I see now you didn't lie.'

'I never lie.'

'That's fairly true, now I come to think of it.'

'It's not to my credit. I can't put a brave face on anything. If I'm miserable I show it. As you know.'

'I never did like these noble selfless women who never share anything important like misery,' he said. 'It makes a man feel left out in the cold. That's one thing you never did with me.'

He hugged me again. With each minute that passed I was sinking back deeper and deeper into my love for him. It gave me a panicky feeling. I'd been congratulating myself during the last few months on the completeness with which I had let him go, just when I needed him most—I *had* felt secretly rather noble and selfless about it, actually. I hadn't wanted to be an emotional burden to him, just when he was beginning to find his feet as a writer and as a man, so I'd waved him an apparently cheery goodbye and gone off to the country with David, leaving Toby to the rigours of his basement flat in Holland Park and his second novel. We'd written occasionally—brief, terse notes from him, ending always 'Love, Toby,' and from me gay, flippant letters which were intended to convey how well I was making out by myself and how free from responsibility he was. It hadn't been too difficult, because I *was* happy most of the time, but whenever I got his letters or sat down to write one to him I would remember with poignant clarity those extraordinary weeks of our love in the L-shaped room in Fulham, a love which had sprung on me from behind, so to speak, and then grown and deepened as naturally as roots going into the earth until he was absolutely a fundamental part of my life. At such times I would feel the stretched-elastic tension still there between us, dragging, dragging . . . and the flippancy and carelessness hadn't always gone easily onto paper.

And now here he was, his hands absently slipping up my arms under the sleeves of my cardigan, his eyes watching every tell-tale change of expression on my face. He did not have to look up or down to meet my eyes, in fact if I leant straight forward it was not his lips I kissed, but the tip of his beaky nose. I did it now, from habit, and suddenly he caught his breath and took me in his arms and we stood there in the little tiled hall, oblivious, kissing and kissing. . . .

'I didn't intend any of *this* nonsense,' he said at last, a little gasp audible in his voice. 'I just came to see you.'

'Of course.'

'And to be fed.'

'Naturally.'

'*Not* to resume intimate relations,' he said severely, like a domestic court magistrate.

'Certainly not. That's quite understood.'

We went into the living-room with our arms companionably round each other.

'How lovely and cosy it is here!' he exclaimed, looking round. 'What a difference after my place! An open fire, and comfortable armchairs. . . . Gosh, if I'd known there was all this, I'd have overcome my natural reluctance to see you and wished myself onto you ages ago.'

'Why didn't you come before?' I heard myself asking.

He grinned up at me from where he'd crouched in front of the blazing logs.

'I had nothing to show you before,' he said.

He reached into his pocket, and brought out a small book with drab paper covers.

'What's that?' I said, although I knew.

In the firelight his face was glowing, and all the shadows struck off it so that he looked about sixteen, or even younger, like a thin, beaky little boy with tousled black hair and his wrists growing out of his jacket. He held the book up to me, his lips curled up in the tight little grin of pleasure.

I'd often wondered about the novel he had been struggling to write when we were both living in that bug-run in Fulham. This, then, was it—the finished product of all those months of driving himself against the grain of his own self-confessed indolence, dredging up the wisdom that lay beneath his apparently frivolous nature, and sweating out a style which could not be traced to the despised articles from which he had earned a thin living. It felt strange, almost it gave me a sensual thrill, to hold the solid little blocks of pages in my hands, to riffle through them and see the black streaks flipping past, each streak a word written by Toby, accepted, acknowledged as worth-while and printed by other, unknown men who had set their favourable judgement on his talent.

I crouched beside him suddenly, hugged his small head in the crook of my arm, and kissed him. I was moved, for a moment, almost to tears of pleasure.

'Do you like the title?'

I hadn't looked at it, but now I did. It was *Brave Coward*.

'Ouch! No.'

He rose on his knees with a roar, 'WHAT!? Why the hell not? What's wrong with it?'

'It's awful, that's all. I hate those two-contradictory-word titles, like I hate those the-this-and-the-that ones they're always using for films.'

'The what and the what? What are you talking about?'

'The-Young-and-the-Squalid, The-Vile-and-the-Sacred, The-Bright-and-the-Brutish.'

'Never heard of them,' he said blankly, looking at me as if I'd gone mad.

'You *know* what I mean—titles like that.'

'But *Brave Coward* isn't——'

'*Toby*. Look, what does it matter? It's a very *catchy* title——'

'CATCHY!' he yelled. 'Christ! It's not a pop tune! Catchy! The publishers said it was *absolutely brilliant*.'

'It probably is. I'm probably crazy.'

'There's no bloody probably about it!'

'Okay, then.'

'Okay!'

There was a long, ill-tempered silence. He took the proof-copy away from me protectively and pretended to be glancing through it. I could almost see the steam rising from him.

'It's a marvellous title,' he mumbled at last.

'Yes, darling.'

Suddenly he turned round, flung the book aside, and with a loud snarl of frustrated fury threw himself on top of me. I found myself on my back on the hearthrug, having my head bumped against the floor.

'Toby! Let go! Get off my stomach, you're curdling my milk!'

'Funny place to keep it. Say uncle.'

'Uncle!'

'Say it's the best title in living memory!'

' "Uncle" is the best title in living memory.'

'Aaargh!'

He rose in disgust and stood over me, the book in his hand.

'You're a nice friend!' he said. 'I might as well throw the damn thing in the fire as show it to you. I suppose you'll pick holes in every blasted line!'

'I won't! I——'

'You won't, because I'm not going to show it to you!'

'Oh, darling——'

'What?'

'I half-think you mean it. You are a baby still.'

'Don't try me too far! Since you knew me, let me tell you, I've become absolutely the most adult adult I know. I'm so mature I had to shave my beard off for fear of it turning white. Is a lioness infantile because she springs to the defence of her cubs, when some crass, callow, invidious, insidious female *jackal* creeps up and tries to bite their titles off? What do you know about titles, anyway?'

'Nothing, Toby. Let's forget it.'

'You're so brilliant, what would you have called it?'

'How can I——'

'Just give me one better one. Anything.'

'*The Brave and the Cowardly.*'

He turned away, waving his arms wildly as if invoking God's aid. Then he spun round, did an elaborate windup like a baseball pitcher, and flung the book straight into the fire.

For a moment we both remained motionless, paralysed. Then, as one man, we flung ourselves forward. I grabbed the tongs, he the poker, and in a second we had raked the scorched volume out of the wood-ash. Toby sank onto the rug again, and closed his eyes. He'd actually gone pale.

'Are you completely potty?' I ventured to ask curiously.

'No. I just can't throw. I meant it to miss.'

He sank slowly down until he was lying with his head in my lap. I stroked his silky black hair and after a while he began purring softly, as of old.

'I really don't seem to have grown up much, do I?' he said humbly at last.

'No, thank God.'

'What do you mean?'

'When I saw you after that long gap—when Terry fetched you and you came to the L-shaped room, the day I had the baby, and when you came to the hospital afterwards—I could see you'd changed. You were so self-assured. I knew it was a good thing, and yet . . . I was afraid you'd got too serious, that you'd disciplined the fun out of yourself. . . .' I leaned down and kissed his mouth upside-down. He reached up to touch my face and said, 'Another thing I haven't disciplined out of myself is wanting you. You do look funny the wrong way up.'

'Let's eat, eh?'

'Good God, haven't we done that yet? I've stopped being hungry.'

'That's temper.'

'It's not.' He drew my head down again and kissed me in a special way he had which made my blood beat suddenly and almost painfully upward, like a steep musical crescendo. The effect behind my closed eyelids was as if a mountain had abruptly risen out of a calm sea, lifting me off the surface of things into a rarefied isolation, all commonplaces sinking below me into unimportance and oblivion.

I opened my eyes and looked at Toby. He was frowning deeply, as if concentrating on subduing a sharp pain. His body was utterly still. After a long moment of waiting, he looked up at me and smiled, quickly and painfully, and touched my arm as if in reassurance. He was breathing heavily.

'No,' he said. 'I don't think so.'

My first reaction was one of unmixed and bitter disappointment. 'Why not?' I cried childishly. He smiled and leaned his face against my shoulder.

'Because, my dear, my darling Jane,' he said softly, 'all it needs is that, for me to be utterly in love with you again, and you, correct me if I'm wrong, with me. And that would be less than wise.' I said nothing, feeling too desolate to speak, and after a moment he went on:

'Apart from anything else, I haven't the wherewithal to keep a wife and son. Or two. Yet.'

'What about this?' I inquired in faint voice, indicating the scorched proof.

'A hundred advance, half on sig, half on pub. The sig half's spent, the pub half's mortgaged to the hilt. Do you know how many novels are published every year? Thousands. You only make money from movie sales.'

Trying to recover from what felt like the deathblow of his

not wanting to make love to me, I said facetiously 'I can see it on the marquees now—Toby Coleman's *Brave Coward*——'

'Cohen, if you don't mind,' he said quietly. He straightened up, pushing back his tousled hair. 'And that's another thing.'

'If you *really* want to insult me, try implying that *that's* a factor.'

He looked at me, all the sparkle gone. 'It can be a factor without you knowing it,' he said.

We stared at each other. Suddenly I shook myself free of the spell of depression I was enmeshed in.

'I can't think why you're going to all this trouble to explain why you can't marry me,' I said brightly. 'I don't even remember asking you.' I saw his face soften and begin to lean helplessly towards me, and I got quickly to my feet. 'My lovely dinner, worth at least three crossed spoons and forks, is now a cinder. Go to the table and wait while I bring you your nice crunchy charcoal.' I went into the kitchen, ran the end of the roller-towel under the cold tap, and held my face in it until the water wasn't cold any more. Then I served the meal. That's the good thing about a pot-roast, it doesn't spoil with keeping, and the wine helped. Toby spent the night in the guest-room and neither of us slept a wink, and in the morning he went away again, leaving the charred novel for me to read. It was so good it hurt me. I wanted to be proud of him but as he wasn't mine, I couldn't. That was when I decided that I would have to go further than Surrey if I were really going to learn self-sufficiency.

Chapter 2

MY FATHER sat down heavily in his favourite chair.

'Jane dear,' he said seriously, 'are you going mad, or is it—it probably is—me?'

'It's me, Father,' I said calmly.

'Well, that's a relief.' He took his pipe out of his jacket pocket, on the outside of which I could see a dark-brown burn mark.

'Have you been setting yourself on fire again?' I asked severely.

'What? Oh, shut up. You're just trying to change the subject. Just a minute while I calm myself, before you burden me with the details.' He drew on his still-smouldering pipe for a few minutes, and took a mouthful of the whisky and water I'd placed discreetly at his elbow. He wasn't drinking regularly any more, but he still liked his dram, and it did him good. I always kept a bottle handy for when he came down at weekends.

'Now,' he said at last. 'What lunacy is this? Who's put this cuckoo idea into your head?'

'It just came,' I said modestly. 'I don't think it's cuckoo, I think it's very exciting.'

Strange how I could talk to him now, argue with him, listen to his point of view on things, and not ever get angry or offended. We had found a new relationship since our trouble had been resolved. It was almost as if we were two different people.

Before, it had all been quite different. A word, a breath of criticism, a chance remark about my hair-style or my choice of a new dress, and I would be apt to flounce from the room, stung to the heart by what I mentally characterized his 'constant carping'. Everything in his manner falling short of total approval seemed to me a deliberate attack on my self-esteem, a further proof that he didn't love me.

Now I was not in any doubt on this point. If he had not loved me, he would hardly have taken to drink during the time when, at his impulsive request, I was living on my own awaiting the birth of his irregular grandchild. He would hardly have treated David with all the besotted affection I had once felt deprived of, and even, as I had heard, boasted about him freely to my rather self-righteous, not to say narrow-minded, uncles and aunts. These were manifestations which, coming from a man like my father, could only have sprung from love. Now I looked at him with unreserved tenderness as he scowled disapproval at me.

'Have another drink,' I urged, unable to think of any immediately effective argument in favour of my unfeasible plan.

'Do you *want* me to die of DT's?' he asked irritably. 'I probably shall anyway, or go loopy, thinking of you in that hell-hole of a city . . . you're not really going, are you?'

'Yes, I think so.'

'But who'll look after David while you're away?'

'What do you mean?—He'll be with me.'

'What!'

'Naturally," I said, calmly.

'Now I know you're mad. Have you even begun to think it through?'

'I've begun. I didn't get very far. I never do—how can one "think through" something one's never experienced?'

'Well, as a starter, you might try imagining what it will feel like to be all by yourself in some tenement block somewhere, surrounded by Puerto Rican thugs with flick-knives. Just so you can be around when Addy's book is published. It's absolute *rubbish*,' he said, getting very heated now. 'What possible use can you be?'

'Publicity.'

'Guff,' he said shortly. 'You're not even the author. What sort of publicity can you supply? Do you think the publishers are going to ask you to jump off the Empire State Building naked into a tea-strainer or something? Stay at home and don't be so ridiculous.'

I was silent. How could I explain the feeling I had, that Addy wanted me to go—not only to keep an eye on her book (to see it, as it were, for her, in its shiny cover, displayed in New York bookshops and perhaps reviewed in New York papers), but to 'do something exciting' with the £400. How could I explain that I wanted to get away—far away from London, even from England, in an effort to escape my need for Toby? If I stayed within earshot, so to speak, one day, when I was low and my need great, I would call, and he would come, and then I would be a millstone round his neck forever. I had to get out of calling-distance. I had to learn to do without him.

Billie Lee also thought I was crazy, though I hadn't told Father this, naturally.

My resolution was becoming impossible to keep up in the face of so much discouragement. I decided there was only one thing to do—go and see Dottie.

I went to see her while I was up in London, or rather, she invited me out for the evening. I left David with Father, tarted myself up for the first time in months, and presented myself at her lovely new flat, feeling like a child going to its first party.

She flung open the door and swept me in, kissing me soundly on the way. The flat was beautiful, and I had no doubt she had done the whole thing herself, but she denied it.

'No, love, not a bit of it,' she declared, sitting me down on a luscious cinnamon velvet button-back sofa amid an array of wallflower-coloured cushions. 'It was quite marvellous what happened, actually. I had this gentleman-friend, who by a happy coincidence happened to be an interior decorator. He rather resented the fact that I wanted to do all the choosing and designing, but after several hideous rows he saw I had taste and gave in, and just did what I told him.' She sighed. 'I think he had ideas about living here himself. But unfortunately the relationship didn't survive the business partnership. Very few do, I find. What finally tore it, was that picture above the fireplace.' She pointed to a large square canvas, thickly encrusted with lime, gold, white and terracotta oilpaint. It didn't mean anything at all, but it was nonetheless very decorative and suitable to the room, which was all whites and browns and yellows, with an olive carpet and lots of copper.

'I like it,' I said.

'So do I,' she said promptly. 'I liked it the moment I set eyes on it, and so, I still believe, did he; but when he found out I'd bought it for a mere thirteen guineas at Catesby's sale, he lost all respect for it and me. I think what chiefly enraged him was that he'd been fooled into thinking it was something "good". When he used that word, I realized then, quite suddenly, he always referred to where a thing had come from. So when he found out I hadn't bought that picture at an art gallery, he flew into a furious rage and said it was a cheap piece of background decoration for mass-produced furniture and told me to take it back. I refused. And that, I fear, was that.'

'Oh Dottie, I'm sorry! Was it really serious?'

'I don't suppose it can have been—I hardly cried at all, except from temper, and when I really care I cry for weeks. Anyway, there are really only two important points arising from him—first, he did the whole flat for "cost" before his walk-out, and second, no one has come along to take his place in my life. The latter is really becoming a matter for concern, since I am not given to the solitary life, as you know.' Dottie was my age, and very like me in many ways; she had always been flamboyant and gay on the surface (one of the things I loved about her) but somehow, lately, this surface had begun to develop a steely gloss which worried me. It was too bright, too shining, too devil-may-care. Dottie cared; she had always cared. She loathed being alone, and looking round at this splendid *milieu* she had created for herself it all seemed, suddenly, like part of the shiny shell of her manner—a gay turtle-plate, designed to disguise and protect the vulnerable softness within.

'Well, and what news have you for me?' she asked, lighting a cigarette and changing the subject.

'Nothing much, except that I'm going to New York,' I threw away casually.

Dottie was an unbeatable audience for things like that. She did a genuine double-take, and gazed at me, her grey eyes wide with astonishment. 'New *York*? You? When? Why? How?'

I explained as well as one can ever explain crazy impulses, while she sat completely immobile, her attention riveted in that gratifying way she had which made her an ideal listener. Occasionally she would nod her head slightly, half in agreement, half, it seemed, in a breathless urging-on. 'Can you understand my point of view at all?' I asked finally.

'Well!' she said, relaxing and drawing on her cigarette. 'Yes. Of course. I think it's mad, but wonderful. I wish I had your——' I think she was about to say 'recklessness' or some such word, but she changed it tactfully to 'courage'.

She looked at me thoughtfully for a while as if she were thinking about something far removed from what I'd been saying, and then jumped up abruptly. 'How's about a drink? We're going to see Ibsen, whom I love, but I need a stiff gin first to appreciate him properly.'

I watched her deftly mixing things at a table in one corner of her living-room. One couldn't call her a beauty, but she had flair—her talent for decorating began with herself. She was every magazine-editor's dream of how a plain girl looks 'after' getting the full treatment, but in this field no expert had been called in to help. Dottie had done the whole thing herself.

Her hair, by nature fine mouse, had not been mouse for many years, though it was only comparatively recently that by process of elimination she had arrived at the delicate streaky blonde short coiffure she had now apparently settled for. It was a happy choice, slightly theatrical without being in the least brassy, and it suited her dark-fringed grey eyes and rather round face excellently. She was tall and slim—her one undeniable natural asset—and had taught herself to dress with elegance and individuality. This evening, for instance, she wore a straight simple dress, in a lichen-green, slightly nubbly fabric, decorated by an asymmetrical silver ornament which hung round her neck on a long strip of suède. The effect was chic and wholly original, and for my part I couldn't help feeling comparatively dowdy. I realized sadly that I had been eating too much good country food and wearing too many loose sweaters and undisciplining jeans.

She didn't mention the New York thing again until after the theatre, when we were sitting in a delightful little restaurant in Chelsea which had opened so recently that only well-known people knew about it, and the prices were still invitingly moderate. From where I was sitting, under a large Edwardian coach-lamp, I could pick out one minor and one major film star, two TV personalities, one MP and a theatre critic.

Dottie ordered what sounded like a terribly expensive meal, opening with oysters which were a passion with both of us, and then settled back. I thought she was going to discuss the play (she was very knowledgeable about the theatre, in fact I often thought that she regretted not having had a go at the stage as a career) but instead she said: 'May I ask the obvious question? How's it going?'

'Baby sans husband? Deceptively okay, so far.'

'No embarrassments? No guilty stirrings? No loneliness?'

'Oh, all of those. But nothing to get hysterical about. The worst thing is trying to anticipate how much worse it's likely to get.'

'H'm,' she said non-committally. 'And—the blackbird?'

I told her about Toby's visit to the cottage, and my feelings about it. She told me straight out I was mad. 'He loves you—you love him. He's not a poor waif or stray any more, he's on his way. Now, baby apart, I fail to see how or why you should be a millstone round his neck at this stage.'

'It isn't the right time yet,' was all I could find to say.

'And is this another reason for the New York project?' she asked astutely (I hadn't mentioned this angle on things before). I admitted it was. 'The trouble with you, Jane,' she said, 'is that you're too conscientious about these matters. You won't "play the game"—the man-getting game. You never were any good at it. Any other woman would have been married to Terry by now.' Almost before I could grimace, she hastily continued: 'Not that I think that would have been advisable, mark you. Clearly you'd have been miserable, but a lot of girls prefer safety to the joys of independence. I often wonder if I wouldn't myself.' She sighed—a faintly overdone sigh, but with a wealth of sincerity in it.

'Don't tell me you've never had any offers.'

'Oh—*offers*,' she said scathingly. 'Every female with her glands fully functioning has had *offers*—of some sort. What becomes increasingly unbearable is the dichotomy between those few you want, and those entirely "other" few who want you. They never seem to overlap at any point.'

I wondered if Dottie had ever had any affairs. I felt sure she must have, since nothing in her bearing and manner suggested the isolation of virginity. If so, they must have been disappointing—and, I suddenly realized, rather recent. There had not been this faintly world-weary smoothness about her even a year ago. The decamped interior decorator, perhaps? I was almost curious enough to ask, but Dottie was not the kind of woman who is only waiting for the right leading question to give her the chance to pour out all. If she wanted to, she would, so that the direct question would seem like the grossest inquisitiveness.

While we ate, she asked a lot about what it was like, living in the country (she was such an urbanite herself that the mere idea filled her with incredulity and wonder, as if one were describing life on a distant planet) and a lot more about the baby. Once or twice before I had had an idea that, despite the circumstances, she rather envied me David—and even what I had gone through before he was born. All through the years of our friendship, she had been the leader, not only because she was slightly the elder, but because she had always been more adventurous, more extrovert and positive in her outlook than I. But now, with a giant step, I had apparently (in her eyes) overtaken her; she now deferred to me in a curious way. I had entered, albeit through the back door, The Club, and Dottie, I knew, felt more left-out than ever before. Her questions were directed at finding out some of the mysteries; but the mysteries of this society are not secret, they're open, a hundred times described and explained, yet still as mysterious and tantalizing to those outside as if no one were allowed to mention them. And there was no denying it, I did feel a certain superiority which I couldn't wholly suppress whenever I thought or spoke about David—a superiority which kept guilt and doubt to a minimum.

Chapter 3

IT'S AMAZING how long it takes to bring out a book. Toby's took nine months to be born, just like a baby; and Addy's, even though it was coming out first in speed-crazy America, was going to take about the same. This I learned from Billie Lee, who, seeing that I was all set to rush off to New York in time for Christmas, told me firmly to go home and relax. 'Next autumn,' she said, 'or thereabouts. I'll let you know the exact date later.'

I was shattered. How would I live for nine months without touching the sacred £400? How, come to that, would I live for nine months even if I *did* touch it? I wondered how Toby was managing during this gestation period of his own. His 'half on sig', he'd told me, was already spent. It was awful to think he might be driven back to hack-writing to keep himself until the book came out. But I knew well how very thriftily Toby was capable of living. I had been raised too soft for such exigencies. I would have to find some way of keeping myself and David in reasonable comfort until the time came to break out and rush over to New York for my heady binge of madness.

My father's relief that the New York scheme was not going into action at once was severely modified when I informed him of my immediate plans. He wrung his hands and moaned: 'Why don't you come and live here? What have I been working hard all my life for, if not to help my only child at a moment like this?' Such melodramatic expressions were no part of his usual lexicon, so I knew he was under great stress, and I was very tempted to give in—it would have been so lovely just to relax into his arms, so to speak, and let him take care of all my problems, as I'd discovered during the short visit I'd been paying him. But once independence gets hold of you, it becomes like an obsession to which you cling when it's impractical and stupid and even unkind to do so.

So I put David in his battered carry-cot, set it on the back seat of the Galloping Maggot, and headed back for Surrey, to think.

It was hard winter now. The track from the village was a crunchy morass of mud and ice; to maintain momentum (the tyres had no tread left and I was terrified of getting bogged down) I had to keep up a speed which resulted in the car leaping and bounding over the hidden ruts—I had to grip the lurching wheel with one hand and reach behind to pin the carry-cot down with the other. I was heartily glad to round the last bend and see the cottage, looking grey and forsaken with its masses of leafless creepers swarming up its walls like some creature about to overwhelm it, and its thatched eaves weeping icicles.

I had been away a scant fortnight, but awful things had overtaken the poor little place in my absence. The last of everything in the garden had died, but that was inevitable, merely a gloomy prelude to what I would find inside. As I opened the door, a thin trickle of water came to meet me. Appalled, I followed it up the stairs, and found—what I might have expected—a burst pipe in the lavatory. The devastation was frightful—the whole floor (wood, of course) soaked and warped, the walls (plaster) soggy, the pipes rusty and a stench of damp everywhere. Going to my bedroom to get into some working-clothes, I made the cheering discovery that I had left the window unfastened; it had blown open in a gale, the bed was thoroughly wet (there was mildew on the eiderdown) and the carpet was apparently ruined. That the whole cottage was bitterly cold goes without saying.

Before I could even think what action to take, David signified that he was chilled, tired and hungry. He was half on baby food now, and he liked everything nice and hot, which there really wasn't time for, so I found a relatively dry spot in the living-room, sat down in it, ripped open my shirt with a distracted gesture and stuffed a nipple somewhat untenderly into his wailing jaws. While he had a snack, I made a plan of campaign.

First, fires. Fortunately I'd left a supply of dry wood

in all the wood-boxes before I'd left, and there were electric fires that I could apply to the wetter areas in bathrooms and passages. Then, mops and pails, oh God! No, first, I'd better get a plumber. But how? I'd no idea where there was one. Oh, why had I been too mean to keep Mrs Griffiths on while I was away? She would never have let this happen! These were the moments when a man about the place seemed not merely desirable, but utterly essential. A man would know, for instance, where the tap was that turned the water off at the main. It was probably outside somewhere, hidden among the frozen wet undergrowth surrounding the cottage. I would never find it, and meanwhile the water from the burst was still flowing.

After bedding David down under a smother of blankets, I put on one of Addy's ankle-length mackintoshes and gumboots and ventured outside. I circled the cottage three times before I located the tap, cunningly hidden beneath an evergreen shrub which was leaning heavily against the wall. The tap, when I had fought my way through to it, was immovably stuck—I had to fetch a pair of pliers before it would budge, and by this time I was in such a temper I did something I hadn't done all the time I'd been living there—namely, locked myself out. Smashing a window would have given me intense satisfaction at that moment, but unfortunately—or rather, mercifully—they were all diamond-pane so it wouldn't have helped much. Instead I climbed back into the car, and drove furiously back to the village, skidding recklessly from side to side in the ruts. It was lighting-up time by then, and the plumber, when I at last located him with the aid of Mrs Griffiths (who, to my relief, had managed not to lose her key in the interim) only agreed to come that night when I wept, wrung my hands, and told him my baby would get pneumonia. His wife, very naturally, took a dim view of the whole thing, and while the plumber was grumbling his way into his coat and scarf she sat silently looking me up and down and just as I was going out of the door said in clear, ominous tones: 'Yers. I've heard of you.' This transparent lifemanship ploy managed to wilt me as none of the more direct comments of my relations had ever succeeded in doing, and I drove back to the cottage in disconcerted silence while the plumber muttered and snuffled self-pityingly beside me, holding his battered old leather tool bag clanking on his knees.

However, while he worked on the pipe, I built a roaring fire and made a hasty but rousing pot of tea. Twice I popped up to give him a chance to remark yet again: 'Bitin' bloody cold in here, isn't it? Take a while to get rid o' this damp. Pity you didn't lag 'em.' At last he came down, shivering ostentatiously. The living-room looked bright and cheerful, with the firelight flickering on the walls and the curtains drawn; knowing I had interrupted his supper, I had prepared a hot toasted sandwich as well as the tea, and there was a discreet glass of whisky near the plate. He protested he couldn't possibly stop, the missis was waiting, and then lingered in the doorway for half-an-hour while I brought the cup, plate and glass one by one from the table. . . .

When at last he'd gone, and I'd shut everything tight and lit all the fires I could produce (including an old primus stove), mopped up as much as I could, and checked that David was all right. I finally flopped down in the cretonne armchair before the fire and had a cup of tea myself. I was suddenly but completely exhausted, and once more close to inexplicable tears. It was not only the crises in the cottage, or what the plumber's wife had said; there had been something vaguely disquieting about the plumber. I had suddenly had a most unpleasant feeling, when I gave him the whisky, that he— well, that he'd misunderstood what seemed to me the most ordinary courtesy when you've dragged a man out on a cold wet night. It was nothing he actually did, only that he straightened himself away from the door-jamb and looked at me through his rather low-slung eyebrows and winked; he took the glass and looked around, saying something like 'You've got it right snug here, I *will* say,' and followed this up with a sort of slow, knowing smile, and his eyes followed me back to the table. Impossible to explain why this made me so uncomfortable, but it did. After that I thought he would never go. He just stood in the doorway, sipping his whisky and watching me and talking slowly about nothing very much. He made me feel I was waiting for him to do something. I was; I was waiting, with increasing impatience, for him to leave, and when at last he did, and I had to offer to drive him home, he grinned again and said, 'Well, bus'll be passing in two minutes—a'course, if you was goin' that way——' and he winked once again.

This, then, was to be part of my 'punishment'. It was what Terry had said—I was 'that sort of a girl', irrevocably, until I either married or started to tell lies about widowhood or something similar. People were very charitable, very kind and understanding, even the supposedly narrow-minded villagers; but there was always this, the implied or even overt predatoriness of the men, and the basic disapproval of the women which of course derived from it. I sighed deeply and swallowed my cold tea. It was part of it. I would have to face it, along with the other things. I could manage. But just the same, I thought of the plumber's sly wink and shivered, and felt the loneliness slide one rung deeper.

Chapter 4

FOR A WEEK after my return to the cottage, I lived in my shell and took stock and thought. David and I slept in the relatively dry living-room while I systematically dried out the other parts of the house.

Outside it rained steadily, hampering the drying process, but effectively immuring me indoors, which was where I really wanted to be. I was so happy to find I *wanted* to be alone. Every day that passed without my being lonely or bored seemed like a feather in the cap of my independence. In a queer way it also seemed like a present to Toby—one more day when I hadn't *needed* him. I wanted him all the time, but not in a craving, grabbing way, not so desperately that my need was stronger than my wish that he should be left alone.

In any case, I had to occupy my mind with more practical details. There stretched ahead of me at least eight months before I could go to America with any real excuse or sense of purpose; that eight months must inevitably be filled with profitable labour of some sort. For hours at a time I lay on my back on the sofa, half-hypnotized by the grey drops running endlessly down the diamond-panes, over the ridges in between and on down at a slight tangent, feeling warm and lazy and broke and happy and alarmed all at once.

My assets were few, but definite. I could type. I had a car. I could act after a fashion, though I hadn't for years—not much use, that one. I could cook, sort of. There was almost no category of work I felt myself to be intrinsically 'too good' to have a go at. But naturally, some things appealed more than others.

At the end of the week, the weather changed; I woke one morning to find a different sort of light in the room. Rising to peer over the back of the sofa, I perceived a pattern of sunlight on the curtains. I hurried to draw them, stopping on my way to prod David, who was keeping the most irregular hours—my hours, almost, which explained why he was still fast asleep at half-past eight in the morning. Outside, the garden was a pale glittering mass of water-drops each cored with a tiny spark of reflected sunlight. I threw open the windows and breathed deeply of the sweet wet loamy air. It was so intoxicating after a week of frowst that I immediately put on my gum-boots and climbed out of the window. It was lovely to sink ankle-deep in the wet earth and feel the mild water stains soaking through my pyjamas as I was caressed by bushes and curled brown leaves.

I wandered about happily, shivering as much with delight as with actual cold, getting wetter and wetter, my gum-boots gleaming like patent-leather. After a bit I went in again and fetched David and a ground-sheet, setting them down together on a bumpy bit of lawn. He promptly crawled to the edge of the rubber and onto the jewelled grass, but I didn't think it mattered much. I sat down beside him a few minutes later and shared my hunk of bread and butter and marmalade with him, washing mine down with a mug of tea while he swigged his usual, his icy hands clutching my bare ribs, his head hidden inside my jacket, his muddy feet stamping a tattoo of pleasure against my thigh. I sat thinking how lovely it was not to care about getting wet and dirty, and not to have anybody around to tell me what a bad mother I was. After our meal, we rolled around together until we were both thoroughly soaked and filthy; then we went indoors, I threw everything we'd been wearing into the sink to soak, and we had a joint bath.

I had no special bath for David; we always bathed together. It was the high-spot of the day. What I used to do was put him down on the bath-mat, climb into the bath when it was really hot, soak myself a bit, and then run the cold in until it was the right temperature for him. Then I'd take him into the bath with me and wash him and play with him, until he'd had enough; roll him up in a towel and put him back on the floor, run more hot in and wash myself, and then get out and dry us both at once. This was a most delightful arrangement for both of us; the only drawback was that he refused to take a bath without me, and several times I had to undress and get in with him even though I'd had my own bath separately.

While I was sitting there that bright morning, holding the baby between my knees and making his plastic duck swim under water, my mind perfectly unencumbered by any thoughts of a practical nature, an idea suddenly popped into my head. What I really needed was a job I could do in my own time, like the typing I'd done in the L-shaped room. I wondered suddenly if I couldn't set myself up as something—preferably something a bit more lucrative and less dreary than typing, possibly something creative. 'Cottage industry' was the phrase that inevitably leapt into my head. The difficulty was, I wasn't really the handicrafts type; I couldn't even knit. Nevertheless, I whiled away a few moments with a pleasant dream of collecting sheep's-wool from the rhimy hedgerows, washing it, dyeing it with vegetable dyes (home-made, of course), spinning it on the decorative spinning-wheel that stood on one of the landings, and then embroidering wool panels of my own designing. And selling them for large sums. I finished the dream off neatly, sighed, and began soaping David's back.

No, but something of the sort. What could I do? Surely I had some kind of flair which could be useful? Abruptly I envied Dottie, an old familiar feeling that I hadn't had for a long time. Dottie had taken herself in hand, channelled her talents, been clever enough to get herself a niche in the fashionable world where they could best be put to use, and where she could embellish them with new skills. Any fool, I suddenly thought, can have a baby. But not any fool can support it.

My early-morning pastoral elation was cooling with the bathwater. I was getting goose-flesh, and not just from being slightly chilled. The lonely feeling, the helpless sense of being too small for the battle, could lash back in a moment, like a bent branch, if one didn't watch it. I clambered out, wrapped myself in a bathrobe which had been warming in front of the oil-stove, and dried David while the water gurgled away with a passionate resonance. The sun had gone in, and I felt rather like having a good cry all of a sudden, which wasn't wise in front of David who had recently begun to sense my moods like a dog and respond to the bad ones with sympathetic howls. So I quickly got him to bed before the mood overwhelmed us both.

It was just about time to dry my eyes and start thinking about lunch when a car drew up outside. My heart gave a little lurch of joy which told me more clearly than the unexplained crying-fit that the feathers were fitted very insecurely into my cap; almost any visitor (except the plumber) would have been welcome just then, even though the house was a mess and I was still looking like the wrath of God in a pair of pregnancy slacks and one of Addy's age-old smocks. When I saw Dottie's behind emerge from the car, followed by the rest of her lugging a large carry-all, I couldn't get outside fast enough to greet her with hugs and glad cries.

She noticed my red eyes immediately.

'What've you been bawling about on this gorgeous morning?'

'I've been bawling because no one was coming to lunch— as far as I then knew,' I said, taking one handle of the hold-all. 'Good God, what have you got in here, geological specimens?'

'Toys for my godchild.'

'I must warn you, his tastes aren't very sophisticated. His favourite thing at the moment is a rather oily length of old bicycle-chain.'

'And bottles.'

'Ah! There you may find a more appreciative response.'

She was dressed for the occasion in tight trousers, tucked into very smart leather boots, topped by a hip-length jacket of tartan wool with a fringe.

'I do wish you'd try to look a bit more dowdy when you know you're going to see me,' I couldn't help saying peevishly.

'My dowdy days are over,' she said. 'Only women like you, with no need for sublimations or compensations, can afford the luxury of dressing badly.'

We went indoors and she flopped down on the sofa. I threw a log on the fire, which was burning sluggishly amid yesterday's ashes, wishing I'd done a bit more housework in the morning.

'How long are you staying?'

'How long can you put up with me?'

I looked at her sharply, remembering quite suddenly that it was not Saturday.

'Indefinitely, but . . . what about your job?'

'What job?' she asked, with a one-sided smile.

'H'm. I sense a crisis. Have a sherry before you begin.'

'Forgive my ingratitude, but this is not an occasion for sherry.' She plunged a hand into the hold-all and came up with a bottle of Black and White.

'I've got no soda,' I warned her.

'Soda's for good days.'

We drank, Dottie eyeing me over the rim of her glass with a rueful, ironic expression.

'Well?' I asked.

'Well! The job has folded. Not the job only—the whole enterprise. Bust—kaput—down the drain. Pity. It was fun while it lasted.' She shrugged, a casual gesture which didn't fool me. Dottie had waited a long time for this particular opportunity, this potentially gold-plated niche within a niche —buyer for a new and wildly with-it boutique in Sloane Street.

'What happened, exactly?'

'The happy young couple who started it with the aid of large wedding-presents from their respective daddies, decided, six months after the nuptials, that they'd "made a nonsense" as they put it. Strange how they both used the same expression, though there the similarity in their stories ended. According to him, she was frigid and neurotic; according to her, he was kinky and wanted to tie her to the bed-posts, among other exotic delights. All very sad. And strange . . . they looked so normal. But then, who's normal these days?'

'I am,' I said. 'I think.'

'Only because you live in the country,' she said obscurely. 'There's no "normal" any more. If normal means average, you're the kinky one, believe me.' She sighed deeply. 'I don't even know if I'm normal any more. Is it normal to choose the chaste life when one could be getting tied to bed-posts or rolling about on grubby mattresses in discothéques every night? I've been told so often lately that I'm a freak that I'm beginning to believe it.'

'Which is what you're doing here.'

'The whisky is making you very acute, Janie. But then,

you always were pretty perceptive, even before you opted for the life of a happy cabbage which I suddenly so envy you.' She poured another drink and stared at the fire. 'What a really wonderful smell that is—wood burning.'

'It's apple and pine, mixed. I agree it's wonderful.'

'And is that actual beeswax I smell on the furniture?'

'No, *Johnson's Glocoat*. But it's nice.'

'Christ, I'm going to cry.'

'No, please, don't you start! It's too much. I've been at it all morning.'

'It's this *bloody* business of being alone,' she mumbled, her face in her hands.

'I know. Do shut up, please, Dottie.'

'You're lucky. You don't know how lucky you are.'

'Yes, I do. But right now I'd give half my luck for half your ability to earn your own living.'

She looked up at me through a ruined eye make-up.

'Is that what you were really crying about—money?'

'Sort of. Partly.'

'I'll lend you some.'

I shook my head. 'Thanks, but that'd be no good. It's not only the cash I want, it's the feeling that I can cope.'

'You've coped up to now.'

'So have you.'

She stared at me. 'Ah. I see what you mean. No, past successes or gettings-by don't really help at crossroads, do they?' She dried her eyes and leaned her head back, staring at the ceiling. We sat silently for a while and at last I said, 'What about food?'

'Not hungry, really.'

'Bowl of soup?'

'Oh, well. . . .'

She fed David for me and seemed more cheerful. I was full of sympathy, and yet I couldn't quite understand why she was so basically upset. She'd been in and out of jobs before, and would surely not find it hard to get another now, though perhaps not quite so close to her heart's desire. I knew it was something deeper, a pot-hole in the long cold valley of being unmarried. It was some days before I pieced it all together from snatches of conversation here and there. It was all fairly

42

hard to pin down or explain, but after my experiences in the L-shaped room, though hers were on a much more sophisticated level, I thought I understood.

'It's the parties,' she said, 'and the dates, and the things you hear at them. It's not just that most of the conversation is shallow and brittle and all the worn-out words for cocktail-talk; there's a viciousness there, a feeling of inner bankruptcy. I sat next to a young writer at a dinner party the other night—the sort of man one thinks one would like to meet, until one meets him. He's very ugly, with a beautiful, aristocratic wife who sat across the table smiling tenderly at him all the time he was telling me in a low, continuous mutter what a shallow, boring bitch she was. On my other side was a politician you often see on television, holding forth on brains-trusts—he's supposed to be one of the white hopes of the future—and he was quite seriously propounding his theory that the best way to control the population in the East was to blanket the Orient in homosexual propaganda and try to turn as many young men as possible into queers.'

'He was joking.'

'Was he? Nobody was laughing. Then at another recent party that I got invited to more or less by accident, given by some tycoon in the rag-trade, one of the guests got a very little bit tight and made a speech about the host, highly laudatory in tone, from which it clearly emerged that both of them were nothing but very successful crooks. The speaker stood there cheerfully making jokes about the dirty deals they'd done together, and the whole room was rolling about with carefree laughter. What's so lousy, Jane, is that while there've always been crooks and bastards and hypocrites and all the other species of human insect, they've never felt free to get up at parties and boast about it until just recently. Nobody's shocked any more—not by anything. It's not done to be shocked. You have to accept everything, like some sort of garbage-disposal unit that opens itself up and makes happy laughing noises while every sort of rottenness and filth is tipped into it. I tell you, I'm afraid to go out with men now. They've all got something disgusting to tell you about themselves. All they want from you is that you shall listen and not be shocked, so they can go away feeling there's nothing the matter with them. Well, I tell you, I won't do it any more. When they start, I just tell them I don't want to hear. If they insist, I don't try to be unshockable—when I'm shocked, I act shocked, and then of course it's their turn to laugh. The ugly, frightened sound of that laughter is something I can't describe. Sometimes I feel they're wiping their dirty minds all over me. That's why I won't go to bed with them any more. It's like acquiescing to them as people, and I don't, not to one in fifty of them, not to one in a hundred.'

Of course this didn't all come out in one long speech, but in dribs and drabs, over a number of days. I was appalled . . . even the L-shaped room, and the denizens of its surroundings, for all their squalor, had not been as sordid as the picture Dottie drew for me of the smart set. The thing was, she didn't strike me as the type that would attract that sort of thing unless it were much more universal than I had imagined. She seemed to be saying it was so intrinsic that it was impossible to avoid —except by burying oneself in the country, about which she suddenly harboured rather unrealistic notions of purity and sanity and vicelessness. As a sort of balancer, I told her about the plumber, but she simply asked if he'd actually 'tried anything' and when I said no, she said in that case the gleam in his eye had probably been a reflection of my own slight guilt-complex and that even if he'd pinched my bottom with his size-4 pliers, it would have been merely a nymphs-and-shepherds type frolic compared to what she was talking about.

During the first few days of her visit, while she was unwinding, we didn't talk much about me, and my plan-making was held in abeyance. She grew more and more relaxed, less and less smart as the few clothes she'd brought lost their immaculate perfection, and (it seemed to me) more and more deeply entrenched and unwilling to return to London. Not that I minded. Though her conversation was frequently depressing, her company in general was a joy; for Dottie could never be gloomy for long, and even her gloom was often shot with humour and mimicry. David loved her, and she him. I began myself to dread the moment when she would inevitably have to depart to renew the battle.

One morning in the village while we were shopping, she

paused to look through an empty bay-window overhung by a 'Shop for Rent' sign.

'What was here?' she asked.

'All-sorts shop,' I said. 'Very dingy, doomed to fail. After all, we have a tiny supermarket now.'

'Don't,' said Dottie, whose current fad was shuddering at all manifestations of urban progress. She lingered on, peering through cupped hands into the dusty interior. 'I have a fellow-feeling for failed enterprises at the moment,' she said. 'Could we get the key and go in and look?'

'There's nothing to see—just an empty shop. A bit sad, really.'

'Still . . . I'd like to.'

She persisted, so I took her to the estate agent's and soon we were standing in the shop. It was, indeed, quite empty, except for some cornflakes cartons stuffed with paper and rubbish, a dusty counter and some broken shelves still festooned with a tatty oil-cloth frill attached to rusty thumb-tacks. The floor was bare boards, the walls papered with a flowered pattern gone dark which reminded me irresistibly of the L-shaped room when I had first gone there.

Dottie was running her hand over one section of wall.

'There's a beam under here,' she said. 'Fancy covering a genuine beam with this hideous wall-paper! You're right, they deserved to fail.'

'I didn't say that,' I murmured. 'Look, there are beams in the ceiling, too. Quite untampered with.'

'How can you say that! They've been whitewashed.'

'What's wrong about that?'

She gave me a look. 'You've got no feeling for places,' she said.

That annoyed me. It was patently untrue.

'If there's one thing I have got, it's a feeling for places!' I said. 'You didn't see the L-shaped room before and after!'

'I didn't see it at all; you never invited me,' she reminded me.

'I'm very good with places,' I persisted.

'All right, prove it. What would you do with this?'

'Do with it? Just what any sane person would do—leave it alone.'

But even as I said the words, I felt a pang. Poor little place!
It shouldn't be so dirty and ugly. The bay window was
marvellous; it came almost to the ground and there was a
semi-circular rostrum inside for arranging displays on. The
floor was pine, and so, probably, was the fireplace, which had
been painted dark green and filled in with cardboard. Stripped
and waxed, they would be beautiful. The counter was an
excrescence, but it could be taken out. It would be an
anachronism to sell food in here anyway, it would need to be—
oh, antiques or something. Lustrous copper, glowing rosewood, fine mellow velvets and stripped oak and those silky
green paperweights full of bubbly flowers. . . .

'You know what would really be interesting in here,' Dottie
said suddenly. 'Scandinavian ware. You know—Design Centre
stuff. Teak, whitewood, enamelled iron, ceramics, glass candle-
sticks, snow-white yakskin rugs, maybe a few rolls of Swedish
fabrics. . . .'

I gazed at her aghast. 'Are you quite barmy? In *here*?'

'Of course! Think of the contrast. The tudor setting with
the brand-new, stark simple goods—it'd be marvellous!'

She sounded so enthusiastic that I looked round dubiously,
trying to visualize it. 'Strip lighting? Show-cases?' I asked
incredulously.

'Possibly—possibly——' She was pacing about with such an
air of purpose that I grew suddenly worried for fear she was
serious.

'Dottie, come on out of it, will you? Are you crazy?'

'No. We've got to do something, why not this?'

'We?'

'You're looking for gainful employment, aren't you? You
should be. And so am I. And this might be just what we both
need.'

'But—but—but—you can't open a shop, just like that!
What about permits, stock, capital, *experience* . . . ?'

'I've got the capital—we won't need much. I've got the
experience, too—well, a bit of it. As for the rest, we can deal
with everything as it comes.'

'I wish you'd stop saying "we"! Include me right out of this,
I've never heard of anything so insane.'

'I have.'

'What?' I said, taken off balance.

'Your New York scheme is a lot madder, it's absolutely certifiable if you want to know, but did I throw cold water on it when you told me? No, I didn't, I even thought seriously of asking if I could come with you. I'm still thinking of it. And in the meantime, it strikes me we might try and do something together, to keep ourselves alive and sane and self-respecting until——' She stopped. We stared at each other through the dust-motes. Suddenly she drooped.

'You're right,' she said flatly. 'What am I talking about? Let's get out of here and go home.'

That afternoon abruptly, she left for London. She was very subdued.

'You can't do anything without a man,' she said dispiritedly. 'You can't even give yourself the illusion of enterprise.'

She kissed David tenderly and then kissed me. 'Take care of him,' she said, and walked swiftly to the car, leaving behind a bottle and a half of Scotch and a very unpleasant emptiness.

I was doing some gardening towards dusk, trying to dispel my depression, when I heard the gate creak and a stranger walked in. He was very London-looking, tweed jacket, whip-cords, Clydella shirt and all. He was also extremely attractive. I hadn't seen such a handsome man for ages, at least not one with such a gloss. I leaned on my spade and tried to look casual.

He doffed his brand-new driving cap and crinkled up his eyes.

'Mrs Graham?'

'Miss,' I said automatically.

'Ah,' he said whimsically. 'Yes. Is—er—Dorothy still on the premises?'

'No, she drove back to London at lunchtime.'

'Ah,' he said again, looking downcast.

A sudden intuition told me that this was the interior decorator. Dottie had told me, among other things to do with her called-off love-life, that he had been tentatively trying to renew acquaintance.

'Just my luck,' he said. 'Must have missed her on the way down here. Damned awful road, missed my way twice.'

'I'm sorry,' I said, quite untruthfully.

We stared blankly at each other.

'Well,' he said, stirring himself. 'I suppose I'd better be starting back.'

'Perhaps you'd like something before you go,' I offered without much enthusiasm.

He brightened. 'Well, that's very sweet of you—if you were making a pot of tea, that'd be just——'

I suppressed a sigh and led him into the cottage. David was asleep in his pram in the hall and we had to edge past.

'Do you share the house?'

'Only with him,' I said shortly, praying he wouldn't say 'Ah!' again, but of course he did, very sagely this time.

I offered him whisky, chiefly because I'd had tea and couldn't be bothered to start making more. He seemed gratified to find some of London's amenities in this rural wilderness. He took his glass and strolled to the window, where he sat on the window-seat and gazed out at the darkening garden. David began to whimper, so I went out and changed him and when I came back about ten minutes later, the young man looked round at me with an expression of some surprise.

'It's quite pleasant, just sitting here, isn't it?' he said.

'Do you mean, not boring?'

'No, really pleasant. Pretty. Quiet. The birds and so on. And the air smells fresh.' He smiled diffidently. 'You can tell I don't get into the country much. Not the real country.'

'Well, the whisky's probably helping.'

He laughed rather uncertainly. 'Are you getting at me?'

'Maybe a little. Quite unfairly. Sorry, I'm in a rather bad mood today.'

'Why?' he asked interestedly.

'Well, I've had Dottie here for a week, and now she's gone.'

He looked at me with a sudden sharpening of sympathy. His good looks became much more actively attractive when he wasn't being blasé and mannered.

'How I do know exactly what you mean!' he said fervently. He drank the remains of his drink and then said, 'By the way, my name's Alan Innes. Without wanting to inveigle any confidence out of you, would you mind me asking if she's ever mentioned me at all?'

I hesitated. 'Not that I remember. But names without faces never stick in my mind. She might have done.'

'Yes. I see,' he said glumly. He looked through the window which was now a series of black diamonds, then back at me with his crinkled-up smile of rue. 'We were very fond of each other once. But it all broke up, unfortunately.'

'Oh?'

'I couldn't have been sorrier myself. It was all so absurd. You know how these things can happen, if one's fool enough to let them—everything's going along beautifully, and then some absolute nonsense happens—something so silly and trivial one's ashamed to remember it later—and it's like pulling out the supporting pillar which brings the whole thing down on one's head.'

He looked at me. I said nothing.

'Idiotic, isn't it?' he said with a wry smile.

'Well. If the relationship is supported on such frail pillars, perhaps it wasn't very strong anyway,' I said, remembering the green and gold picture which had brought this particular temple of love tumbling down.

He sighed. 'P'raps you're right. Felt quite strong at the time.'

He stared into his empty glass in what might have been a gloomy reverie or a broad hint. It had begun to rain outside, rather heavily. I excused myself and went out to put away my gardening tools, returning after a while rather too wet for comfort. I put some more logs on the fire, realizing as I did so that this might create just the sort of cosy atmosphere which, together with the rain and the whisky and Mr. Innes' melancholy mood, might make it even more difficult to get rid of him.

It did. He sat on and on, until another small drink became a necessity of good manners. I made it as small as I could, and then left him again, this time to feed David and put him to bed. I was gone some time, and when I came back I found my visitor stretched on the settee reading a book with his shoes off, looking mightily at home. The glass, which looked slightly fuller than when I had seen it last, was on the floor beside him. He gave me a most appealing grin as I came into the room.

49

'I say, I've taken a diabolical liberty,' he said, holding up the glass.

'So I see.'

'I do hope you'll forgive me. I feel incredibly at home here somehow. Funny, that. Not my *milieu* at all.'

'Well, it's Dottie's whisky, as it happens. I'm just a bit concerned about you finding your way home in the dark.'

He got up reluctantly and padded to the window in his socks. 'It's coming down in buckets,' he said, sounding more cheerful than he had any right to. 'What's worrying me is not finding the way, but the fact that I shall be doing it in an open car.'

'What do you mean, open? Can't you put the roof up?'

'No. It's broken.'

I felt so annoyed I could scarcely hide it. Did he expect me to put him up for the night? If so, he was in for a rude disappointment.

'You've got a car full of water by now, then,' I said.

'Oh, no, that's all right—I've got a bit of canvas over it. But it'd be pretty wet trying to drive through this lot.' He looked at me. The winning grin still played about his lips. His whole manner was that of a man accustomed to getting things his own way. Something in it made me stubborn.

'I'm awfully sorry,' I said. 'I'd offer to put you up here, if you were a female. But as you're most decidedly not, I'm afraid I can't.'

The smile slipped briefly, and was restored. 'Oh, Jane, don't be like that!' he said, throwing in my name so casually I wasn't sure I'd heard it. 'Are you worried about your reputation, or your virtue? I assure you, neither will suffer from me spending the night in your spare bedroom! Or even down here on that most comfortable settee.'

'I'm sure my virtue, what's left of it, is quite safe in your hands, Mr Innes,' I said. 'I wouldn't flatter myself so far as to think it might not be. As to my reputation, you're quite worldly-wise enough to realize I've nothing much to lose there. However, nothing much is better than nothing at all. This is a village, and I have to live in it. They naturally expect the worst of me because of my situation; I take a rather perverse pride in not fulfilling their expectations.'

His face had changed and now he came towards me and put his glass down on the table. 'How long have you lived here?' he asked curiously.

'Six months.'

'And in all that time—you've never let a man stay the night?'

I stared at him, as if winded. From feeling utterly in control of the situation two minutes before, I now felt as out of countenance as I had felt in the face of the plumber's sly wink. My thoughts flew to Toby and latched to him like a burr. But how can the man you love protect you if he is not there?

'You poor little thing,' said Alan Innes, and took me in his arms with practised tenderness.

Some dim instinct told me not to struggle, that if I stood there coldly and let him kiss a dead mouth he would be insulted and lose interest. But it didn't work, for two reasons. One, he was very strongly inclined to spend the night in my warm bed and not driving through the rain in his open car, and he was not really sensitive enough to notice or care whether I reacted to his first kisses or not. But the other reason was the one which was shaming to me. I despised him; but I was not, it seemed, physically indifferent to any man so good-looking and sexually able. His mouth, hands and body compelled me to a response, a response so treacherous and despicable that nausea damped down the sudden blaze in my body as soon as he let me go.

He looked into my eyes with simple triumph for a second, then with admirable adroitness took me off balance with a turn of his foot and the next moment I found myself in a highly connubial position with him on the hearthrug.

I don't really know what would have happened if he had managed to down me on the settee instead of the floor. But the floor before the fire was where I had lain with Toby.

Galvanized by this sudden recollection, I began to struggle fiercely, as if I'd just woken up to find an irresponsible erotic dream to be quite terrifyingly real and imminent. He had me at a severe disadvantage, moral as well as postural, having just distinctly felt me return his kiss, and being thus certain of victory he held me down and laughed in my face—a not entirely lover-like laugh. It alarmed and infuriated me. I got one hand free and pushed him sharply in the mouth with it.

51

This hurt him enough to make him want to hurt me, which he did by kissing me with most unpleasant violence, biting me painfully at the same time.

'Is that what you wanted?' he asked me, with what I can only call a leer, and without further ado wrenched at my shirt, tearing the first two buttons off it.

God, I thought, he's going to rape me.

It was too ridiculous—too bizarre. How could this have happened? The polite, ultra-correct young man who had climbed, so immaculately dressed, out of his car two hours ago was now swarming all over me and pawing me like a savage, literally panting with lust, his neatly-barbered fair hair falling over a suddenly sweating brow. I felt panic rising in me and pulled his head back by the hair as hard as I could. He let go of me just long enough to slap my face. I could feel his knee working its way between my legs, and I suddenly thought: well, thank God I've got slacks on, anyway, he won't find those so damned easy to navigate.

This thought returned me to some faint sense of proportion. No woman, surely, can be assaulted by one man against her will, and the whole enterprise by this time was thoroughly against mine. But since I didn't fancy a lengthy continuation of this undignified struggle, I decided to try a ruse. I suddenly went limp, rolled my eyes, stuck my tongue out, arched my back, let out a gargling sound, and went limp again.

It worked. He dropped me like a hot brick and clambered hastily off my apparently unconscious form.

'Jane——' he began, uncertainly.

I was on my feet in a second and making for the door. Before he could gather his wits to follow me I was locked in the hall lavatory. I sat down there and put my head between my knees. I felt sick and rotten.

He knocked on the door. With his fist.

'Come out, you bitch,' he said harshly.

'Not bloody likely,' I replied in kind.

'You can't stay in there all night,' he said after a moment, in a slightly less vicious tone. I made no reply, but stood up shakily and gave myself a drink of water. 'Come on out. I won't make love to you if you really don't want to,' he said, merely sullen now.

'You call that making love?' I said. 'You poor ignorant bastard. Go home.'

I always was inclined to stoop to abusive language when upset, as I was now, exceedingly. I always regret it later and wish I had been dignified and ladylike, but by then it's too late.

Unfortunately, he had this in common with me, and there followed a perfectly unprintable string of filth from which I inferred that he thought a woman in my position (only he put it more graphically) who invites men into her house and fills them with whisky is asking for anything she gets, and should be grateful to get it from somebody like him and not from some passing yokel who'd probably murder her afterwards. From his description of the poor mythical yokel's crime, I came to the firm conclusion that Mr Alan Innes was a none-too-well-sublimated sadist.

I sat on the john with my plastic tooth-mug of water, feeling more and more ill and appalled as I listened helplessly, wondering how long it would go on and whether I'd really brought it on myself. I suspected I might have done. It was easy to see now what had set Dottie off on the downward path to disillusion and cynicism. Strange she hadn't mentioned any of this.

Perhaps as she was not 'a woman in my position' he had treated her with more restraint. I sincerely hoped so.

At last he withdrew, snarlingly. I heard the front door slam, but I wasn't falling for that. About ten minutes later I heard it close again, more convincingly this time, and shortly afterwards came the angry roaring of a car engine being revved up with merciless violence. It drove away, and a beautiful silence fell, broken only by the patter of rain on the roof and my own somewhat unsteady breathing.

I emerged from my haven, and stood in the hall, fighting the desire to bolt and bar every entrance to the cottage. Never had the spectre of the demented chalk-pit worker loomed larger.

Eventually I settled for the chain. Then I went to see David. On the threshold of his room a sudden most ghastly fear came over me—what if Alan should have . . . ? But of course he hadn't. David was peacefully asleep. I woke him up, quite needlessly, and fed him, quite selfishly. I remember holding him tightly and rocking him with tears of wretchedness and reaction running down my face and saying Toby's name over and over again, like an incantation to hold off the fear.

Chapter 5

THE NEXT MORNING I telephoned Dottie long distance from the village call-box and said I'd been thinking about her shop idea and was prepared to think about it some more if she had been serious.

'What changed your mind?' she asked at once.

'I've decided living alone isn't such a good idea.'

'Why?'

'I had a visitor last night—your charming friend Mr Innes.'

There was a pause, and then she said, 'Oh. Did he behave himself?'

'No,' I said.

After another pause, she said, 'Did you, by any chance, let him have anything to drink?'

'Yes. Your blasted whisky.'

'Oh, God! I'd have warned you, if I'd thought for a moment you'd ever meet. He's practically a schizo. Did you manage all right?'

'I lost the first battle but I won the war.'

'*God*, I'm sorry you had that through me! Do you want me to come down?'

'Yes, but not just to give me moral support. I think you're right. I think we ought to try and do something together, down here. I don't know about your shop idea, but something.'

She thought for a moment, and then said: 'Are you all right by yourself for another night or so?'

'Yes, of course.'

'Then give me a few days to make some enquiries and do some thinking. Meanwhile, you find out a few more details about that place, what's the lowest we could rent it for. By the way, if I haven't enough in the bank, what about your aunt's £400? Couldn't we use that?'

'No,' I said. 'That's for New York.'

'Are you still set on this New York business?'

'Yes.'

'You're crazy. All right. I'll see you on Friday or Saturday.'

Actually it hadn't only been loneliness that had prompted my change of mind. It had also been a letter from the bank that morning, to say I was overdrawn, but much worse than I had thought. Of course I knew I should put the £400 in to get myself out of the red, but if I did that it would be gone in no time. I was deeply determined not to spend it on day-to-day living.

So now I had an insane long-term plan (New York), a dubious middle-term plan (Dottie) but no recourse at all for the immediate present. How, for example, could I go to Acre's General Grocery today to get my week's supplies, to be paid for as usual by cheque, when I knew there was more than an even chance the cheque would bounce? The bank's letter, couched though it was in the usual refined verbiage, had indicated as much. Mr Acre had always been kind enough to cash a weekly cheque somewhat larger than my bill, to allow me some spending money. I really couldn't risk abusing his touching faith in me. On the other hand, I had to eat. If I didn't, David wouldn't, and from the cries which were even now resounding from his carry-cot in the back of the car, he wouldn't take kindly to any drop in milk-production.

The situation called for drastic action. After sitting in the car for ten minutes in futile thought, I went into the post-office and asked Mrs Stephens, who kept it, if she knew of any job-vacancies.

She knew of several. A button-factory in a town twenty miles away had a sign up—she'd seen it last time she passed. Or one of the wealthier local farmers' wives was looking for help in the house. No? Well, several of the probationers from the local cottage hospital were down with 'flu, she knew . . . not a very *nice* job, of course, the probationers only did the floors and the bedpans and were shouted at by everybody, but . . . ? No? Well, what did I have in mind?

I asked if she, herself, needed an assistant.

She stared at me with her voluble mouth a little open. Clearly, such an idea had never come to her. She said she had

56

always run the place alone, post-office, sweets, papers, greetings-cards, tobacco and all. There was hardly room for two behind the all-purpose counter. But, I said, I'd seen her run off her feet at certain times, with a queue protruding from the door. What if I were to come in, not all day, but just at those busy hours, to lend her a hand, for, say, ten shillings an hour? She could then concentrate on the post-office part, and leave all the sundries to me.

She argued that it wouldn't be worth it, since there would be no increase in business to cover the cost of employing me. I said, wouldn't it be worth it in terms of better service and efficiency—and less work for her? She shook her head very doubtfully and said she would have to speak to Mr Stephens.

Mr Stephens, I knew, was usually kept out of sight in the musty little flat behind the shop. He was considerably older than his wife, old to a point where, frankly, his advice on any matter more taxing than whether he felt hungry or cold was scarcely worth asking. But Mrs Stephens, who tended him devotedly, frequently scurrying through the dividing door to guide him away from his favourite pastime of turning on the gas-taps, maintained the saving fiction that he was her *eminence gris*, controlling her and the business from backstage, so to speak. The village maintained it with her, and the neighbours stood by to call the fire-brigade or turn off water at the main should Mrs Stephens's sixth sense of her husband's 'little mischiefs' fail to warn her in time.

So when she spoke of consulting him, I knew that what she really wanted was time to think it over herself, and that the answer would probably be no. Nevertheless, I said I'd call back again in the afternoon to see if she'd arrived at any decision. Meantime, I went into the Swan, next door, and asked its burly proprietor, whom I knew only as A. Davies from the name on his framed licence in the saloon bar, if he needed a part-time bar-maid.

His astonishment was quite comic. He actually reared back his head and made his eyes pop. Then he began to laugh.

'What do you know about drawing pints, my love?' he asked. 'It ain't s'easy as it looks, y'know!'

I told him it didn't even look easy, but that I thought I could learn. The idea evidently tickled him even pinker than

57

his normal shade, and before I knew it he'd lifted the hinged partition and urged me in behind the bar.

'Come into my parlour, said the spider to the fly! Now then, have a try, go on, just you have a try!' He gave me a pint-pot and positioned me opposite a three-handled pump. 'Draw that gentleman a pint of mild and bitter. That's the mild—that's the bitter—don't you worry, Ben, you won't have to drink it, we'll make her drink it, eh, love? You'll pull all the better with a pint inside you.'

At my first attempt I spilled just enough to satisfy him that the whole business was just as highly skilled as he said it was, and pleased him further by drinking half the overflowing pot down in one go, though it nearly killed me as beer is not my drink. However, my effort drew cries of 'She's a good 'un—open your throat, love, tip it down—you see, Alf, you don't have to drive her to it, she's willin'!' and a scattered round of applause. When I raised my face from the mug, and had received the laugh due to me for my foam moustache, Alf was looking at me with a gleam of speculation in his small eyes.

'Have another go, my dear,' he said in a quite different tone.

This time I drew a perfect pint, basing my timing on what I remembered from a vast tea-urn I once presided over during my waitress days in Yorkshire. Alf watched me narrowly. 'A shade too much bitter,' he commented.

'Never mind that,' said Ben, a rotund farmer with a whiskery jowl. 'I'll settle for that one. Never seen one prettier pulled'n that, neither. Give 'er the job, I would.'

'Come through into the private,' said Alf.

I finished the day with two jobs under my belt, 'Mr Stephens' having decided his dear wife needed a helper after all. The hours were as complex as a jig-saw puzzle—10 a.m. till opening time in the post office. The Swan till 2.30, lunch to be eaten on the hop, then a break until 3.30 when I returned to the post office until it closed at 5. I was also to do special duty in the evenings at The Swan on Saturdays and other occasions, as and when Alf needed me and I could manage.

Fitting David's schedule in with this was going to be none too easy. I sat at home in the evening and worked it out at Addy's desk. What it amounted to was that I was going to have to start weaning him—well, at $6\frac{1}{2}$ months that was no tragedy, but the truth was I adored feeding him myself and rather envied those primitive women who go on suckling their children till they're walking. Of course I realized there was something a bit Freudian and perilous in this. I had been unable to help noticing the distinctly erotic element in the delight engendered by that eager, nuzzling mouth. Sometimes, in the sleepy hours of the night when I had taken David into my bed and, propped up with pillows, had found myself drifting off to sleep in the middle of a feed, I had been guiltily aware of the intrusion of some highly unmaternal images. My memories of Toby's caresses were still concrete enough to need very little stimulation to revive disturbingly.

All in all, the necessity of abandoning the two middle feeds of the day and combining them, with luck, into one milk-plus-solids meal which could be given to him by kind Mrs. Alf, or me if not too busy, seemed an excellent plan. I only hoped it would seem so to David.

The first day worked out splendidly. I fed him an hour early, an arrangement which surprised but did not seem to dismay him, and took him, sleeping peacefully, in his carry-cot to Mrs Stephens's where I found a corner for him behind the counter—raised from the floor on four pillars of glass containing Sunny Sparklers, Treacle Bon-Bons, Lemon Sherbets and Dolly-Mixture respectively. There wasn't a peep out of him all the while I was learning the secrets of weighing sweets, taking newspaper orders, pricing cigarettes and locating stationery, a minor line relegated to some dusty boxes on a top shelf. The only bad moment was when I saw Mrs Stephens's grey Persian cat stealing towards the cot, its eyes narrowed with fell intent. I let out a roar which caused Mrs Stephens, two steps down in the post-office section, to drop one of the parcel weights on her foot, and the cat to leap affrightedly into a box of jelly-babies which fell all over the floor.

'What is it, what is it?' I heard the wheezing voice of poor senile Mr Stephens pettishly inquiring. 'What have I done now?'

'Nothing, dearie, it's nothing, just the pussy!' Mrs Stephens called gaily, whispering to me, 'Don't cry out like that, dear, it does startle him.'

'But the cat was going to jump in the cot!'

'No, no, I'm sure Muffy would never do such a thing!' she cried, much shocked. She scooped the cat, whose name was Mufferpaws, up in her arms and put her face into its long, suffocating fur.

'Isn't there somewhere else we could put the baby?' I asked.

'Well . . . there's the bedroom. Even with the door closed, we could easily hear him if he cried.'

We carried him through between us, and I saw Mr Stephens for the first time. He was sitting in a cretonne-covered wing chair before a tiny black range which included a minute fire of glowing coke. He was covered from bedroom-slippers to shoulders with an ancient rug, and his white head lolled against one of the wings, though his eyes opened and observed us blearily as we passed through.

'It wa'n't me this time,' he muttered rather smugly as we passed him.

'Of course it wasn't, lovie,' said Mrs Stephens briskly. 'You sleep a bit more, it'll soon be time for your dinner.'

We put the cot in the middle of the pink satin bedspread on some newspapers. There was a stifling odour of old flesh and old clothes and chamber-pots in the room and I sidled over to the window to open it. Thick lace curtains, brown with age, obscured the light, and the window stuck after being opened the first inch or two. Also I was none too happy about the proximity of the room to the wandering old man.

As we went out, I noticed a key in the door. 'Should we lock it, perhaps?' I asked tentatively.

Mrs Stephens stiffened. 'There's no need for that,' she said shortly. 'No need whatever.' And she paused on her way back to the shop to kiss the palsied head of her husband over the back of the chair with defensive tenderness.

The rest of the morning passed without incident. Mrs Alf, a broad-beamed dark-haired blonde who, until the birth of her own baby recently, had helped her husband with great skill and joviality behind the bar, came round sharp at 10.55 to help me carry David to the pub. I was glad to get him out of that frowsty bedroom and into the open air. Mrs Alf suggested we leave him out with her own baby in the small garden behind The Swan, so we set the cot squarely on a defunct fountain.

Both babies, my little dark one and the Davieses' fat red-cheeked fair one, were fast asleep. Mrs Alf folded her large arms across her bosom and remarked with perfect seriousness: 'Don't they make a lovely couple?' I agreed that they certainly did, and she added, 'Now don't you worry, Jane duck. Just as soon as yours wakes up, I'll give him his dins. Got everything there?' I handed her the hold-all containing the ready-made formula in a thermos and the two tins of baby-food. She looked at the thermos disapprovingly. 'The bottle should be in the fridge,' she said. 'Easy to see you haven't had much to do with bottles. Now mine, she had a bottle from the start.'

I glanced at her large, soft, maternal bosom in surprise. She caught the glance and laughed.

'Oh, it's not that I couldn't've,' she hastened to explain. 'Just that I wasn't having any. Such a nuisance! Well, what I mean to say, having 'em's one thing, but givin' up your whole life to 'em's another. This way anyone can feed her, and I can get out in the evenin's. Always was one for a bit of a gay time,' she added, cutting a clumsy caper on the grass.

I wondered what Alf thought of this arrangement. If his wife was free to go out in the evenings, was she not equally free to stay at home and resume her duties behind the bar? But for the moment, her frolics were my bread and butter, so I was not inclined to argue.

The work in The Swan was a great deal harder than that in the post office, but also more lively. It was the local for many farm workers as well as those who worked up their thirsts in the village shops and businesses. It interested me to see how they divided themselves—the farm workers in their reeking overalls considerately placed themselves in the public bar, together with the blacksmith, the odd builder's labourer and grimy coal-heaver, while the farmers themselves, however they, too, might reek, occupied a place in the saloon bar in company with the men of property and stature in the neighbourhood—the coal merchant himself, for instance, though frequently as engrimed as his men, thinking it no shame to give them a hand with the sacks, evidently considered it unseemly to drink with them.

The tiny private bar, carefully screened off by frosted glass panels and not even visible indirectly via the huge mirrors behind the bottles, was for the local ladies (though these generally preferred the more matey atmosphere in the saloon) or for visiting gentry—the Alan Innes type driving through the village with their chic women in Jacqmar headscarves and sheepskin coats, who dropped in for gin and tonic or a lager and perhaps a Scotch egg, or a ham sandwich which it became my job to make.

The Davieses lived, like the Stephenses, behind their premises, but there the similarity ended. The pub might be furnished in the traditional fashion—horse-brasses, pewter mugs and well-rubbed leather seating were much in evidence—but this clearly did not represent the Davieses' personal taste, which burst upon anyone walking through into the living-quarters with all the force that extreme contrast could lend it. From the sober darkness of the pub to such a dazzling welter of 'contemp' always gave me a slight shock, especially in that building, which had been untrammelled Queen Anne before the Davieses took over. Not a wall but was papered in a contrasting pattern; not a vase lacked embellishments of twirling glass tendrils; the furniture was lacquered whitewood (now getting scuffed) upholstered with rexine and speckled with contrasting cushions; the pictures were many and featured a certain study of a green Chinese girl that I had seen in a number of branches of W. H. Smith but never before in anyone's home. The lovely old fireplaces had been blocked in and replaced by flickering electrical monstrosities and the diamond-paned windows were effectually cancelled out by curtains of a much bolder cubist pattern.

Despite all this, there was an atmosphere of cosy hospitality about the place which defied the décor. Mrs Alf, whose real name was Dora although nobody ever called her that, was a very gregarious woman, as indeed she needed to be, since her husband had probably chosen his business in deference to his own need for constant companionship, noise and activity all round him. There was no such thing in the Davieses' household as a 'quiet evening at home', which would have been death for both of them. They entertained from morning till night, if not in the way of business, then privately, and if the licensing laws were not actually broken they were decidedly bent by Alf's own system, to which I was soon made a party. What happened if customers or friends (Alf regarded the two as more or less synonymous) 'came visiting' out of hours was this: Alf would offer drinks from his own cocktail cabinet, a monstrous piece of furniture made of high-gloss maple and white formica with glass panels inside, and the visitor would partake, on the clear mutual understanding that the next time he called during pub hours his bill would be enlarged to include what he was drinking now. The scheme paid dividends in goodwill, but I don't know how much profit it could have shown in actual cash, since when serving drinks in his own home Alf considered it bad manners not to drink too—that, he said, would look too much as if a friendly visit were being exploited for business. Alf was a gargantuan drinker and could put away pint for pint or tot for tot more than twice what any average man could manage—I suppose it was some form of professional immunity.

The Davieses had been married for ten years before the longed-for child was born. 'Bashin' away to no avail,' was how Alf put it. Actually, it was he, and not she, as I soon realized, who had so much wanted a family—Dora was too gay a girl, too proud of her figure and too fond of her freedom, to sink readily into motherhood. From one or two of the broad hints she let fall, I guess that the unavailingness of the bashing had not been entirely a natural accident, at least for the first five years. After that, she probably co-operated spasmodically, according to her mood—she was very fond of Alf, and no doubt sometimes felt guilty that she was depriving him of the 'nippers' he wanted so badly—'But after all,' as she said to me, 'it's not men that has to do all the doings, not just having them and that, but after.' Adding without the least hint of cattiness, 'As you well know, poor ducky!'

Chapter 6

WELL, ALL IN ALL, it was a terrific 'shvitz' as Toby used to say—a mad rush—but worth it, if only in terms of having enough to pay cash to Mr Acre at the end of the week. Actually, I enjoyed it. I'd forgotten how naturally gregarious I am—living alone is pleasant in a way, but it's certainly much pleasanter at night by contrast with a dayful of people. But still, I felt I was only marking time until Dottie arrived and gave me my marching orders. I felt certain she would somehow take me over and get us both organized.

I found time to nip into the local estate agents (which was also the local lawyer's office) and enquire about the shop. The rent was so high that I just stood aghast, but the man gave me a reassuring wink and muttered something about that being the asking-price and that the asking had been going on for a long time. I said, 'Well, what's the paying-price?' but he looked quite shocked at that and said he really couldn't undertake to say. It's obvious that bargaining is just as necessary in the property business as in any oriental market—if you don't want to bargain, they don't feel you're a proper customer or that the deal is a real live deal.

I was serving in the saloon bar on Saturday evening, while David slept the sleep of the full-bellied in the Davieses' nursery. He was getting so active now that I was afraid to leave him alone to sleep in his carry-cot, but this was a minor problem that the practical ingenuity of Dora soon overcame. Her own baby was equipped with the largest drop-side cot I'd ever seen, of which she occupied perhaps 10 per cent of the groundspace; so we simply waited till they were both asleep and then dumped them in together at opposite ends. Since Alf was constantly in and out to see that Eleanor (the baby) was still breathing, there was little danger of their suffocating each other. 'Or of any other untoward incidents occurrin',' as Alf put it with his innocent leer. 'Dunno what's happening to the younger generation these days,' he pursued relentlessly. 'Start shackin' up together in the cradle.' Dora, in the Public, gave a shriek of laughter and insisted upon telling the customers that her daughter was already sharing her bed with a gentleman-friend.

I heard the door of the Private swing to, and slipped through to see who it was. It was Dottie, and there was a man with her. They were deep in conversation and he had asked her what she wanted, she had told him and he had given me the order before she noticed me. She stared at me from between the high wings of her sheepskin collar. Then she affected to be not at all taken by surprise and remarked, 'Oh, there you are, Jane. We were just talking about you!'

'This is her?' asked the man in some amazement.

'Isn't it marvellous?' I said to Dottie. 'Six pun' a week and it's not my only job. Rare roast rib for lunch tomorrow, and steak tonight, if you can wait that long.'

'You're terrific!' she said, with a genuine admiration which warmed me since I did feel a little bit embarrassed about it (oh God, how one's middle-class conditioning haunts one even unto the grave!). 'However, it occurs to me to wonder if you're one of these bar-maids who stand gassing all day and forget what they're there for.'

'Oh! Yes, madam! Beg pardon, madam!' I fixed their genteel drinks (no trouble at all, of course, after pulling pints; my nightmare always was that someone from the sophisticated world beyond the village would come in and ask for some complex cocktail, like a Backlash or a Blue-tailed Fly, that nobody had ever heard of). The man, whom Dottie introduced as Henry Barclay, offered me a 'noggin' but I thought better not and hurried back to the Saloon, which was still unattended since Eleanor had just been heard to give a tiny cough.

Dottie and her companion stayed until closing-time, consuming quantities of alcohol and seeming none the worse for it, talking away with their heads close together over the solitary table. Nobody came into the Private to disturb them. Even I didn't; I was worked nearly off my feet as the rush-hour built up. It was my first Saturday and it practically killed me. Dora said she didn't know how they'd ever managed without me. I didn't either, unless it was because Dora had had to work harder previously than she did when I was there. She seemed to spend her time rubbing noses and exchanging cackles with her favourite customers while Alf kept the swing-door between the Public and the Saloon constantly whupping to and fro, doing most of the work, occasionally giving Dora's ample behind an indulgent pat when it impeded him in his progress.

At last time was called, we mopped the bar, and Dottie, bless her, ducked under it, put on an apron and helped wash the myriad glasses while Henry Barclay had another gin-and-lime and looked on, watching her with a bemused expression. I still had no idea what their relationship was, but it was clear he was rather taken with her. He was a somewhat unimpressive figure, no taller than herself, stocky, with a square, ruddy face and a flat top to his head covered closely by hair of the same colour and pattern as a beach when the tide is far out—little shallow, regular sandy waves. He didn't smile much and from this, and his rather po-faced reaction to my job and Dottie's timely help, I adjudged him to have little or no sense of humour and to be possibly somewhat of a stodge. However, I couldn't have been more wrong.

When we'd cleared everything up, I collected David, put him in Dottie's arms in the front seat of my car and drove off, leaving Henry Barclay to follow in his rather new Triumph. I had to have a private word with Dottie to find out how the land lay and why she'd brought him.

'My dear, he's a find!' she began at once. 'Don't be deceived by his looking like Dick Tracy,' (I hadn't thought he did, which just shows how different people look to each other) 'he could be the answer to our prayers. Actually, what he is, is a sort of private money-lender. You know, he's got a bit to invest and he doesn't want shares, he wants to put it into something he can take an active interest in. No, no, now don't put that face on! He's just what we need.'

'I thought you said you had enough capital.'

'Well, I haven't. I had no idea then what things cost. Anyway, why should we put our own money into it if somebody else is willing?'

'Because it's better to lose our own than somebody else's.'

66

'Is it really? You must be mad. If money's going to be lost, let it be someone else's every time, say I! But there's no reason to suppose we'll lose it. We've got the know-how——'

'Have we?'

'I have,' she said with superb confidence which quite swept me along with her. 'I've spent the last three years selling things, arranging things, buying things to sell. I know how it's done, Jane, and I'm telling you, there's gold in them thar hills, providing you've got two things—the money to get started, and flair.'

'Flair. . . .' I didn't care for the word, somehow. It had a reckless sound.

'Henry has £5,000—' (I gasped)—'which he's willing, subject to finding everything satisfactory, to put into a modern fancy-goods shop run by us——'

'God, what's a modern fancy-goods shop? It sounds ghastly.'

'Nonsense, it's what I told you. Glass, wood, ceramics, hand-woven fabrics—toys, perhaps. Since David was born I've been looking at a lot of toys. I've had a million ideas. Maybe we could find some old craftsmen in the countryside near here who hand-carve things or weave and make pots and so on, whom we could employ in a sort of cottage-industry way to supply us. Of course we'd have to show them exactly what we wanted—no fusty old tat, everything's got to be bang up to date.'

So she rattled on. Her enthusiasm was dangerously in-fectious. By the time we had bounced over the last splashy rut, I could almost see it all myself—the little shop cleaned out and stripped for action, its basic beauties revealed or high-lighted to provide the best possible background for our wares, which Dottie would arrange in the finest Heal's tradition of display. The wares themselves would combine Dottie's intrinsic love for the finest in contemporary urban elegance and taste, with her new-found desire to patronize and nurture the simple talents and produce of the countryside—hand-carved dolls, hand-thrown white-glazed pottery, hand-woven wall-hangings and rugs, hand-hammered iron and copper-ware. Not to mention hand-painted pictures. 'Because as I see it, it will be part art-gallery as well as shop. I mean, if Catesby's can use oil-paintings as background dressing, and sell them too, why can't we? We can seek out local artists—maybe uncover an unknown primitive like that marvellous man who does the suits of armour in little dots or those gorgeous steam-engines.'

'They aren't primitives.'

She brushed this aside. 'Jane, this is going to be wonderful. I know it. Henry falling into my net like that is a sign from heaven that it's going to be a success.'

'How *did* you capture Henry?'

'Ad. in the *Times* Personal.'

'Yours or his?'

'Oh, his. I wouldn't have thought of it.'

'So you fell into *his* net, really.'

'Don't put it like that! Henry's not a bit like a spider.'

'And you're not a bit like a fly. Still, he doesn't look to me like a manifestation of the Heavenly Will, either.'

'You know what I mean,' she said impatiently as we climbed out of the car. 'Why aren't you being more excited?'

'Sorry,' I said. 'The whole thing's moving too fast for me. I hope you haven't forgotten that in less than a year I'm going to New York?'

'Oh, that. . . . Well, you never know, you may not want to go by then.'

'Oh, yes I will. And then you'll be annoyed at my going off.'

'It may well be running on its own momentum by then.'

Henry drove up behind the Maggot and climbed out backwards, bringing out a small, neat, overnight bag.

'You can put him up for the night?' Dottie whispered.

'Yes, if he doesn't object to the sofa. Here, we must get David to bed, it's cold for him out here.'

We were soon sitting round the fire eating underdone steaks from plates on our knees. Dottie was chatting away, I was answering in indistinct monosyllables due to extreme hunger, and Henry was keeping very quiet. I hadn't got Henry's number at all yet. He had vaguely asked if there was anything he could do, but in the end had taken no for an answer and had let me light the fire and get the supper while he sat staring rather moodily into the flames with a glass in his hand. He had brought his own bottle, though, for which I gave him points, even though Dottie had probably told him to.

After the meal, Dottie announced that Henry had to leave

after lunch the next day to spend Sunday afternoon with his mother, and that we must begin talking business. She said this very briskly and authoritatively and then looked from one to the other of us expectantly. A long silence followed.

'I'd like to look at the—er—premises,' said Henry at last. 'In the morning, I mean, of course.'

'Of course,' said Dottie. 'We can get the key from the agent, he's sure not to mind, even if it is Sunday. And then we'll start negotiations right away. I'll go back to town with you tomorrow, Henry, and we'll finalize everything. Then I'll drive back, Jane, and while you earn our bread and butter in the pub, I'll drive round the countryside tracking down sources.'

'Er,' said Henry tentatively.

'What?' asked Dottie, raising her eyebrows in surprise that even such a timid hesitation should be shown.

'Well, only—I mean—you want to finalize everything *tomorrow*?'

'What's the point of waiting?'

'Of course I don't know a great deal about business, but isn't that a bit . . . I mean, wouldn't that be pushing it a bit?' He spoke with a fairly marked Cockney accent—not gorblimey but quite noticeable. It made him more interesting, because his clothes were so tweedy and Austin Reed—he even had a matching waistcoat on, and very conservative shoes that looked as if he'd had them for years and polished them every night. It was hard to place him—town or country, posh or com, rich/idle/shrewd/thrifty/Lib/Lab/Tory, or permutations of the same, it was impossible to tell. He didn't, for instance, look the type who would hurry home from a business meeting to have Sunday tea with his mum. I found myself watching him closely for clues, at the same time thinking how Toby would have enjoyed doing the same from a writer's viewpoint.

Dottie looked jarred, like someone whizzing blithely downhill on a toboggan and hitting a submerged stump.

'Look,' she said, with half-concealed impatience. 'This whole thing is such a wonderful idea—and everything is falling into place so perfectly—it's obviously destined to be *on*. Can't you see that?' She looked from one to the other of us. I tried to look encouraging but at the same time not wholly committed.

69

Henry looked worried and rather mentally windblown. 'I can't see the point of delays!' Dottie exclaimed, stubbing out her cigarette. I saw Henry look along the length of her straight, tense, slender arm and stop at the thick silver bracelet on the wrist. There was a faint, puzzled frown on his face; it could have been simply unease at the way Dottie was pushing him into something he wasn't sure of, but to me it looked like the frown of a man who is beginning to feel something that he never wanted or expected to feel and doesn't know how to cope with it. He suddenly got a pair of heavy-rimmed glasses out of his top pocket and put them on, then leaned back with an air of greater assurance as if wearing them made him invisible and he were now free to observe us and the situation from a position of immunity. The glasses became him; I suddenly saw that for all his stockiness and lack of expression, he was not unattractive—he looked like a nice cuddly koala bear in his hairy brown tweeds, and his rather large ears added not unpleasingly to the likeness.

'I think,' I said, 'that we shouldn't plan too far or too definitely ahead. Let's look over the shop tomorrow and then see.'

'I agree,' said Henry. 'After all, it's no use worrying about "sources" until we're sure we'll have a market. It's only a little village, after all. Who's going to buy the stuff?'

'Oh, nobody around here, probably,' said Dottie airily. 'Not at first, anyway. But look at Tenterden.' She grinned at us triumphantly, like a child who has done its homework.

'Who's he?' asked Henry unwarily.

' "He" is a village in Kent,' said Dottie. 'It's full of antique shops. Super ones—I drove out there the other day. It's a lot further from London than this, but people flock there to buy antiques.'

'Dealers.'

'Not only. *And* it has a modern fancy-goods shop, which the locals now go to—thriving. It's all imported stuff there, too. Ours would be local products, cheaper, *nicer*. And think— we'd be helping to prevent local crafts from dying out. I read somewhere that there's hardly anybody left who knows how to make real rocking-horses any more.'

'What about all those ones in toy-shops?'

'Factory made,' said Dottie scornfully, as if they were some-how fakes.

'And very nice too,' said Henry unexpectedly. 'I hope you're not going to turn your nose up at everything that hasn't been turned out by some doddering old bugger sitting on a sunny bench whittling away with a bowie-knife.' I snorted into my brandy and received a frosty look from Dottie.

'What's wrong with that?' she asked him.

'Everything. I've no objection to a few bits of handicrafts dotted around the place, but the main bulk of the stock's obviously got to be manufactured. I may as well tell you,' he went on, now warming up—it seemed to be a side effect of the glasses—'that if I go into this—*if*, I said—I'm going into it as an investment. I got this bit of money by working damn hard for it and there's no more where that came from; I'm not planning to chuck it away on any airy-fairy artsy-craftsy nonsense. I'll have another of those,' he said to me, passing his glass.

'Help yourself,' I said admiringly, passing him his bottle. He did so, liberally, while Dottie gazed at him with totally new eyes.

'I think I'll have another one too,' she said faintly.

'You shouldn't drink so much,' he said.

Dottie was now flabbergasted. 'Who says so?' she asked dangerously.

'I do. It's not womanly.'

'Don't talk cock,' said Dottie distinctly.

This shocked him into temporary silence. Dottie reached for the brandy and deliberately poured herself a fair old tot. I couldn't help finding all this by-play very amusing, and was watching it with a faintly maternal smile when Henry sud-denly turned the full force of his new-found belligerency on to me.

'And what about you?' he said. 'You're keeping dead quiet, I notice. What's your contribution to all this going to be?'

'I don't really know,' I said pleasantly. 'Work, I should think. You know, nothing skilled—just black-work. There's bound to be some of that, isn't there?'

'There's black-work behind every success,' said Henry tersely. 'I know. I've done some.' Clue! But it didn't lead to anything. It seemed Henry was an early retirer, because although it was only just on midnight he suddenly jumped up and said, 'Here, it's late! I want to get up early tomorrow and I must get my sleep. Can you show me my bed?'

'That's it you've been sitting on,' I said.

'Oh, well, that's fine,' he said, and stood rather awkwardly waiting for us to take ourselves off. I brought him sheets and blankets and showed him the downstairs loo, and then Dottie and I went up to my room feeling rather ousted; if we'd been alone we'd have undoubtedly sat talking for another couple of hours at least.

'There's more to that one than I thought,' said Dottie rather grimly as we closed the door of David's room behind us.

'Who, David?' I asked wickedly.

'No. 'Ennery.'

'Did you think he was just a fall-guy?'

'Really, Jane! One would think I was out to rob him. I only mean I expected him to be a sort of—well, *sleepy* partner, if not actually a sleeping one; I mean until this evening he hardly had a word to say for himself.'

'What were you talking about then, all evening in the bar?'

'Oh, he wasn't talking at all. I was.'

I believed her. 'Do you like him?'

'How?' she asked at once.

'That way.'

'No, of course not! With those ears? With that funny hair?'

'He likes you—that way.'

'Too bad,' she said callously. 'Or rather, no, it's good. Useful.'

'Dottie!'

'Oh, don't look so shocked. I'm fed up with men using me. I'm going to do the using in future.'

'Even if it's somebody nice?'

'Show me a really nice man,' she said, 'a really *nice* man, and I'll use him—till death do us part. But Henry's not it. He's too damn *chutzpahdic* for one thing.'

'Where did you hear that?'

'You're not the only one who's had a Jewish lover,' she said as she climbed into bed.

72

Chapter 7

I WAS MORE than surprised the next morning, on tottering downstairs in my dressing-gown with David draped over my shoulder and my eyes only half open, so find a brisk and busy Henry, dressed except for his jacket, and neatly shaved, an apron tied under his armpits to protect his waistcoat, washing the supper-dishes at the kitchen sink. The kettle was steaming and various bits and pieces had been brought out of the fridge which indicated that when the ground was cleared he had proposed to begin making breakfast.

'Good morning,' I said in dopey astonishment. 'You don't have to do that.'

'Well, I want my breakfast. I always eat well in the mornings. I hope you don't mind,' he said as an afterthought. 'I've already had a cup of tea.'

'Of course I don't mind. You make me feel a bad hostess, that's all. But after all, it *is* barely seven o'clock.' I put David in his Babysitta on the table where he could watch us.

'You put him on the table, do you?' asked Henry, disapprovingly.

'Yes,' I said rather shortly, starting to prepare his morning cereal and orange juice.

'Doesn't he ever pee on it?'

'Babies of that age don't pee very copiously. And he is wearing a nappy.' I find people who are too fastidious very hard to take in my own house.

Now that I'd arrived, Henry allowed me to take over. It would have been nice if he'd finished the dishes, but instead he stood in the middle of the kitchen, his hands in his pockets, gazing at David expectantly as if waiting for him to perform.

'My mother's is rather like him,' he said musingly. 'But then I suppose they all look much alike.'

I stopped dead and stared at him. He was hard on forty, must have been. 'Your *mother's* got a baby?'

'Step-mother, I mean, of course.'

'How old's your father, then?'

'Sixty-four.'

'Good for him.'

'Well, why not?' he asked defensively.

'No reason at all! I said—good for him.'

'Thought you were being sarky.'

'Is it your step-mother you're going to visit today?'

'Yes. They live not far from here. Dad's retired. They've got a little house near Walton.' The accent was sounding more and more incongruous. It would have led me to expect a dad on a council estate in Roehampton. My trouble, one of them, is that I'm a sort of snob. I mean, I'm inclined to stick labels on people according to what used to be class, and now that one can't do that any more, I'm often at a loss. Fortunately I'm beginning to like it that way; much more interesting than being able to pigeon-hole people as Shaw's Professor Higgins was able to. Henry really intrigued me, and I liked him for that. In a sudden rush of affection for the unwonted mental activity he was unwittingly supplying, I said, 'Do sit down. I'm going to make you a huge breakfast right away. Bacon and eggs?'

'Fine. Any left-over potatoes, have you got? I like a few fried-up potatoes in the mornings.'

'I've got a left-over steak, if you want it,' I offered jokingly.

'Fine,' he said, not jokingly at all.

'Oh,' I said. 'Well, perhaps you wouldn't mind feeding the baby?'

'Who, me?'

'It's easy. You just spoon it into his mouth.'

'Can't your friend do it?' It was clear he thought that was woman's work.

'Dottie's still fast asleep and likely to remain so until she hears the toast being scraped.'

'Oh, hell. Oh, all right. Let's be having you,' he said to David, who was staring at him, mouth ready agape. 'Here,' said Henry plaintively a few seconds later. 'It all comes out again.'

'Scrape it off his chin and put it back.'

'Ugh!'

'Oh, don't be such an old woman!' I couldn't help saying rather sharply.

'It's just because I'm not an old woman,' he retorted, 'that I'm not accustomed to this kind of thing.'

'You wouldn't make a very nice husband if you insist on such distinctions.'

'I would have made an excellent husband for any woman who didn't mind *being* the woman and letting me be the man.'

I let this go, because all possible responses would have been either trite or inquisitive. It was only later that I wondered about the tense he'd used.

We drove into the village in Henry's car in the middle of the morning. Henry was ready and aching to get started hours before we were; he sat or stood about, not troubling to hide his impatience, and yet watching with the same puzzled look in his eyes as Dottie wafted somnolently about, her long, elegant house-robe billowing in the draughts and her streaky hair attractively tousled. At last she went drifting upstairs to make a leisurely toilet while I tidied up and got David and myself dressed in warm slacks and an anorak apiece. He really looked very fetching in his little red one; his hair was long enough now to fall in a silken fringe across his forehead under the hood, and with his great dark eyes and solemn mouth he looked like a little Eskimo.

'Isn't he a darling?' I couldn't help asking Henry rhetorically, just because I had to say it to someone.

'Will he pee on my upholstery?'

'Oh Henry, do stop about him peeing! What a fuss!'

'My step-mother's peed all over the back seat. It took two weeks to get rid of the smell.'

'Your car's obviously a new thing in your life.'

'Well, I've waited a long time for one,' he said rather sheepishly.

We got the key out of the agent without difficulty and drove to the shop. Dottie had now completely woken up (it usually took her about two hours, three cups of coffee and a bath to achieve this) and was on top of her form; she looked stunning in her suède boots and a startlingly short scarlet topcoat which reminded me of the time she'd been my only visitor in hospital when I'd nearly miscarried with David. Now she walked in ahead of us and immediately began swooping to and fro like a swallow engaged in nest-building, gesturing and explaining and painting mental pictures for us to such an extent that I, at any rate, soon forgot the present unpromising appearance of the place. But Henry was made of sterner stuff.

'I expected something much larger,' he said flatly when she paused for breath.

'What do you want for £5,000, Liberty's?' she asked indignantly. It was obvious she regarded the place as her own and resented any slight upon it.

'There's scarcely room in here to swing a cat. And it's pitch dark. You'd have to use artificial lighting all day—that's damned pricey.' He looked up at the ceiling, about which Dottie had just been reverently making plans. 'Dare not touch that,' he said. 'Start stripping off the layers of varnish and the whole lot'd likely come down. It's only the paint that holds the plaster up.'

'But the lovely old beams!'

'Never mind them. Let them stay up there under the paint and do their job as long as they can. One thing though, we'll have to get an expert in to see if there's woodworm or dry rot. There's bound to be, I suppose—always is in these shaky old buildings. Depends how extensive it is. If it's at all bad, there's no use touching it. We'd just have the whole thing ready to go and one of us'd walk in one day and fall through the floor.' He walked round the room, bent over, apparently examining the skirting-boards. 'Here, look at this!' he said, more, it seemed, in triumph than dismay. He showed Dottie his fingers which were tipped in white. 'Damp. Bet the place has no damp-course at all. Have to lay one down—very expensive business.'

This went on for about ten minutes. By the end, Dottie looked rather like a flat tyre—all the joy had gone out of her. She was just sitting on a box in a dark corner looking as if she might burst into tears.

There was a silence and then she sighed, stirred herself and lit a cigarette. Then she stood up and moved to the door. 'Let's go,' she said forlornly.

'Where to?'

'Take the key back and then home.'

'What's the matter, have I put you off the whole scheme just by being a bit realistic?'

'Well, you're obviously not interested, so what's the sense?'

'Really,' he said, 'you are a silly girl. Did you expect me to join you in your never-never-land of dreams? If you wanted someone who just wanted to get rid of his money, you should have looked for someone with plenty of it. Anyway, you told me you needed a man, to take over the practical details. And when I do so, you get all damp and tearful.'

'I am not damp and tearful!' retorted Dottie furiously. 'I thought you were giving up on the whole thing!'

'Well, I haven't yet. But I don't promise I won't. If there's dry-rot——'

'Oh, shut up about dry rot!'

Henry cast a speaking glance at me which loyalty forbade me to acknowledge. Instead I said tactfully, 'It's nearly opening time.'

'I can see you are going to be useful,' said Henry. Dottie swept out ahead of us and he was forced to take the other handle of the carry-cot.

'Actually she's more of a problem than the dry rot,' he said in an undertone. 'Talk about easy glum, easy glow! What's the matter with her?'

'She's an enthusiast, that's all,' I said—more shortly than I would have done had I not also privately thought Dottie was acting rather childishly.

Alf served us in the saloon bar with a somewhat bleary Sunday-morning air as if he'd been taken by force away from his Colour Supplement. 'Nice to see you the other side of the bar,' he said. 'How's the nipper then? Sleep well, did you?' he asked David. 'Not so nice on your own, is it, my lad? Chilly-like on these damp nights.' He enjoyed his joke until he looked at me and thinking, I suppose, that this might be a sore spot in my own life, stopped chuckling abruptly.

The drinks hit home and did us all good. Dottie cheered up as Henry bluntly told her *his* plans. He proposed sending

77

out experts early in the week to inspect the place and make estimates for putting it in order. When he'd seen those, he said, and only then, would he be able to make a decision. On mature reflection, and a double whisky, this could not but seem perfectly reasonable to Dottie.

'I can see you're exactly what we need, actually, I mean apart altogether from the money,' she said. She was sitting in a very fashionable position with her legs stretched out and her toes turned in, and was twiddling her glass on her knee, where the base left a round, wet medallion on the patterned stocking. 'I'm sorry I behaved like such an idiot. I can never take having cold water poured on my infant enthusiasms.'

Henry, sitting in his stiffly upright position, well-shod feet planted apart, and the feeling about him that he should have a watch-chain festooned across his waistcoat, glanced at her in surprise, and his eye got stuck to the wet place on her knee. 'Oh—forget it,' he said uncertainly. Then he looked quickly back at his glass, at me, at the bar, at the door. Suddenly he stood up, tossed back his drink and said abruptly, 'I must be off.'

'Now? But you said after lunch.'

'Well . . . I don't go in for lunches much. I'll drop you at your place on my way.'

He whisked us back to the cottage, and before we quite knew what was happening we were watching the cream rear of the Triumph vanishing down the lane.

'Impulsive, isn't he?' said Dottie, sounding puzzled.

'Is he frightened of women, do you think?'

'I don't know—he certainly didn't give that impression this morning.'

'I didn't mean as business partners, I mean as females.'

'Dunno. Don't care much. . . . Come on, let's eat, that whisky's gone to my head.'

On Tuesday morning the first of the experts came roaring down from London to investigate the shop. I was working of course, so Dottie dealt with them. Dottie was causing quite a stir in the village. Her clothes were 100 per cent Mary Quant and King's Road in general—not too far out, but far enough for the village to find her pretty hard to swallow and pretty interesting to talk about. Even Alf, who flattered himself he was with-it, could be seen waving his heavy eyebrows about a bit at his male customers whenever she entered the pub, and Dora said enviously, 'Is that what they're wearing in the Smoke now? Makes you feel right out of it, living in the sticks AND being too busty and hippy even if you didn't. She's got a nice figure, your friend.' However, she couldn't resist adding that blonde tips and streaks went out years ago.

The experts, as I say, came and went, but not before Dottie had charmed them all with her enthusiasm. 'I believe he *did* find a spot or two of dry rot,' she mentioned on the Wednesday evening. 'And some tiny holes which he insisted were made by some insidious beetle or other. I said the holes were old and the beetle was probably dead long ago, but he put his ear to one and said he could hear them chewing. Never mind. When I explained what we were going to do, and how badly we needed him to give a promising report to Henry, he sort of made scratching-out motions with his pen in his notebook. He was making a joke of it, but still, I think he'll play it down. He was quite a sweetie as a matter of fact,' she said coolly. 'Easy to work on.'

I looked at her anxiously across the supper-table. Alf had asked me to go back and help out between 8 p.m. and closing time, so I was rushing, but more and more there was this thing about Dottie now that was worrying me. She was different—tougher. I didn't like it.

'But you don't want Henry to invest his money in something that's going to fail, do you? I don't know how he made it, but it's all he's got and he said there's no more where that came from.'

'Well, that's all rot, to start with. He's a young, active chap, not some retired old grandad handing over his life's savings— *if* he came a cropper over this, why couldn't he earn some more? But anyway he's not going to lose it. All this fuss about a few beetles and a bit of damp! The building hasn't fallen down for 400 years, it's not likely to collapse in the next five.'

'What "next five"? Dottie, I told you, I'm in on this for exactly the next eight months or so, then I'm off.'

'We'll see.'

'We *will* see. I'm going.'

'Why are you so set on it, anyway?'

'I've got to do something exciting with the £400.'

'Wouldn't starting a business be exciting enough?'

'It's not the right kind of thing. I can't explain.'

'What if you met someone and wanted to get married?'

I was struck dumb with surprise. Could it be that Dottie hadn't understood about me and Toby? But of course she had! She noticed my expression and interpreted it correctly.

'Oh, I know all about *that*. But sometimes things like that drag on until one finds one's missed the boat. When you get the ball you have to play it quickly or it just turns to lead in your hands. I think you and Toby may have dropped the ball already. I mean, how long since you've seen him?'

'I don't know—I don't keep count like that.'

'Well, that doesn't sound as if you're still in love.'

'In love. . . .' The words rang strangely in juxtaposition to Toby's name. In love did, indeed, mean counting days, rushing for the mail, peaking and pining. Toby was . . . how to put it, even to myself? I wasn't in love with Toby any more. Toby was part of me. You don't get in a lather about someone who is simply a basic essential in your life. He was just with me all the time. I thought suddenly that even if he died, it would still be like that.

'Could you have an affair with somebody else?'

The question came from Dottie, but I might have asked it of myself. The answer, based with all honesty on my experience with that grisly Alan, had to be a qualified yes, and for the first time I understood how men can have affairs and claim that it has nothing to do with their marriage. But that's not to say I would have felt right about it, or enjoyed it more than marginally, or that it wouldn't have damaged me, and me-and-Toby.

'Could you?'

'I don't know—perhaps. But not—but never—marry.' I felt like adding, *I am married*, but it would have sounded stupid.

'Whatever happened,' Dottie asked suddenly, just as I was going out of the door, 'to the black man?'

'John? He's working in a club in London.'

'Could you have an affair with a negro?'

'Dottie, what on earth is all this about?—No.'

'Why not?'

'I'd feel strange about it. I must go.'

'Go on, then. I'll take good care of David.' I was outside and climbing into the car when I heard the window open and Dottie shouted after me: '*I* could!'

'What?'

'Have an affair with a negro!'

'Well, you're out of luck in these parts.'

'I might go and hunt up John. He was a really nice fellow.'

I slammed the car door eloquently and drove away, thinking: a fat lot of good darling old John would do you or any woman. I didn't like the taste left in my mouth by the conversation, somehow. Was Dottie getting frustrated? It was something I could well sympathize with, though it didn't take me like that—sexy conversations and so on. And being nervy. The way I coped was to lie in bed at night, or in my bath, and imagine Toby and me in all sorts of lovely pornographic situations—on rafts at sea where he had to lick my lips to keep them moist, or in steaming jungles with us both naked and slippery, or just back in the L-shaped room doing the things we actually did. I liked reading sexy books, too, and identifying myself with the protagonists. The trouble with so-called dirty books, of course, is that they usually *get* dirty—I mean, the lovely sex gets mucky and perverted instead of just being normal, the way I like it. For instance, I adored *Fanny Hill* and got a lot of purely physical, sublimationary pleasure out of it, till it got to the mucky bits about whips and idiots which made me feel absolutely sick. What the hell is the matter with people that they need that sort of thing? And what was the matter with Dottie, that she needed to start talking about having affairs with negroes in that rather peculiar, lip-licking way? I loved Dottie. I really cared about her. It worried me very much when she did things or said things that were not in keeping with what I thought I knew of her.

Chapter 8

SEVERAL WEEKS PASSED. I saw little enough of Dottie, and nothing of Henry, except once he drove down to go into a huddle with Dottie over the estimates. He left again without even waiting for a meal, but Dottie was far too excited to notice. It was clear, without anything specific being said, that he had decided to include himself in.

I was kept busy following my complex schedule; sometimes I felt as if David and I were moving parts in some kind of involved puzzle—one of those how-to-get-from-A-to-Z-by-the-longest-possible-route things. I settled into the routine as well as I could, and found it just worked, though the transition from the frowsty back bedroom at the Stephenses to the ever-colder air in the Davieses' back garden gave David the first cold of his life.

This made for worse complications, since Alf was appalled at the idea that Eleanor might catch this cold and die. So for several days David, muffled up to the eyebrows, had to travel round the countryside in the back seat of Dottie's car. We arranged a sort of baby-trap of fish-netting over the top of the carry-cot so that he couldn't roll out, but in any case he slept most of the time; when Dottie stopped somewhere for food, usually frugally at a country café or pub, she would get the bottle out of the thermos and feed him on her knee, stuffing a few spoonfuls of mashed vegetables or rice pudding into his mouth from her own dish for good measure. I'm sure that David's cast-iron stomach and willingness to eat absolutely anything dates from those days when he had to fit willy-nilly into his godmother's business life.

In the evenings we would both stagger home in a state of near-exhaustion, and usually Dottie would prepare a scratch meal while I crawled into a bath with David and got him off to bed. Really, if he had been a difficult baby in any way I simply don't know how we'd have managed, but he was quite angelic and didn't seem to mind what sort of hours he kept or how many of them were spent in different localities or bumping about in strange cars.

Then Dottie and I would sit down together by the fire (which in those rushed weeks I often treacherously wished was a simple electric one which didn't need raking out, laying and lighting) with our suppers on our knees and the radio, with luck, playing soft, soothing music, and I would listen to her day's doings. (There was little enough to relate to her of mine, in which the dramatic highlight was likely to be something like Mufferpaws having misbehaved under Mr Stephens's chair, leading to a horrible misunderstanding, or Eleanor cutting a tooth.)

I had to hand it to Dottie. She really was getting down to cases. I was amazed by how many sources of talent she had run to earth in how short a time. One person interested in some form of handicraft seemed to lead to another.

At first, whenever she enquired for people who could make things, she was directed to Old Mrs Crabbe who knitted lovely little jumpers, or Miss Dogsbody who was famous for her upside-down cake at bring-and-buys.

Far from turning up her nose at these suggestions, she always meticulously followed them up; sitting in Mrs Crabbe's parlour watching her hands flash nimbly over half-finished weeny garments, her quick eye would be roving the walls and corners; and there, sure enough, she might see a rather ghastly, but beautifully executed, embroidered picture or firescreen or cushion-cover. This she would admire, and be told that this was just something Mrs Crabbe's married daughter did 'to fill her hands' while she watched the telly in the evenings. So then Dottie would repair to the home of Mrs Crabbe's married daughter, and ask whether she would be prepared to alter her style a little—relinquish the nasturtiums and hollyhocks and crinoline ladies, and embroider according to a design which Dottie would supply. When Mrs Crabbe's daughter learned that there would be money in this which could be made in her spare time, she agreed readily. So then Dottie would make a note in her little ABC notebook under E for

Embroidery, and come home and tell me: 'Now what I've got to look out for is an artist who can design small modern tapestries. They're all the rage now, in London—I saw a marvellous wall decoration a few weeks ago in a friend's flat which turned out to be a piece of embroidery based on a small Sutherland.'

'Sew-your-own-Coventry-Cathedral,' I suggested.

'Don't mock,' she said severely. 'It'll sell.'

She said the same of pictures made of scraps of material and nylon stockings, which a middle-aged maiden lady in the district whose talents had so far been limited to making patch-work tea-cosies had rather doubtfully agreed she would try her hand at; and dolls made of polished straw or corn-cobs and dried leaves, 'in the tradition of the American craftsmen,' as Dottie loftily put it; and children's basket-chairs with hoods, which the old basket-maker she had tracked down had told her he'd almost forgotten how to make because there was no demand for them.

But all these were small fry. Pictures and dolls would not fill the shop, or our pockets. She had to lay on 'the hard stuff' as she called it. So she asked round and consulted local suppliers and telephone directories and all sorts of other ingenious sources, and made a list of all the professional carpenters, potters, weavers, blacksmiths and glass-blowers she could find out about. Actually there were no glass-blowers, which was a heavy blow to her; the nearest glass foundry was in the Midlands, and she gloomily supposed they would be working full-blast mass-producing objects of singular monotony and hideousness, like the vases which flourished in the Davieses' apartment, all without a flaw or a sign of having been touched by a warm, skilful human hand (or rather, blown into by a warm human mouth).

However, doggedly determined, she set off one morning in the car to drive North and see if she couldn't find some smallish factory with a few craftsmen left who might blow her some nice thick lopsided bubbly objects with silken textured sides and 'that marvellous rough blob at the bottom where they've been broken off the pipe', which she could display and sell as works of the glass-blowers' art. I watched her go with a sense of affection and pride, but also a feeling of despair;

she cared so desperately—not just about the shop, but about this whole concept she'd developed, this hatred of mass-production, the almost sensuous desire to propagate the work of skilled hands.

I knew she was struggling against the tide, and I felt certain that, well as she had done in a small way so far, today she was doomed to disappointment. Lost in the grimy stews of the industrial Midlands, she might see and realize what she was actually up against; they might laugh at her; she might, probably would, come back that night worn out and with a destructive inkling—which I had had from the outset—that, however enthusiastically we might start out, however noble our aims or hard our efforts, by the very nature of our times, our enterprise was doomed.

Sure enough, she arrived back at eleven p.m., desperately stiff and weary, and with nothing concrete to show for it except one slender hope. I'd kept supper for her, and as she sat by the fire, almost too tired to eat it, sipping a much-needed whisky and relating her story with her head back and her eyes closed, she told me that, in the course of as dismal and depressing a day as I had foreseen for her, she had met one man with broken veins in his cheeks and lips like a trumpeter who said he had once worked for a private foundry on the outskirts of Birmingham, where what he called 'glass artists' used to come in on Saturday afternoons before the fires had cooled, and 'blow all manner of queer things, animals and that sometimes, but other times they just blowed lumps.' This sounded exactly what Dottie wanted, but of course it was too late by then to go all the way across to Brum, so she planned to go up there in a day or two, and see if she could find the place, if it still existed.

'Probably doesn't,' she said in a flat, weary voice. 'It's probably a supermarket or a "proper" factory by now. That's what that ex-craftsman called the soulless junk-producing monolith where he works now—a proper factory.'

She filled the next few days with visits closer at hand, though often she would drive fifty miles to talk to a craftsman she'd heard of in a distant village; sometimes she would spend hours just trying to find their workshops or cottages; some of the villages were even so small they were not to be found on any map, and these, she said, were where one frequently turned up the best people; it was as if the less contact they had with the world, the less likely the world was to have laid its corruptive finger on them and taken away their skills.

One day she drove all the way to the Cotswolds to unearth an old man whose carving she'd seen in a junk-shop in Esher. This time she came back elated. 'Gloucestershire's the place!' she exclaimed happily, tucking into a vast meal at 10 p.m. (Her appetite fluctuated according to the sort of people she'd met during the day.) 'I tell you, the further away from the big city centres they are, the better they work, and the nicer they are, too. Simple, unspoiled, gentle, kind, marvellous, marvellous people. We're ruining ourselves, Jane, that's what we're doing, we poor city idiots, clogging our bodies with poisons and cramming our souls and hands with ugliness. That old man today made me feel ashamed of myself, ashamed of my slick silly clothes, ashamed of the way I talk and the way I think and with practically everything about the way I live except the fact that some drive in me had led me to be sitting there with him, drinking cider and handling his *beautiful* work. You know? His tools alone, the clutter of old, worn, practical, creative tools on his work bench, was something you could paint or photograph from a hundred angles and have a picture worth hanging on your wall every time. And the *quiet* there —the utter peace! Every single thing in his cottage was old and well-worn and lovely to touch—mellow, smooth, integrated. I could have stayed there forever. Well,' catching my eye, 'of course that's not true, but the fact that I couldn't, means there's something wrong with *me*. That old man had something that——' She put a big chunk of stewed lamb into her mouth and chewed it blissfully. 'Food,' she said, 'is wonderful when you've earned it. Oh, I should have been a farmer's boy-oy-oy . . . have we any beer? No, don't laugh at me. Or, yes, you may if you like. I don't care. The old man has agreed to make tables for us. Not just ordinary tables. Irregular nests, each one a slightly different shape; and little kidney-shaped ones for children, with the chairs to match. In oak and pine and rosewood. He does the finish himself—satin. No varnish. Wait till you see what he gave me—a wonderful knife-box, with a lid that fits exactly like a glove. Just to open and close it gives one a sensual thrill. He carves a little thistle on all his work, it's his trade-mark, like Grinling Gibbons's mouse.'

She set off for Birmingham at the crack of dawn next day, before I was even awake, and despite the fact that she'd had only about five hours' sleep. I couldn't help worrying about her driving up the M1 like that, in case she got sleepy, but she'd gone by the time I thought of warning her to take a thermos of coffee. I went off to work as usual, and was in the middle of serving a little boy with a box of liquorice allsorts when the post-office door opened and in walked Toby.

'Three tuppence-ha'penny stamps and a Mars bar,' he said without batting an eye.

I served him with a straight face and a heart nearly bursting with joy, while Mrs Stephens looked at him curiously from behind the jars. He was subtly changed once again. His clothes were better—gone the threadbare corduroy jacket and the jeans-like trousers, and in their place a nice pair of off-the-peg flannels and a very nice polo-neck sweater. My eyes slid carelessly past this to his hair, which happily he had not allowed to grow to a fashionable length, and then snapped back again sharply. The sweater definitely had a hand-knitted look.

'Where did you get that?' I asked, much to Mrs Stephens's surprise.

'Ah-ha! Lost none of our acuity, I notice,' he remarked, unpeeling the Mars bar and taking a bite out of it. 'Want a bit?'

'No thanks, I want to know where you got that sweater.'

'Well, as you obviously spotted, it was knitted for me.'

'Who by?'

'We literate authors say, by whom? What are you doing in here?'

'What are *you*? And don't change the subject.'

'If you mean, how did I know where to look for you, Billie told me. She's a great admirer of yours—and mine, by the way. I've got lots to tell you. When do you get off?'

'From here, at opening time. Then I move across to the local.'

He raised his eyebrows. 'You are a busy girl,' he said in a

87

disturbed tone. He lowered his voice. 'Is all this really necessary?'

'And how.'

'Where's the baby?'

I gestured over my shoulder. Several customers were waiting. Toby took the hint. 'I'll wait for you in The Swan,' he said, and edged to the door. There he stopped and, while I was trying to listen to the next customer's order, distracted me by a series of gestures indicating that the maker of the sweater was a luscious, shapely siren. With a last erotic roll of his eyes he went out, but stood for some time peering through the window making faces at me. He sloped off at last, leaving me to cope with my feelings and a crowd of customers and Mrs Stephens's curiosity.

'Friend of yours, dear?' she asked as soon as there was the smallest opportunity.

'Yes, a very old friend.'

'He doesn't look very well-fed,' she remarked.

'He's a writer.' I knew that, to Mrs Stephens, that would be self-explanatory.

'Ah! I see,' she said wisely.

At 11.30 I carted the cot, which seemed to grow heavier every day, across the road. Christmas was hard upon us, and the pub was thickly festooned with aged paper-chains and fretted bells and balls, with a daily-increasing number of cards tacked to the edge of the awning above the bar. Toby jumped up as I came back in, lugging the cot, and helped me to set it on one of the benches. He stood for some time then, staring down at David, who stared back up at him.

'He's huge,' he said at last in a rather subdued voice.

'Well, that's good, isn't it?'

'Oh, yes . . . it's just that . . .'

'What?'

'I'm missing so much of him.'

I glanced at him quickly. If he meant this as it sounded, it was perhaps the nicest thing that had been said to me for some time.

He seemed to pull his eyes away from the baby and said to me, 'Have you time for a quick one before you start serving them?'

The pub was almost empty still, so I ducked under the bar and got us both a drink. As I passed him his, Toby leaned across the bar and kissed me quickly. 'You,' he said gently.

'Yes, me,' I said with too much briskness because I instantly wanted to be in bed with him. 'Now what about this sweater?'

'Ah yes,' he said. 'Watch closely.' He reached into the neck of the sweater and slowly drew out a girlie magazine with the head and naked bosom of a gorgeous blonde on its cover. By the time he'd completely withdrawn it it concealed his own face and looked as if the girl were emerging from the polo neck.

'Brilliant,' I said sourly. '*She* can't even knit for herself, apparently. Come on, who was it?'

'Well, she's very young—seventeen as a matter of fact. The most delectable age. She's trim and slim and small and red-headed and she wears skirts up to here and bells round her ankles. . . .'

'Stop making it up.'

'But it's true! Every word. As a matter of fact, she's Billie Lee's daughter.'

This rang so true that suddenly I was really jealous. I knew —I hoped—I had no cause to be, but I was. How dared she knit him a sweater? What could be more intimate, more of a declaration? The fact of my own incapacity in this field made things worse.

'What's her name?'

'Whistler.'

'I beg your pardon?'

'Her real name is Melinda or something frightful, but she's always called Whistler. And don't ask what that makes Billie. She's rather had that joke.'

'And she's keen on you—obviously.'

'Why obviously?'

'Well, I mean to say! It's a cable-stitch.'

He looked blank for a minute, then burst out laughing. 'Well, as it happens she *is* a bit struck. They get these crushes at that age. I go round to Billie's quite a bit—she's not just an agent to me, she's much more a friend and believe me, she's been quite wonderful through many a tight spot in the last year. I don't think I'd ever have finished the first novel if she hadn't been around to push me.'

'I'm sure. Now about Whistler, of all the bloody silly names.'

'Don't be like that.'

'I *am* like it. Didn't you know?'

'No.'

'Well you've never given me cause before.'

'Sad, but true. I can't even say "that's all you know".'

'Are *you* struck?'

'Madly. She's young, tender, dewy-eyed. . . .'

'Shut up.'

'Darling!'

'Sorry. Just tell me the facts.'

He looked into my eyes and then down into his drink. '*Facts*. You know I'm a man of fiction. But she's very pretty—that's a fact.'

I left him to serve a customer. My eyes were burning. I felt angry and miserable. I was more angry with myself than with him, because what was it all about, what was I living alone for, and not making demands on him, and trying to make myself believe in leaving each other free, if the second I thought the unthinkable—that he might, just might, in my absence look at another woman—my possessiveness came back with such force that the words 'He's mine, he's mine, he's mine,' were beating through my brain like the very tides of my blood, and I wanted to tear the sweater off his back and throw it into the pretty face of its loving maker? I wanted to hang a label round his neck saying 'Taken' and chain him to my bedpost and never let him out of my sight again. And from these primitive feelings I knew that I had no more cured myself of wanting to own him than if I had just grabbed him and held onto him right at the beginning.

When I went back to him, it was as if, by silent mutual agreement, we had decided to drop the subject. He had meant it as a sort of teasing game and I couldn't take it like that so we dropped it. He told me things were going well; he'd sold a short story to the *Saturday Evening Post*, which was at one time the absolute height of his ambition, and he'd started on another novel. He said Billie had persuaded him to leave the Holland Park basement and move to a more habitable abode, so he'd got a big studio-room for himself in a house in Earl's Court—'Lovely area, such variety! Food, shops, newspapers, nationalities—you name it, we've got it. All the vices and virtues catered for—the world and the city in microcosm. The house I live in is a micro-microcosm.'

'Like the house in Fulham?'

'God, no! Thank heaven, it's a good step up from that. The room's big and gaunt and practically empty, but it's very much what I wanted. Now I'm sort of into the way of working properly, I mean so many hours every day, I don't feel I have to keep my surroundings quite so austere. You remember how I wouldn't let myself have a radio or pictures or even books except for what I needed for reference and a few of the classics? It was necessary then, or I'd have sat about all day letting myself fall into any distraction that offered itself. You know I'm naturally bone bloody idle. But one can get into a saving routine, a habit of work, and then you're like a cured alcoholic, you're afraid to backslide, you remember the horror of not working and you're afraid to let a day drift by . . . I've done a tremendous bulk of work in the last nine months or so, and some of it's beginning to sell, and now Billie makes me keep it up by ringing me every few days to ask how many pages I've written. But it's not so essential any more—I can do it for myself. So I'm free to let myself have some of the amenities I've never had but always wanted.'

'Here, Jane! Don't you work for us any more, girl?'

I rushed through into the Public to help Alf, with an apologetic air, but kept nipping back whenever I could to the end of the bar in the Saloon to hear the next instalment. Between midday and 2.30 I caught up on all his news. I heard about the few things he'd carefully bought for himself in markets and antique shops ('Well, junk shops really, I can't run to antique-shop prices, even the Earl's Court Road ones.') I heard the book was coming out in January, that the next was half-finished. I heard some very funny stories about other people living in the house. And I heard about John.

'You know, I often wonder what will become of John. After all, what's the future for a chap like him? He'll never marry, never have a proper home; he's so gentle and innocent he'll never really get on in the world of night-club bands and so on. And I do care about the old black bastard, I mean I'll never forget how he mothered the pair of us when we were all imprisoned together in that grim house. And how we hurt him by falling in love! I think he was half 'n love with both of us. In the end he completely got over my jealousy and only wanted us to marry and be happy. I never knew a queer could be so natural in his outlook towards marriage and children. He hasn't a clue, you know, that there's anything wrong with him, I don't suppose he's ever heard of queerdom or would be anything but horrified if anyone told him he wasn't normal. I hope to Christ nobody ever does! I try to see him as often as I can. He always asks wistfully about you and the baby; he can't understand why we're not together.' He took hold of my forefinger and pushed at the nail with his thumb and muttered, 'When I talk to John and sort of soak up some of his simplicity about love and babies, I can't understand why myself.' He looked up at me with that utter candour that came over him whenever he wasn't fooling around. 'Would you like to? I mean, shall we?'

I stared at him. I should say no, because I could see that he was functioning under John's influence and that he, by himself, was not sure. I myself was not entirely sure—of him. Would he really be able to love the baby and forget it wasn't his? Would he be able to work with a wife and child in the house? Would he be able to keep us, or endure not being able to keep us, and my having to help? I should say no . . . but what if he never asked again?

In the space of those few seconds, other urgent considerations rushed through my mind. I had never, till now, thought for one moment of the possibility of his meeting someone else. But now I thought I'd been a fool. Toby was hardly suited to a monastic existence, however he might be disciplining himself; he was a very normal, hot-blooded man, and as he wasn't getting it from me, where was he to get it? He couldn't go on not getting it forever.

Sooner or later he'd form a relationship, probably meaning it to be one of those transient oh-be-joyful things that goes up like a rocket and leaves nothing but a gratifying smell of spent sulphur in the air afterwards; but knowing Toby, it might very well not stay like that, because he wasn't that kind; if he liked the girl well enough to make love to her in the first place, he probably liked her enough to get really involved later on. And if he got really involved with any other woman I would want to kill the pair of them, but that wouldn't help much, since it would be entirely my own responsibility. Especially now that he'd actually asked me in so many words.

'Toby,' I began carefully.

'Last orders, please!'

We looked at each other and laughed as the rush to the counter began. 'The finality of that!' said Toby. 'Nothing on earth should sound that final.'

Chapter 9

DOTTIE went to Birmingham on the 23rd, and came back late on Christmas Eve—having stayed overnight at a long-distance drivers' stop-over *en route* for home and had several hair-raising adventures; she hadn't had much luck and was feeling disappointed and depressed. The foundry was still there, and still operating, but under new management—no more 'glass artists', but a production line which went on day and night, turning out every sort of monstrosity that can possibly be formed of glass.

At first she couldn't even find anybody there who wasn't a white-collar worker—not an overall, not a burst cheek-vein, not a blow-pipe, not even a furnace was in evidence. She sat in a clean grey cubicle and spoke to a clean grey woman who merely smiled thinly when she told her what she wanted. On her way out she went scouting round the back and found some men who looked as if they might, in the course of their work, occasionally see glass in its molten state, eating sandwiches in a patch of cold sunshine which fell miraculously through the black net of the surrounding chimneys onto a packing-case. She asked them if they'd ever heard of anybody who knew how to blow glass and they laughed and eyed her up and down in her bright trim coat and long London boots, and said how could you have a glass factory without people who knew how to blow glass? They all knew how. But, said Dottie, did any of them know how to *work* glass, to make something of their own? 'I know how to make mistakes!' said one man. 'Do you know how to make mistakes, miss?' They all roared.

Dottie, setting her teeth, waited silently for them to stop, and then asked the same man, 'What I mean is, could you make something out of glass that was quite different from anything else?' 'Like what, for instance?' he asked suspiciously. She pulled out a couple of pages from her pet American magazine, *Craft Horizons*, showing some beautiful, smooth, irregular shapes. The men crowded round to look. 'What's this, then? Here, Ron, look at this! What magazine's this, then?'

They examined the pictures with wonder, and read the captions. They seemed to be struck dumb. 'But what is it?' asked one of them. 'It's not a vase, it's not a jug—some kind of ornament, is it? But it's not symmetrical.' 'That's the whole point—one of them. It's art. Like a statue. The man who made it is trying to say something—with glass. Not simply to make something useful.' They were silent, staring at the unfamiliar contours. 'Could any of you do anything like it?' They shook their heads slowly. 'Don't see the point of it, meself,' said one. 'You'd never sell it. Who'd want a thing like that?' 'Somebody did. Somebody paid nearly five hundred dollars for that one, for instance.' The men whistled. Then one of them said, 'Ah. But that's Americans. They'll buy anything.'

In the end, she wrote her address on a bit of paper and gave it to the one called Ron, who took it and slipped it into his pocket with a lewd look which caused his mates to burst out laughing again, and Dottie to wish him in hell. 'Crass idiot!' she said to me afterwards. 'I must have been mad to bother with them! But I thought they might hear of somebody. That's the kind our much-vaunted affluent society is evolving from the once-proud ranks of the working classes!' She was joking, but not entirely. Somehow I felt she really was nostalgic for the days, before she or I were born, which we'd both heard our Conservative-minded parents (who had not been working-class) talking about—the days when a worker took a pride in his skill, when he was honest, sober and industrious—'And usually hungry,' as I reminded Dottie. But she wasn't in the mood for my socialism just then. 'Some of them, a relative minority, may have been hungry,' she retorted. 'Why wasn't it possible to rectify *that*, without transforming them all into prosperous, ogling, idle, ignorant yobs?'

'Don't come over all right-wing today, it's Christmas Eve —Good King Wenceslas and all that crowd,' I reminded her. She groaned and put her head in her hands. 'I can't stand

Christmas!' she muttered. 'Why did you have to remind me? I hoped we were going to let it pass completely unremarked.' 'I never can—can you?' 'Yes. For three years running, I have.' 'Last year you came to visit me in the hospital and told me severely that one couldn't not do anything about Christmas, or spend it alone.' 'That was good counsel for you because you'd just nearly had a miscarriage and were living in a slum and I thought you ought to come and visit me.' 'Well, this year you're visiting me, so we do things my way.' 'What way's that?' she asked suspiciously. 'The lot,' I said simply. She slid limply off the chair onto the floor and lay there, her hands over her head, twitching.

After a while, she looked up hopefully. 'But it's too late!' she said. 'Shops are all shut!'

'I've got everything.'

'Everything?'

'Everything,' I repeated firmly.

She dropped her head resoundingly on the floor with another loud groan. 'But it's absurd!' she croaked. 'Two grown women! I suppose you'll make me hang up my stocking while you dress up as Father Christmas!'

'Henry will be Father Christmas.'

She looked up sharply. 'Henry? Why Henry?'

'Because I've invited him to come down and spend tonight here on the way to his parents.'

'But what did you do that for?'

'Because I like him, and we need a man around.'

'To fill our stockings?'

'And drag in the yule-log, and fix the star on top of the tree, and be the baritone voice when we sing carols after dinner.'

She stared at me, then burst out laughing, rolling on her back and kicking her shapely legs in the air. 'I can just see Henry! Wow! Has he been told the programme? Old Po-Face! A natural-born Scrooge, if ever I saw one.'

'We'll see.'

'When's he coming?'

'Any time now.'

She lay on her side and watched while I began to arrange Christmas cards round the room, and pin up the holly which

I had culled in the garden that morning. 'Where's the mistle-toe?' she asked sardonically.

'Here,' I said, holding it up.

'God! You really have thought of everything!' There was a pause, and then she said, 'Except one thing.'

'What?'

'Well, you kindly invited Henry, for me, presumably. What about one for you?'

'You mean Toby? He's upstairs, asleep.'

She leapt to her feet in a moment, her eyes alight. 'The Blackbird's *here*?' she cried. 'Oh really, you are a bitch! Letting me lie here spouting nonsense when all the time . . . How long has he been here?'

'Only since you left for the North, obviously.'

'But that was yesterday.' She looked at me, eyes popping, mouth ajar. 'Jane! It was *yesterday*.'

'Yes, dear.'

'You mean, he was here—last night? All night?'

'Yes. Do take that look off your face.'

'Jane. Jane. You know I never pry, never hint, never ask, never interfere. You know that, don't you? Did he sleep with you?'

'Is that any of your business?'

'Of course it isn't, you idiot. But if you don't tell me, I shall go out of my mind.'

'Yes, he did, as a matter of fact.'

She spun on her heels and dropped straight backwards onto the sofa, where she lay sprawled with a look of utter bliss on her face and her eyes closed. '*Thank Christ* for that!' she murmured with what sounded like genuine reverence.

'That is to say,' I went on carefully, 'he shared my bed. You know how imprecise English is.'

She opened her eyes and fixed them on me as one who hears something incredible and unspeakable. 'What,' she said, 'exactly, are you saying? That you went to bed together——'

'And talked for an hour or so——'

'And then went to sleep?'

'That's right. What about helping me in with the tree? It's outside the back door.'

'Bugger the tree. Why didn't you?'

'Do you really have to know?'

'Yes. I'm a student of human behaviour, with a particular interest in explanations for the inexplicable.'

'There's nothing inexplicable about this.'

She stood up and paced about. 'Jane. I thought we were alike. I only have women friends who are reasonable facsimiles of myself. If I were in your shoes, and were—incredibly—lucky enough to have a man friend whom I loved and who loved me, and if I had a baby to raise, and if the said friend was no longer penniless, and if he was, by some miracle, as generously-minded as you told me Toby was—is—hell's teeth! You get the message. If such a situation existed in my totally barren sex-life and said friend turned up one twenty-third of December when I happened to be alone in the house, and . . .' She turned to face me, hands spread out. 'Why? Just tell me why!'

'It's perfectly simple. I've got the curse.'

She closed her eyes tightly, grasped the sides of her head, and let out a sound that can only be represented by the comic-book stand-by 'AAAAUGHHH!' She held the pose, head thrown back, elbows in the air, for some moments, and then walked quite normally to the table and poured herself a drink. 'Never mind,' she said matter-of-factly. 'There's always Christmas Night.'

'He'll have gone back to town by then.'

Dottie looked as if she honestly wanted to cry. 'Oh my God, Jane.'

'Would you tell me something? Why are you so anxious to re-open *my* affair with Toby?'

'Because,' she answered, promptly and without any self-pity, 'one of us at least has got to marry and be happy. And since you've got David, it had better be you.'

'Why not you too? Or you instead?'

She didn't answer for a minute, but stood quite still, looking down at her drink. She looked very pretty in the firelight, not at all thirty-ish. 'Look,' she said at last, and now there was no exaggeration and no playing games. 'I'm a very down-to-earth girl, as you know. I mean, I don't normally get "pre-monitions" or any nonsense like that. But I can't help believing a bit in fate. I think you can come to turning-points in your life, when you do the right thing—or at least, the thing that will make you happiest in the end—or you do something else, and after that you get swept along in the wrong direction and you can never turn back. Maybe you find other things, you can make the best of it, and that's what I mean to do, that's why I'm simply plunging up to the neck in this shop business, because I think—I'm pretty sure in fact—that I'm destined, or doomed if you like, to be a career woman and never to marry. I took a boss-shot at a turning about two years ago, and I think that was it—my chance to marry, I mean. I thought I didn't love him quite enough, or something like that, anyway I backed off and backed off until he got fed up and married someone else. I don't mean I'm now pining for him or even that I think of him very much, but I do have the feeling that—however many affairs I may have (and I haven't sworn off affairs really, even if I wish I could sometimes), none of them will ever lead to anything.'

'Well, I'll tell you now what I think. I think everyone who is capable of love at all, has one—at least—really big thing in their lives. Early or late, it comes. And although I don't know who this chap was that you say now you should have married, I don't believe he was your big thing, or you'd have felt more at the time and you'd be feeling more now than just a sort of luke-warm academic regret.'

She was watching me with the most intense interest, possibly, that I had ever seen, even on her always acutely receptive face. 'You really think that? That I've still got my big thing—up ahead of me? Even though I'm thirty?'

'Thirty! Thirty's nothing. Thirty's a beginning.'

She was quite silent for a long time, still looking at me. In the flickering firelight I read all sorts of things into her expression; I thought I saw depths of pain there that one would never guess at from her flip behaviour and her cavalier manner. 'I wish you were the Delphic Oracle,' she said at last. 'But even if you're not, I'll try to believe you. You can't imagine how badly I want to.' She gave a shaky little laugh. 'You haven't a clue about me, actually, I mean about what a fool I've made of myself from time to time in the course of The Search. Well, you met Alan. Mad, horrible fellow. But I considered him. I seriously considered him. Even after I'd seen him like *that*, I still didn't wholly dismiss him, because whenever I've started going to bed with a man I always feel I have to justify it by at least trying to make it—work. You know—permanently. That's my whole trouble. I don't seem capable of living for the moment. It's as if the future threw back a shadow—a great black shadow of years of loneliness, and it terrifies me so much that I keep lighting little futile lights to try to drive the shadow away.'

'You won't have to live alone, Dottie. There are always husbands for women like you.'

'Like me?'

'Attractive. Clever. With something to offer.'

She heaved a monstrous sigh. 'It seems to me those are just the ones who have to do without, because, in the final analysis, they *can*. And men basically want women who can't live without them.'

A cold shiver passed over me. 'That's not true!' I said, much louder than I'd intended. 'Men—the best kind of men—don't want empty-headed clingers! They want independent women, women with lives of their own, women who *don't* need them all the time! Don't they?'

'Can't say I've ever noticed it,' said Dottie.

We stopped talking then because Henry arrived, and after that we were busy and pretty happy the whole evening, forcing him to do all the things I'd planned and plying him with unaccustomed quantities of whisky to get him into the Christmas spirit—which I must say proved unexpectedly easy. Toby played along with his usual enthusiasm, lightly tinged with irony, and every now and then he caught my eye and said, 'Do you remember last year—dyeing the pop-corn? And Doris's pot? And John helping? And the party?' And we would laugh gaily or ruefully, whichever was called for. We even thought of trying to get hold of John, but we couldn't think how to do it, and the sudden thought of John alone somewhere, also perhaps remembering the silly, friendly, intimate threesome that was Christmas of last year, plunged me into temporary depression. But John wasn't really at the bottom of it. The real trouble was that the whole evening, through the turkey dinner and the crackers and the carols and everything, I kept on thinking, *My God. What if she's right? And what if Whistler is the needing kind? And doesn't mind admitting it?*

A surprising sidelight on the evening was how well Toby and Henry got on together. Two more disparate personalities could scarcely be imagined; yet they took to one another almost at sight.

I don't think Henry had ever said anything consciously funny in my hearing since I'd met him, but quite suddenly there he was, festooning the tree with Toby, handing him things with deft twists of the wrist and saying in a dead-level voice, 'Scalpel—forceps—sponge—icicle . . .' and later on doing a very undergraduate but, with the mood we were all in, extremely funny imitation of a monkey as he clambered up the ladder and appeared about to start swinging from the upper branches, the star between his teeth. When we'd all had a bit to drink he began telling jokes. I'm always a bit nervous of men who don't usually tell jokes, and who suddenly begin to when they're tight; the jokes which then emerge are often more revealing of their libido than amusing. But Henry turned out to be such a good *raconteur* in his cups that even Toby, who prided himself in this field, was impressed. Henry even knew one Jewish joke that Toby had never heard, and Toby is the man that *writes* the Jewish jokes.

The sleeping arrangements that night were mildly complicated. Having only one spare room, there had to be some doubling up somewhere, but it soon sorted itself out—Dottie shared my bed and Toby had the spare room while Henry dossed down on the sofa. He said he was used to it (whether he meant my particular sofa or sofas in general, I wasn't sure) and in any case was so well-fed and soporific with drink that he didn't mind where he slept.

It really had been a very good evening—even Dottie had enjoyed herself and entered, although somewhat laconically, into the spirit of it all in the end. She was a bit aloof at first, but Henry absolutely teased her until she relented, and at one point when we were clearing the dishes away and bumping into each other, singing carols and behaving just like children, he suddenly took her arm and said, 'That up there's mistletoe unless I'm mistaken, and I want a kiss from someone tonight.

I think it better be you.' With that he kissed her very firmly on the cheek before she could gather her wits to elude him. She went abruptly red in the face and so did he and she made some most gauche and un-Dottie-like remark about that being a funny way to do business; he said, 'Well, I'll apologize if I ought to,' and she said, 'Oh, never mind! It wasn't that sort of kiss.' To which he replied, 'No, that's true, regrettably.' Dottie gave a sudden shrill, London laugh, which I recognized with an instinctive flash of something very like matchmaking acuity as a defence against unexpected emotion, or at the very least, physical reaction; but Henry didn't know this, and let go of her arm as if it had suddenly become too hot. However, this was only a brief interlude in a multi-faceted evening, and might have passed completely unremarked if I hadn't had good reason to remember it later.

When we were all in bed, I was tired enough to want to drop off at once; but Dottie was terribly restless and kept tossing and turning in the narrow bed, waking me up with every movement, until at last, getting exasperated, I asked her if anything was the matter.

'Is there no decent way I could change places with Toby?' she whispered.

'Oh, Dottie, really! I'm far too tired anyway. Go to sleep.'

. . . I woke somewhere near dawn. Something had wakened me. Had it been nothing but Dottie getting out of bed and leaving the room? Anyway, she was gone. But somehow I didn't feel it was that. I still felt half-doped with sleepiness and I had to force myself to lie awake for a few minutes, wondering hazily if I could have heard David cry. I felt I should go and have a look at him, but I was so heavy-limbed and thick-headed I didn't want to move; the whole cottage was quiet now; I had leapt out of bed so many scores of times, my heart in my mouth because I thought I had heard a whimper or, at the beginning, that perhaps he was suffocating in his blanket or something, and I was compelled to go and check that he was all right. He always had been. . . . I rolled over and plummeted back into the depths of sleep, scarcely even asking myself where Dottie could have gone. . . .

When I next woke up, Dottie, looking radically different, was bending over me.

'Jane, you must wake up. David's ill.'

I literally fell out of bed onto all fours; when I stood up, my head spun and Dottie had to steady me.

'Look, don't panic. It may be nothing much . . . he's been sick in the night. . . .'

I didn't wait for the rest, but ran into his little room. It stank of vomit and the deeper, more frightening smell of baby's diarrhoea. He and his bed were clean, but the soiled sheets were bundled into a corner. He wasn't crying, just lying there looking awful; he actually looked as if he'd lost weight off his face in the night. His eyes were big and he gazed up at me; when I touched him, he was damp and hot.

'Thank you for—cleaning up—have you taken his temperature?'

'I didn't know how to, but Henry did. It's 101.' My blood congealed, but just then Henry came in, neatly dressed and shaved, and said calmly, 'It sounds a lot, but it's nothing much for a baby with salmonella. Don't be unduly alarmed. Just give him lots to drink. The main thing is not to let him get dehydrated.'

I simply stared at him.

Dottie gave a little strained laugh. Even in my state of near-panic (David had never in his life been really ill) I registered that laugh—it was so different to her laugh the night before. 'Isn't he amazing,' she said. 'Just like a doctor. You should have seen how he took over.'

'How do you know it's—what you said?' I asked thinly at last.

'It's going the rounds just now. Amanda's just had it—my step-mother's. She nearly went out of her mind—my step-mother, I mean, not the baby of course. But it was all over in two or three days. Antibiotics. You need to call a doctor and get him started on them right away.'

Dottie turned to me, horrified. 'Oh, but you mustn't give him that stuff! It'll poison his system—set up immunities—then if he ever really needed them——'

'Don't be so daft. He really needs them now. He's been crapping and spewing half the night. Go on, Jane, you give him more to drink while I go for your sawbones—what's his address?'

It was so long since I'd needed a doctor that I couldn't remember, but fortunately I'd had the sense to write it down in an address-book in my desk. There was a few moments of stifled terror as I scrabbled for it but it turned up mercifully quickly and in a very few moments Henry's car was bucketing down the road. It was raining, and I remembered, as I held David up to drink and it all came spouting out again in an evil-smelling fountain, that it was Christmas morning. My mind was quite dark with guilt and despair. To think of him, losing liquid like that for God knows how many hours of the night, while I slept like a fat pig in its sty, oblivious. . . . I was sure he felt lighter . . . patiently I coaxed more sugar-water into him. Dottie had disappeared, taking the soiled sheets, and reappeared quite quickly with cups of tea.

'Where's Toby?' I remembered to ask.

'I don't know. I suppose he's still asleep.'

I thought, *How could he!* But that was ridiculous.

'Did you hear him being sick? Was that why you got up so early?' I was prepared to be horrifyingly angry with her if she had failed to waken me; but my fog of wretchedness was pierced by her sudden look of confusion as she said, 'No. . . . I got up because I was restless and I wanted to wander about.' I let it go, though later I wondered: where does one wander to, on a pouring wet night, in a five-roomed cottage of which every one except the kitchen contains somebody asleep?

The doctor came. It was Christmas Day and he had a large family and was a good deal more grumpy than the plumber had been, but he did come, and my respect for Henry sky-rocketed when the official diagnosis proved to agree in every respect with his. 'Don't try to give him milk. Just sugar-water, or weak sweet tea—whatever he'll take. Plus a teaspoonful of this three times a day for ten days.' He gave me a bottle of thick yellow medicine which was the antibiotics. Dottie curled her lip at it, but I grabbed it gratefully and stuffed the first dose into him as quickly as I could. 'Liquid, liquid and more liquid,' said the doctor. 'If he seems prostrated, get him to hospital. I'll come in again this evening.' He sighed as he said this, and I knew then how serious it was.

When he'd gone, I suddenly said, 'But the car's not working.

How could I get him to hospital?' I looked desperately at Henry, who hesitated only a moment and then said, 'I'll stick around. My people will understand.' I felt as if he were my dearest, closest friend, the most reliable, kind and beloved person in my life. I wanted to hang round his neck and kiss him and thank him. I suppose something of this must have shown in my expression, because he became quite embarrassed and said it was nothing at all, absolutely nothing.

Chapter 10

IT WAS an unspeakable, unforgettable Christmas, the worst of my life. I don't know how I'd have got through it at all without Henry. It wasn't so much what he did; he did very little, other than sit in the living-room keeping the fire going and steadily reading his way through all the previous Sunday's papers. It was his calm words of reassurance, which he had the patience to repeat every time I reappeared downstairs on my way to the washing-machine with a new bundle of soiled clothes—as often as not, my own, for David was sick on me every time I fed him or picked him up, and the insertion of the thermometer inevitably produced an even fouler jet which frightened me so much that I stopped taking his temperature and just guessed at it from feeling him.

'Don't worry. It's always like this the first day. How many times is that? Only four? That's nothing. Amanda was sick four times in an hour on her first day. The weight simply fell off her, until the old cynto-mitsetin got cracking on her. They put it all back amazingly quickly when they get the bug out of their systems.'

Dottie drifted about, half being a great help and half getting in the way. I had been overtaken by the most violent attack of possessiveness about David, probably as a reaction to my guilt-feelings; I didn't want to depute even the meanest tasks to Dottie or anyone else, and even resented it when she wanted to help me change the bed-linen. In the end she kept her distance, looking hurt—almost dazed somehow—but clearly trying to understand, and contented herself with doing the cooking and tea-brewing.

As for Toby . . . what can I say about the way I behaved to him? There was nothing he could have done, yet I perversely found the fact that he found nothing to do extremely irritating, and held it against him. It was so unfair, yet I couldn't help it. Henry's sitting downstairs like a tweedy Buddha, far from exasperating me, had a most soothing and comforting effect; he knew what this was all about, everything he said was consoling, his very casualness reassured me. Also, his presence, relaxed as it was, was purposeful—he was my means of getting David to hospital if he had to go. But when Toby dared to sink into a chair for a few minutes and reach tentatively for a paper, it was as much as I could do not to shout at him: 'How can you sit there and read? Don't you know what David's going through, what I'm going through?' I didn't say it, but I looked it, and he dropped the paper and got uneasily to his feet, asking for the fifteenth time if there was anything he could do. There was nothing—except somehow share in my anguish of mind, as only a father and a husband could have done, instead of merely standing there, limp and depressed, as helpless and empty-hearted as any casual by-stander.

By evening the tension I was generating had exhausted us all. The doctor returned, examined David very carefully, with particular attention to the skin on his stomach. Henry had already explained that there was nothing to be really worried about until the skin there began to lose its elasticity from dryness. In my eyes David looked terrible, as if he really might be going to die; but it was, I suppose, only because he looked different from his normal smiling active self. Anyway, the doctor said he wasn't any worse, that the first day was always a trial, tomorrow might be very little better but not to worry because the third day would show an improvement. I privately thought another day like the one just past would be the finish of both of us, but after the doctor had gone, Henry ambled upstairs and said, 'What did I tell you? Now come down and have a strong drink, you need it. Dorothy, make some coffee, she'll want to stay awake with him most of the night to give him a drink every time he wakes up.' He took me by the hand like a brother and led me downstairs; leaving Toby to keep watch by the cot. I had the prescribed drinks—whisky followed by coffee—and they both did me good in their respective ways; sitting by the cot did Toby good, and making the coffee did Dottie good. I became more and more sure that

Henry was one of the most wonderful men I had ever had the luck to meet.

A little later we were all sitting in the kitchen for a few minutes. Henry was talking in his flat, matter-of-fact, faintly off-voice about the rate at which Amanda had put her lost pounds back on again, still holding my hand in an unemotional, almost medicinal grip, when I interrupted him to say suddenly: 'Henry, I've ruined your Christmas—I'm so sorry——' and burst into tears. Henry rather awkwardly put his arm round me and said, 'There you go, have a bellow, it won't hurt. . . .' Dottie stood up abruptly and left the room. Toby stood up too, his face a queer mixture of feelings frozen into a sort of angry mask. The sight of it made me stop crying very quickly and sit there staring at him. Henry took his arm from my shoulders with a little cough. I felt a most peculiar atmosphere in the room, of which Dottie's absence was a component; but I was too wrought-up to even attempt to unravel it.

Both the men left that evening. Henry was going to his people, and Toby asked, in a cold crisp voice I didn't recognize, if he could have a lift as far as the nearest large town from which to get a train back to London. I watched the two of them off the premises and was appalled—even frightened—to find myself saying goodbye to Toby quite coolly while having to restrain myself forcibly from kissing Henry and thanking him with the utmost effusion of warmth for the simple fact of his presence during the past twelve hours. Dottie was not around for the leave-takings, but called a remote goodbye from the kitchen. Henry seemed inclined to hang around a bit, as if expecting her to appear, but quite soon he and Toby were both climbing into his car and driving away. I had the distinct impression, as I looked at their two heads side by side in the front seat, both facing forward, that despite their cordiality with each other the previous evening they would not find two words to exchange on the journey.

What had happened?

David had been taken ill—that was all that had happened as far as I was concerned. But as Dottie and I sat down to a scratch meal on trays at the top of the stairs, just outside David's room, both just as gravelled for words as I had

imagined the men being, it was borne in upon me that a lo·
had been going on for other people which had passed me by
I had assumed, for instance, that the extraordinary difference
I had noticed in Dottie's appearance early in the morning when
she'd woken me, had been solely due to her concern for David.
Now as I looked at her, her head bent over her tray, picking
desultorily at her supper and avoiding me as completely as if
she had left with the others, I realized I'd been wrong.

I tried to make conversation: 'I'm afraid I've been awful
today—I hope you understood—you see, he's never been ill
before, and—I wasn't there when it started——' But it petered
out for lack of a reaction. Dottie stopped eating, stood up with
her tray and started downstairs without so much as a word.
I got the clear impression she was crying, or trying not to. I
looked in on David and, finding him safely asleep, hurried
down after her. I felt an unspecific renewal of guilt. Was my
touchy manner all day really responsible for this withdrawal?

Dottie was in the kitchen putting dishes in the sink, but
almost ran past me into the living-room as I came in. She
looked quite strange—white and wretched. I knew she didn't
want me, but I couldn't stop myself following her.

She stood with her back to me, both hands gripping the
mantelpiece. As I came into the room she said in a high-
pitched nervy tone, 'My God! I hate living in other people's
houses! There's no escape!' Her voice squeaked and scraped
on the edge of tears.

'Dottie, what is it? What's the matter?'

'Nothing!'

'Is it something I've done?'

'No, for God's sake, no!' She sounded so distraught I was
taken completely aback. It couldn't be my fault, I really
hadn't done or said anything which justified this. I tried once
more:

'Can't I do something to help?'

'No you can't,' she said shrilly. 'Except go back up to David
and leave me alone for five minutes.'

Alarmed, hurt and disconcerted, I obeyed. I had never seen
Dottie like this in all the years we'd known each other. I could
hear her right through the floor-boards, sobbing her eyes out.

I sat up most of the night with David. Every time he stirred,

I put a bottle to his lips, and usually he drank a little, mostly in his sleep. He wasn't sick again until he woke up in the morning. I heard Dottie coming slowly upstairs, in the middle of the night, and going quietly into the spare room. The next I heard from her was when she brought me a cup of coffee early the next morning. I had dozed off and hadn't heard her going downstairs again. She looked about as haggard and worn-out as I felt, and avoided my eyes, but she had brought two cups and sat down to drink hers with me, which seemed a good sign.

'How was he in the night?' she asked. She sounded very subdued, as if she'd cried herself empty—I knew that feeling.

'All right—fine really.' At that moment he opened his eyes, lifting his head and was sick right through the bars of the cot. We both jumped up and this time I had no objection to Dottie's helping. We cleaned up in silence and then sat down to finish our cold coffee. The light coming into the room was cold and grey. I saw Dottie shiver in her elegant, but now sick-stained, house-coat. I put my hand out very tentatively and touched hers. Her cup rattled in her hand as she put it down and turned to me. 'What on earth can I say? I've got to say something and say it quickly, but I'm damned if I know what.'

Her eyes were really so exhausted and pathetic that I simply hugged her. 'Don't say a word—you idiot—it's all right——'

'But I'm so ashamed——'

'Oh, nonsense, love, don't be ridiculous. Please forget it.'

'I can't even explain. No. Don't ask me anything. I'll tell you sometime, perhaps. I can't now. Let's—if you could just pretend—this whole ghastly Christmas—didn't happen. Help me to pretend it didn't happen!' She began to cry again, weakly and desperately, leaning against me—suave, poised, self-controlled, Dottie. I marvelled, and at the same time I burned, let me be honest, with an almost intolerable curiosity. It *must* have something to do with Henry. What? But friendship demanded, not the patient willing ear, but deafness and denial of my own powerful desire to know.

Chapter 11

THINGS WENT BACK to being the way they'd been before. Well, not quite, but it was a pretty good surface imitation. David got better; he had lost three pounds and Dottie said his new slimness became him, but I worked on him night and day to put it back, filling him with cereals laced with butter and cocoa, chocolate biscuits and any other fattening things I could think of. I understood for the first time Alf Davies's behaviour towards Eleanor—now every slightest sound sent me rocketing to David's side, and I realized how fantastically carefree and almost unreal my motherhood had been until now—how can you be a mother if you've never had a moment's worry or fear?

Dottie's preoccupation with the shop continued as before, in fact she intensified her activities to a point where I began to wonder anxiously whether she wasn't seriously overdoing it. She drove about the countryside like a maniac, seeing people, ordering samples, drawing up contracts; on other days she would spend every daylight hour in the shop itself, supervising and even helping with the redecorations. She would usually arrive home at night too tired to eat. It looked to me like a deliberate campaign to keep herself too busy to think. She never spoke about whatever it was that had happened. There were other areas of silence, too. For instance, she had completely stopped her occasional outbursts of sexy-joke-sessions about men. Men as men were never mentioned. If she missed them in her life she never hinted at it any more.

Henry had to be around more and more frequently, and quite soon he found himself a little flat in a new block on the outskirts of the village, an excrescence on the landscape which Dottie had frequently deplored; it was, by village standards, a miniature skyscraper, built by the local council to give housing mainly to 'immigrants' (to the locality, not the country) who were employed at a new little factory nearby—a concession by the village to the needs of the century, to wit, industry to bring in money and restrain some of its own young people from the otherwise inevitable drift to the bigger towns. Henry invited us to his flat as soon as he'd settled in. He wasn't over-excited about it, but seemed to think it quite adequate. Dottie, however, as I could plainly see, was aesthetically outraged.

She hid her feelings from Henry, and pretended to admire, though temperately, his arrangement of the highly nondescript and utilitarian furniture (which came with the flat) and the view from the fourth-floor windows over the as yet unsullied countryside. He gave us a rather touching self-cooked meal of omelettes and tinned soup, and we sat around afterwards discussing the shop; but I could see Dottie was hard put to it to hold her peace and behave as if nothing were wrong. As soon as we were on our way home, out it burst.

'How could he live in a place like that!—an *egg*-box. Those stone stairs and landings! And the front doors, all the same colour! You can hear the people in the next flat breathing! How doesn't he want to scream?'

'But it suits him fine. It's convenient, modern——'

'He's got no *right* to be suited by it! Nobody has,' she added lamely, trying to make it a matter of general principle. But something very personal in her anger with Henry made me murmur, my curiosity awakened:

'What sort of place do you think he ought to have?'

She didn't fall into that one, though, She merely said shortly, 'Something very different from that.' I sighed silently, balked. I had thought she might unwarily describe the sort of characterful dwelling which only she could devise for him, and then I would have known for sure she was in love with him, instead of only suspecting it.

His feelings about her were even harder to determine. The little signs and symptoms I had observed at the beginning—his bemused expression, the way his eyes would fix themselves to some part of her and have to be wrenched away, the sudden spasms of nervousness and inclination to escape—all these were now absent. When they were together, a more practical, mundane, down-to-earth business relationship could not have been imagined. They seldom even laughed in each other's company, although their now entirely mutual enthusiasm for the project should surely have generated the kind of excitement which, in their 'shop' talks, would inevitably have led to laughter. It was left to me to listen to, and appreciate, Dottie's witty stories about her often bizarre encounters, setbacks and small triumphs; if Henry got to hear about them, it was from me. Sometimes I'd repeat, as well as I could, some anecdote of Dottie's in front of her, presaged with the words: 'Did you tell Henry about . . . ?' Sometimes even my pale re-telling could make Henry's quiet, withdrawn, rather square features burst into one of his delightful smiles; then he would say, 'No, she didn't tell me.' Dottie would remark crisply on these occasions, 'It was only a silly fringe-thing, not important enough to waste your time with.'

Looking for signs of love, I could find only indeterminate negative ones. Why should two people who were really indifferent to each other, go to such pains to display their indifference? Why should Henry so seldom come to my place any more for friendly evenings. Why were all meetings so strictly business? And why, one evening when he did come and when a 40-mile-an-hour gale, blowing mixed snow and rain parallel to the ground, suddenly developed, which should have made sleeping on our sofa the natural thing to do, did he refuse all my blandishments and insist upon climbing into his car and struggling back to the other side of the village to his own place? Dottie's behaviour on that occasion was very odd. She said nothing, but when I woke up in the middle of the night, thinking I had heard a noise from David's room and went in to him, I found her sitting there in a chair by his cot. She had fallen asleep, and when the passage light fell on her face she started awake with a look of guilty dismay, as if she'd been caught out in an act of complete self-revelation. I could not just pass over this because my first thought was that some untoward indication from David must have brought her in; but when challenged, she simply said, 'You know I love this little boy very much and there are moments when I like to be with him, even if he is fast asleep.' It was a very simple—perhaps over-simple—matter to sub this down to

'Tonight I needed to be near to someone I loved.' But there was no way of being sure about anything, except that if they did care for each other, things were not progressing in any kind of positive direction. This in itself was a contra-indication, because it implied some impediment, and although I actively racked my brains I couldn't imagine what this could possibly be.

I am not by nature as interested in other people's affairs as the foregoing would indicate. I, too, was looking for a kind of sublimation. . . . I infinitely preferred to occupy my mind with Dottie's problems in this field than be forced to face up to, analyse and deal with, my own.

My own all but passionate devotion for Henry, kindled abruptly during David's illness, did not survive it, though it left a very warm residue; his relationship with me was certainly a very pleasant one for us both, easy, friendly and affectionate. I liked him, in fact, more and more as I came to understand his strangely withdrawn temperament better and to perceive the sterling qualities of reliability, kindliness and dry humour that lay hidden. What I never could understand was why the façade was so necessary to him, why the wit and warmth had to be winkled out of him or observed in flashes when it slipped out unawares.

And meanwhile, what of Toby?

I heard nothing from him, did nothing about him—except feel a good deal. The predominant feeling was of bewilderment. I didn't know what had happened, but something had: something serious, moreover, and possibly (though I was too afraid of the thought of this to countenance it) even permanent. He was no longer the constant warm, secure presence bolstering up my life; he came and went, as it were, in my thoughts, and I could no longer get any real sense of security from summoning him to my mind and talking to him there. It was as if he had gone away from me and came back only intermittently, and uncertainly at that. The two-way current of love which had been flowing circuitously between us for over a year, seemed now somehow to have been damaged.

It wasn't, of course, until this happened that I fully realized how heavily I'd been depending on him all the time I'd been living alone. I was forced to the conclusion at last that I had not, in essence, been living alone at all until now. Now I was. Dottie hardly counted. True, she was company of a sort; but our separate, private preoccupations, so sedulously kept secret from each other, prevented any real sense of intimacy. I missed her; I missed Toby—that is, I missed what I had had with both of them. Now I really and truly felt alone for the first time since leaving Toby, and it was paralysing in its power to frighten and demoralize me.

Late one cold mid-February afternoon, before opening time, I popped next door from Mrs Stephens's to our shop to see how things were going. I used to go in about once a week, and could usually perceive a decided advance. To tell the truth, I personally had been so little connected with the shop that the whole project still had an aura of unreality for me; my weekly visits there were partly therapeutic, to remind myself that very soon life would change again and I would find myself transmogrified into a shopkeeper.

The premises were nearly ready; a drastic change had been wrought since the first time we'd gone in there. Many of the features Dottie had envisaged had come to pass: the removal of the counter, the scraped and polished floorboards, the refurbished fireplace, the clean paint and some rather startling but decidedly effective wallpaper. Strip-lighting had been installed, and did not look at all out of place. Henry's practicality had triumphed with regard to the beams, damp-course and various other matters; he had also insisted upon a mild form of central heating. Before a single saleable item was installed, the shop was already radically different from any other interior in the village, especially on a dark, frozen winter's afternoon; warm where others were chilly and damp; white-bright where others were gloomy; discreetly exuding an atmosphere of London where the rest huddled in unrepentant musty parochialism.

Dottie was there, a vivid electric-blue spark, jumping from point to point. She had begun to dress very smartly again lately—to match the shop, she said, or perhaps it was to match the brittle, businesswoman character she was developing. When she saw me she darted over, and took me through to the back to see the strip-pine trestle counters which had just arrived.

'The workers will be out in three days,' she said, rubbing her hands. 'That's nearly a week inside their original estimate. Have you the faintest idea of how miraculous that is these days? Of course it's all my doing. I've been a thorn in their sides, a remorseless goad. No threats, nothing so crude—just my constant, infuriating presence, lightly, gaily, charmingly telling them how it could be done quicker and better, forestalling their inefficiencies, subtly refusing them tea except as a reward—and, of course, dishing out discreet but generous bonuses for extra-quick work. They *hate* me. Never mind— it's done, and one week from this very day we open as a going enterprise.'

'A week!' I was taken aback. It wasn't that I liked either of my present jobs very much, and as David grew older it was proving a very difficult and taxing routine; but change scares me; I can never foresee myself fitting into a new situation, and to leave an old one, however uncongenial, is always a wrench. 'I'd better give my notice in, then—I suppose.'

'Good Lord, yes! Haven't you done that yet? I wish you were free now! All the goods are going to start arriving tomorrow, Henry's bringing some and I've hired a van for the farther-afield stuff, and what would be grand is if you could get a day off and help me sort it all out and arrange it.' This appealed to me strongly, and I promised to try to get off at least for some hours on the following Saturday morning. Then on Sunday we could work together all day until I had to go into the Swan for the evening.

'Do you have to work out your notice? Couldn't you just quit?'

'Not really. Alf and Mrs Stephens have been so nice.'

'Rubbish! You've earned it.'

'I've earned my wages. Not necessarily all the extras, putting up with David and so on.'

' "Putting up with David", as you call it, is a privilege.'

I said nothing to this. The fact was, if she had but noticed, David was no longer quite the angel-baby he had been to begin with. At eight months old he was rapidly developing a will and a personality very often at odds with what I required of him in the way of co-operative sleeping, eating and travelling. He had now come to the conclusion that what I wanted him to do was not always what he wanted; and when this happened he knew how to express his opposition unmistakably, both vocally and physically. I hadn't liked to draw Dottie's attention to the fact that he now employed such techniques as biting, kicking and hair-pulling to obtain his own way. His screaming she must have noticed, but chose to ignore. She was so busy lately, and so seldom at home at his bedtime, that this was not impossible for her.

Sometimes, when I was tired after a long difficult day and he refused to go quietly to sleep at bedtime, I was startled and alarmed to find myself getting unwontedly quite furious with him. I'd never really understood how a mother could possibly have even a faintly violent impulse towards her baby, but after he had been screaming for an hour and I had found it impossible to discover what he wanted, other than to be picked up and allowed to continue playing as if night had not come, I was ready to bang my head against a wall—or even his, if it would just stop the noise. As soon as he finally fell asleep all my love for him came rushing back at once, mingled with an agonizing remorse for ever having entertained thoughts of savagery; but it did occur to me to change my dogmatic views on the subject of nannies. How lovely it would have been, when I was really at my wits' end, to be able to hand him over to some capable woman the very touch of whose experienced hands would instantly soothe him and bring him to order! Or, better and much more wholesome, to a father. . . . Babies, I had heard, often sense the superior strength and nervelessness of masculinity and respond to it. But David just had to make do with me, and very often these days I was too tired and miserable to be the quiet, patient, stable mother he needed.

'I don't quite know how we're going to arrange it,' I said now tentatively. 'I mean, when the shop's running. Where will David——?'

'Oh, don't worry about that. There'll be no need for more than one of us to serve in the shop at once. We'll organize a rota, one day off, one on. Except that on my days off, I'll have to be scouting round the countryside for talent. . . . Oh well! It'll work out all right, you'll see.'

'And Henry?'

'Henry hardly fancies himself as what he calls a "counter-jumper" type. He'll stay in the background, organizing, keeping me on an even keel, and incidentally of course paying the bills.'

'What did he do before?'

'Before what?'

'I mean, how did he earn all the money to pay our bills with?'

'He was in his father's business, I gather,' she said, going vague, as she did whenever Henry came up in conversation.

'Which was?'

'Oh, something in London. When he retired, his father I mean, he sold up and gave Henry his share, and this is how he's chosen to use it.'

'Odd, somehow.'

'I don't see why. Have you seen these high box-shelves? They're for the toys and the fabrics. Did I tell you I've found a marvellous woman to make things like traycloths and tea-cosies—and lovely weird-looking toy animals with the scraps.'

'It's odd,' I persisted, 'because one would have expected a man of Henry's practicality to invest his capital in a longer-term prospect—something safer, that would give him an occupation a little more . . . I don't know, solid, permanent, *regular*-sounding than ours.'

'He knows what he wants, no doubt.'

'After all, he can't be more than forty——'

'He's thirty-nine.'

'Thirty-nine, then. Is he planning to spend the rest of his life living in that egg-box, as you called it, doing a little organizing, a little fetching and carrying, a little advice-giving? It seems very undemanding for a man like him.'

Dottie said quietly, 'Jane, hasn't it struck you I don't specially want to discuss Henry's affairs?'

'I'm sorry,' I said, ashamed, for of course it had.

'Where's David?'

'Asleep in the car.'

'He'll freeze. Come on, let's lock up. I'll take him home and put him to bed for you. He's too big to be larking about with that nubile Eleanor any more.'

Chapter 12

IT WAS ACTUALLY another fortnight before the grand opening. Dottie realized it would take at least that to have everything ready, and also to lay on the opening itself, which
involved inviting 'the right people' down from London. I
would have thought of none of that, of course; I in my
ignorance imagined one simply opened the doors of one's shop
one day and hoped people passing would come in to buy. But
Dottie knew all the wrinkles. She not only sent very grand-
looking invitations to literally scores of people, in and out of
the trade, but spent the better part of the final week up in
town, renewing contacts as she called it.

I couldn't resist asking if it were not distasteful to her, having
to spend time with the corrupt, over-sophisticated city-society
that she despised; she refused to be drawn, however, and
simply said, 'I've no principles against using them and their
glamour and their money. It's all they're fit for, after all—
commercial exploitation.'

During the week she was away, I was so shockingly lonely
—having given up both my bread-and-butter jobs, I was at
home alone all the time—that before two days had passed, I
had no alternative but to ring Henry up and beg him to come
for a meal.

He was very busy—Dottie having left him plenty to do in
and around the shop—but he kindly came in for lunch one
morning on his way to pick up some stuff from a nearby
blacksmith's. As usual, his quiet presence restored my sense
of proportion. I told him about going to America. I hadn't
mentioned this to anybody for months and it had somehow
lost some of its tangibility for me—I felt I had to talk about
it again to re-solidify it before it turned into a chimera and
wafted away.

Henry watched me steadily as I outlined my plan, and then, after chewing his way through three mouthfuls, asked: 'But what'll happen about the shop?'

'I always told Dottie I could only come in on it very temporarily.'

'But if you go, she will then be left to run the place all by herself.'

'What do you mean? She'll have you.'

Henry drank some beer and said slowly, 'Well, but not indefinitely.'

Taken aback, I said, 'Why not? I thought——'

'Well, you know, I never really thought of this as being—— forever.'

This put a very new complexion on things, and I thought about this new prospective hole in Dottie's business, not to mention personal, future for a while and then asked, 'Does Dottie know about this?'

'Yes,' he said, 'I've told her.'

'But surely you wouldn't pull out in less than—a few years, I mean if it's a success?'

'I don't know exactly when I shall pull out.'

'Will you take your money out as well?'

Henry grinned and said, 'No, only myself.'

'Even so . . . it means so much to her. If we both walked out on her——'

'Well, you might change your mind. In any case, there's no reason to talk as if she'd be left entirely alone in the world. She could find a partner——'

'You were the one who was startled when I said a few minutes ago that I was leaving in the autumn. Why not admit you were counting on me staying, just as I was counting on you?'

He got up from the table and took his beer to the window. His four-square figure looked remarkably solid and masculine, standing there in outline, and in one of those disquieting flashes of disloyalty which I had lately experienced about Toby I compared Toby's fragile-looking slender body to this stocky silhouette, and felt such a pang of sadness as I did so, that I looked away and clenched my teeth. Such moments were quite involuntary, yet I paid for them as if I had willed them.

What did they mean? Was I falling out of love with Toby? Has he, wherever he was, fallen out of love with me? I got some abstruse comfort from the unendurable sense of loss this very idea gave me.

'Look,' said Henry. 'Dorothy's not a baby, though I know she behaves a bit like it sometimes. There's no real need for either of us to fret about her. She's taken care of herself through some tough times before this, I imagine, and she can do it again if she has to. It's just . . . just that I wouldn't want to be the one who brought it on her.' He turned back into the room and sat down by the fire, getting out his pipe. 'Anyway, she's been warned—both of us have warned her. There's not much more we can do, since she decided to go ahead anyway.'

'And what about the shop itself? Do you think it'll succeed?'

This time he didn't answer for a very long time. At last he finished fiddling with the pipe, put it in his mouth and raised himself a little in the chair to get out his matches. His eyes met mine and were rather grim. 'No,' he said flatly. 'I don't think it stands a dog's chance.'

I was shattered, and so surprised I didn't know how to react. I simply stared at him.

'I'm telling you this,' he said, 'because you've asked me, and because I think one of you—you, it'll have to be, since she couldn't face it and it wouldn't be fair to make her face it, right from the start—ought to know that—well, it's a lovely idea, it ought to go, but it won't. It can't. Not here—not now. Maybe if she'd agree to rely more on factory goods . . . but that'd be to take away the whole point of it for her. The way she's set on doing it . . . well, these days there aren't the sources and there isn't the market for them. Why, does she think, thatched roofs and hand-carved rocking-horses and patchwork quilts are practically obsolete? Because people don't want 'em any more, that's why; they prefer tiles and pedal-cars and candle-wick. You can't revitalize a taste for old things, however beautiful, when it's been overtaken by a taste for new stuff, however hideous. Oh, here and there, perhaps. But not enough. The hand-made stuff takes too long, it costs too much, there isn't enough of it. And even if there were, there wouldn't be enough people who'd want it.' He mumbled the last of this through his pipe-stem and then settled back, blowing out a long thin stream of aromatic smoke. 'No,' he said. 'I'm afraid as a scheme it's doomed to failure.'

Utterly bewildered, I could hardly think what to ask first, but settled for the obvious. 'Then why on earth are you letting her go ahead with it?'

'Because she wants to so badly. Because it's damned well worthwhile. Because, at certain times and in certain ways, I'm a ruddy fool.'

He'd said it was preferable to tell me the truth than Dottie; but in fact I found it almost as hard to face. I was sure he was right; I'd suspected it from the start, and besides, when Henry said something, one instinctively believed it. And I felt a bitter disappointment. But I felt even more worried about Dottie, because now I understood very well Henry's understated anxiety about how she would manage alone. It's one thing to leave someone with the problems of running a successful enterprise on her hands; but to leave her to face a failure and to pick up the pieces by herself—that's something different.

'If you're right,' I said, 'and I still hope to God you're not, then one or other of us must stay until—well, until the crash. Hell, how appalling to be talking like this before the thing even starts! I do wonder if you shouldn't have stopped her before she'd got in so deep.'

'I wonder too, believe me.'

'You were sure, right from scratch?'

'Look, I'm not omniscient. How can I be sure? I hope I'm wrong.'

'And if you're right, you'll lose all your money.' I remembered suddenly.

'Well . . . *lose* it . . . no. Losing means wasting, getting nothing back. I won't have it any more, that's true. But it will have gone on something, and somebody, that matters.'

I let the 'somebody' pass, though I got a secret warm pleasure from it. 'Why is a man like you so keen on something like this —a piece of anachronistic feminine quixotry that most sensible, practical men would just dismiss as pure folly?'

He threw back his head suddenly and roared with laughter. It was a rare and marvellous thing to hear Henry really losing himself in laughter. 'Anachronistic feminine quixotry!' he shouted. 'Oh, that's great, that is! Yes, indeed. Yes, indeed!

That's exactly what most sensible, practical men would call it.'
He leaned over and patted my arm, his eyes full of appreciation and humour. 'Jane . . . you're very good for me.'

'Well, that's odd. I always feel it's the other way round.'

He leant back again and looked at the ceiling, one forefinger resting on each side of his pipe-bowl. 'You see,' he said, 'I'm a reactionary. Not so much politically, but constitutionally. I react away from things. This whole business is in the nature of a strong reaction—that's the only way I can possibly explain it, even to myself.'

'A reaction against what?'

'Well, from two things. One's private. The other's what I've been busy at for the past twenty years of my life. More than twenty. . . . I was only seventeen when I went into my dad's business, and I've been hard at it ever since until he retired last year—not one moment too soon to suit me, I may say. God knows how I stuck it so long.'

'What was it?'

He looked at me, his eyes twinkling. 'Don't laugh. A shop! Several, as a matter of fact. We built up quite a little chain, mostly in South London. Dad started off with one little store in Dalton, and I started off behind the counter, as delivery boy, van driver, then buyer, branch manager . . . in the end I was running most of it for Dad. He was a good employer, and the whole thing was a steadily increasing success. When he sold out last year, he cleared something like £75,000 net profit. Of which he generously gave me five. I suppose he was right in a way. He said it was pretty cushy severance-pay, and a good pension by any standards for a chap of my age. . . . I didn't resent it, or at least I wouldn't have done if I hadn't privately known that that £5,000 was paying me for twenty years of soul-destroying work, of which, looking back on it now, I know that I hated every single day.'

'And yet now you're putting that money straight back into another shop.'

He nodded. 'That's right. But of a very different kind.'

'What kind did your father have?'

He took the pipe out of his mouth and said succinctly, 'Junk.'

'Junk?'

'Oh, not what you mean—not rags and bottles and old bedsteads, I think I might have quite enjoyed that. I mean real rubbish. Gew-gaws, trash. Tin ash-trays and table-napkin holders, cheap prints of girls with rosebud lips and chiffon dresses lying beside bright blue lakes surrounded by fairies, vases and tea-sets with flowers stamped on them, cutlery that bent and broke, plastic trays, plastic cruets, plastic waste-paper baskets, plastic lampshades, plastic doilies. . . . Of course we had our better lines, too. Front-door chimes, plaster wall-plaques—very pricey, those can be—and a long list of "novelties", things you hang in the windows of your car to cause accidents, musical cigarette-boxes that go wrong within a week, practical jokes, jewellery embellished by what my Dad cynically called "Irish rhinestones", artificial flowers, brass nut-crackers shaped like girls' legs. . . .'

'Enough!' I begged. 'It's all perfectly clear to me now.'

'Yes. Well. There you are,' said Henry. 'And what made it worse was, Dad gave me a pretty fair education beforehand. Nothing posh of course, he couldn't afford it then—though no doubt Amanda will go to Eton, or whatever's the female equivalent—very hot on education, my Dad. Gave me a taste for a bit of quality, and then surrounded me for twenty years with rubbish and never saw anything wrong. Three times I tried to get out, and three times he had heart attacks. Real ones. . . . I never have known quite how he managed it. He always recovered completely as soon as I'd recanted. He's a clever chap, my Dad is.'

'I've heard of mothers doing that. Never fathers.'

'It's got nothing to do with gender. It's widowed mothers who do it to only sons or daughters, and widowed fathers do it for the same reason.'

'Loneliness?'

'Fear of. Same thing.' I suddenly thought how Father had gone on the drink after I'd left home, pregnant. Was that a species of aborted moral blackmail, which he was too basically decent to actually bring to my attention?

'You don't like your father much, I gather,' I remarked.

'No, I hardly like him at all. But I love him,' he said, with a lack of self-consciousness which was surprising. 'Anyway, he's much nicer since he married Joanna. That's my step-mother.

She's nearly thirty years younger than him. She's marvellous and very attractive. Wouldn't have minded marrying her myself. I even asked her once, but she was utterly honest about it. I had £5,000 and Dad had £70,000.'

'How can she be marvellous if she'd do a thing like that?' I asked indignantly. But Henry looked as if I'd disappointed him.

'Here, don't you be so silly, Jane! Joanna was 37 when she met Dad. She'd been trying for years and years to make a living on the stage. Security was what she was looking for, and she wasn't ashamed to admit it. She put it to Dad quite straight—you make me safe and comfortable, she said, and I'll make you a damned good wife, and even give you a baby if I can. Well, she could and she did, and Dad's tickled pink. Dad and I, you know, we'd hardly spoken a word except in the way of business to each other for years until recently; but the atmosphere in that house is so happy that it's a pleasure to go there. I think Joanna's terrific, so lively and honest and warm, and Dad gets the overspill of my liking for her. We're quite matey now, him and me. Funny how things happen.'

So it was that in this one conversation I learned more about Henry than in the three previous months. He was still just about the last person I'd ever have expected Dottie to fall for, and yet if she had I could completely sympathize. Sometimes I felt so fond of him myself it was almost like a kind of being in love.

Dottie returned, full of glad tidings. She'd had acceptances from a number of very 'useful' people, including the *Vogue Shop-Hound*, and a whole lot of other magazines, plus a string of 'names' which meant nothing to me but which she said had enabled her to set off a chain-reaction—on the strength of the names she had got the magazines interested, and vice-versa, though quite often, she said, she had been sort of buying on margin—mentioning a name to a magazine before she'd secured it, in the hope that the magazine's 'yes' would inveigle the name. It usually worked. The guest-list for the opening was now so lengthy and impressive that I—and Henry too, I think —began to feel a little alarmed.

'Are you sure they're not going to get a disappointment when they've dragged themselves all the way down here?' I asked nervously.

Dottie bridled as if I'd stabbed her. 'Disappointment?' she echoed. 'They're going to see wares they've never seen in all their lives. Anyone who's disappointed is a mere clod who *deserves* to have had his journey for nothing.'

'I hope the entertainment isn't going to be purely aesthetic,' said Henry somewhat dryly.

'Don't be silly,' said Dottie.

It turned out she'd engaged one of the best caterers in the West End to do drinks and snacks. Henry blenched when he heard the amount of the estimate, but Dottie swept him aside. 'Think big,' she kept saying.

'Have I any choice?'

'Leave this to me, now, Henry. I know exactly what I'm about.'

'You're about to ruin me,' he answered, more dryly than ever.

But Dottie had more news, which I must confess was of greater interest to me than anything connected with the shop could possibly have been. She waited to impart it until we were alone in the shop, frantically rearranging the displays to accommodate a last-minute delivery of hand-carved salad bowls and spoons from the old carpenter in Gloucester.

'I saw Toby,' she said without preamble.

I was relieved—overjoyed, almost—to feel my blood jump in my head.

'Oh?' I said.

'What "oh"? Have you gone off him?'

'No. Tell me.'

'Well, I wondered, because . . . actually I made a point of seeking him out. I looked up his new address in your book before I left.'

'Why didn't you just ask me for it?'

'I don't know quite . . . some intuitive reluctance. Anyway, I just arrived one evening, and a—a sort of girl answered the door.'

After a long blank moment I found I had just come to a stop, like a motor which seizes up. I had to force myself to ask, 'What do you mean, a sort of girl?'

'Well, the sort of girl who looks a bit like a boy. You know, jeans, man's sweater, short hair, scrubbed-looking features. *Very* young. Not more than sixteen I shouldn't think.'

'Seventeen,' I said.

'You know her?' asked Dottie in surprise.

'I know of her. Her name's Whistler, isn't it?'

'She was introduced to me as Melissa Lee.'

I nodded. 'That's Whistler.' I felt faint but kept my voice normal with an effort. The blood in my ears was banging curses into my head: 'You fool, you fool, you god-damned bloody stupid bitch, it serves you right!' I could hardly hear what Dottie was saying.

'Toby didn't seem specially gratified by my visit, which was understandable. He and this hermaphrodite were just sitting down to supper, which she'd evidently cooked. . . .'

'What was it?' I asked ludicrously.

'Steak,' she replied promptly. 'Very tough, with baked potatoes slightly burnt. The salad looked good though.' She reported all this with meticulous care and accuracy, as if unaware of what it was doing to me—yet I knew she wasn't unaware and I stood leaning against a trestle, understanding why Cleopatra murdered the messenger who brought the news about Antony's marriage.

'Go on,' I said.

'I hadn't prepared anything, I mean my reason for coming, and I had to think of something feasible quickly, so I told him —of all things—that I'd come because you'd asked me to get John's address. That was his name, wasn't it—the black man?' I nodded. 'He gave it to me, and then asked me to have a drink. I must say he was very nice. The girl could have sliced my head off. I sat there until everything was cold, making bright chat. I felt that was the least I could do. Eventually she lost her temper and said, "I hope you don't mind but I'm hungry." Whereupon she sat down and furiously devoured her meal. I couldn't help feeling a bit sorry for her. She was almost crying.'

I was almost crying myself but managed to ask, 'Did she seem to be living there?'

Dottie made a startled movement behind my back and answered, 'That I couldn't say. But surely not! She's hardly dry behind the ears——'

'Don't be fooled. She knows it all.'

There was a long silence while I fought a desperate battle to control my feelings and not start having hysterics. Dottie finally came up to my shoulder and asked without touching me, 'Does it matter that much?'

'It seems to.'

'Then you'd better get up to town and do something about it. Only,' she added, 'please, love—not till after the opening.'

Chapter 13

THE ADVICE, though selfishly motivated, was good. If I'd rushed off then and there, as I half wanted to, God knows I might have done something really awful, made a complete fool of myself somehow. As it was, I waited three days, and they were full on two levels: physically, with the preparations and the opening itself, and mentally with an endless succession of compulsive mental screen-plays—duologues and triologues which filled my brain all day and most of the night, and left me in no sort of doubt as to whether Toby was still the man I wanted. But now I took no comfort from this assurance, for my instincts tormented me with the conviction that he no longer wanted me.

The opening thus passed for me in a haze of confusion. I remember one moment when I was standing in a group of etiolated, superbly-dressed, shrieky people, all too thin and too well-groomed to seem quite real, and all of us (as I thought) were taking part in some fatuous conversation over our dry martinis when suddenly one of the men, who was wearing a ruffle-fronted pink shirt and no tie, leaned to my ear and whispered, 'Hey, come back to us!' I snapped my head round to him in astonishment and asked what he meant, whereupon he bared the splendid teeth of a finely-bred racehorse and said, 'Darling, you were so far away you'd all but vanished from view.' At that moment, as it happened, I had been actually confronting Toby and Whistler in *flagrante delicto* and had been on the point of flying at Whistler's throat, so I had to blush and apologize to the young man, for whom, as I vaguely recalled, Dottie had especially asked me to be responsible. (It must be added here that all my imaginary encounters did not take such a violent or dramatic turn; in most of them I tried to be reasonable and civilized, and in my more hopeful moments my imagination contrived a tender and acceptable outcome. I think the heady atmosphere of Dottie's party, not to mention the mixture of champagne cocktails and gin, was to blame for the sudden lapse of control over my libido.)

If the party was for me no more than a blur superimposed on my thoughts, it was certainly a blur of the brightest and most dazzling kind. I have a montage of recollections: the whole of the village high-street lined with costly cars on both sides; the bow-window encircled by a solid frieze of curious local children peering in from the outer gloom to the inner brilliance which jiggled with colour, noise and movement like a sort of audible kaleidoscope; Dottie, radiant, vital and poised as a kingfisher, swooping from group to group, her hands always filled with one of her hand-wrought wonders, her face alight as she turned it about, demanding from her audience appreciation for its beauty. Henry, alone but at ease, leaning against the fireplace with his inevitable tankard of ale in his hand, apparently dispassionately surveying the scene but in reality (unless I was mistaken) following Dottie with his eyes; only when she was lost to him in the crowd did I see him stir himself, stretching his neck a little or shifting his casual stance until he located her again. Once I saw her dart up to him and they stood together for a brief moment; she put her hand up towards his chest in one of her impulsive gestures, as if to emphasize a point, and I saw the hand stop short and stand by itself in the air for a brief, raw moment before she drew it back. This aborted movement focused my wandering attention, and I experienced a sudden little blow over the heart like an electric shock. I didn't know what it meant; it was as if I'd spied on a private moment in an intense personal drama. The next instant she had turned back into the crowd and Henry was alone again.

The whole business seemed to be over remarkably quickly; if Dottie hadn't explained that this particular 'set' was accustomed to driving all over the countryside to attend any function from a house-party to an auction, I would have been amazed that so many sophisticates had found it worthwhile to come so far for so short a time.

Abruptly the cohesion of the clot of colour crowded between

the trestles broke up; groups drifted to the door, calling good-byes; Dottie signalled to me to attend her and I stood at her side smiling and jabbering adieus while the white-jacketed caterers helped the women on with their furs.

I now noticed that many of them carried our Dottie-designed carrier-bags, a vivid creation in purple, green and blue with the name of the shop—'Us and Them'—emblazoned on it. I thought these people must have been buying things, but Dottie later explained it was bad form to take money at openings; she had merely given away a pile of these distinctive bags, each containing a tiny polished straw doll, as a publicity gimmick.

She had, however, unobtrusively accepted several very lucrative orders, and all in all was in such a state of elation when the last of the guests had roared away down the high street that we had to forcibly seat her and make her calm down for fear she would twirl herself into a state of collapse, like a victim of the Wilis.

We had to assure her repeatedly that it had been a wonderful success, that the chronic vacuity in the eyes of the rich and influential guests had cleared, at least momentarily, releasing gleams of wonder and dawning aesthetic delight at the taste and craft on display, that 'Us and Them' could scarcely have been better or more truly launched. I was really quite tight by this time and so was she, and soon she was laughing hysterically at my rather overdone sallies of praise, and then gradually the laughter changed and she began to cry.

I thought Henry might have been a bit impatient with this, but half Henry's charm was his unpredictability. He came straight off the table where he was sitting and went over to her, lifting her quite gently and saying, 'That's enough, now. It's been a busy day. Time to be getting home.'

He led her quietly out of the shop, leaving me to turn out the lights and lock up; I lingered a bit to tidy up, and after a few minutes Henry returned alone and threw me Dottie's keys. 'I'm taking her home in my car,' he said. 'Could you bring hers?' I said of course, and just as he was going out he paused in the doorway and said indistinctly, without looking at me, 'And if you can manage not to hurry. . . .'

'Henry. . . .'

'What?'

There was a pause while I tried to think how one says things like that when one is not sure of one's ground or even of one's hearer, and then mumbled gauchely, 'I could sleep at your place tonight, if you liked.'

He hesitated a moment, and then said in a rough, angry voice—but not as if he were angry with me—'No. No, don't.' His manner softened apologetically. 'I want a chat with her, that's all.' Then he went off again; I saw him walking quickly past the bow-window with his funny, short-man's step, a slight spring in the toe as if trying to make himself feel taller. His face was hard and the whole set of his body looked rigid, as if he was holding himself in.

I made my superficial tidying-up into something a bit more elaborate, until everything was ready to open the doors properly the following Monday. The caterers, albeit the best in the West End, had left quite a mess, so it all took time, but I wasn't sure at the end if it'd taken long enough, so as it was still only nine o'clock I wandered into the local cinema, of which the box-office had already closed, and watched the last three-quarters of quite a good film for nothing.

The champagne had made me light-headed enough to be able to push my unhappy thoughts of Toby right to the back of my mind and sink without trace into the pure escapism of that movie—an hour and a half of total relaxation which couldn't have been equalled (judging by the past two wretched nights I'd passed) even in sleep.

I emerged at a little before eleven, feeling almost happy. I walked slowly back to where Dottie had left the car, passing the post office and next to it the darkened bow-window of our shop. I stopped a moment to look up at the façade with its freshly-painted name, in bold clear purple letters outlined in gold. The frontage itself had all been stripped to the wood and varnished. A street-lamp showed me the display on the rostrum inside the window—Dottie had cunningly used a plain white packing-case with its lining of natural straw, on its side, with goods spilling out of it in well-organized confusion like a practical man's cornucopia.

Hanging on a plain board at the back were a craftsman's tools, not new ones, but old and well-used. Swatches and hanks of unbleached wool, straw, bamboo, raffia and cane hung from the ceiling. On a succession of small shelves on one side wall were objects like paint-pots, brushes, a few unbaked crocks, even a small blow-lamp, and finally a glass-blower's pipe, for although there was no hand-blown glass in the shop Dottie had not given up hope of getting some and had put the pipe there for luck. In the window was a hand-written sign:

You will not get plastic objects from *Us*.
Try *Them*.

I personally did not care for this touch, but it was Henry's only personal contribution to the decor and Dottie had allowed it because, I suppose, she knew his history and understood as well as I did why it mattered to him, like a definition of his creed.

I arrived back at the cottage to find everything quiet and a dry note from Henry on the hall table:

'Have driven Mrs G. home' (Mrs Griffiths had been baby-sitting for me, I'd forgotten about her) . . . 'you needn't have stayed out so long. H.'

I went upstairs. Dottie was asleep, and so was David. I had never felt so wide awake in my life; sleep would be quite impossible. I made myself a cup of strong coffee, as if on purpose to banish sleep still more decisively. For a long time I sat in the kitchen, not reading or doing anything except sip my coffee and stare into space. My whole body seemed to be trembling with the need for some action, and suddenly I knew what it must be.

I went upstairs again, changed out of the glamour-rags Dottie had picked out for me into a skirt, sweater, warm tights and anorak. Then I went into the spare room and crouched by Dottie's bed.

I had to shake her shoulder to bring her even half way awake.

'Dottie, listen. I'm going up to London. Can I leave David with you, just for tomorrow? I'll be back tomorrow evening.'

'Isn't it the middle of the night?'

'Yes. It's better. Less traffic. Anyway, I must.'

At the door her voice stopped me. 'Jane——'

'Yes?'

'Take John's address.'

'I won't have time——'

'You might. Take it, it's on a piece of paper in my bag.' Irritated by the delay, I rummaged about till I found it, and stuck it into my pocket.

Chapter 14

A LOT OF OTHER MOTORISTS besides myself seemed to
have imagined it was easier to drive at night, and it took me
the best part of another hour and a bit to get to Hammersmith.
I glanced at our house—that's to say, Father's—as I went past;
it was dark. I hadn't seen him for months, though we dropped
each other notes occasionally. I had a sudden feeling of panic
about where I was going, and a craven desire to turn into our
drive, get Father out of bed, sit and talk for an hour, and then
go to sleep in the room where I had spent my not-very-happy
and yet now, somehow, strangely attractive, because safe,
adolescence. However, the pull was not quite strong enough,
and in any case, I thought: 'It isn't far from Earl's Court—I
can always come back—afterwards.'

I drove on.

The Earl's Court Road was quite alive; there were several
coffee-bars still open, despite the cold weather. However, the
subtle plimsol-line between respectable day-time occupancy of
the area and the emergence of disreputable-looking night-
denizens had been crossed, and the streets had a strongly
sinister atmosphere in which even quite ordinary people took
on a faintly lupous appearance and seemed suspect.

I drew up under a lamp-post, near the side-turning which
would take me to Toby's street. Now I was so close, I was
grimly unsurprised to find that my burning desire to confront
him was wavering. What if Whistler were there . . . ? It hardly
bore thinking about. This was one occasion when I was quite
determined to behave with dignity, and not have any loss of
self-control with which to reproach myself later. But to ensure
this, and also to gather my courage, I needed a minute to
sort myself out. I looked at my watch. It was a quarter past
one.

I thought: If I go to Toby's now, it will be patently obvious that I've come to check up on him because of Dottie's report; perhaps he'll even think I've come to catch him out with the girl, and if he's not sleeping with her he'll have every right to be very angry. After all, it could have been just a casual supper together. On the other hand, if she *is* there, it'll be (my mind went blank at this point. Sober, I couldn't really visualize a scene with Toby in bed with Whistler as its focal point). Better to go by day, when I can easily explain my visit as a simple dropping-in, and bring up the subject of Whistler in some more or less natural way. I reviewed my behaviour towards Toby the last time I'd seen him, and remembering clearly only one thing—the look I had thrown at him when he had tried to sit down with a newspaper—I shrivelled in my skin. If he were to plead that look alone as a reason for turning his back on me, I would be totally at a loss for a defence. In any case, what use was it to defend myself? Love lost by one moment's explicit unfairness can't be won back by trying to justify it. My only real hope was that I was wrong; that it was only my guilty conscience telling me that that look had been such a fundamental thing. It deserved to be; but one doesn't always get one's deserts. On the other hand— there was his silence. Two months of it . . . but I hadn't written either . . . perhaps he was waiting for a sign from me . . . perhaps he would be overjoyed to be confronted by me on his doorstep at one in the morning, we would hold each other, talk for a bit, everything would be explained, and then, as naturally as water sinking into thirsty earth, we would go to bed. Once, he had drawn back from making love to me because he was afraid it would bind us together again, give us renewed responsibility for each other. The next time, we had slept together, actually slept in each other's arms, but without making love, due to the comic and annoying physical accident about which I'd told Dottie. But the mere fact of being so close to him must have reminded him, as it did me, that our love was a permanency, only waiting for him to grow and develop enough to take hold of it and accept it fully. *I* was ready—God knows, I'd been ready all the time. I was readier this moment than ever before, and surer; but perhaps that was only because I had had such a fright and really had to face the fact that I might have lost him altogether. All self-doubts are apt to fly before such an eventuality.

The torment of not knowing almost drove me to change my mind again and go bursting in on Toby that night. I went as far as the house where his studio-flat was. Never having been there, I couldn't be sure which window was his, but as the whole house was in darkness it made little difference. I sat in the car for ten minutes, debating with myself. Several very dubious-looking characters drifted by, every one of them pausing to peer in through the windows, I suppose in the hope of surprising some couple in a pornographic position on the back seat. When they saw it was a lone woman, just sitting there in the dark, several of the men knocked hopefully on the windscreen. I hated this so much that eventually I blew a terrific blast on my horn, which made the latest applicant for my services jump and run.

Eventually a policeman came strolling along, and this, oddly enough, alarmed me more than the lubricious strollers and made up my mind for me. I moved off. Driving away from Earl's Court with a feeling of the deepest misery—Toby so near me, yet unreachable, unmerited, perhaps no longer loving me—I drove aimlessly through the streets for a long time, too wretched even to wonder what to do and where to go. I supposed dimly that I would wind up at Father's, but as it grew later and later I became more disinclined to arrive there and have to wake him up and explain. I thought of going to a hotel, but dismissed the idea—I loathe hotels, especially cheap ones in the middle of the night, not that I've ever had any experience of them, but London altogether at that hour is so sleazy and frightening that I wanted more than anything just to find somebody I knew—somebody kind and undemanding and not too curious—yet who could one disturb at this hour who would not be curious?

Hot on the heels of this question came the answer.

I pulled up once again. I was at Little Venice, and the water of the canal glinted golden from the street lamps; the leaves of the old trees fringing the banks moved with a soft sound which I could just hear between the intermittent roars of passing cars. It was as nearly peaceful there as one could hope for, and certainly not at all sinister, perhaps because there were no people. I took the bit of paper out of my pocket and opened it in the light from the dashboard. It gave an address in Paddington. I got out my A-to-Z and looked it up. It wasn't more than a few minutes' drive from where I was.

I started the engine up again, rather reluctant to break the relative quiet, but it didn't break it for long because it died almost as soon as I'd choked it into life. I glanced at the petrol gauge, which was silly of me, since it had been pointing to zero ever since I'd inherited the car from Addy. I tried the starter a couple of times without result. Then I pulled my anorak hood over my head and, thanking God there was no rain, abandoned the car and started walking, carrying nothing but my A-to-Z and the bit of paper. I'd even forgotten to bring my wallet.

The street was a sad one, one of those neighbourhoods which has known much better days but which is now just one rung up the ladder from a slum. The houses were, or had been, beautiful, and their frontages still had a certain magnificence, although the moulding, pilasters—even the window-sills— were crumbling away and it was many years since any of them had been painted. But they had a splendid Regency uniformity, a whole terrace built at once with an integrity of design which had retained its splendour through every degree of indignity and neglect.

I found the place easily, though the number on the pillar at the top of the flight of wide, once-gracious steps had been chipped away and defaced. The blistered and peeling front door was not locked, and swung open when I fell against it, stumbling over a roller-skate on the porch. At first I was too nervous to venture into the dark, murky-smelling hall, but then I realized I would have to—there were no individual bells; I really had no notion of how I could possibly locate John in this large warren, filled to bursting-point, I could sense, with sleeping humanity. The hall was almost pitch-dark, but as I got used to it I found enough light came in through the front door to prevent me bumping into two or three prams, a push-chair, a child's waggon and two bicycles that all but made even that spacious hall impassable. Several tiles were out of the marble floor and I had to make my way slowly and with the greatest care to the foot of the curving stairway, whose stone steps, once adorned with carpeting, now bore no traces of it except one forgotten stair-rod which nearly caused me to break my neck by rolling under my foot, and clattering musically down to the bottom.

A door opened on the first floor and a woman's voice whispered querulously, 'That you at last, you bit of stopping-out dirt?' I stopped in my tracks in momentary terror, but then, realizing this might be my salvation from the hell of knocking on strange doors, I hurriedly groped my way up the last stairs and confronted a dim headless wraith in a long pale garment. The head, which was there but too black to perceive, made itself manifest by opening its white eyes very wide. 'Who you?' it asked.

In a low, polite whisper, I said I was looking for John.

'What John you wanting? There's three Johns here. My son's name John. You not looking for him, I hope, cause you won't get to him this time of night.'

'The John I want isn't anybody's son. He plays the guitar.'

'Oh, him. Third floor front. . . .' The sleeve of the pale garment raised itself apparently without human agency and an invisible hand indicated the general direction. The disembodied eyes watched me curiously as I felt my way round the banisters, and answered with a suspicious roll when I turned to whisper good-night.

The stairs were apparently endless, curving onward and upward; there are few things bleaker and colder than uncarpeted stone stairs. The only light came from the huge curtainless windows at every landing; it felt like an empty house which has been filled up with refugees who are not involved in any part of it except their own rooms and corners.

On what I judged to be the third floor I groped to the only door I could see and knocked on it very softly. By this time I had quite decided that I was suffering from a rather prolonged fit of madness, but having pointed myself in this direction, crazy though it undoubtedly was, I couldn't seem to turn aside. I knocked again, and this time I heard a movement in the room—a grunt, the squeak of a bedspring; then a well-remembered voice said, 'Who that? Somebody out there?'

'John!' I hissed joyfully. 'It's me—Jane!'

I heard the padding of large bare feet, and the door was

unbolted and opened a crack. We stared into each other's faces in pitch blackness for several seconds.

'Jane?' John's voice asked incredulously.

'It's me, you fathead! Let me in!'

In another moment I was being clasped against a vast expanse of chest. 'Jane! Jane!' he kept saying exultantly. 'You come to see me! You come back again!' He almost carried me into the room and instantly switched on a single ceiling light, holding me, almost off the ground, out in front of him.

He hadn't changed much. Well, not at all, really; it was just that I had hardly ever seen him in any other surroundings than my room or his at Fulham, except a few times at the hospital after David's birth. This big, rambling, underfurnished room was such a contrast to the little cupboard at the top of the house in Fulham where he had lived next to mine; now I saw him in a room big enough not to make him look like a giant in a gnome's cave and I realized he was not so enormous as I had always thought. His big black face was split from ear to ear with a smile of simple delight. He rubbed his hand back and forth over the top of his woolly head and with the other held my shoulder and rocked me violently to and fro while we both laughed like idiots.

Suddenly an irritable movement at the other end of the room caught my eye, and to my astonishment I saw that there were three beds in the room, and that two of them were occupied. I clapped my hand over my mouth. John followed my eyes and said in a normal voice, 'Oh, don't mind them! They just share the room, that's all.'

'But we'll disturb them!'

'So what? You think they never disturb me? Ain't no prizes for guessin' which from us three does the less disturbin'.' He led me to a rickety kitchen chair, took his guitar and a pile of dirty clothes off it and made me sit, 'They got their lady-friends comin' and goin' all night, every night. You the first lady-friend I had to visit me since I moved in with them randy bastards.'

'Shh!'

'What "shh"? I talk how I like. I don't owe them nothin'.' He picked up his guitar and struck a loud, deliberate chord. The hump of grey blankets in one bed didn't move; the other heaved and a dark voice from the depths said peevishly, 'Can't a man sleep without the damn radio playin' half the night?'

'That ain't no radio, boy!' retorted John, strumming louder. 'Won't hear nothin' that good on no radio!'

The other man sat up in bed sharply and said, 'Kill it, frigger, before I slit your black skin from your neck to your navel!' He was wearing a flannel sweat-shirt with the words 'Go Man Go' written on it.

John laughed and said, 'Since you asked me so nice——' and put the guitar aside. The other man turned his back, lay down and went to sleep with a deep sigh.

'Why do you have to share a room?' I asked. 'Money?'

'Not that so much. I got a goodish job now, same band I with before but they move up in the world and me with 'em. Now we get lots of dates, lots of good places; you know what's a debutante?' I nodded. 'Very rich kind of girl with stinkin' rich daddies. Well, them kinds of people gettin' very liberal now, want to show they ain't colour-prejudiced, and besides we play good; so they engages us to play for their dances. Big deal! Best hotels, sometimes in their own country houses, some even send a car for bringin' us. Some of them's real democratic, we even get champagne to drink and same food as the guests; but that ain't every time of course. It's more often beer and sandwiches and havin' to play five, six hours on the trot, take your break when it's not your solo. Them kids, though, Jane! You look at 'em, start of the evening, in their lovely clothes, and you think how pretty they are, how clean, and how their riches make 'em look somethin' better than humans, different somehow. And everyone's so nice to each other, so polite, you know what I mean —cultured. You feel like you're playing for a bunch of angels. And then they start dancin' and every time it give me a shock to see how they dance, *wild*, like anybody, like I seen these two here dancin' with their whore-women, only it looks worse in them long dresses. I'll tell you somethin', when their daddies and mummies gets up to dance, what do they do? Same kind of wild twistin' and Bosanovarin' and stuff as the kids do. I seen one old mummy, her crown fell right off and got kicked clear across the floor before she could bend her old self over to pick it up. False teeth and glasses falling off you often see, but when one of them little diamond crowns falls in among all them jumpin' feet it gets you.' He shook his head sadly. 'I asked the other boys, that time—what we blowin' for? Just to send these people? Look at what we're doin' to 'em! They ain't theirselves no more, they gone back to the jungle they say we come from. Because of course they don't talk so liberal when they get a bit of that champagne inside their bellies, then you get to hear what they really think, and they don't mind you hearin' neither, sayin' things like—well, I wouldn't tell you what they says, but personal, real personal. And some of them pretty dressed-up little debutantes, they gets to feeling so curious, there ain't nothing they won't do to satisfy theirselves about . . . and some of our boys don't stop at nothin' neither. Course, I don't—lower myself—to doin' nothin' like that, Jane. Somehow I don't even like to think of it. But these fellows here—' he jerked his big thumb over his shoulder at his sleeping room-mates—'they'd take three or four of 'em out into the bushes or into the back of a car in their beer-break and come back after it and tell the rest of the boys in the band all about it while they're shakin' the wet out of their saxes.'

'Are they in the band—those two?'

'Naaa—they're just fellows, they got no music, no nothin', they just work anyplace. They're big black bodies with heads on 'em but nothin' inside the heads, you know what I mean? I hate 'em,' he said dispassionately, 'and they hate me because I ain't like them.'

'But John, then why do you live with them?'

'Jane, you can't understand. It's hard to find a place where to live in this white man's city. Oh, there's places, there's houses, but they're mostly like this—broken down, nobody carin' for nothin' except the rent. I told you I wasn't doin' so bad for money, but I couldn't rent this room for my lone self. You know what each of us is shellin' out for our third share? Four pound. And for what? Well, look around and you'll see. One bathroom downstairs which the bath is always full of dirty water, cause the drain's blocked, no cooking allowed for the bachelors, no privacy, no nothin'. Four pound a week.'

'God!' I said, appalled. 'Wasn't it better at Doris's?'

'Better?' he cried. 'I tell you, I look back on that bug-run like you'd look back to paradise. Them days, Jane—last year, with you and Toby and old Doris, and Charlie, and that funny woman, what was her name, the nosy one——?'

'Mavis——'

'Yes, her. She died, did you know that?'

'Mavis? Died?'

'Yeh. Fell down them damn stairs, poor old woman. I was real sorry, even though she wouldn't have no dealin's with me on account of me bein' a spade. She was kind to you though, wasn't she?'

'Yes,' I said. I was very shocked.

'That happened before I left. We all went to her funeral— Doris cried just like a baby. I cried too, but I was cryin' mostly because she reminded me of them good times with you and Toby.' He gazed at me through sad yellow eyes. 'They was the best times I ever had. And you two was my best friends. I won't never have no friends again like you two.'

I took hold of his huge hand and played with the fingers, dark brown on top, sort of beigy-pink underneath, with a brick-like callous on the side of the thumb from strumming. 'Why did you leave Doris's?'

'Lonely. I tried to be friendly with a girl who came to live in your old room, but she didn't want no truck with me, she was scared stiff of me, used to run if I spoke to her. She pretty soon married a young fellow who had Toby's room after Toby left. Then they went and some awful people came, I think they were gangsters or somethin'. I was never so sure they didn't have somethin' to do with that poor old woman fallin'. Maybe they bust in on her and scared her or—well, I can't be sure, but they were real ugly people, the two of them. I used to hear funny conversations through the wall. Whispers —you know; like plannin' somethin', with just a few words comin' plain when they didn't agree 'bout somethin'. One night I was practisin' some music real soft, and suddenly that little window—you remember, high up between the rooms— that got smashed right to bits and this fellow put his fists in with a whole lot of bits of razor blades stuck between his knuckles. He shook it at me and said, real quiet and threatening, from behind the partition, "If you don't stop that row you black animal I'm going to kick that door open and flay the skin right off your face." Well, I'm no hero. I believed him, so I stopped. And couple of days later I moved out. Doris was sorry in the end. She was scared of these white boys, and I guess she'd found out I was harmless. Funny how she'd come round to me. But with you and Toby and Mavis and me gone, I could see what she was thinkin'. The house'd fill up somehow with the real bad types and there'd be her and Charlie, never knowin' when they was goin' to get done up in the night.' He shook his head again, really concerned for Doris. 'That poor old cow, she never had no judgement. It was just her good luck she got people like us.'

'*She* probably looks back on that time as *her* golden age, too. After all, it was when she married Charlie.'

But John was pursuing his own thoughts. 'Maybe you ain't noticed it so much, livin' in the country,' he said. 'But this bad world is gettin' worse and worse all the time. The people's gettin' worse. Better at hatin', better at grabbin'. I tell you somethin', I'm real scared to go out alone some nights.' He sat back on his bed and looked at the two recumbent figures behind him. 'You ask me why do I live with these two randy spades and I tell you, money. But that ain't the only thing. I wish I could find somebody nice to live with, but I can't seem to find nobody real nice that ain't fixed up with a wife or somehow, and I sure ain't aimin' to live on my own no more. These two ain't much, but they better than nothin'.'

'Even though they say they're going to slice you?'

'Ah, that's just talkin'. Ain't like that white boy—he meant it. We been livin' here now, the three of us, for near six months, and ain't hardly been one day we haven't said we'll slice each other. Ain't nobody so much as brought a knife out yet, 'cept to cut his bread. And sometimes when they had their fill of women and they feelin' good they get me to play and they dance and sing and this whole old house starts jumpin', and we have a good time together. Sort of. But it ain't real, like with you and Toby, because them and me, we ain't alike in our hearts, and under the music and drink we looks down at each other, we're on the hate-kick same as the rest.'

We'd been talking non-stop for nearly an hour; it was 3 a.m. and he hadn't asked me a word about myself or why I'd come so late or anything. Sitting there in that sleazy room, half-frozen, too tired to feel like sleeping, I felt the most tremendous love for John and cursed myself for not having written to him or come to see him before. I wondered if Toby had been any better.

'Do you see anything of Toby?'

John brightened. 'I see him, time to time. Couple times he's invited me to his place for a meal. Them's the times I look forward to! Toby's a good friend, But afterwards I got to come back here to these two pails of slops which got no conversation 'cept women and cursing the whites and somehow I feel more worse than I did before. Still, it's worth it to see Toby in that big nice studio-room of his and talk about you and old times.'

'You talk about me?' I couldn't help asking.

'Sure we do,' he said, surprised. 'I always ask about you.'

'When did you last see him?'

'Dunno. Couple months, maybe.'

'Not since Christmas?'

His face changed a little and he said, 'Let's don't talk about Christmas. That was my worst, most loneliest time I ever had.'

'Oh John! We thought of you!'

He looked at me curiously. 'You was together—you and Toby—Christmastime?' I nodded. 'Where?' I told him. 'You had a tree?' I nodded again, unable to speak for remorse. He stood up and walked to the door, opened and closed it aimlessly, wandered around a bit among all the clutter littering the floor and slowly came back to me. He sat down without looking at me. He sat with his knees wide apart and his head hanging down looking at the floor. 'You want to drink somethin'?' he asked me after a long time.

'No thanks, John,' I muttered, almost crying.

'I could make tea.' He looked up at me and said more cheerfully, 'That's a good idea, you know? Tea? It's cold in here. I'll make some, like I used to when you was pregnant in the mornin's.' His mood had changed. He was as volatile as a child. Now with something to do—the begrimed electric kettle to plug in on a table several layers thick with food and kitchen crocks, mugs to find and wash in a bucket of water under the table, a lot of business with tea and sugar and condensed milk in a tube—he seemed quite happy again and chattered away about debutantes and clubs and the café where he usually ate, where dope was peddled as a sideline: I asked him if he 'smoked' and he said yes of course, with an air of surprise, and explained that when he said dope he meant the hard stuff which he never touched. The two bodies slept on, impervious to light and voices, and I asked if they touched the hard stuff and John said one of them did and was in fact sleeping off a fix right now. The other had a shot now and again but wasn't hooked. Their names were Frank and Leroy and they were both West Indian. . . . I listened to their whole histories while we drank our tea, which smelt faintly of dirty dish-cloth but which, being very hot, strong and sweet, was comforting. I hadn't realized how really cold and empty I was; I had sort of gone numb.

I had to bring up Toby again.

'So you haven't seen anything of Toby since—for two months?'

'About that. It was winter, I know that, 'cause he'd just got himself a new kind of heater that blew hot air along the floor, and he gave me his old oil-stove. There it is,' he pointed to it standing in a corner under a pile of old *Daily Mirrors*, 'only it run out of oil just after I brought it back and I ain't never got round to buyin' any. Still, I like havin' it, somethin' of Toby's.' He took a long drink of tea, looking slowly at me over the rim. 'What's with you two people? Ain't you never goin' to get married?'

I looked at him and wondered how wise he was. Of course he wasn't at all clever, but he had a certain basic wisdom about some things.

'Do you think Toby's strong enough to marry?'

The golden whites of his eyes didn't flicker or change. 'Oh yes,' he said without hesitating. 'Toby strong enough. Question is, if *you* strong enough.'

My first reaction, after the first stunned moment, was: He's crazy! He doesn't know the first thing about either of us! Even so, I was oddly hurt—almost insulted. Too much so to ask what he meant or for any further elaboration. I just went on staring at him until he said, quite gently, 'You been thinkin' it was the other way round?' I didn't answer, and he went on: 'Who run away? Who all the time don't want? Toby wanted. He'd married you after the baby, before the baby, any time you was willin'. But you run.'

'I wanted him to be free!'

John laughed, a soft, kind chuckle, and ran his finger round the rim of the cup. 'You can make music like this,' he said, 'with glasses.'

'I didn't want to hang onto him! I didn't want to tie him with my need!' But even as I cried the words, they sounded false. Completely.

John didn't look up at me, just shook his head and finished his chuckle. After a moment he said, 'You know what they say about me?' He indicated the sleepers with his head. 'They call me a fag. That's a fellow only wants it with other fellows.' I gasped, but covered it with a deep, shaken breath. 'It's true I don't go after women much, but I ain't a fag, not what they mean. I never wanted Toby that way, and I loved Toby like I never loved anybody—'cept maybe you. And another thing. I know how a man feels. Not men like them—they ain't real men, they're just a pair of walkin' John Thomases. I mean real men, like Toby. You say you didn't want him to know you needed him. Well, I'll ask you. What you think men want from women? That's why I say you the weak one. You too weak to let him know how weak you are. He been waitin' all this time for you to come to him and need him. I tell you somethin', Jane, I don't know how much longer he goin' to wait. He's strong, but he ain't that strong. No man ain't that strong, to go on forever without nobody that needs him.' He lay back on the bed and looked straight up at the ceiling. 'I thought about it a lot. I mean if I was a fag or not. And I found the answer in one thing. Why was them months at Doris's the happiest I ever was? This'll sound real silly. It was because you was sick and you felt better when I brought you cups of tea. And because Toby was sick a different way and used to talk to me a lot. Half he said I couldn't understand, that's the half I just had to feel. But just the talkin' did him good, he said so. You both needed me, and I felt good. And that was a man's kind of feelin' good. Which is what you ain't givin' Toby, cause you're afraid to.'

Chapter 15

I SLEPT IN JOHN'S BED for the rest of the night, while he lay on the floor beside me on a mattress of newspapers and blankets and periodically made me jump by putting up his hand to feel if I was still there. His bed smelt very strongly of male sweat, and the near proximity of John's randy room-mates made it quite difficult to sleep soundly; besides, I had too much on my mind.

Anyway, after three hours or so it was morning—Sunday morning, so the sleepers slept on while John and I, both feeling befuddled but laughing hysterically a good deal, staggered up and prepared a breakfast of sorts from the unappetizing assortment on the table. I had some stale sliced loaf and marge with condensed milk on it, and more tea, and John partook of cold sausage and the remains of a tin of Mulligatawny soup, most of which had solidified round the tin to a sort of black paste.

We had the radio on and we did some P.T. to try and get warm, and then I had to pay a visit to the communal lavatory on the floor below—a very sobering experience. Then we drank more tea, and still the sleepers slept, and still John had asked me nothing; but it was getting on for nine o'clock and I was sitting on nails, half longing to go over to Toby's at once and half dreading it, no longer sure even of my own most basic feelings, let alone my moral justification which had already been on shaky ground.

At last I said to John, 'Let's go and visit Toby,' and it was out before I knew it, the 'let's'. His face came alive like a child's and he jumped to his feet at once. 'I get dressed!' he announced, though so far as one could see he was dressed already, and presumably went to bed every night in the same attire—a sweat-shirt, long underwear, a pair of jeans, and thick socks. But he dug some cleaner clothes out of an overcrowded cupboard and danced into them while I, keeping my back discreetly turned, made his bed and tidied his small section of the room perfunctorily.

When he looked round and saw what I'd been doing he laughed loudly and pointed with his thumb to the other two beds.

'Now they know for sure I'm a fag!' he said. 'Ain't nobody here made his bed in six months!'

'On the contrary, they'll see you've had a woman here and they'll be completely confused.'

We left the house quietly and were lucky to meet none of the other inhabitants except a small clot of children playing jacks on the front porch. They stared at us and did not move an inch to let us pass, so we had to pick our way between their thin little arms and legs. As we went down the steps one boy whispered, 'Whitey, whitey, took off her nightie——' John whipped round with an angry movement, but confronting only five closed mouths and innocent pairs of eyes, allowed me to tug him away.

'Wasn't never like this couple years ago,' he muttered. 'Where they learn things like that?'

'From their elders,' I said. 'Where else?'

'Nearly ain't no white people left in this street,' said John. 'Couple old landladies won't move out or sell, but even they only got black tenants. Can't get no white ones now. We people just ruined the neighbourhood.' I glanced at him expecting to see that he was joking, but he wasn't; he looked serious and regretful. 'Ain't our fault though,' he added. 'We got to go somewhere.'

We got a series of buses back to Earl's Court and then walked up the Sunday-silent street to Toby's. I was even more than Sunday-silent; I was terribly scared, actually quaking. I had the feeling that this was a vital turning-point in my life and I was absolutely unprepared to meet it. John, who had no way of knowing what was in my mind, sensed my inner turmoil as we neared the house and quietly took my hand. This was too much for me and I pulled him to a stop.

'John, he—he may have a girl there.'

'Ah,' he said, and stood still for a moment. 'Well, if so, then we don't stay long.' And with that he drew me forward again.

Toby's flat was at the top of an ugly two-storied Victorian house. The attic had been reconstructed to make a studio room. He had his own bell outside his door with his name on it, T. Cohen. I hung back from the door, absolutely shivering with apprehension, while John, still holding me in case I fled, boldly rang the bell.

While we waited, he said, 'If Toby got himself another girl——' But I never knew what he was going to say because just then Toby opened the door.

My relief that it was not Whistler was so great that for a moment I felt as if all doubt and uncertainty was at an end. But I watched his face with care and saw a strange, unreadable series of emotions play quickly over it, and when none of them could be interpreted as unalloyed joy every drop of the spurious relief vanished in a moment and I saw his face as if it were looking at me from an old photograph already fading. In those few seconds before anyone spoke I thought: it's over, I've lost him. And a desolation greater than any loneliness I've ever experienced swept into me like a heavy wind and made me shut my eyes and hold my breath.

But it was not to prove so simple and absolute. Toby grasped a grinning John by his free hand and exploded into a welcome which sounded to my frightened, over-sensitive ears a shade too hearty.

He passed John into the room and that left him facing me, and I summoned all my courage to look at him. His face was sober and there was no pretence in it. His eyes told me directly that something had happened, was happening, but now, looking at him, I felt a glimmer of hope. I don't know what it came from, but something in his expression must have shown that he retained some strong feeling for me which could be worked on.

It was so like him not to dissemble, like an ordinary man caught between two women. He said quietly, 'Did Dottie tell you?' I nodded. Here my eyes must have flickered uncontrollably over his shoulder because he said, 'She's not here now. She's never here in the mornings.' Which told me only the crudest part of what I had come to learn, and I found no relief in it, only a deepening fear because he spoke of it so openly. I knew it must be important and that her living with him or not hardly mattered.

150

We went in. It was a high room with sloping ceiling—walls cut into by a floor-length studio-window facing the street—a vast window, uncurtained and cold grey on this winter morning. It lit the room, every corner of it, with a lucid, bleak light. The furnishing was sparse and simple, a big bed in an alcove, a lot of bookshelves on either side of a blocked-in fireplace, some chairs and a sofa, a huge scrubbed kitchen table in the middle of the room, littered with papers and with Minnie, Toby's beloved typewriter, reposing in their midst with a white tongue of foolscap sticking out of her roller. The floor was boards.

The whole effect would have been very stark had it not been for a number of unmistakably feminine touches which I observed with a—well, you couldn't properly call it a *pang* of jealousy since that suggests a pain which comes and goes quickly, whereas this started like a stab when I saw the Come-to-Greece posters and just went on and on. The posters themselves couldn't have been more juvenile, I mean stuck to the wall like that with Sellotape—nobody does that any more except abroad-struck students. I tried to despise it, but it had been done out of love by a seventeen-year-old girl, who probably *had* been to Greece, for a thirty-year-old man who certainly hadn't ever been able to afford it. It seemed as if she were not merely trying to brighten the barren walls of his room but giving him a glimpse of the world, a goal as it were, or perhaps simply trying, in a touching, childish way, to share something with him.

Confused by the inability I felt to hate her, I forced myself to take in the other items in the room which were obviously her doing—nearly all had that glowing out-of-placeness which things bought abroad bring to English surroundings: the only rug in the room, a sort of long-haired tapestry ablaze in hot reds and pinks and tangerines which looked Spanish; a Delft coffee percolator, still on the table full of cold morning coffee; a row of unmatched mugs of varying shapes and colours which had the appearance of a collection fed by many trips; a cylindrical lamp-shade of glass beads strung between brass rims which had a look of the Middle-East. The sway-backed sofa was draped in a large bedspread-length of African batik in very masculine colours, and there was a pair of carved wooden tribal masks on the wall and a leather pouffe in blood-and-earth tones, evidently from the same part of the world.

She's been around, this girl, I thought grimly, and remembered she was the only daughter of one of the most successful literary agents in London. Young; rich; travelled; full of generosity and love. . . . And her need not hidden, not even disguised, for who gives such gifts except as frank tokens of a desire to be loved in return? I knew she had beaten me and that I deserved to be beaten, for she was a wise woman no matter what her age, and I was a blind and bloody fool.

I sat down on the batik and from somewhere came the strength—just enough—to appear composed while Toby chatted to John and John chatted back. Toby didn't look at me and I felt it as a deliberate kindness on his part, which hurt me worse than anything. He's expecting me to be feeling just exactly how I am feeling. I thought, he knows me so well, and he isn't looking at me because he doesn't want me to see that he knows, or perhaps he is too embarrassed . . . but the idea of me *embarrassing* Toby with my emotions was too unbearable and I stared at the jungle masks and fought to be still and controlled and above all not to cry.

This whole situation was somehow, still, despite all the evidence, all the mental preparation, unthinkable—Toby and somebody else. But he's mine! He's mine! I kept thinking despairingly. I don't believe any more passionate feelings had ever passed through me than I experienced as I sat on that sofa and stared blindly at those masks, hearing Toby's voice talking cheerfully and normally and knowing he loved somebody else.

This went on for a long time during which I don't think I spoke a word, and at last when it seemed I couldn't bear the ordinariness of the men's conversation another moment, John stood up and said, 'It's nearly lunch-time. You got what to cook, Toby?'

'A few tins——'

'Not for us! This is a big day, us three together again. I go out and buy something and cook.'

At this I jerked myself to life and said, 'John, Toby may not want——' thinking Whistler might be coming, but Toby quickly interrupted and said, 'Oh, but I do. I can't think of anything nicer. Here, we'll all contribute. Got any money,

Jane?' I said no, and John said that was good, women shouldn't pay when there were men around, and he gave me such an ambivalent wink that I nearly smiled. He accepted a pound note from Toby and found a shopping-basket in the kitchen, which was down three steps. (The basket was also from Whistler.) 'But it's Sunday,' I protested weakly, frightened now the moment was nearly on me, wanting John and me to just quietly leave together and not see Toby again ever.

'There's a Jewish delicatessen on the main road,' said Toby. 'You can pick up anything you want there, and get a bottle of wine at the off-licence on the corner.'

'Yes!' crowed John. 'That cheap red stuff we used to drink at Doris's!'

Too quickly, Toby said, 'No, not that.' He laughed awkwardly. 'We can do better than that now. Get a bottle of something reasonable.'

'I like the cheap stuff best,' said John regretfully.

Then he was gone, and Toby and I were alone.

He came at once and sat beside me on the sofa and we looked at each other. 'We've got about half-an-hour before he comes back,' he said. 'Do you want to talk now, or shall we put it off?'

'Better get it over,' I said, frightened and hopeless but absolutely determined not to do or say anything that would embarrass him. If it *was* as bad as I feared, at least I could behave well over it—it was the last thing I could give him.

'What—what did you come here to ask me?'

One cannot be anything but direct with this sort of a beginning. Anyway, there was no room for prevaricating or pretending.

'Do you love her? Is it serious? Have you stopped loving me?'

He stared at me for a moment and said curiously: 'Then you recognize the possibility that I might be able to answer, quite truthfully, yes, yes, and no?'

'*Is* that your answer?'

'Yes.'

'That you love us both?'

'Can you accept that as a premise?'

I looked away from his steady eyes and stared at the ceiling. The accursed tears were coming and I couldn't stop them.

But I tried. I did try. I said, 'If you tell me it's true, of course I believe it. But I don't know—how to behave about it.' When I moved my head the damn things at once spilled down my face and I stood up though it was too late because of course he'd seen. I stood at the window with my back to him and the dreary winter roofs blurred and fused and I hung onto the strings of my anorak like a drowner and there was a long—an interminable silence.

Then Toby came up behind me and touched me very gently on the elbows and said, 'We're wasting our talking-time. Come on back. It doesn't matter if you cry.' He brought me back to the sofa. I held myself as stiff as a rock so as not to throw myself into his arms; my throat ached so much I could hardly talk and I had to blow my nose which I felt to be an indignity. That in itself was something new and terrible. Once Toby and I could have done anything before each other; there was no need to think in terms of the impression we were making. Now all that was gone, and I literally didn't know how to behave. How could a man love two women at once? I believed it without in the least understanding it. Sleep with, yes; but love?

'Ask me; I'll tell you anything you want to know.'

'But wouldn't that be like—betraying her?'

'I don't really expect that kind of question,' he said gently.

'Does she know about me?'

'Of course.'

'What does she know?'

'That you exist, and that you were—and in a way still are —the most important person in my life. She's very much aware of you as a rival, although she doesn't understand quite what she's fighting since she never sees you and she knows I don't either, lately. All these things that of course you've noticed'— he indicated the décor with his eyes—'are her weapons against you, as well as her bids for me.'

'Do you give her presents?'

'Yes, sometimes. She's so generous she's made me generous too.'

'Why did you and I never give each other presents?'

'You gave me that typing-paper for Christmas. It was me that didn't give you anything.'

'But you never got that! You went away before I could give it to you!'

'John told me, ages afterwards.'

'But in general—we never gave each other——'

'Jane, don't talk such nonsense. You know exactly what we gave each other.' There was a long silence and then he said, 'You and I were always too poor for things like that. Whistler's rich, she's not happy unless she's spending money. Anyway, it doesn't matter, presents or no presents. It only matters if it shows that you're mean if you don't give, or conniving if you do. Neither applies here. Whistler can't help giving; very often I wish she wouldn't, but it would be cruel to try to stop her.'

'Does she want to marry you?'

'Yes.'

'She's *told* you that?'

'Yes. She's even proposed to me. She says she'll come and live here with me if I don't want to get married.' He said it without a trace of conceit.

'And—don't you?'

He hesitated and then said, 'It's difficult. You see, for so long I didn't think about it much because I just took it for granted that if and when I married, it would be to you.'

'But you never asked me!' I blurted out, despite my resolves trying to make it his fault that everything was lost and spoilt and wasted, because I couldn't possibly bear it if it were really all mine.

'Asked you?' he said blankly. 'I must have done! You knew I was willing any time you were. Yes, come to think of it, I asked you very recently. In the pub.'

I remember it only too clearly, my last chance. I had already known about the threat of Whistler; instinct had warned me it was a dangerous one. Why had I ignored it? Utterly impossible now to know—unless of course John was right, and I was afraid to marry Toby.

No more questions came into my head for a while; I just sat silently trying to come to grips with it, but I seemed to be quite empty of thoughts. It was like that electric-shock therapy which, they say, seems at first to have knocked a hole in your brain that has to fill up again slowly. At last another question did seep into the raw empty space.

'All this—did it start after—because of—the way I behaved the day David was ill?'

Toby stood up and went to the table for a cigarette. 'Jane,' he said at last, 'if you're trying to find out what went wrong, or whose fault it was, I think you're wasting time. Things like this—love-relationships—need a certain minimum of proximity to keep them going. We've seen each other exactly three times, very briefly, in the past eight months. I'm not prepared to say whose fault that is—I'm obviously more mobile than you at the moment, and I should have come to visit you much oftener, but I've been trying so hard to work concentratedly . . . at first because I wanted to prove something to you, then because I had to prove it to myself . . . then because I found it was the only way I could be happy. But I thought of you all the time, not so much consciously although I mentally "talked" to you a lot, but subconsciously you were always somewhere close by, the way you really used to be when you lived over my head in Fulham and I knew I only had to climb a few stairs to reach you.' I was crying openly now, and he was holding my hand, but he was holding it the way you hold an ill person's hand, to comfort them. 'But then I suppose little by little it began to—get weaker, somehow, because it wasn't fed by anything solid. And Whistler appeared. I met her at a party of Billie's. She was only a child, I thought at first; I remember wondering why Billie let her come to one of her swish parties in dirty jeans and with her hair looking as if she'd hacked it off with a razor. She was only sixteen then. But she just latched onto me somehow. Kids that age nowadays are either terribly sophisticated and devious, little trained coquettes, or they're like Whistler—utterly open, straightforward, honest—none of those words really describes her. She told me she loved me three days after we met. Of course I didn't take her seriously . . . But Billie soon realized . . . Billie's terribly worried. . . . Do you know something? I think if I had to weigh it up, it's much more because of Billie than for any other reason that I've so far kept Whistler out of my bed.'

John came back then, and I went into the bathroom to wash my face while Toby took him through into the kitchen and showed him where things were. John was absolutely lit up with happiness, and had obviously forgotten what I'd said to him as we arrived. I glanced at him as he was passing through the main room, clutching two huge paper sacks under his arms, and he gave me a great uncomplicated grin which somehow plunged me into even deeper loneliness.

The conversation had been broken off at such a vital point that it was not hard to resume it. While I was in the bathroom I had thought of the only other thing I really wanted to know, but before I could formulate a question Toby began again:

'You mentioned the day David was ill. I won't deny that did something to me. The helplessness I felt. . . . You needed something from me. I even knew roughly what it was, but I couldn't give it to you because. . . . Well, look—and I don't know if this'll make any sense. When David was born and I came to see you in hospital I had a look at him, but it didn't mean much. Even though he was yours. I was a bit shattered about that. I thought maybe seeing him, knowing he'd come out of you, knowing what you went through to get him and all that—it might make a difference; but there it was, he was just a rather ugly little scrap of human being and I couldn't feel anything special for him. The feeling of failing you somehow started then, because I knew that if we did marry, I would have to feel like a father to David. And I didn't. . . . Later I felt better about it, because I found out that real fathers often don't feel anything much for their children at first; it's something that grows as you share in bringing them up. And that's what I haven't had. Do you see? David's not mine. Not in any way. I've missed nearly a year of his life, a very important year when we should have been getting to know him together. So when he was so ill that day I couldn't feel what you wanted me to feel. I could only have felt it if we'd been together, the three of us, ever since he was born.'

'And if we had been—oh, but Toby, it's not fair! You mean we should have got married right after the baby was born. But you weren't anything near ready to marry me then.'

'Nonsense, I'd have married you like a shot if you'd just insisted a little.'

'Insisted a little! In other words, bullied you into it!'

'Yes, if you like.'

'But who wants to have to push a man into marrying her?'

'I don't know about that. But from what I can see, hardly

any man gets married without a bit of pushing. Especially in those circumstances.'

I stared at him. 'You mean, when the woman has an illegitimate baby?'

He flushed. 'Not that exactly. But when the man isn't very sure of himself.'

'I wanted you to be very sure of yourself and—everything else, before you married me.'

'Well . . . one way to increase my self-confidence might have been to show me you needed me then.' I sat in stunned silence. 'Did you?' he asked at last.

'Christ almighty!' I said under my breath. 'I've needed you every hour of every day for the past year. Did you really have to be told that?'

'Yes,' he said quietly.

'And your writing,' I said, beginning now to feel something else, strangely like anger. 'It never crossed your mind I was refraining from—pushing—in order that you should be free of domestic concerns and able to find your feet as a writer?'

'Of course I realized that, and I was very grateful.'

'Grateful? Were you really? But that didn't interfere with your beginning to love me less?'

'On the contrary, it made me love you more—to begin with. But damn it all, I'm only——'

'Human——'

'Yes. I was grateful, I appreciated you for not making demands, but as the months went by, I wanted—well, gratitude and even the realization that you'd been right in a way, I mean that I couldn't have worked as well as I did on the novel if I'd been distracted by a family, it didn't stop me from getting very lonely.'

'You were lonely,' I said. '*You* were lonely. Well I'm sorry. What I should have done of course was to dump David onto a neighbour every three days and drive up here to sleep with you. That would have met the situation I should think—no ties, no restrictions, just frequent bouts of loving, undemanding sex.'

Now it was he who stared. 'You're talking rubbish. You must know me well enough to know that wasn't even remotely what I wanted.'

'I'm just beginning to wonder if you know what the hell it is you do want!'

'Men do manage to combine a domestic life with writing. . . .'

'Yes,' I said from the depths of utter fury and despair. 'Men do.'

As soon as the words were out I knew I'd finished everything. But, oddly, I no longer cared. At least, not for that moment. I'd worked so hard on myself, trying to grow, trying to be independent, trying to be strong and unselfish. It had been so damned difficult, so against my grain; but I'd done it all for him. And my reward now was to be told I should have been weak and clinging and dependent. The very qualities I'd been trying to develop had lost me the thing I was working for. All desire to cry had gone. I sat there shaking with rage, watching with actual satisfaction as his face turned white, then scarlet.

'So you don't think I'm much of a *mensch*,' he said quietly.

'I'd never doubted it till this moment. But of all the feeble, pusillanimous——'

'Yes,' he interrupted. 'Quite. Well, who knows? You may be right.'

We sat in silence, and the rage withdrew slowly, like a wave, leaving desolation. The pain of losing him began again and I bit on it hard, like a bad tooth.

'So what are your plans now? I suppose you'll marry Whistler.'

'Yes, I suppose so, when she's a little older. If she still wants to.' There was another long pause in which we could hear John—the sole reason why I couldn't leave the flat and run and run as fast and as far away as I could—singing and banging about in the kitchen, making us a celebration lunch.

'There's one thing,' said Toby abruptly. 'She's Jewish.'

I snapped my head round to look at him in amazement. 'So what?'

He didn't look at me but at the point of his cigarette as he said, 'I've had the strangest feeling recently that I'd like to marry a Jewish woman. To be—more Jewish than I've been. Don't ask me to explain. It's just a feeling.' He added after a moment, defensively, 'After all, I *am* a Jew.'

He met my eyes. His were defiant, sheepish somehow, as

if he realized the underlying weakness of what he was saying. I thought, John's wrong. I'm no spiritual Hercules, but at least I know who I am. And on that belief, plus three glasses of wine, I coasted smoothly through the celebration lunch as if on the crest of an artificial wave, and it was Toby who lay below in the trough and didn't say a word.

Chapter 16

WHEN YOU'VE LOVED SOMEBODY for a long time, and then it stops, it's akin to an amputation in that you go on feeling the cut-off part long after it's been taken away. All sorts of nervous and emotional impulses set out to travel to their accustomed stations, and when they come up against the new, raw barrier, they're carried through it by their own impetus, and only then, finding themselves shooting through empty space, do they dwindle and die away. In the same way, when somebody dies—I noticed this a lot with Addy—you keep projecting your thoughts towards them as if they were still alive.

And so it was with Toby.

My love-impulses kept going out towards where he had been; I kept leaning against the relationship which for so long had supported me like a plaster-cast, and falling flat on my face because it wasn't there any longer to hold me up. As a result, after a few days I already felt bewildered and exhausted; by the end of a fortnight I was as emotionally battered as I would have been physically if I had fallen over and over again down a flight of stone steps which it was somehow beyond my power to avoid.

Because the pain of this was so awful, I began to hate him, and there's nothing, of course, more damaging and hurtful to the psyche than that—searching grimly for things to despise and revile in a person you once loved. You may destroy the beloved image but at the same time you destroy part of the basis of your self-respect, plus a whole vital chunk out of your past. Because, if he is hateful now, what aberration once caused you to waste so much love on him?

While I was actively at work on this project of demolition, I kept remembering something he had once said to me in bed:

'We have to do this well, this, and everything that goes with it; and we have to go on doing it well. And if by any unforeseeable chance we ever want to stop, we must do that well, too. Because if a love-affair doesn't stay sweet in your mind forever, it just wasn't worth it.' And, perhaps on another occasion, but linked to the same philosophical idea: 'If the ending is messy, one doesn't remember anything good about any of it.'

Perhaps it was the intrinsic rightness of this that angered me now; but out of my developing sophistry came the pretence that it angered me because it was false and worse than false. Because (I reasoned) there is no such thing as a 'good' ending. There is only one way to make it 'stay sweet' and that is to continue it until one of you dies, and even *that* inevitable conclusion will probably spoil the mental picture through its shocking finality and sorrow.

I felt this new cynicism seeping through me like sewage: nothing lasts, nothing is worthwhile, the cost of every emotional indulgence is too outrageously high; but in any case nobody deserves anything better or more permanent. Certainly not Toby, and certainly not me with my egocentricity and destructive outbursts of anger. (It would take me a long time to forgive myself for the contemptuous 'So what?' when Toby told me Whistler was Jewish. But it was many, many months before I was prepared to acknowledge that.)

Toby became anathema, my whipping-boy. When I felt angry with anything or anybody—when the baby cried too long or the vacuum cleaner backfired or I dropped a hot casserole full of stew; when Dottie went off 'talent-hunting' for three days, leaving me in the shop on my own, with only the sketchiest idea of how to cope with any but the most straightforward sales and Mrs G. at home breathing 'flu germs all over David and actually letting him fall off the sofa and bang his head; when the local women came sniffing round the shop with no commercial intentions other than the satisfaction of their curiosity, and made their telling exits with remarks like 'All a bit grand for me, dear; but then I suppose you've been used to *very* different ways all round in London, haven't you?' When any of these things happened, I gathered my rage into a little hard ball and hurled it at an Aunt Sally figure in my mind which had Toby's head on it. He ceased, in one sense, to be a living person, even in memory, and became a receiver, a receptacle, for all my aggressions, all my misery, all my loneliness. He got the blame for absolutely everything.

I'm quite certain, looking back, that I have never seemed so utterly detestable to myself as I was at that time. The more I made myself hate Toby, the more it rebounded, though I tried my utmost to make myself feel like a poor victim. And as I whittled away at the foundations of my life, feeble and shored-up as they were already, of course, I became less and less able to cope with even the simplest daily disciplines. Everything, but everything, became too much trouble—getting up in the morning, getting myself to bed at night, and everything in between. I just seemed to shuffle through the days, begrudging every effort, seizing on every chance to fly off the handle, to sulk, to cry in secret, to take it out on people.

Only with David was I able to maintain some kind of balance, but even he got shouted at and untenderly picked up or dumped down, quite often. And of course, poor Dottie got the worst of it, because she was handiest. And she was definitely not in the mood for it just then, which, looking back on it with what I know now, is what makes me most ashamed of it.

Approximately five minutes after I had arrived back from London that Sunday afternoon, having borrowed money from John for petrol, and driven all the way in a state of blind, stiff-jawed, unreasoning rage and despair—Dottie realized that something awful, and terminal, had happened.

I remember that when I stamped and slammed into the cottage, she and Henry were sitting on the floor drinking tea from mugs and rejoicing, in their nice way, over the fact that David had just arrived at a sitting position by himself. 'Amanda couldn't do that till she was ten months,' Henry commented, presumably solely to gratify me. I hardly heard him; I sat on the sofa staring at David, sitting there crowing, without seeing him properly, just hearing Toby's words about marrying Whistler going on and on in my brain like one of those sleep-teaching machines.

Dottie offered me tea and added, 'You're not going to credit this, but I've actually baked a cake. You have to eat it with a teaspoon but it tastes rather marvellous.'

'No thanks,' I said shortly, and got up, took David in my arms and went out of the room. It must have looked ridiculously like a melodramatic exit, but was in fact uncalculated. I had suddenly realized that even David being able to sit up alone at under eight months didn't give me the smallest kick; I had just had the shattering experience of sitting there looking at him after a whole day's absence and not feeling anything, no lifting of the heart, nothing, and the veil of protective rage lifted for a few seconds to show the great yawning fearful black emptiness that lay on the other side.

No Toby. No more Toby. . . . I went upstairs with David and sat on my bed with him in my arms and just rocked to and fro gripping him tightly and keeping the veil drawn. Just that, no tears, no feelings; rock, rock, rock, and stare at the corn-flower pattern on the wall. . . . I was trying to hypnotize myself, I think, and then Dottie walked in and the spell of relative painlessness was broken.

'What's the matter, love, what's happened?'

'Nothing. Go away. Leave me alone.'

It had happened before, only with the positions reversed. In a few minutes I, like Dottie on Christmas night, would be sobbing myself empty; I longed for the release of it, but David was lying there on my knee gazing up at me unwinkingly and I looked at him and *for the very first time* I thought, 'He's got no father. I've got an illegitimate baby.'

Before I could check myself I said wonderingly, 'He's a bastard.'

'Who is?' asked Dottie, and I answered, still in a sort of daze of suddenly awakened shame, 'He is—David.'

The really remarkable thing was that Dottie understood—just from that. It amazed me more later than at the time. She sat down on the bed beside me and said, after a long silence, 'You'll find another father for him—better and stronger.'

I turned on her, not appreciating her perspicacity and kindness and wisdom, 'I don't want anyone else! I only want Toby!' That was about the last honest, unperverted word or thought I produced about him for months. It sprang straight out of naked pain, which is one of the main sources of un-tampered-with truth; when you begin stifling the pain, you twist and muffle the truth at the same time.

I don't know how to describe the weeks that followed. I would undoubtedly be even more ashamed of my behaviour, if it were not for the odd conviction that I was, as they say, 'not myself'. It is like remembering another person's experience, or something one once read about and felt, deeply perhaps but vicariously. In other words, I think I was a little mad.

One lesson I learnt stands out clearly, however. Work, that supposed panacea, the great Taker-of-Your-Mind-Off, proved just about as totally useless and in fact irrelevant as those 'Easy Childbirth' theories are in the face of the real thing. The work was there, and I had to do it—housework, baby-work, and the new and—one might have expected—energy- and mind-absorbing work in the shop. In fact I seldom stopped working; but the queer thing is that the only times I was at all at peace were when I did stop.

The shop did a lot of business during those first weeks after the opening; customers actually did come all the way from London as well as from surrounding districts, and when it was my turn to be on duty I was kept on my feet a large percentage of the time. But while my body was active, so was my brain, seething in its poison; and the times I look back on now with some recognition of myself are those when there was a break and I was able to go into the back of the shop, where the storeroom was, and a tiny kitchenette arrangement, and sit there motionless among the packing-cases staring out of the glass panel in the back door at the minute yard, where a tree grew out of crumbling paving-stones beside a blackened incinerator surrounded by an old board fence.

That view, uninspiring as it was during the bleak winds of March and April, has imprinted itself on my memory so that at any time I can cast myself back there and feel the wooden rungs of the chair pressing into my back and see the leafless branches of that struggling tree tossing to and fro against the sky. It was as if the violence of the tree's agitation took over the frenzy of my brain for a little while; contemplating it, yet hardly aware of it, I would feel myself growing calmer, the bitterness simmering down like boiling milk lifted for a moment off the heat. I remember I used to sigh, deeply and repeatedly, as if the madness had been using up too much oxygen, and feel gradually much better. Then I would be startled by the ping of the door in the front being opened; automatically I would jump up and hurry through, and at the same time my brain would jump to attention too and go back to its beastly work.

Dottie didn't ever ask me again what exactly had transpired in London—I suppose she guessed. But Henry, of course, had no way of doing that, and he was fond of me, so that seeing me getting thinner very rapidly (something I only manage to do when I'm desperately unhappy) and more and more silent, he naturally became concerned, and one day when we were alone in the shop together, he suddenly said, 'Suppose you tell me what's happened to you.'

I said, 'Why should I?' which was in keeping with my general rudeness at the time, but Henry was hard to offend, and replied, 'First, because I'm very curious to know what can possibly have changed you so radically. Second, because you never know, I might be able to help.'

Two months had already gone by since that fatal Sunday, and perhaps I was ready to talk, because I said, after only a short hesitation, 'Do you remember Toby?'

Henry said he did, with some pleasure.

I began to prevaricate to the effect that it was all very hard to explain, but then his honesty temporarily revived mine and I realized it was not hard at all, merely wretchedly painful, so I said, 'For a year I thought he was going to marry me, and now I've found out he's going to marry somebody else.' Put baldly like that it seemed extremely simple; I marvelled at the twisted complexity of my reactions to it.

Henry now asked the obvious question. 'Is he David's father?'

'Didn't Dottie tell you?—No.'

'Dorothy and I don't discuss your business. Then where is he?'

'David's father? I have no idea. Possibly in Paris.'

'What sort of chap is he?—I hope you don't mind all these questions.'

'Not specially.' Actually since the subject of this unexpected enquiry had shifted away from Toby, I didn't mind at all. I really don't think I would have minded any questions from Henry; it pleased me obscurely to find him showing such a sensible, human interest in somebody else's concerns. I would have expected him to have found such manifestations of curiosity rather beneath him. (It was not for ages afterwards that I found out from Dottie that of course she'd told him the whole story long ago, and that he was presumably only asking me about Terry to change the obsessive focus of my thoughts for a little while.)

I told him briefly about my affair with Terry, and our mutual antipathy after it. Henry listened with his usual patience and then said, 'And out of that, all that stupidity and futility, you got that nice child that you love so much. Zero plus zero equals any amount you like to name. It's all very strange.'

'So you think Terry and I are zeroes?'

'No, no, that's not what I meant.' He looked up at me and smiled through his pipe-smoke. 'You're a fair bit of a chump at times, like now for instance, but you're not a zero. Oh dear no.' And he picked up my hand and held it for a moment so hard that it hurt, then put it down unselfconsciously as someone came into the shop.

A little oasis in the wilderness. After it, the dark mood of misery and brooding and tumult closed in round me again; but I remembered that warm squeeze and his funny, old-fashioned way of saying 'You're not a zero, oh dear no!' Even while I was helplessly behaving like one, I remembered sometimes that Henry didn't think I was; and it helped. A little.

But it was Dottie who dragged me out of it in the end. I hadn't been noticing Dottie very much recently, or asking myself how things were with her; it was all part of my current malaise of introversion, because in fact had anyone asked me I would have said that Dottie mattered to me more than anybody still remaining in my life, except David of course. But one couldn't have guessed it from my behaviour towards her.

For weeks we hardly exchanged a friendly inessential word; she tried—God knows she tried—to bring me out of it with her usual flow of entertaining anecdotes, but that was just at first; no one can go on telling stories to someone who patently is not listening, let alone reacting. So then she withdrew into a sort of brisk, waiting silence, at first patient, later impatient, gradually becoming irritated and at last furious. She had good reason for this; my help and support in the shop were so essential to her that my virtual disappearance into my own private purgatory struck at the roots of all her plans, not only the business ones but also, as I was to discover, her plans for her survival through the crisis in her own life, which depended entirely on the shop and its success.

The crunch came when I had been in charge at the shop all one day while Dottie went to Birmingham. The reason for this trip was both unexpected and highly exciting to her; she had had a letter from Ron, the glass-worker with whom she had left her address all those months ago. It was neatly written on a small sheet of lined paper, and said in a very businesslike way that if she cared to come along, he might be able to show her something to her advantage.

It was actually her turn for shop-duty the following day, and I had been looking forward to the sort of quiet day at home with David which was the only kind I found tolerable any more—a morning getting the housework out of the way, and an afternoon spent sitting in front of the fire watching the flames, just as I watched the tree behind the shop, letting all the vicious inner knots untie themselves.

So when Dottie, showing an unusual degree of animation, announced her imminent departure and begged me to take over for the day, I sank into a deep slough of gloom and grudge and scarcely brought a civil word out of my mouth all evening. Whereas I felt she could just as easily have waited till the following day, when I was due to be at the shop anyway, she clearly felt it impossible to wait even twenty-four hours longer to find out what Ron had to tell her, and expected me to understand this.

We both indicated our points of view in a terse conversation which ended with Dottie saying, with unaccustomed edge: 'Look, like it or lump it this shop is our livelihood. You think it's enough just to put in a few hours selling every second day. Well, that's okay for shop assistants; it's not enough for the management.'

'Fine. Well, you be the management and give your whole life to it. I'm prepared just to be the shop-girl. After all, you haven't got a baby to look after.'

'No, that's right, I haven't,' Dottie retorted. 'I haven't got one to raise, either, or I might have the grace to be damned grateful for someone who'd do all the work of setting up a business of which I was getting equal shares while doing about a fifth of the labour.'

There was no possible reply to this, so I merely shrugged coldly and went on washing the dishes. How I hate remembering it now!—although she wasn't being entirely fair either; true, she did far more than half the work to do with the shop, but the house was my job and here she scarcely contributed anything except very occasionally a meal or a bit of washing up.

Mrs Griffiths was nearly always called in on the days when Dottie was supposed to be at home, and when Dottie had nowhere to travel to and actually did stay in the cottage with David, she did the bare minimum necessary to keep him clean and fed, and then let the housework go to hell while she did her accounts, wrote letters, drafted advertisements, or had Henry over for a conference. Often I'd get home tired at six in the evening to find the fire out and supper not even begun. I'd learnt to pick up a large packet of fish-and-chips or a frozen pork-pie on these occasions so I wouldn't have to set to from scratch.

Anyway, this pointed exchange led to a chill evening, during which we sat locked in our private silences and I, at least, spared a thought for the past and asked myself (but desultorily) whether there was any hope of ever reverting to the *status quo ante*. But at the time this seemed as hopeless as trying to rebuild a house from which the foundations have been blasted away.

So the next day Dottie set off early by road for Birmingham and Ron, while I left David (as usual in shrieks of outrage at my departure, which always started the days at the shop off on the wrong foot) and drove into the village. It was the beginning of May, but there were few signs of spring, apart from new leaves and some flowers in the garden which persist in coming to birth no matter how inclement the weather.

Just before climbing into the car I obeyed an impulse to throw a gardening fork into the back. I thought if the day were not too hectic I might find the energy to fulfil a promise made long ago to Mrs Stephens, to dig the little plot behind their shop, which was next door to ours. Since the day was spoilt anyway, and since I had a slightly guilty conscience about Dottie which I wanted to expiate with sweat, I thought I might get around to it, though it seemed doubtful considering my present aversion to hard work.

The day was so gloomy and blustery, with gusts of periodic rain, that the shop was very quiet. It was also ominously cold; something had gone wrong with the central heating. I phoned Henry to tell him and he said apologetically that he was awfully sorry, he had a stinking cold that day and was cosseting himself indoors, but that I was not to call in a professional to look at it—'No point in shelling out, it's probably something I can deal with easily.' He advised me to light an oil-stove for myself and stick it out for the day. This hardly commended itself to me; to begin with the oil-stove stank abominably and to go on with, it heated an area approximately one-fifth of what was needed. Everything outside that area, which included my little corner of the store-room, was left to freeze, and me in it.

At about 3 p.m., when there still hadn't been a single customer, I got so fed up and miserable that I pulled on my coat and went out through the back door, leaving it open so that I could hear the bell. I climbed easily over the dividing fence with my fork and at once began thrusting it brutally into the clotted earth of the tiny flower-beds surrounding a patch of grass the size of a night-club dance-floor. After a short time, Mrs Stephens's permanently-startled face appeared at a back window between the dingy crocheted curtains, and then she came running out, tutting and jumping flat-footed in her carpet-slippers through the puddles, to exclaim over my hardiness, offer thanks for my help and cups of nice hot tea. I refused without stopping work, and remembered, only as she was withdrawing backwards due to admiration entirely misplaced, to make a perfunctory inquiry after Mr Stephens's health.

'Oh . . .' said Mrs Stephens vaguely. 'Not what it might be, dear. The poor lamb is not what he was, I'm afraid.' She had spoken very softly, her voice barely carrying to me on a gust of wind, but even so she glanced nervously over her shoulder as if expecting to see his old ear glued to the window to hear whatever disloyalty might be spoken of him.

As I worked under the dark grey, sullen skies, shoved about and rumpled by the wind and slapped across the face by occasional spots of rain, I fell into a dismal pattern—digging fast and feverishly in an effort to escape my mood and my thoughts, while the thoughts raced faster and more vividly in an effort to keep up. Thoughts about Toby. . . . I still have them. But they're infinitely different now, thank God. Then, my mind seemed like a festering sore, an all-absorbing pain, drawing all my attention in towards itself, like the skin round a wound. I seemed to see nothing, even the good clean earth I was digging, and I certainly heard nothing other than the endless, exhausting conversations going on in my imagination.

Suddenly Henry was looking at me over the fence.

'What are you doing?' he asked, with nothing in his voice but incredulous curiosity.

I dropped the fork and stood still, panting and worn out as if I'd been running.

'Are you all right? You look strange.'

'I'm all right. . . . What time is it?'

'It's five o'clock. I've been phoning and phoning. . . . Didn't you hear the bell?'

'No.'

'How long have you been out here?'

'I don't know . . . since about three, I think.'

'Since three!' He didn't look angry, just amazed. 'But what about Billings?'

'Who?'

'Billings. The health-restaurant man. Didn't Dorothy tell you?'

It came back to me with a tingling sense of shock. Of course she'd told me. She'd particularly told me about Billings. He was a man after her own heart, though his field was quite different; he was what Henry called a muck-and-mystery man, a farmer with an obsession with natural methods of crop- and stock-raising who had now decided to go into—or rather, put his son into—the restaurant business, as a subsidiary enterprise to his own farm. The farm would supply the restaurant with free-range chickens and eggs, unsprayed fruit, vegetables

171

grown in farmyard manure, and wholewheat bread, among many other things such as honey made by bees who had never soiled their feet by settling on a chemically-treated flower. Dottie had been full of Billings for the past week, the more so since he was the biggest potential customer we had yet had.

He had visited the shop, listened to Dottie expound her principles, and liked them, finding them very akin to his own, as indeed she found his; and he had virtually promised to return and order all the furniture needed by the restaurant from us—small pine refectory tables, heart-backed chairs, darkly glazed ceramic bowls for barley soup, wooden plates for meadow-raised beef steaks, baskets for the chickens, rush mats for the floors, and possibly a great many secondary items such as cruets, table-napkins, and purely decorative times.

I remembered now, with a flush of guilt, that a lesser reason why Dottie had hurried off to Birmingham was because she needed to find a source of ordinary glassware—jugs and glasses for the fresh vegetable juices. And I remembered too that there had been a strong possibility that Billings would call by between three and four this afternoon, and that I had been specially told to be ready for him and to welcome him with every encouraging courtesy.

Henry was gazing at me with a sort of wonderment, his head cocked to one side, a slight frown between his eyes. He was waiting for me to speak, but what could I possibly say? I stammered something about having promised Mrs Stephens, no customers all day, forgot about Billings, was sure I could have heard the bell. . . . Henry's face didn't change.

'I'm only asking myself,' he said slowly, 'what Dorothy's going to say.'

My blood quite literally ran cold—I turned clammy all over. Was it conceivable that I was afraid—afraid of Dottie? Of course I was hopelessly disgracefully in the wrong, but still—that didn't explain goose-flesh.

'Maybe he didn't come,' I said with sudden hope.

'But he did.' He handed me a note. I took my gloves off—my hands were shaking. The note, written on a page torn from a pocket pad, simply said, 'Called at 3.30 as arranged. Could have walked off with all your stock. J. S. Billings.'

'Oh my God,' I said faintly.

For the first time in ten weeks, something other than Toby occupied my thoughts to the exclusion of all else. I was appalled by the prospect of Dottie's return, and of having to confess. A totally new kind of duologue now took up all my creative slack. My end of it sounded unimaginably thin. I must have been mad, I kept thinking to myself, wringing my hands. It didn't occur to me then that I had been more or less mad for ten weeks.

She arrived back sometime after eight, absolutely glowing with triumph as I hadn't seen her glow since the mysterious events of Christmas Eve. She flung her coat off and rushed into the kitchen, where in an agony of guilty anticipation I was trying to get some supper. She stood in the doorway and flung her arms wide. 'Ron!' she cried. 'Ah, Ron of the licentious ogle, of the sneering lip, of the cretinous demeanour! Ron of the once-sober-and-industrious and now degenerate Lower Orders! Ron, my creation, my angel, my *craftsman*! I love you!' She disappeared with a flourish, returning a few seconds later with a large box which she set down on the kitchen table. With a conjurer's gesture she removed the lid and reverently lifted to the light a little green glass horse. It was very roughly made, the sort of thing a child might form out of taffy, teasing limbs and ears, a ruffle of mane, a switch of tail, out of it before it grew cold and hard. But there was something very attractive about it.

'Infantile,' said Dottie, but lovingly. 'Too literary, too explicit. But a start. A start in the right, unblueprinted, original, creative direction.'

She produced several other little animals of the same sort. They didn't look professional enough to offer for sale, but they had something, and Dottie said Ron was so excited about them himself that it surely wouldn't be long before he 'developed' the technique to a point where they would be good enough.

'It started with lumps,' Dottie explained, pouring herself a huge beaker of cold milk, her eyes burning with an almost fanatical enthusiasm. 'I showed him something when I was there before—a picture in a crafts magazine—he said it was nothing but a lump. Only afterwards he started to think about it, and he said it haunted him. So he began to pick up lumps of glass, left-overs, throw-outs, around the factory, and kind of look at them. He kept one on his mantelpiece at home for weeks, he said, and he kept staring at it, and handling it, until his wife got furious and slung it out. He was so angry at losing it, he realized that you could get fond of a lump. "It gave me all kinds of funny ideas," he said. "And not *that* kind, either." Oh, he's marvellous, is Ron! I adore his awful smutty way of talking! So then he started making lumps in his spare time. Just letting blobs of hot glass fall as it would. Then he began blowing bubbles into it. Then shaping it. Of course he dared not let any of his mates know what he was doing—they'd have thought he'd gone bonkers. Then one day a lump turned into something like an animal, and that was how he got started on this line.' She made the horse gallop across the table-top. 'You know what I told him? I told him to go back to just plain lumps, and not try to make them look like any-thing except the kind of lump his wife threw away—the kind you can get fond of.'

She dipped into the box again and produced a lump, which she weighed in her hand. It really was rather a beautiful lump —like a piece of crystallized ocean. One immediately wanted to hold it. I reached for it instinctively and Dottie, grinning, held it away.

'Ah ha! I knew it! It draws the hand. It even draws the face.' She smoothed the cool thing with her cheek. 'He was so shy about showing me this. When I raved, he thought I was having him on. I love him. I mean it. I feel I've started some-thing up in him, like Pygmalion.'

'Is that whole great box full of Ron's lumps?' I asked.

'No, no. The bottom's packed with the samples of the nicest coarse-glass tumblers and jugs I could find for my dearly beloved Mr Billings.' My heart sank into the region of my knees. 'Did he call? Did he make a firm order?' I said nothing, and she asked again, 'Did he come?'

'Yes,' I said.

'Well? Tell!'

'I wasn't—there.'

'What? What do you mean? Where were you?'

'I was out at the back, digging the Stephens's garden.'

There was no question of *her* face not changing. It froze for a second and then went white. I knew I was for it and I shrank. I thought cravenly, I can't face a row with Dottie, not now! I began gibbering out excuses but she cut me short.

'Dear, kind, loving Jesus,' she said softly. 'You've bitched it. Trust you.' She had a glass in her hand, a nice square tumbler with a solid glass bottom with a bubble in it and very thick sides. For a moment I thought she was going to throw it straight at my head, and then I thought, No, she'll smash it on the floor. I could see the impulse tremble through her arm and be checked when it was almost overflowing into her fingers. But then she put the glass carefully back into the box and packed Ron's things on top among the wood-shavings and newspaper. She closed the box down, keeping her head bent. I stood still, waiting. But she merely picked the box up and carried it out of the kitchen. I heard her put it down on the hall table and go upstairs. I'd never seen her even half as angry; I felt physically sick from watching it and knowing that I'd caused it.

She stayed in her room all evening with the door shut, and I put David to bed in a wholly unaccustomed silence. He tried to induce me to play his usual games but I couldn't. He went to bed whimpering resentfully and I sat by him, still silent, until he fell asleep. Then I wept with shame.

When that was finished, I went to Dottie's door and knocked.

'What do you want?' she asked after a moment.

'To come in.'

'I wouldn't if I were you. Better wait till I've had a night's sleep.'

'It's tempting, but I'd rather get it over.'

There was no answer, so I turned the handle and went in. She was not undressed, but was sitting by the window. When she turned, I could see she'd been crying too. Her face was quite drawn.

I sat opposite her on the window seat. 'Say it,' I said. 'Please. We'll both feel better.'

She gazed at me for a long moment, and then sighed from her depths and turned back to the window, leaning her chin heavily on her hand. 'What's the use,' she said in a tired voice. 'I could give you hell, but it wouldn't change anything. Not a thing.'

'Dottie, nothing like it will ever happen again, I promise.'

'It's not only that. You don't know. You don't know.'

'What don't I know?'

She didn't answer for a moment, and then said wearily, 'Oh, it's—it's a whole lot of things. I mean, even if you turned overnight into a model partner, conscientious and single-minded, it wouldn't change the fact that you basically don't give a damn about the whole project, that you don't believe it stands a chance. You never have, really. At first I thought I had enough enthusiasm for us both, or at least that self-interest would drive you into some semblance of caring, but I see now things don't work out like that. You're not—with me at all. I sometimes wonder if even Henry really is, or if in his heart of hearts he isn't smiling pityingly at my cavortings and waiting around to pick up the pieces. . . .' She dropped her face into her hand for a second, then straightened it quickly, throwing a bit of hair out of her eyes and keeping her fingers over her mouth so that her voice was muffled. 'I didn't realize,' she went on, 'what a damned lonely business a business could be.'

It's terribly easy to fall prey to the conviction that your own loneliness is the worst in the world. Except occasionally, Dottie always seemed so strong and resilient, so self-sufficient, it was hard to believe that her loneliness went as deep and hurt just as much as mine or anybody's. Feeling sorry for Dottie always seemed like an affront; that saved one the trouble; one could always tell oneself she didn't need sympathy, and go straight back to pitying oneself. But now I looked at her averted face and realized some part of her misery, and how akin it was to mine, and felt a shame much more poignant than the one I had felt about my default over Billings.

'Listen,' I said at last. 'First, let's get Billings out of the way. All's not lost. I'll go myself and see him and explain—crawl if necessary. So long as he knows it wasn't your fault, I'm sure he'll come round.'

She didn't move a muscle and I knew for sure then that she'd left Billings a long way behind in her thoughts, that she was now struggling away alone in some dark secret place, far from the shop and from me. She seemed to have curled into herself and the knuckles over her mouth were white as if her hand were holding back some pressure that was trying to burst out of her. 'Dottie,' I said, actually managing to forget myself completely for a moment and beginning to shake a little from the tension of pity and anxiety.

She looked slowly up at me over her hand. Her eyes were desolate, and glassy with tears. 'It's all right,' she said indistinctly. 'I'm not angry any more about this afternoon. I know how you've been feeling. I know how terribly you miss Toby. I'm so sorry for you. Forgive me if I haven't seemed very sympathetic. I had such dreams. . . .' She broke off and stared at me. Then in an altered voice she said, 'But it's not so bad for you. You had Toby. He's still *somewhere*, your mark will always be on him, no other woman can ever wipe you out of his mind whatever happens. And you had him, you had him for a whole year, just when you needed him most. I don't know why *I* should be feeling sorry for *you*. Maybe at bottom I'm just wildly jealous of you.'

'To be remembered by a man, or to remember him, is hardly what one wants, or what anyone has to envy.'

'I envy you that year. No one can do you out of that.'

'Someone *has*.'

'But you *had* it. You've had *something*.'

'But it's spoilt, it's gone. If you've never had it, at least there's no—aching empty gap where it used to be.'

'There's an aching empty gap where it ought to go. And the growing conviction that that place, in your body and in your life, is going to stay empty until it, and you, shrivel up.'

'I'd change places with you this minute.'

'No you wouldn't. Don't say that.'

'I wish I'd never seen Toby, never loved him.'

'Blasphemy,' she said. Her hand came away from her mouth and she reached for a cigarette.

'All I can feel is the pain. I can't remember any tiny part of it without bitterness.'

'Then you're a fool. You've got to learn to live with it. What if your affair with Toby is all the love you're ever due for in your life? Are you going to soil it and spoil it just because it didn't last?'

I suddenly knew what she had meant, long ago, by the backward shadow, the shadow of the lonely future flung back on the present and filling it with fear. Dottie had been living in that shadow, and now I must live in it too. All the little specific pains and terrors were swept away in a great wave of horror. To be alone always!—through youth, middle-age, dotage . . . no one to share with, no one to keep you warm, no hand to hold, no other half of your organism to fill you and fulfil you. . . . Then I remembered David. He was an added cause for fear in a way, the unsharable responsibility, the unsharable joy. But although not the right one, he was someone, to love, to be loved by, the need and the needy. . . . (Why had I been ashamed of my need for Toby, why had I tried to fight it, what had I thought I could bring to him which would satisfy him more? And yet, how dangerous to bring that exclusive need to one's child, one's son. . . .) On a tempered impulse of relief I said to Dottie, 'You're right. You're right to envy me. I've got David.'

'Be careful of that feeling.'

'I know what you mean—but still.'

'Yes,' she said. 'Oh, yes.' She smoked for a while and stared at the blank window-panes and after a while she said, 'And I've got the shop.' She looked at me and gave a little rueful laugh, to which I responded. 'It's all very well to laugh,' she said. 'But at least it's safer to pin one's hopes and dreams on a shop. Not safer for me, but safer for the shop. *It* can't turn queer because its mother dotes on it too much.' We both laughed again at this, but thinly, whistling in the dark. 'One has to have something,' she said, 'if only to take up one's slack. Cold baths and runs over the moors and lime-juice and deck-scrubbing. Not just the sexual slack, of course. The shop's really not much good for that! Energy, time, thoughts—enthusiasm. That most of all. It's the caring. One needs a cause. That's why I was so angry. Because I need someone to share my cause with me, and you don't share it. And neither does Henry. You've both got causes of your own.'

'What's Henry's?'

'Henry's cause?' Her eyes came round to mine very slowly

178

through the film of smoke. She was half-smiling, a grim, grim smile that stopped my breath for a minute. 'Shall I tell you? I promised him not to.'

'Then you'd better not.'

'But I want to. Then you'll understand. You'll understand why you mustn't say, even impulsively, that you'd change places with me or anyone.'

I said nothing.

'Henry's cause,' said Dottie, 'is dying well.'

I didn't understand a word of what she had said. 'Dying well? What do you mean by that?'

'Henry is dying,' she said very quietly. 'And he wants to do it well.'

Chapter 17

I CAN'T REMEMBER now the exact details of Henry's illness. He had only one kidney and there was something wrong with the other—something like that; it makes no difference now, anyway. Apart from having to take it easy, and follow a regular course of treatment, there was nothing he could do, and the disease was not incapacitating or even specially uncomfortable. It was simply a matter of waiting.

What I do remember very clearly is the effect this incredible piece of news had on me. It wasn't exactly that it made my loss of Toby seem less important; it was merely that it knocked all thought of that or anything else right out of my head. I went about for several days reeling mentally as if I'd just been given incontrovertible proof that the law of gravity was about to start working in reverse, or that two and two make eight. Dottie said afterwards that I wore a deep frown all the time, not of sadness or anger, but of serious puzzlement. I was trying to come to grips with it—Henry dying, and knowing it, and behaving as he did, and had, and continued to do; and, hardly less bewildering, Dottie, knowing it too, being in love with him and knowing that he had at best a year to live, a little, little year, of which every hour through which we were all living together was one hour less.

My personal acquaintance with death at that time was limited to Addy and Mavis, and Mavis hardly counted, though that news had given me a sharp momentary shock. Addy's death had of course been a bitter blow and one from which I took months to recover; but at the same time, unexpected, unbelievable as it had seemed at the time, on reflection I had to realize that Addy was old, and that some part of one's subconscious must always be prepared for the death of an old person. But Henry was 39 years old, and moreover I don't think I've ever in my life met a more robust, solid, indestructible-looking man. To think of him with the seeds of death already sprouting in him was ludicrous. But there it was.

Getting accustomed to this, at first, wholly unacceptable situation, then, proved to be a full-time emotional and mental occupation. It left little time or energy for my own sorrow. I watched with a dreadful, an ignoble fascination, as Dottie and Henry proceeded with their daily lives in an atmosphere of unassailable calm. How was it possible? They were in love with each other; Dottie had said so in a perfectly level voice as if announcing the state of the weather. They had been in love since Christmas Eve, the night when Dottie, acting, she said, on an irresistible impulse, had got out of bed and gone down to talk to Henry in the middle of the night. 'I wanted,' she said, 'to explain that brainless laugh.' So driven was she by the sudden need to speak to him that she had actually woken him, crouching by the sofa where he lay asleep in front of the last red embers of our Christmas log. And, half-waking, half-sleeping, undefended, unmanned by the whole evening and Dottie's sudden unlooked-for appearance, Henry had put his arms round her. In that moment, she told me, she knew her 'search' was over, that here she had found her refuge and her companion, her cause and the end of the terrors of the backward shadow, all in this man whom she had once sneered at to me for his funny hair and short body. For the length of that one kiss, she experienced the exquisite relief of safety, the safety of finding one's love at last centred in a basically good person who loves you in return—the thing we're all constantly looking for.

And then he woke up properly, and sat up holding the covers round him, and let go of her. She said she felt ice-cold where his arms and his lips had been, and could remember the exact physical sensation even now, long afterwards. And suddenly she saw it was no good. She could neither believe it nor accept it, and so she begged him, Dottie, who would sooner die than humble herself, she begged him to love her. Then he —rather than let her think the kiss had been false—told her the truth.

Dottie, in that first moment of knowing, filling up slowly with horror and pity for them both, offered herself on any terms at all, and he said, 'On my terms only.' His terms were, no marriage of course, no bed, no kisses even, no physical intimacy at all, because he knew that would draw them closer and closer to a point where the inevitable, when it came, would be the breaking of her; but a business relationship, a sharing of a project outside themselves that would allow them contact and partnership under the strictest sort of self-protective controls.

She had promised. She had had to, she told me, because otherwise he told her that he would go away. Privately it seemed to me that this would have been the best thing to do, but I remembered many little things I had noticed about Henry's behaviour at the beginning and I knew that in his quiet, undemonstrative way, he loved her deeply and probably couldn't have left her although he wanted to spare her as much as possible. Although I rebelled at first against the idea of his having told her the truth like that, so brutally, I soon saw it was the kindest, the only way. She had a year's pain to face while he was still alive to modify the pain with his presence, but then when the time came, she probably wouldn't suffer so much because she would be accustomed to the idea; in a way, by then, his actual death might come as a sort of relief.

But meanwhile, they behaved incredibly bravely and well. I watched with almost unbearable admiration how they stuck to their bargain. 'He's the strongest man living,' Dottie had said. And to me she became his counterpart in strength—she told me it was almost easy; because he had demanded it of himself, he expected no less of her, and so she had to be his equal in courage and control. Even when they were alone, she told me, they only talked business or about everyday things; they didn't so much as look straight into each other's eyes. Yet all the time she was consciously aware of how much she loved him, how much she wanted him, with what degree of despair she felt the passing of time. Every night as she got into bed, however exhausted she had made herself, she always thought: Another day less of him. Yet she seldom cried, even secretly, and sometimes she could rouse real happiness in herself, such as on the day she went to see Ron. She had the basic health to realize that these occasions were not disloyal to Henry, but a tribute to his wisdom. 'Could I have even those little moments of detachment if we'd been sleeping together? He was right. I haven't the strength to survive if we had been even one fraction closer to each other. As it is, there's hope for me for afterwards. Sometimes I can't see it, but it's there.'

As I watched, I shrank in my own eyes. And Toby shrank in proportion. I felt him slipping away from me finally, and cried new tears, because now I was really losing him, losing even the bond of hating him; it had been an entirely false bond, fabricated by me out of my need to wean myself away from him, but now that I began to find I had no strong feelings at all about him any more I felt an exhausted, empty sadness, different from anything that had gone before.

I went to see Billings the following day, as I'd promised, but I was in a sort of daze and perhaps because of that I didn't find the right words to apologize and convince him that we were reliable. He was friendly enough; a bluff broad-bodied farmer with health and good sense written all over him except in his eyes, where fanaticism gleamed inconsistently; he smiled and patted my shoulder and said of course, of course, he understood, it could happen to anyone, but I could see him mentally adding; to anyone half daft and wholly amateur, that is. In the end he said good-naturedly that he'd order the accessories from us, linen and table-napkin rings, place-mats, maybe cruets if we could show him something 'really earthy' that took his liking; but the big stuff, no. Better find a good carpenter and order direct—cheaper too. Sorry and all that, and he wished us the best of luck.

I went creeping home with my tail between my legs; knowing that Dottie would not now blast me but would suffer her disappointment silently made it worse. I vowed a solemn vow, that I would put my very heart and soul into the shop from now on, that even if no such titanic opportunity again presented itself, I would make it up slowly by taking every possible advantage of the little day-to-day ones. I began to look for things to do, to put my mind to it; I realized I had never contributed one single original idea, and since I had always flattered myself that I am good at things like that, this seemed doubly a pity. I often looked round the shop, saw how very well done it was, and felt envious and regretful that I couldn't credit myself with any of it, at a time when a bit of credit was exactly what I most needed. Totting up in the small hours, I realized I had nothing to show for the past ten months except a healthy baby, and after all any dim-wit can achieve that, given reasonable conditions.

Business, having fallen off after the first rush, picked up a bit as spring advanced and the weather improved, but of course fell right off again with the start of the summer holidays. David's first birthday was a pretty gloomy occasion for us, because the day before happened to be quarter-day and Henry's week's work on the accounts had succeeded in showing only that we had passed some sort of graphic peak and were now —only temporarily, we hoped, but still—on the downgrade. We owed quite a lot of money to various suppliers, which Dottie insisted on our paying immediately since most of them were 'struggling artists', as she called them, who depended on our prompt payment for their very livelihood. ('How have they been managing up to now?' Henry asked, to which Dottie retorted, 'That wasn't our responsibility. This is.') The end of Henry's £5,000 was rather closer than just in sight, and although he said very little, I could see he was worried.

'What shall we do when we run out of liquid assets?' I asked uneasily.

'Borrow more,' said Dottie shortly.

I looked at Henry. I seldom did this directly any more, for fear he should somehow divine that Dottie had broken her word and told me. But this time he refused to meet my eye. Instead he said quietly, 'I don't like that idea much. Surely there are some other assets we could cash in on. My car, for instance.'

But Dottie flatly refused to hear of that. There was a silence, and then I said, 'Are we really desperate? Because there *is* Addy's £400.' Henry said, 'It's not come to that yet,' but I caught Dottie's swift, grateful look at me. I was gripped with a mixture of satisfaction and regret that I had spoken the words. I knew I had done, or rather said, the right thing, but I could hardly bear the thought that I might have to make it good. The situation was so confused and miserable now, that the thought of a line of escape which had been laid down too early for it to count as desertion, was sustaining me more than I cared to admit. Yet how could I even dream of running out on Dottie, as things stood? That night in bed, I lay awake trying to think, to plan. The plain truth seemed to be that I was deeply afraid of Dottie's suffering. I was afraid to be left alone to cope with it after Henry died—to be so close to another person's pain was worse in a way than anticipating one's own. I didn't know how it might take her. If the positions were reversed—if Toby had died, say, at the height of my love for him—I could well imagine myself wanting to die too, or at least retreating so far into myself as to be unreachable by all around me. Perhaps Dottie would start to drink, perhaps she would run wild with all sorts of men; it was impossible to predict. I felt guiltily that such thoughts were unjust to her, considering how well she was behaving now; but fear seldom takes justice or loyalty into account. I even went so far as to wish she hadn't told me about Henry, so that when autumn came I could go off to America with an easy conscience, not knowing what I was leaving Dottie to face. Perhaps—perhaps she had told me the truth about Henry in order to inhibit me from this very action? And if so, who could blame her? In her situation I would have moved heaven and earth, and put aside all scruples, to avoid being left alone. Besides, if I really loved her as a friend should, how could I contemplate leaving her?

When I look back on it now, to do myself justice I think I really had done my native decency and courage, such as it is, an injury with those months of trying to destroy my relationship with Toby. By the time this awful time of 'dis-ease' came to an end, when the fire inside me burnt itself out, there was very little left, for the time being, of such strength of character as I had once had to draw on. What an irony it seems now! All my efforts to build myself into an independent person for whom loneliness held no terrors, with reserves of strength to offer the person I loved, had themselves reduced me to such a sickly, craven condition that I was prepared to run away from the only real friend I had left in order to avoid having to support her through an ordeal far worse than mine.

It was around this time that Father paid me one of his ever-more-infrequent visits, and told me that he was going to have to go abroad for his health.

'All the quacks seem to be agreed,' he said with seeming

gloom. 'This climate isn't for me.' He was sitting in the living-room in front of a fire which I'd hastily lit, even though it was the beginning of July, because he looked so frail and cold. It was barely a month since I'd last gone up to town to see him, but in that time he had somehow got smaller in his clothes; his normal robustness, the almost military set of his shoulders, seemed to be thawing into a kind of flabby limpness and I felt frightened. Could he, too, be going to die? I felt a sudden pang of foreknowledge of how old people must feel, when the friends and acquaintances of their lives all begin dropping away one by one. But Father hastened to tell me that it wasn't a matter of life and death—'It's only a precaution. Frankly, I wouldn't have taken any notice of them, if I hadn't rather fancied the idea of living somewhere warm,' he said. 'I'm retiring this year anyway—get my pension—which will just about keep me in drink and cigarettes. . . . H'm, I've just thought. The drink will presumably be wine where I'm going. Supposed to be good for the stomach. Personally I've always doubted it.' But I could see the idea didn't really displease him. The only thing he didn't like about it was leaving me.

'Listen, couldn't you come? Sell your share of this shop enterprise and the cottage, and take David to a place where you don't have to muffle him up like an eskimo half the year? Think of him crawling in and out of the Med, pottering about in the nude—you too. Be easier for you in all sorts of ways. Couldn't you fancy it?'

I could and did. There was nothing, at that low-water-mark of my life, that I fancied more than a life of soporific warmth, a total change, new surroundings, in a word—escape. I let myself play like a child with the idea for a whole day and night, tossing it about in my head and in conversation with Father—a bright-coloured irresponsible ball; I didn't bother about details like the fact that I would have to get work there, that neither of us spoke any language but English, that we could certainly not afford to live anywhere near the white-sanded shore we were dreaming about but would probably find ourselves in some hot, dusty flat, in the middle of some unfriendly provincial town somewhere; it was not worth spoiling the game with such unwelcome realities because I knew all the time that I wouldn't be going.

By the time Father had kissed me goodbye at the station, the bubble had been duly pricked and I drove home through a sudden chilling squall feeling deeply and newly depressed. The prospect of losing Father—of his being out of reach—added a new dimension to my encroaching sense of solitude and feebleness. Was there to be nobody left to lean on? Life seemed intent upon knocking the props out from under me one by one, saying maliciously as it did so: 'You wanted the chance to be brave and independent, didn't you? Well, here it comes, and I hope it chokes you.'

Chapter 18

JULY WASN'T A BAD MONTH as far as the shop was concerned, and our busy-ness disguised, for the moment, the growing undercurrents of tension between the three of us. The
weather treated us kindly; David spent most of his days out
in the garden, stumbling about in the long grass of our shamefully neglected lawn, and happily pulling out flowers and
weeds with great impartiality. He was a baby no longer; his
puppy-fat fell away and he showed himself tall and sturdy and
slightly knock-kneed, with strong, up-springing darkish hair
and great eyes 'the colour of a beer-bottle', as Henry said,
though Dottie demurred and said it sounded better to say they
were the colour of fine ale. 'Yes, Watney's brown,' said Henry.
He was always good with David, and it worried me to see him
romping with him, letting him clamber over him, kick him,
and jump on him as if he were in perfect health. But when I
glanced once at Dottie in veiled anxiety, she simply shook her
head.

One day Henry invited his father's family to visit the shop
and us. Joanna, Mr Barclay's ex-actress wife, had been begging
to come for a long time, but for some reason Henry had put
her off; I guessed it was because he wanted his father to see a
successful-looking concern, and not one which was in its infancy
and might be expected to collapse at any moment. He gave
a great deal of attention to the displays and to the whole
appearance of the shop in preparation for the visit, and dropped
me several lively hints that he would appreciate the putting-on
of all possible dog in the way of lunch.

Fortunately Dottie had just received a consignment of glass
from Ron, including some very original and attractive things.
Plus a new line in ceramic tableware from the local potter,
hitherto an amateur, who had fallen total prey to Dottie's

charms and had been working day and night for her to produce a matching service of bowls, plates and serving-dishes with a marvellous sort of speckled sludge glaze. These were on show in the window, and as soon as she saw them Joanna fell for them and demanded that Henry's father buy them for her as a gift.

He was clearly reluctant, on all counts: first because he thought them drab and hideous, an opinion he voiced without restraint—' 'Aven't you anything a bit more cheerful? Looks like that lot's been laying out in a ditch.' Secondly, because he obviously felt embarrassed and put out at being forced to buy anything from his son. He made several pointed and elephantine jokes to the effect that a father shouldn't have to *buy* things from his own son's establishment; but Henry blandly ignored them and smilingly promised that the whole set would be packed up ready to take back with them when they left, and that he was delighted Jo liked them. He didn't even offer to make a special price. I watched him, patently enjoying himself as his father looked grudgingly round at the elegant good taste of the interior and the hand-made quality goods, and suspected that time was bringing in one of its sweet revenges.

Ted Barclay was a tough, chunky little Cockney in his sixties, beefy-cheeked from uncountable pints and with thick, stubby, capable hands like Henry's own. These hands he seemed unable to keep far from Joanna.

I saw at once what Henry meant about her. She was tough, too, but only inwardly; physically she was delicate-looking, almost fey, with an aureole of fine blonde hair and a make-up —all fragile pinks and peaches stamped with strongly-lashed eyes through which a determined character struck out at you —which looked still like a stage make-up carefully toned down. Her clothes were in excellent taste, the country gentlewoman, though not tweedy of course—that wouldn't have suited her; powder-blue linen, all crisp and simple, with a frightfully smart chunky white cardigan ending neatly at the waist and with short sleeves.

I could see Dottie admiring her. I wondered if Henry had told her that he had once wanted to marry Joanna. I could understand it—she was very attractive, very warm and lively, and only stagey enough to keep everyone's eyes riveted on her without its seeming overdone. She had a peculiar trick of appearing to say the exact truth all the time with no evasions or social compromises, though I suppose this is an impossibility. Anyway it gave one a breathless feeling of waiting to see what she would say next, and to analyse her gift of being so forthright without ever being cruel or offensive. I was at last able to see how she had been able to put it up to Ted Barclay, cold-turkey, that she would marry him for his money, and emerge from the negotiations not only with a husband but one who respected her for her honesty.

She spent about an hour and a half in the shop, just wandering about looking at everything, handling things sensuously, holding lengths of curtaining fabric up against herself, rubbing her cheeks and lips against wood and glaze finishes, playing with toys and once in an absent way trying a tea-cosy on as a hat. Nobody laughed—she looked very good in it. She never put anything back where she'd found it, and Henry followed her round, indulgently tidying up after her, throwing little pacifying glances at Dottie and leaving me to handle the few customers who happened by while they were there.

His father sat rather heavily on a whitewood milking-stool looking very uncomfortable and bored except when Joanna spoke to him or showed him something. It was perfectly clear there was nothing here for him, and he watched the growing pile of things she wanted to buy with wry incomprehension.

'All very nice,' he grumbled once or twice. 'But where's the customers? I don't see the customers.' He turned to me. 'Here it is,' he said, 'Saturday morning, and the place is empty. Who's been in?—a couple of old trokes from the neighbourhood and one posh couple from Town, and between them they bought two china mugs and a glass ashtray. You're not likely to double your capital in two years, son, like I did, if you carry on with stuff like this. Unless of course I bring Jo in every week to buy up the shop.'

Henry smiled imperturbably, though I thought I saw a gleam of annoyance in his eyes. 'As it happens, I'll double it in one year, if we go on as we've started,' he said, which was the first lie I'd ever heard him tell. 'Most of our big sales aren't over the counter at all.' I thought about the muck-and-mystery man and felt grim all over again. 'And we're working on the possibility of a tie-up with a big shop in London—our own section.'

Dottie and I looked at him. I was about to exclaim 'First I've heard of it!' or something stupid when I realized that I'd just heard him tell his second lie. 'Which shop's that then?' asked Ted rather disgruntled. Henry was stuck for a moment and all might have been lost, but for Dottie who quick as a flash said 'Heal's of course,' as if there were no other shop. Ted grunted non-committally but he shut up after that and wrote out the fat cheque for Jo's purchases with no more than a token protest.

We didn't normally close on Saturday afternoons, but that day we did, and after a fairly elaborate lunch at the cottage, which I'd spent most of the previous night preparing, Ted took us all out for a drive in his really very magnificent Bentley. David came too, sitting on my knee, and Joanna sat next to me in the back and we had a long child-bore conversation which lasted until each had convinced herself that her own child was superior. In the process we felt oddly close, and I decided I could really like her, despite the fact that I knew she was as hard as nails; she was also very honest and a lot of fun.

Dottie meanwhile, poor thing, sat beside us and stared out of the window, though she was actually trying to listen to what Ted and Henry were talking about in the front. I gathered that Henry was continuing to string his dad the most amazing line about the success of the business, and that Ted, though he said very little other than grunts, was obviously taking it all in.

Joanna must have been taking it in too, out of the corner of her ear, so to speak, in the way that good wives often can, because she suddenly lowered her voice from the pitch it had reached a moment previously in describing Amanda's latest achievements in the field of mobility and said, 'Henry's enjoying himself, bless him. He must have been looking forward to this for a long time.' 'To what?' I asked, as Dottie turned her head slightly to catch this turn in a conversation which had previously left her cold. 'Showing Ted that quality pays,' she said with a chuckle. 'He won't fully convince him, of course, no matter how hard he tries; but he's not doing so badly. I can see my old man's not unimpressed, in spite of himself.'

We stopped for tea at one of those mock-Tudor places with tables set out on a lawn in front, spoiled by striped umbrellas with some brand-name emblazoned on them, and ate scones and jam and an assortment of little cup-cakes covered with shiny pink icing and blobs of unreal cream. Ted got into a slightly better humour; it was such a pleasant day, we were all enjoying the drive in his splendid car and had told him so several times, and there was a big dog there which took a liking to him. Of course this is always flattering, and I rather warmed to Ted for going all soggy when this great slavering beast came and put its head on his knee. 'Why *can't* we have a dog?' he said to Jo, in a plaintive voice, like a child who has pursued the matter naggingly for weeks, as indeed it appeared that he had, for Jo dismissed him with the words: 'I've told you a hundred times, a, I'm scared of them. And b, they're dirty. And, c, it might bite Amanda.' 'Oh, don't talk so daft! Dogs don't bite babies, they protect 'em!' 'So you always say, but I'm not prepared to risk Amanda getting rabies in order to settle the argument. And that's final.' Whereupon Ted lapsed into glum silence and rubbed the resident dog wistfully behind the ears.

In the short silence before general conversation started up again, I had time to wonder suddenly and shockingly if Ted and Joanna knew about Henry. I instantly decided they didn't. They couldn't possibly, and behave as they had, somehow. And yet—we knew, and how were we behaving? What if Joanna, who was sitting very still with her eyes resting on Henry's face as he drank his tea, was at this very moment thinking: 'What would these two self-immersed girls think if they knew what I know?' I tried to read her expression as she looked at him. Was I mistaken, or was there a look of tenderness, of sorrow . . . ? No. It was nothing but a casual glance —a moment later he set down his cup and she leant forward to refill it and began chatting away about the things she had liked in the shop, which caused Ted to get heavily to his feet and say, 'I think I'll take a trot round the premises and see what they got in their beds that I haven't.' 'In their whats?'

asked Dottie, her eyebrows rising. 'Flower-beds, ducks. Cor, what a mind these young girls got these days!' And he strolled away, snapping his fingers surreptitiously for the dog, which lumbered obligingly after him.

As soon as he'd gone round the corner, Joanna leant back in her wicker chair and looked at Henry again, a different look this time, sharp and knowing and humorous, even a little bitchy perhaps. 'Well! Now he's out of the way, p'raps you'll tell me how the business is *really* doing.'

Henry looked decidedly startled, but then he, too, sat back, answering her look with a rather rueful grin. He appeared relaxed for the first time that day. 'Might've known there'd be no fooling you,' he said.

'That bad?'

'No, no. Just a rather dicey patch, that's all. We've done pretty well taking things all round, up to recently; let's just say things are not quite as rosy as I painted them for Dad's benefit.'

'So I supposed. But you'll be all right? I mean, that marvellous business will thrive, in the end, won't it?' She looked at Dottie. 'I think I'd weep if it didn't,' she said, sounding perfectly serious.

Dottie shrugged lightly. 'We've done our very best. Now it's in the lap of the gods.'

'Henry?'

'It certainly ought to go,' he said, lighting his pipe with lowered eyes.

' "But we'll do more, Horatio—we'll deserve it." ' Henry looked up at her questioningly, and she gave him the whole quote in a slightly teasing, sing-song voice: ' 'Tis-not-in-mortals-to-command-success—you *know*. It's my philosophy of life. Unfortunately it doesn't always work out right. It's bloody, but it doesn't. Sometimes the *better* you deserve it——'

'That's fine, cheer us up,' said Henry. 'Anyway, you certainly did your bit today.' He looked at her with suddenly narrowed eyes. 'I hope to Christ you really liked all that stuff,' he said, 'and didn't just buy it to——'

'Shut up,' she said sharply. 'I don't *ever* do stupid, meaningless, dishonest things like that, and you should know it.'

We drove home, and Henry expansively invited them in for

supper, which caused me sinkings of the heart because I hadn't planned on that; but Joanna, who I imagined to be a thoroughly experienced hostess, took one quick glance at my face (which may well have paled slightly) and chipped in with a grateful but firm refusal. 'Baby-sitter problems—you *know*,' she said cosily to me.

We were standing in the lane outside the cottage gate; Ted, with lumbering courtesy, and entirely masculine tenderness, was helping her on with a very glamorous off-white trench-coat lined with dark real fur which, when done up, only showed discreetly at neck and cuffs—an overstated understatement of wealth and restraint. Through this wrist-ruff her thin expressive hand extended itself to shake mine warmly. 'It's been gorgeous,' she said. 'You must come to us and bring David. And if you can't or don't, I'm coming to see you again soon.' She shook Dottie's hand more reservedly, and then kissed Henry. She was so petite that she had to stand on tiptoe to do it and watching Dottie I could see that she did know that there had once been something between them (I think I would have guessed it myself from that brief moment even if I hadn't known) and that she minded. I understood it so well. She had so little of him, she begrudged any form of sharing. And Jo was the sort of woman you would always have to feel a little wary of, however married she was. And I somehow felt that, despite everything, she was very married.

Then Henry shook hands with Ted, who said grudgingly, 'Well son, I can't pretend it hasn't surprised me a bit, to hear how well you're making out with that posh ice-cream-and-oysters business of yours. If you really get a concession from Heal's, you're away, I suppose. Funny, I thought you'd be sure to come a cropper, trying to flog stuff like that . . . maybe the public taste's improving.'

'Let's hope so—it's time it did.'

'So long as you're giving 'em what they want, that's the way . . . like I always told you. No good trying to educate 'em. Find out what they want and lay it in by the gross.' He looked thoughtfully at his brogues for a minute. 'Funny somehow, to think of my five thousand going on stuff like that.'

'*My* five thousand, Dad.'

'I mean, that I made.'

'*I* mean, that *I* made.'

Ted looked at him a moment, and then laughed and gave him a sort of hug. 'Yes, well, you've learnt something from your old Dad, anyhow. Eh?'

'And let's hope his old Dad's learnt something from him,' put in Jo briskly. 'Eh? Come on, Ted, we must away.'

After they'd gone we sat about the living-room and Henry suddenly got up and, after asking my permission, poured himself a large whisky and soda. He went back to his armchair and sat drinking it, looking, I thought, remarkably contented, at least until the drink was finished. Then his conscience started bothering him.

'Maybe I shouldn't have told all those whoppers to the old man,' he said. 'But I couldn't let him have the laugh on me.'

'He surely wouldn't have laughed!'

'Oh ho! Would he not! You don't know him.' He looked over at Dottie who was staring into the fire with a fixed expression. I knew she was thinking about Jo; I hoped Henry didn't. 'But there's one thing. Moments of desperation can throw up some good ideas. That one about Heal's—we just might be able to make an honest man of me about that. It's worth looking into. Eh, Dorothy?' Dottie came to with a jolt.

'Heal's? Yes. Yes, I thought when we said it that it would bear investigating. I'll write and make an appointment—enclose some cuttings from the opening press.' She got up. 'I must go to bed,' she said shortly. 'Goodnight to you both.' She gave us a vague salute and went upstairs. She looked awfully tired.

Henry echoed my thought. 'She looks tired,' he said.

'Yes.'

'Just the same, eight p.m.'s pretty early to be going to bed.'

We said no more. I realized it was the first time for ages that I'd been alone with Henry and I wished I didn't feel so uncomfortable with him, now that there was nothing to keep the conversation going. I was tired myself, and half-wished he would go; but when I thought of his austere anonymous little flat, and his aloneness once he shut the door after himself there, I felt glad he seemed to want to stay awhile. To be alone and to think about your own death coming closer. . . . Addy had done that, deliberately. But Addy was as strong as a weathered oak, and the commoner forms of loneliness were unknown to her. Henry always appeared very self-sufficient, but there was a vulnerable place inside him that made the way he was behaving all the more admirable.

'Do you want some supper, Henry?'

'Thanks, I don't mind.'

'It's only left-overs, I'm afraid.'

'Left-overs of *that* meal would grace a prince's table,' he said, and added, 'Thanks. For the lunch, I mean.'

'Was it all right?'

'Spot on.'

He smiled at me and, incredibly, I caught myself wanting to love him—to go to him that moment and kiss and caress him. The attraction of the doomed, I thought, trying to disgust myself, to shake off this extraordinary feeling. You don't really find him physically attractive, what you feel this moment is an unworthy mixture of pity and morbidity, not flattering to him really. But I went into the kitchen and stood there for a moment, quite shaken by something very much like desire, and unable to pull myself away from it by any kind of crisp rationalizations.

However, by the time I'd hashed up some supper for us it had faded almost into total quiescence, only interfering subtly with my actions. For instance, I wanted to lay a rather special sort of table in the dining-room with candles and so on but I stopped myself, of course, and instead threw a few bits of china and cutlery onto the kitchen table. I went too far the other way, and made it all too casual and sloppy, which drew a faintly caustic remark from Henry about eating *al fresco*.

I mollified him by opening a bottle of his favourite lager which I always kept handy in the fridge, and we had a pleasant enough supper. During it Henry talked about his father and Joanna and how it never failed to strike him as rather unnatural that their marriage appeared so successful.

'It's not only the age thing, it's her being so delicate and him so—well, gross.' I said he wasn't gross at all, but very spare and trim for a man of his age, but Henry said, 'Not physically. I mean coarse, really. When you think of them in bed it's like thinking about a butterfly and a gorilla.' We munched in silence for a bit and then I said, 'Do you think about it often?'

And he said, in what seemed to be a *non-sequitur*, 'I'm quite a normal chap, you know, whatever Dorothy may have told you to the contrary.'

It took me a moment to digest this, and still I had to be very cautious.

'Dottie hasn't told me anything.'

He looked up at me over a forkful of food and a sudden piercing silence fell which seemed to make a buzzing in my ears, like a silent echo of my own lie. 'I think she has,' he said at last.

He went on eating, but more slowly, frowning slightly, bent over his plate, putting the food into his mouth deliberately and washing every third mouthful down with a gulp of beer. I had a sense of something—it came over me, as it had earlier; the way he moved, the way he ate, calmly and deliberately. And yet . . . he did this every day in his flat, quite alone, with no one for company and no distractions, this and a thousand other little everyday actions . . . did he perform every one of them in awareness of the shadow? Could there be such a thing as an automatic action when one *knows* how near death is? Surely he must look at his very hands performing the movements of lifting the fork, cutting the meat, and feel a coldness of anticipation come over him as he imagines them lying rubbery, icy and abandoned, at his sides, in such a little while? Didn't the food curdle in his stomach as he thought that his body was so close to corruption? 'This sensible warm motion cease on a sudden. . . .' Yes, that was what the ordinary simple mechanics of life were—warm, sensible, unutterably pleasant and comfortable, no, *comforting*, and to think—to be forced to think imminently of that all coming to a stop—what would it do, what new patterns of thought would it overlay upon everything one did?

I stared at him with a pity that was so deep it was almost revulsion. I, too, suddenly saw him in a new way; his death was so sure, so close, that it was almost as if he had no life even now, as if he were a monstrous doll going through the motions of life; for just as a disease is not a disease if you have the cure, so life, suddenly and horribly, did not seem to be life when its term was near and known. Fear of the unknown is part of disease; and joy of the unknown—of the unknown length of time ahead—is an integral and necessary part of life. Life without that, is death begun early. And at that, I began to understand Dottie's philosophy, if one can call it that, of the backward shadow, the thief that destroys by reaching behind it, which deguts the present from the future. For loneliness, too, is like an illness; and it's not true loneliness if you know, or can even hope, that it will have an end. Missing someone who is going to come back is not loneliness. And if one *knew*, knew beyond doubt, that one's loneliness was going to last forever, if it was beyond hope of remedy, that would surely be the same kind of death-in-life which Henry was living through moment by moment. . . .

'How do you bear it!'

I hadn't meant to ask, or to say a word. The words burst out of me as one might be unable to prevent oneself asking a miracle-worker how his miracles were done. For I was certain that I myself would go mad if I were living in Henry's situation, and yet, here he was, sitting in front of me, eating his dinner—there he had been, all day, entertaining his father, enjoying his little moment of triumph, worrying because he had not been entirely entitled to it . . . normally. Normally! 'I'm quite a normal chap you know. . . .' But how, how, how? And so, out of my uncontrollable admiration and bewilderment, the words came out.

He finished eating, wiped his mouth with a napkin, and sat back. 'How do I bear it,' he repeated slowly. 'Well, thanks for asking. I think myself it's pretty remarkable how I do bear it. Perhaps it helps that I've always been rather phlegmatic, I suppose you'd say. But it's hard, and it's hard not to show that it's hard. One sometimes longs to talk about it. Like telling war stories. If one were really grown-up, really brave, one wouldn't need to. I despise myself for wanting to, because I'm afraid that what I really want is—people's pity. I have such a lot for myself, you see, but it doesn't seem to be enough. And yet, of course, at the same time pity is the last thing on earth that I want. Because what I can see now in your eyes, Jane, it just—makes it more real, easier to believe. You're looking at me as if I were a corpse already! The only *really* good moments, of course, are when I stop believing it. Like today, while we were sitting at that tea-place, and the three of you were looking at me, you, Dorothy and Jo, three attractive women, and for a long moment while I was drinking my tea I forgot. I just thought how pleasant it was to be sitting like that being stared at by the three of you and that after all I must have something. . . .' He laughed aloud. 'Silly, isn't it! You were all staring at me thinking "Poor old Henry, he's going to croak" and I'd forgotten and thought you were all under my spell. . . . My God!' he cried out suddenly, and I was struck by an unnamable fear that something, some long-held control, was going to break, and that then whatever tremendous force lay behind it would overwhelm me. 'What a fool I've been! The time, the chances I've wasted! That's the very worst thing about it. Thinking of all you've missed. Do you know that in the whole of my life I've only had three women? And one of them was a tart. And the other two didn't matter, they weren't anything, just stupid creatures I fell in with and did it with because they seemed to expect it. . . . But nothing real, nothing *proper*! Jo wouldn't, and with Dorothy it's me that won't. My Christ, that's hard work if you like, *that's* something to be proud of, not taking her, putting her first. I must stop, I must shut up! Talking will take all the good out of it. But you don't know how I want her! I never wanted anyone like that, and there she is, there she is. . . .' He put up both hands and covered—not his eyes as I expected, but his mouth, as if to stem the flood of revelation which seemed to be frightening him as much as it was me. He bent his head low over the table till I could only see the top of it, his 'funny hair' as Dottie used to call it, little sandy waves running across from his neat parting, unmoved by his emotion, as orderly as something machine-made . . . so typical of him outwardly, the order, the almost rigid calm, while at the same time—under those trim flat waves, behind that sedate waist-coat—violence, fragility, mortality. My hands reached out. He brought both his down like clamps dropping, clutching my wrists, and I could feel the deep inner trembling. He held me like that for a minute, still staring down at the table and then he said harshly, 'You won't go to New York and leave her, will you? I want your absolute promise that you won't go.'

I didn't answer. I don't think I really registered until after-wards what he had said. I was still half inside his skin, feeling his fear and his courage battling; the very walls of him shook with the force of it. He looked up at me and repeated: 'Jane! You've got to promise me you'll be here to look after her!' And all I did was to get up somehow and go round the table and stand as close to him as I could get.

He looked at me for a moment very austerely, then a sudden expression of intense surprise came over his face as if he felt something twist inside him, something totally unexpected beginning to get a grip on him. And abruptly he took hold of me, clenching his fists on the clothes at my waist, and put his face against me.

He didn't move or speak, but I felt such a pressure of silent anguish in him that I had a spasm of terror that he would somehow burst through my fingers, that he would lie in a moment or two like a blown tyre, in broken chunks round my feet. I felt more for him in that dreadful moment than I'd ever felt for anyone in my life, more than for Toby, even more than for David, who might one day—God forbid—need help as terribly and ask for it as silently and rawly, and then turn away with a wrenching, sobbing groan because neither I nor anyone else could give it to him.

I took him in my arms as well as I could—poor, stiff, defence-less, terrified, admirable man. His hands, so male and protective and capable, now kept clenching and opening, clutching at me as if he were plummeting through emptiness, and I felt my heart break. I'd have given anything—my body first of all —to help him, and I tried to let him feel that; but I think he was beyond understanding anything so earthy and ordinary as the offer of what is, after all, the most basic life-thing. A little while before, he had needed this, he was within reach of its help; but now he had gone beyond it. He didn't need or recognize any of the more refined feelings or desires; the one great lust which was firing and rending him was the final one, the violent, passionate, undefeatable will for life itself.

Everything changed for me in those extraordinary moments. I felt myself expanding inside, as if the wind of Henry's suffer-ing were blowing my soul up like a shrunken rubber balloon. I felt that, till then, I'd known nothing, seen nothing and been nothing—I had hardly scratched the surface of life. Perhaps— is such a mammoth irony possible?—one never does taste life until death is closing in. Henry has been dead now for five years, and inevitably I've forgotten many things about him, including his face (incredibly, no photograph of him seems to exist). But his hands at that moment I can remember precisely, down to the last hair, the last small callous beside one flat, practical thumb-nail. And I remember the weave of his jacket across the shoulders, the sandy bristles on his neck, the wet feeling of his tears through my shirt. Exactly, I remember them. And when I do, I feel myself beginning to cry as one only cries for a dead person whom one deeply loved, and loved with a special intensity. When I think of him now, and of Toby, both lost to me, I think perhaps I loved Henry more; certainly the pain of remembering and longing for him is just as acute. Perhaps it's because I loved him *better*; nothing ever spoilt it until his death. But then, with Henry things were relatively simple.

For a long time after the tears stopped he just sat there, passive and exhausted, his head on his arms on the table, with me touching him fearfully here and there—I couldn't bring myself to stroke or kiss him; I didn't know what to do with him. I loved him and pitied him so much that my skull ached and my skin crawled; I was afraid to look at him, afraid he would be ashamed to look at me. But after a long time he slowly and stiffly sat up, took out his handkerchief and blew his nose, and then got awkwardly to his feet, leaning against the table.

There was a great emptiness in the air between us, the emptiness of a question—what could we say now, what could we do—what could we even safely feel? He stared at the black window and I sat down limply, worn out and still aching from that moment of sudden growth. And so we stayed, still and apart, until the knocking began.

Henry turned, and our eyes met for the first time—for the very first time, it seemed to me. The looks we exchanged simply said, 'Who's that?' and 'I don't know.' But with that much said, our eyes clung together, fascinated by the depths each saw in the other's, now that we were truly friends.

More knocking came, heavy and urgent. Henry, suddenly calm and controlled, came across to me and gave me his hand to help me up. We stood for a moment, facing each other, close together, and he held my hand very lightly and we stared at each other; the kisses I had for him then, and which he knew about although I kept them back, were the same sort that I gave to David.

The knocking stopped for a moment, then began again. Henry dropped my hand. 'I'll go,' he said.

When he walked away from me, I was left there, staring at the wall. Something tremendous had happened to me. I didn't know what it was then. I recall a pang of guilt that had some connection with Dottie, so perhaps, in the bewildered aftermath of that emotional explosion, I was confused enough to wonder fearfully if I were in love. But I need not have worried. It was love all right, but not—if only she had realized it!—of a kind which threatened Dottie. It was something right outside the experience of both of us, unfortunately. It seems to me now incredibly sad that she and I, who could have sworn that the word 'friendship' applied to us, didn't know the real meaning of the word, at least not until later. Friendship, like other kinds of love, has to be tested in the fire. Henry's and mine was born in it.

The knocker was a policeman who had come to tell us that the post office was on fire and that the fire was threatening to spread to our shop. Dottie, warned by some sixth sense—I wondered why it had not functioned with respect of Henry—that something menaced her treasures, was already dressing, white-faced and jittering, when I rushed up the stairs to call her.

With Henry already in the police-car, and Dottie half-way out to join him, I hesitated about leaving David alone. But he never woke in the night and the emergency was so great that I had to leave him. It was a ridiculously, an outrageously wrong decision. I should have stayed, but luck was with me in this at least. When we returned, hours later, he was just as I had left him.

We drove at what seemed a fantastic speed back over the pitted roads to the village. The whole place was awake; we could see the glow from the far end of the High Street, and the crowd, like clotted flies on blood, against it. Dottie was out of the car before it had stopped and was forcing her way through, threshing and hitting out like a madwoman. I didn't see her again for some time. The fire-engine from the neighbouring town must have had a breakdown because it had still not arrived; the post office was well alight, and in fact the roof fell in just as we got there, sending up a vast curling blast of smoke and sparks and a deep, baying grunt from the crowd as if from a blow in the stomach.

As the people in front pressed backwards, the policeman, Henry and I managed to wriggle through to the front. There was a wide open space between the crowd and the shop, but even so their faces were infernally lit up like something out of Hieronymus Bosch, with gaping holes for mouths and the effect of their hair being ablaze. The sparks and bits of burning wood were raining down on the roof of our shop, which was separated from the post office by the narrowest of passages.

The policeman was shouting to another, who was ineffectually standing in front of the crowd, 'Have you got them out?' I thought he must mean all Dottie's beautiful things, some of which I could see in the darkened window when the glare was not reflected on it; the heat was ferocious, and I shielded my face, feeling Henry close beside me; I was quite quiet inside. Then the other policeman said, 'Yes, they're both out,' and I suddenly knew he meant the Stephenses. He went on shouting: 'The old boy started it, of course—dotty —I always said he should be put away——' Just then some other part of the house's interior fell in, and the increased blast of heat sent us all cowering a pace backwards.

I looked round for Dottie, and spotted the two old people. They were in the centre of a little knot in the crowd rather thicker than the main body of it. I sidled over towards them, trying to protect that side of my face from the heat.

Mr. Stephens was sitting in the road on a chair from somewhere; a rug had been thrown over him and he was staring blankly at the inferno he had caused, only his hands twitching and dancing like two rabid animals on his knees. His wife was beside him, gripping his shoulders. Unlike his, her face as she looked at the burning building was alive and full of horror and shock. Neighbours were clustered round, some obviously trying to urge them to come away, but they remained there, caught and ossified, as it were, by the awfulness of the scene. They both wore nightclothes with coats on top; her hair was all undone and wild and her face was black with smuts. Shock and the violent glaring light had wiped away the lines of age for the moment; she looked like a grubby, horrified little girl in her nightgown.

Suddenly she seemed to come to herself a little, and began to turn her head this way and that, looking for something in a dazed sort of way. She saw me, her eyes slid past then snapped back. 'Jane!' she screamed out. 'Jane!' The crowd moved to let me get to her side, and she clutched my arm, shaking me and saying something that, because of the general hubbub, I couldn't hear at first. But then she put her mouth to my ear and shouted: 'Mufferpaws! Where's Muffer! He's not in there, is he?' I shouted to one of the bystanders, 'Where's their cat?' Nobody knew.

The old woman clutched me with both hands and began to cry. All at once she looked old again, the illusion of childishness was gone and she looked old and ugly with rage and pain. 'If he's killed my cat, I won't forgive him! I won't forgive him this time!' Then she actually turned on the old man, sitting there helplessly, and screamed at him, 'I told you to leave the matches alone! Now see what you've done, you old villain, you've been and killed my Muffer, I shan't overlook it this time, not this time I won't! You'll see!'

He turned his half-empty face towards her slowly, and gave her a piteous look, like a scolded child fearing nothing so much as the loss of its mother's love. His slack, trembling mouth framed the words, 'I didn't mean to——' and suddenly Mrs. Stephens doubled over, holding her waist as if in some unendurable pain, and began to run blindly towards the fire.

For a second nobody moved to stop her, so I ran after her and caught her easily. 'What——' she gasped, weakly struggling against me, 'What have I done—what did I say to him—oh, somebody save us—save our cat or I can't go on, I can't go on like this any longer——' She began crying, feebly and helplessly, shaking her head to and fro heavily between her hands.

'You stay with Mr. Stephens. I'll try and find Muffer.'

I handed her back to her neighbours. I knew I had offered to do the impossible—looking at that fiery interior left me in small doubt that the poor little beast was charred to a cinder by now. But still, cats are supposed to have a strong instinct for self-preservation. If it were not actually trapped, it might have escaped. I couldn't help feeling it was terribly important to find it if I could; only by putting the creature unharmed into Mrs Stephens's arms could I save her from hating that poor old man forever.

I remembered that the only window in the house that was ever opened was at the back—the larder, or what had once been the larder, where the cat slept. Getting to the back through the passage was quite impossible—one couldn't approach the building from the front at all, since the wind was blowing the heat that way. But by running down to the end of the block and turning left twice, I came into a narrow alley which led past the bottoms of the tiny gardens. From here things did not look half so bad. The back part of the house was in silhouette from the blaze in the front, but it seemed to be intact, and so, I noticed, did our shop on the far side. Things were uncannily quiet here too, compared to the uproar in the front, to which was now faintly added the belated clanging of an old-fashioned fire-engine bell.

I scrambled over the fence into the Stephens's back garden, falling into the soft earth which I myself had loosened on that fatal Billings day. Standing there in the eerie, spark-filled dimness, wreathed in stray curls of smoke, I called urgently for the wretched cat. 'Muffer! Muffer! Sh-wsh—wsh—Come on, pussy, come on——'

I couldn't see a thing. I found my way to the back of the house. The smoke was thicker there, and all the windows seemed to be closed, but I got my fingers under the sash of the larder one and it jerked open. I expected the cat to come shooting out, but nothing happened. Apart from the smoke, and the crackling, it was hard to believe the front of the building was ablaze. Here, everything was dark and still. I felt quite safe in climbing in over the sill.

The cat wasn't in the larder. I opened the door, and a gust of smoke billowed out and nearly knocked me over backwards. I choked and coughed and wanted to clear out, but there was no sign of any flames so I thought I'd just make sure the cat wasn't in the kitchen. I got down on hands and knees and crawled forward; there was much less smoke near the ground, and I could breathe all right, but it was pitch-dark and I bumped into several pieces of furniture before I reached another door on the far side.

This time I did hesitate. The ominous crackling was very loud now, and I remembered that the front part of the building, the shop part, which was now only one room away, had collapsed. I touched the door; it was hot. I knew that a sudden draught going through the house might bring the whole lot down in a moment. But then I heard the damn cat mewing in the living-room. It was a dreadful sound, quite unlike the ordinary voice of a cat—it was a high-pitched all-but-continuous miaow which convinced me that animals, too, can reach a point of despair. I really couldn't leave it there. It wasn't because of the Stephenses any more. It was the cat itself, and I don't even like cats, but you can't turn deaf ears to anything that's crying like that, in such hopeless terror of abandonment and nameless death.

I half-stood up and opened the door a very little. A lot of things seemed to happen at once. A terrific roar met my ears, like a furious live animal about to leap on me. After an eternal moment, the cat came bolting out with its fur full of sparks, its tail like a brush, fairly screaming from a wide-open mouth. It flashed past me and was gone, heading unerringly for the only escape route. The smoke seemed to fall into the room as if the opening door had released a great weight of it which had been leaning against the other side. I bent double and ran, my eyes clenched shut, stinging and burning, and not daring to breathe. I don't think I breathed again till I had fallen out through the larder window head first into the open air.

I lay stunned for a minute—I had actually fallen partly onto my head—and then picked myself up and fled down the garden and over the fence. I spotted the cat almost at once, and it was as well I did, because its coat was smouldering and its tail was actually alight in one place. I caught hold of it quite brutally and rolled it over in the dirt and damp grass behind the fence. It sank its teeth and claws into me, of course, and for a second I had a brilliantly clear flash of memory—Mavis's cat clawing me as I let it out of its basket. Then I picked it up round the middle and carried it, kicking and struggling and raking my knuckles with its back feet, round the corner and into the main street again.

The crowd had increased considerably in the interim, and in the midst of it was the fire-engine, the men, their hoses already linked up, playing quantities of white foam all over the front of the post-office, or where it had once been, and, incidentally, all over the front of our shop as well. For the first time I noticed that the door of this was open and I caught a glimpse of Dottie, appearing briefly in the doorway with a huge crate which she handed to someone and then vanished again into the blackness—the electricity must have failed. Henry was nowhere to be seen, but a torch was playing around the inside of the shop, as I could see through the descending cascades of white foam which were pouring down the bay window. I had a sudden longing to be near him, and wondered how I could have left his side for so long.

Looking round desperately for the Stephenses, or for anybody on whom I could unload the terrified cat, I saw a policeman, a very youthful one, gaping open-mouthed at the wonder of a shiny fire-engine. He came to himself with a jerk when I spoke to him to ask where the Stephenses had gone. He directed me perfunctorily to the chemist's across the street, from which lights were now shining, and then went back to his fascinated contemplation of the fire, hands behind his back, face aglow with innocent enjoyment.

When I went into the chemist's the door-bell tinkled and everyone looked round, and then there was a general gasp, the reason for which I understood only when I caught sight of my face in the large mirror behind the counter. I had not realized at all that I was quite filthy, face, clothes and all, and furthermore rather bloody—I had a cut on my head and my hands were quite a mess where that idiot cat had savaged me for my pains.

When Mrs. Stephens saw it she let out a shriek and flew towards me, embracing me and the cat together. Then she took the poor scorched brute away from me, and cradled it passionately in her arms: 'Oh, poor pussy! Poor pussy! Mother's poor little pussy then! Did it get burnt, poor girlie, did it get burnt?' She carried it tenderly to the chemist, and looked up at him wordlessly, her eyes red-rimmed from smoke and tears, her hands all the time in motion, fumblingly stroking and gentling the cat, who now lay quite still in her arms—so still that I had the awful thought that it might have died of shock. The chemist gave a deep sigh, but he didn't argue. 'Bring it behind the counter, dear, we'll see what we can do for it.'

Everyone crowded round and watched with fascination as the cat's hurts were anointed and neatly bandaged. Then the chemist turned to me and said, 'Now we'd better clean you up, miss.' He winked. 'Sorry, but you see how it is. First things first.' With that the tension broke, everyone burst out laughing, even Mrs. Stephens, and the old man, who sensed somehow that a crisis had passed, could be heard cackling away in senile merriment, his mischievous hands once more innocently at rest on his knees.

Chapter 19

IT WAS AFTER MIDNIGHT before we got home. The same policeman took us back in his car. Dottie sat in the front with him and I in the back with Henry. I wanted to hold his hand, but mine were too painful to touch, even in the bandages. A doctor had been found who had given me a shot of something against infection and I was feeling pretty woolly and absolutely deadly tired as well. I was scarcely aware of what was going on any more, only of Henry's steady, comforting presence beside me, and Dottie's head, kerchiefed and still miraculously erect, silhouetted against the windshield in front of me. She and Henry, with some help from bystanders, had had to shift everything back again into the shop after the danger had passed. Our shop had not caught fire. I didn't stop to think beyond that. If I had any anxiety it was for David, but this had been nagging at the back of my mind all the time and now that I was heading back for him I already felt easier about it. I fell asleep almost at once from the motion of the car. . . .

I have a dim memory of Henry helping me up the stairs; I seemed to be completely befuddled by that time, but I did go in and make sure of David before dropping my outer clothes on the floor and falling on the bed. I was already asleep again when Dottie woke me.

'Jane,' she was saying in a harsh, loud voice, shaking me by the shoulder. 'Jane! You've got to wake up.' I peered up at her through a haze of sleep and resentment.

'What is it? I'm dead beat. Won't it keep till morning?'

'No, I've got to talk to you now, I can't possibly sleep until I've talked to you.' She sounded like a stranger, her voice rough and violent, scraping on some jagged edge of hysteria. I heaved myself up in bed, wincing at the smart of my hands.

209

'What's wrong?'

'Wrong!' She gave a shrill laugh which might have sounded theatrical if I hadn't known her very well. 'Plenty. You didn't see the shop, did you? Where the hell were you, anyway?'

'Saving the Stephens's cat.'

She hesitated, not sure if I could possibly be serious. 'Christ,' she said. 'A cat! Never mind, it's too late to go into that now. We managed—Henry and I.' Her voice softened and relaxed a little at the conjunction of names. I said, 'I'm sorry, it all sort of overtook me. But the shop's all right, isn't it?'

'No,' she said, 'it's not bloody well all right. It's not burnt to the ground, and that's the only all-right thing you can say about it.'

'How do you mean?'

'You want it item by item—tonight's damage?' Her hands were clutching my eiderdown and kneading it as Mrs Stephens had the cat's fur. 'The wall on the fire side is scorched black and four or five shelves fell down with everything on them, most of it breakable. Most of the fabrics are ruined by the soot and smoke. The paint's black and blistered. Most of the window panes cracked with the heat, and the foam came in and damaged the floor and a lot of other things.' I stared at her in horror. 'We'll have to start more or less from scratch,' she said.

I couldn't speak. I had had no idea. It was awful! Worse than anything I'd imagined when the policeman first came to the door. Surely the total destruction of the place in one fell swoop wouldn't be quite as appalling as this disaster, which obliged us to decide whether to pack it all in or, as Dottie said, start again from scratch. The thought of doing that fairly winded me.

I reached up and switched on the bed-light to see Dottie better. What I saw really frightened me. She looked distracted, half-mad. I don't think I had fully realized until that very moment what that place meant to her—the shop itself and every piece of work it contained were vital to her, integral, as if she had done every single part of it herself, as in a way she had.

A look at her pale, pinched face, drawn so taut that there were suddenly age-lines all over it, led me to expect her to burst into tears, but she didn't.   Her eyes, wide open and wild, were dry; she showed no signs whatever of breaking, though her body and manner were so taut and tense that she seemed to quiver all over. It was I who cried, because again I had failed her. I put my head into the bandages and sobbed.

'Stop that, stop it!' Dottie said fiercely. 'What does that help? We've got to plan, to. . . .' She stopped abruptly and then went on, her voice slightly altered, 'Jane, I want your four hundred pounds.'

I stopped crying and looked at her. Her eyes pinioned me, glittering. She had the look of a fanatic and I knew she would never give up.

'All right,' I said, not giving myself time to think or bid goodbye to my dream, which had become a stupid and unworthy one anyway.

'You mean it? You won't change your mind?'

'No.' It was hopeless, the least I could do. I pushed away—temporarily—the sadness, the sense of loss. It was worth it, for the moment of the gesture anyway, just to see her face lose a little of its desperation, her hand unclench on the eiderdown, leaving deep creases.

'Thank you,' she said, very formally, as if in a bank or a lawyer's office. She stared at me for a long moment, and then stood up and said, 'I must get some sleep. It all begins again in the morning, and I suppose you won't be much help, with those hands. Never mind. We'll cope somehow.' She went to the door, her back like a ramrod but her legs so out of control that she stumbled twice. Before she went out she stopped with her back turned to me.

'You're sure you mean it about the money? You promise?'

'Yes,' I said, trying not to realize that her caution was entirely justified.

'There's just one more thing.' She began to turn towards me, decided not to look at me and stood in profile, staring at the carpet. 'I noticed Henry looking at you tonight, when we got home. I don't blame him for anything, ever. I wouldn't blame him whatever he did. I understand everything about him. But I just want to tell you that if you let him come anywhere near you, I'll—I won't bear it. I'll do something terrible. Don't say anything,' she said quickly. 'I'm only warning you. We're all three in the same boat—anything could happen between us. Just be careful, be very careful, because——'

She stopped talking and went out of the room, leaving the sentence in mid-air.

I lay there stiff with shock for several minutes after she'd gone. What had she meant, 'We're all in the same boat?' What boat? Perhaps it was her backward-shadow thing again. We were all in the backward shadow of fear of the future. Dottie's fear was of a spinster's eternal loneliness. Mine was of insecurity, moral, emotional and material, in the raising of David and my own personal subsistence. Henry's—death, of course. How very petty ours seemed in comparison with his! Or, on second thoughts, was it not the other way round? Which was worse, to suffer agonies of fear and regret for a year and then be out of it, or to have to face endless years of struggle to keep your identity from flying apart from the lack of a love to hold it together?

That Dottie had so misinterpreted Henry's look as an intention to make love to me somehow didn't surprise me after the first shock. Somehow it was inevitable that she would perceive something altered in Henry's and my relationship, and equally inevitable that she would fail to understand it. This sudden, or no, not too sudden, flowering of love for Henry combined with my horror of the inevitability of losing him, seemed, in some part of my sub-conscious not too far from the surface, to overwhelm all other considerations whatever. But at the back of my mind, in some other place, waiting, was the disappointment, the crushing anticlimax, of the whisking away of my dream trip to the fantasy city of New York. The huge Aladdin's cave which had been hovering there filled with glittering tinsel and fairy-lights for so long was now black-dark and empty. My £400 was pledged. New York was henceforth no more to me than any other distant unattainable city. And reality—the dog-days of slogging, inescapable, problem-choked, discipline-demanding reality—were here again.

Chapter 20

THE NEXT MORNING there was the shop. Thank God in a way that there *was* the poor shop, blackened and soiled and looking somehow confused and ashamed of itself, to be commiserated with and looked after and nursed back to health. When I saw it I really felt with Dottie for the moment that nothing else mattered, except restoring its self-respect. Shades of the L-shaped room! How many times in one's life can it happen that a mere place, bricks and cement and windows and doors, with its illogical subjective demands, can come to one's rescue and save one from the lower depths of folly? Once or twice during the hectic weeks that followed I found myself wishing that the fire, if it had to happen, had happened right after my last meeting with Toby. I would certainly have pulled myself together a whole lot faster if it had.

As it was, the work, the mutual effort to heal the shop, drew us together *as a trio*. None of us seemed to have time or even the desire for personal relationships *à deux*. Dottie never again spoke about Henry and me; Dottie and Henry were virtually never alone together; and Henry and I . . . we were almost never alone together either. Henry saw to that, not me. It would be untrue to say that I didn't try, in the beginning, to be alone with him. If I still feel the tug of longing for him now, so many years later, how much stronger must it have been then, so close in time to our solitary emotional encounter! But he was having none of it. Only once was anything said. I remember the details lucidly; I can re-live the conversation as one re-lives an occasion by looking at an old photograph.

We were on our knees one morning, re-waxing the floor after laboriously cleaning it. I was a little ahead, applying the wax, and Henry was crawling along after me, concentratedly, steadily rubbing back and forth along the planks, working with the grain. Dottie was off somewhere ordering replacements. David was there, I remember, sitting in a corner of the bow-window, making a tower out of broken pieces of ceramics.

I was so bloody tired I could scarcely keep moving, and I had to keep my eyes fixed on the floor in front of me because any time I looked up and around and saw the state everything was still in I just felt like lying down on my stomach and crying my eyes out. It's hard to explain how I felt about it. It was almost as if the state of the shop represented the state of my own life, to wit, utterly squalid with disorder and mess and confusion, and to have that condition prevailing both inwardly *and* in my surroundings was just too much.

Suddenly I heard Henry stop rubbing and I turned round and saw him get up slowly and go and sit on a chair which happened to be in the middle of the room.

'Henry?'

'It's all right, don't fuss. I'll start again in a minute. I'm entitled to take a break, after all we're not in the bloody Union. Besides, I'm a dying man.'

I sat on the floor stupefied, not so much by what he'd said as by a sudden agonizing realization that if Toby, funny, wise, darling Toby, had been mortally ill, he, too, would have made jokes about it in just that tone. I remembered that Dottie had first started to be in love with Henry the night that I had made the startling discovery that the two men had the same sense of humour. Perhaps *my* loves—the one that was going to finish and the one that was stealthily beginning—began their overlap at the same moment.

'Let's both have a break—I'm just about whacked. I'll make some coffee.'

'Tea for me.'

'Okay. Want some milk, David?'

'Na,' he said scathingly, which meant that he did.

I brewed up in the kitchen at the back. My mind was a blank of weariness, but I was conscious of a deep pull towards Henry, an aching desire to go to him where he sat motionless in the middle of the ruined shop and embrace him, warm him, recover him somehow, drag him back up the steep hill. . . . I made his tea and took it in to him, and it seemed that it was an effort for him even to raise his hand to take it.

'Henry, this is ridiculous. You mustn't go on working like this.'

'Oh, what's the odds? A bit longer, a bit shorter . . . one can't opt out just for the sake of a few extra weeks or months.'

I had no answer for this but to put my arm round him. I felt the empty eye of advance grief opening up inside me like a lens. He said, 'No, don't do that.' I took my arm away, stung. 'And don't do that, either—don't be hurt. Don't be hurt! I don't want anybody to be hurt.'

'I do love you, Henry,' I said. It was the only time.

He sighed deeply without looking at me. 'It makes you wonder, you know. You say you love me, Dorothy I know loves me although in a quite different way, Joanna gives me funny long looks. . . . When I was healthy and thought I had a future, do you think any woman of the calibre of you three would have looked at me twice? Well, I don't know, maybe they would, but they didn't. Now it all seems such a waste, such a nuisance. I don't want anybody to be hurt,' he repeated harshly. He took my hand and squeezed it roughly, still without turning his head. 'Not you, not anybody. Let my old Dad cry for me, let him do the funeral honours—that'll be enough. Look, I'm damn sorry for what happened—you know, that night. My fault. I got taken short with a sharp attack of *temps perdu*. But that's no excuse. Forget it.'

'I don't want to. It was too important to me.'

'Try. Be a good girl. I can't help wondering what would happen if they let condemned criminals loose to wander about for the last few weeks or so before they topped 'em. They'd probably be killed in the rush.'

'Henry, I really can't let you go on thinking that I—that we only love you out of some sort of morbid——'

'It must have something to do with it! I mean it's obvious. Look at me. I ask you. Just look.' I looked, and he did something amazingly funny to his face—as if by tightening a few muscles he had subtly turned it into its own caricature. It was an exaggeration of all the features that Dottie had once said made him 'funny-looking'. 'I've got a face like the Idris lemon,' he said plaintively. 'You think I don't know? I have to shave the damn thing every day!'

There's nothing worse than being forced to laugh in the very midst of despair, to laugh aloud at the object of one's love and grief. I didn't understand this until much later; I didn't understand why the laugh I gave was so painful. I learnt it with Dottie at his funeral . . . but I'm jumping ahead. All my memories of that time are telescoped now; the laugh I gave then, Dottie's laugh at the funeral—all are jumbled together under the huge black memory-shadow of his death. Anyway, that was all there was to my intimacy with Henry. That laugh, the sudden tears that followed it interrupted by David spilling his milk . . . that was its sum and its finale. Short, deep, permanent in its effects, like a stab wound. And the terrible thing is, I suppose I shall never know whether he was right—whether my knowledge that he was going to die did have anything to do with it. On the other hand, does it matter? The memory, the loss, the dull, accepted ache, are facts.

Very soon after the brief episode in the shop—a matter of only a week or so, I think—Henry found he couldn't go on working and took to his bed. He said he was very sorry, but he was just too tired. We should have been relieved that the anxiety of watching him doing things that were a strain and very dangerous for him had been removed; but that he had given in was frightening. It also doubled our work, for as well as cleaning and scrubbing, buying and selling (for Dottie had insisted upon 'business as usual' after the first couple of days) we now had to go in turns over to Henry's flat to take care of him.

But before long, Joanna appeared on the scene. 'This situation is absurd,' she said crisply. She brooked no argument, but simply packed Henry's suitcase and bore him away in her car. 'I shall be able to look after him better than you can, with the shop and everything,' she said firmly. I saw her and Dottie exchange a long, straight look, and then Dottie nodded.

That night when we crawled home from our day's work, Dottie drank whisky until it put her to sleep. It was the only time I've ever seen her drunk, and then you wouldn't have known it wasn't just exhaustion. She sat in front of the fire, steadily drinking, and I suddenly seemed to catch her thoughts as if they were floating through the air between us: *The shop comes first*. Or perhaps it was just what I would have been thinking, in her place; for she could always have just given up the shop and devoted all her time to Henry, and she hadn't, and couldn't, and what sort of person did that make her, in her own eyes?

She came to terms with it, as I suppose we always do with whatever is wrong with us. Every few days she would go over to see him and tell him the latest news. These visits were hell for her. Of course she didn't say so, but the strain of them told on her. After one of them she would come back so plunged in depression that it seemed impossible to pull her out of it.

But she was extraordinarily resilient. If she could bring herself to lie down on the floor and romp with David for ten minutes, or if she had work to do in the evening, even paper-work, connected with the shop, she would make a fairly quick recovery. But this resilience, too, had its negative side, because it troubled her conscience that she could so quickly become lively and 'happy' again. Once I remember she caught herself laughing and talking baby-talk to David while he was having his bath, and she stopped suddenly and said in a subdued voice, 'I'm rubber. I'm not flesh and blood at all. What's the matter with me?' And she ran away from David quickly as if he menaced her somehow.

Sometime early in September I had a letter from Billie Lee, asking me to come up to London to see her. I assumed it was something to do with the imminent publication in America of Addy's book, about which I had heard nothing for ages, yet there was something indefinable in the tone of the letter which gave me a vague hint of what was actually coming.

It was very inconvenient just then to take a day off, and if I had not had this strange feeling that Billie wanted to talk to me about some personal matter, which could only be concerned with Toby, I would have telephoned her instead of going up. But as it was, I got Dottie to drop me off at the station on her early way to work and took the train up to town.

Billie received me with singular warmth, remarking what

a lot of weight I had lost and asking after David and the shop with great solicitude. She gave me a tulip-glass of excellent sherry and came round to sit with me on my side of her big desk in the smart office lined with the colourful jackets of her clients' books. When I asked, she said oh yes, that my aunt's book was coming out the following month—there'd been a slight delay due to a printer's strike in New York— was I still planning to go over there? No? Pity in a way, the publishers were exceptionally nice 'guys' and would have been glad to entertain me. . . . I suppose she saw from my bleak expression that I didn't want to hear more in this strain for she quickly let it drop and we sat for a while chatting rather strainedly about this and that. . . . There was, I noticed, a large portrait-frame on her desk with its back to me, well within my reach. My hand moved several times of its own volition to turn it round and look into the face of Whistler, but I always drew it back.

At last I decided that even this rather mannish, efficient woman could do with a little help, so I said, 'How's your daughter these days?' She gave a little quick cough, as if of surprise, and set her glass down with a click on the desk. 'Melissa?' she asked, though I knew she had only the one. 'Oh—she's—fine. Very well. You knew she's on the point of getting engaged?'

'Is she?'

'You did know?'

'I suppose I did, in a way.'

'To—er . . .'

'Toby. Yes, I know.'

There was a pause. She tapped her beige-polished fingernails on the desk and her charm-bracelets shivered with a gentle clinking sound. Her aquiline profile was turned to me. She looked softer and less garish now that fashion had decreed a more natural look in make-up and her lips were not so violently red, though her hair still was, rather brighter if anything than before.

'Look here,' she said at last. 'I have to—I mean, I've been needing to talk to somebody who knows him. I don't know at all how you feel about all this. I know you were fond of him at one time.' She paused, but I said nothing, so she went on. 'He's very talented—there is that about it. And funny, and charming. I like him a lot myself. The only thing is . . .' she paused, glanced at me, and looked away again. 'The only thing is, he strikes me as sort of—unsubstantial. I don't know if that's really the right word. Unsolid, somehow—lightweight. What I mean is—she's only seventeen. I don't have to agree to her marrying yet. I could make them wait.'

'Then why don't you?'

'God, I'm not sure! Perhaps because I don't feel certain she would. She loves me and we're close, but—she's absolutely mad about him, she wants him, she thinks of nothing else, the —the sex thing is pulling her apart. . . . God, Jane,' she said suddenly, 'you're lucky to have a son and not a daughter! You can't conceive how difficult it is to be a parent nowadays! The bombardment! That's what I call it. They're bombarded, day and night, from every side—hoardings, books, television of course, plays and films and newspapers and friends' conversations twenty-times-of-course . . . there's no escaping it. . . . To be seventeen and lovely and a virgin is absolutely unheard-of, the pressure to do something about it is too strong for any young personality to withstand, especially when . . . well, he *is* attractive, little and thin and all as he is, even I can see that. The question is, would I rather she got safely married to him, even though I'm not sure how reliable he would be in the long run, or have an affair with him that can be got out of?' She sighed from her depths and lit a cigarette. 'You see? Even I'm affected by the bombardment. I couldn't have dreamed of such a thing ten years ago—my own daughter! But now it's irresistible, the very air's contaminated with this—moral looseness. Even my generation begins to latch on to the current solutions, the notion that self-control is non-existent, that passion is *ipso facto* irresistible, purity an encumbrance and an anachronism.' She began to walk slowly up and down the room, her short sharp heels making little dents in the mustard coloured carpet. After a long while she looked at me, and with a wry half-smile. 'Sorry, stranger,' she said. 'It's only because you know him—so much better than I do. Tell me. Can I trust her to him?'

The irony of all this—that I should be in a position of withholding or giving a reference to Toby as a potential husband—

struck me very forcibly. Toby's image for me was, at that time, overlayed by my feelings for Henry, though the two have sorted themselves out since into two distinct and very different patterns. But listening to Billie talk about him forced me to bring him out of obscurity and look back at him over the gulf of undeserved hatred that I had dug to separate me from my desire for him. And now, in all honesty, I could only think what a very fortunate person Whistler was, I could only feel a sort of stifled impatience, almost anger, against Billie for not realizing it, not appreciating him, my Toby. . . .

'He could have seduced her, you know. Any time he'd wanted to,' I said.

She stopped pacing abruptly and looked at me, her face turning a bright mottled pink, which clashed with her hair and gave her a very unpleasant appearance. Her thin, nervous hands clenched and for a moment I thought she was going to be furious with me, but she was too fair in the long run to allow the truth to sting her into more than momentary anger. After a moment her colour receded and she sat down again with her cigarette twisting in and out between her fingers.

'That's true,' she said flatly. 'That's perfectly true. And he hasn't. I'm sure of that.'

She sat for a long moment in silence, and then looked at me and smiled thinly. 'Well, thank you. I suppose you've given me the only kind of recommendation that I could have accepted. Once it would have meant nothing at all, for a thirty-year-old man *not* to have seduced an innocent seventeen-year-old girl who loved him. Anyone who did, would have been a bastard. Now anyone who doesn't is either an idiot, a eunuch or a saint.' She laughed. 'He's certainly not the first two, so we must give him the benefit of the doubt and presume that he's nearer to the third.'

Being in London was painful, somehow. I'd planned to do a lot of things while I was up, including going to Father's house to make sure his tenants were looking after the place properly, as he'd asked me to do before leaving for Spain; and perhaps going to visit John. But the conversation about Toby had disturbed me too much to let me do anything more which brought memories into sharper focus. I did go to John's place, mainly because I felt so vulnerable myself that I could wince from imagining how hurt he would be if he knew I'd come up to town without going to see him. Not that he would have found out, but still. . . . I was relieved to find he was out.

By day, that house, which had once been my refuge, seemed unrelievedly squalid and it smelt of human uneasiness. The same children who had shouted after me that morning were playing on the steps again. They weren't thin or anything but none of their clothes seemed to fit, they were grubby and their eyes were distrustful as they looked up at me. I have never hated my times as Dottie did, and as Billie seemed to; but the look in those black children's faces was the look of them-and-us which gave me a feeling compounded of guilty conscience, resentment and even fear. I left a note behind the broken door of John's letter-box in the hall and got away quickly.

I was actually at the station when I thought of Heal's. It came to me quite suddenly and I stood stock still in front of W. H. Smith's and thought about it. There was nothing on earth I wanted more at that moment than to do something that would help Dottie and give her a lift. The blunders I'd made in the past *vis-à-vis* the shop still weighed heavily on my conscience and I wanted desperately, too, to please Henry—though the last time I had been over to see him he had looked so ill and seemed so listless that I had fleeting, stifled doubts whether even a fillip for the shop would have power to rouse him to anything like his old enthusiasm. However, as I considered it I remembered that I had all the cuttings and several brochures with me. The cuttings I had wanted to show Billie (but had forgotten), the brochures were advertisements and a handout that I had in the bottom of my shopping-basket after a visit to the printers.

I took stock of my personal appearance, which usually left almost everything to be desired, though Dottie insisted I dress smartly when I was serving in the shop; but today I had outfitted myself carefully for my interview with Billie; one always armours oneself for encounters containing the potential of emotional uncertainty. I looked all right.

I left the station, knowing I was missing the only train for two hours, and got a bus to Tottenham Court Road. Once in Heal's exquisite entrance hall, surrounded by sights of sweet perfection and the odours of seasoned wood and dressed cloth, I was assailed with misgivings. Business people don't just arrive for important interviews without an appointment, surely? Besides, looking about at that great store it seemed hard to imagine they would be impressed by anything we had to offer. But words of Dottie's came back to me: 'Some of our stuff is as good as anything anywhere.' I looked around again, and saw that it was so—I had nothing to be ashamed of. I found my way to the business manager's office and requested an interview.

Chapter 21

THERE'S NO PARTICULAR NEED, five years after the event, to go into the details of Henry's death. Something known and inevitable, however tragic, can't be very moving to read about, or even interesting. It happened, in any case, very soon after the visit to London which resulted in our landing a contract with Heal's. It comforted me quite ludicrously at the time to feel that I had managed this coup in time to give Henry the knowledge that the shop was back on the upgrade—I remember him saying to me, on one of my last visits, 'Knowing you and Dorothy have that Heal's thing has given me a hell of a kick. It's going to make all the difference to her. . . .' Neither of us was with him when he died; it was Joanna who held his hand and listened to his voice fade out right in the middle of a sentence about Dottie. It was typical of him that he died with his brain, and his heart, still working.

But if his death was somehow unterrible, the funeral cancelled that. I can't recall it even now without horror. His body going sliding through those silent little doors to the bleat of organ music—one expected to see the brilliant white-hot glitter of the furnace between the discreet little curtains. It's hideous, so euphemistic. . . . In India at least you see the flames; it's all out in the open air and everybody wails and you smell the fire and don't pretend it isn't really happening.

Ted arrived late; we found out from Joanna later that he'd been sitting outside in the hire-car, unable to pull himself together enough to show his face in the chapel. But then at last he came in, near the end, his face mournful and somehow simian above the impeccable morning dress with its grey waistcoat and shiny top hat. And *spats.* . . . Dottie's and my mutual wretchedness that day was so acute that it needed only those spats to send us both into suppressed hysterics.

Dottie actually had to leave the chapel, and I followed her when I'd managed to get hold of myself; I found her in the graveyard outside standing erect, her whole body heaving with sobs, the tears washing down her face from red, anguished eyes.

When she saw me coming she turned away from me with a moan. 'We laughed!' she got out at last in a whisper of awe and shame. 'He's dead, and we laughed! We're ill, we're damned, we'd laugh at anything!'

In vain I told her to let herself off, that it was perfectly natural, I even ventured to say that Henry would have been the first to understand and even join in. . . . Stupid of me, for she froze like a rock at the words and said coldly, 'Don't talk about him like that as if he were alive. He's dead and finished.'

I left her alone for a while after that, but when I saw that she was not able to forgive herself I tackled her again. It was two weeks or so later, and she was much calmer, but it was an icy, lifeless sort of calm, and she answered with no hint of emotion, 'It's strange, but any time I've allowed myself to feel superior to anybody, about anything, it's always been proved to me later that I am no better, or am even worse than they are. I used to despise my acquaintances in London because nothing was serious to them, nothing shocked them, nothing really mattered to them, and the sign of this was—they laughed, they laughed at everything, they made jokes about everything —God, the bomb, the First World War, Belsen, cruelty to children, cancer. They say it's the English saving grace, but I think it's our current vice. I loathe it. And yet at Henry's funeral, with him being burnt, I laughed. I laughed at nothing, at something not at all funny: his Cockney father who had dressed in the best he could hire or buy for the occasion. I didn't look at his face, because his tears would have shattered me; I looked at his feet—and I laughed. And so I'm just like those others. No better than those repulsive cynics and shallow gigglers. I degraded my goodbye to Henry to that level, because I just hadn't the *depth* to cope with so much sorrow. That's what's hard to face.'

There followed an awful period, still blacked-out in memory, when Dottie and I had to struggle along somehow with the shop, which chose that moment to start doing such good business that we couldn't abandon it as we both wanted to, and just go into retreat.

But Dottie suddenly took against it. It must have been because her passion for it had prevented her being with Henry, looking after him, during the last weeks of his life, and I suppose she began to feel about it as a man might feel about a tawdry, ravishing mistress who has kept him from his sick wife's bedside until it's too late. Anyway, she began to hate the place, and to curse it instead of cherishing it as she had before. First the little necessary extra bits of effort were dropped, then gradually she began positively to neglect the essential work. If we hadn't had the Heal's contract by that time, I really think the whole thing would just have folded; but that side of it had somehow become my baby, and I managed, despite a few initial blunders, and with Dottie's increasingly desultory but nonetheless vital help and advice, to keep this up and make a go of it.

I think it was the saving of me; quite incredible how the gods of fortune will help you sometimes when you most need it. I clearly remember one extraordinary coincidence, which was that the day of Toby's wedding to Whistler—a huge splashy affair in some big synagogue near Marble Arch, all so dreadfully un-him that I immediately felt an air of doom over the marriage—was the day the 'Us and Them' boutique opened on Heal's first floor, so I simply didn't have time to feel anything about the wedding. And that night, which I had thought would be a major private hell (deep down somewhere in my subconscious, Toby was still mine in the most primitive physical way) I slept like the dead and my imagination with me. By the next morning the worst was over, though even the best of that little lot was not very funny, and the pain—dull, but constant—went on literally for months.

About now Dottie grew downright impossible; she withdrew; she grew surly, sulky, bad-mannered, bad-tempered. She was not drinking, but she behaved as if she were. She did as little work as possible, and that with very bad grace. Her contacts with suppliers fell off, and I found myself having to make furtive journeys round the countryside renewing them and often having to smooth out rudenesses or bad impressions

Dottie had left, either by unanswered letters, unpaid bills, or hasty visits made in a bad mood.

As to her relations with me, they were all right at first—I never took her to task about her failure to pull her weight in the shop, I felt it was only fair after all the months when *I* hadn't, and anyway I understood only too well what was the matter with her. But suddenly one horrible evening she turned on me over supper.

There was no warning; we were just sitting there eating in what I had fondly supposed was a mutually sympathetic silence, when she abruptly looked at me and said icily, 'I must ask you to stop apologizing for me.' I was completely taken aback; I really didn't know what she meant. Though I happened to have spent most of the previous week doing just that, I had no idea that she knew it. There followed an awful sort of one-sided row, with me being very pacific and she getting angrier and wilder until I realized that my lack of appropriate reaction was only making her worse. Then I let myself start shouting too. It was as calculated as that, to begin with; but fatal of course, because as soon as I let go of the tight rein I had had myself on, I found out that I really had been resenting her behaviour, although I had thought I was being so damned Christian and noble about understanding it.

To excuse myself a little for losing my temper as I very shortly did with her, I have to say I was functioning under some considerable strain myself; Henry had been dead barely six weeks, Toby married less than three; and I was feeling the full brunt of running a business and raising a baby for the first time virtually without any support or help from anyone.

The end of it was almost unbearably ugly. Suddenly I saw that it wasn't just a row, she was actively hating me. I stopped shouting and asked what was really the matter? Whereupon she started shaking all over and her face went foreign; I can't think of another word to describe it; I hardly recognized even her *type* for that moment. And then she screamed something mercifully incoherent into my face, and after that. . . . Well, after that she began to hit her head against the wall and smack her own face over and over again and I was so horrified and shocked that it was several minutes before I could do anything about it. I'll never forget the feeling of her wrist when I caught hold of it, it was completely rigid and as strong as iron, she just kept slapping and slapping herself viciously, and I remember shouting at her, 'Slap *me*! Slap *me*!' and frantically trying to redirect her hand. I can't bear to think about it, even now.

She collapsed in the end, teeth chattering, face all shades of grey, eyes rolling, sweat standing out all over her. . . . I put coats over her and called a doctor, but by the time he came she'd recovered a bit and I'd managed to get her upstairs to bed. He gave her a sedative and told me it looked like the onset of a nervous breakdown, which is what it was, of course; I should have seen she was heading for one but I didn't know what a nervous breakdown really was until then.

Later that night—I was sitting beside her bed, frightened to leave her alone although she was fast asleep—she suddenly came wide awake for a few minutes and stared straight at me through the half-darkness and said, 'Did you sleep with him?' 'No,' I said. 'Swear it.' 'I do swear it.' 'How can I be sure? How can I ever be sure? I know you wanted him. If he refused me and took you——' She broke off with a sort of sudden crack like a branch breaking, and instantly closed her eyes and fell asleep again.

So that was it, and I hadn't properly understood after all, until that moment.

She was laid up for a long time and I tried to look after her and run the shop. I couldn't, naturally enough, so I compromised by getting a nurse in, and also engaging an assistant for the shop, a wretched brainless little girl who was the best I could get for what I could afford to pay. She distinguished herself the first week by breaking a supposedly unbreakable casserole, losing two important customers through sheer incompetence and—as I discovered much later—laying the foundations for a profitable sideline, pinching half-crowns from the petty cash.

The nurse was little more successful; she was efficient but chilly, and Dottie just lay there and didn't even look at her. I began to have terrible fears about the actual extent of her breakdown, remembering that moment when I had not recognized her eyes or her face. She was certainly mad at that second.

Sometimes when she withdrew and couldn't be roused, I really feared for her reason. At that time I remembered nothing but good of her, her sweetness, her inexhaustible energy, her irrepressible wit and good cheer and—I knew it all the time— her genuine love for me which had lasted over years of rough going for one or other of us.

I would sit in the evenings and do my accounts on the end of her bed, while she sat propped against her pillows and smoked and seemed either a little nearer or a little further away, according to some inner syndrome which I never fully understood or could predict. She never linked Henry's and my names again.

Once I was working and she suddenly leaned right forward in bed and put her hand over mine as I was writing figures; I looked up and she was gazing at me with an extraordinary expression of tenderness and regret. . . . I jumped up at once and went to hug her. I thought in that moment everything was better, but I found it wasn't that simple. That impulse, that look, the gesture even, had been, as it were, sent through some kind of barrier, the barrier of her illness, and when I tried to get close to her, physically and mentally, the gate clanged almost in my face and she pushed me away, her eyes tightly shut as if something had escaped from them while she wasn't on her guard.

That whole time—the time following Henry's death, Toby's marriage and Dottie's breakdown—was a time of seasoning and trial for me. That I have never worked so hard, or felt so deeply, or travelled as far in an inward fashion, hardly needs saying. And all the time, except when I visited London on business, I was living in the same tucked-away little backwater. Addy's cottage was my home and my retreat, though it had lost its feeling of safety since Dottie had lodged herself and her strangeness like a cuckoo's egg within it. I realize now that, although I never acknowledged it at the time, I was more than a little afraid of her then. It was almost a superstitious fear, as if I half-expected her to metamorphose again into a wild-eyed stranger; yet I never cared for her so much, nor so strongly sensed in her a desperate dependence on me. Sometimes this would show itself as simply and directly as it would have done with a child; she would look at me as I brought her a meal or helped her to dress (she was physically very weak at first) and say 'Thank you, Jane' over and over again, very softly and politely. At other times she would suddenly get panicky for no special reason and say 'Don't leave me, will you?' in the sort of voice she might have used if she'd been hanging over a cliff.

Even as she began to get better, and some of her old independence and spirit returned, she would still have moments of humble and embarrassing gratitude to me, speaking as if I'd saved her life. She never, at any time, then or since, referred to the scene in the kitchen. I've always hoped she doesn't remember it.

During her illness, I really think David was of more active, therapeutic help to her than either I or the doctor or any other single factor. At first I tried to keep him out of the room, for fear of disturbing her, but one day he wandered in by himself and when I went looking for him I found she'd pulled him up on the bed with her. He was lying with her, stomach to stomach, and they were pulling faces at each other, and he was laughing and saying 'More! More!' When I lifted him off, he reached for her and said her name, I think for the first time. Later when I came back to her alone, I heard her from outside the door repeating, with his inflection, 'Do-tie. Do-tie.' When I came in, I found she was crying. It was the first time since the funeral—months. The doctor had said, 'Where are her tears? That's what she needs, she needs to cry, healthy tears, you understand.' And there they were, gently washing those hard, dry, wild eyes as she said her own name over and over again.

After that I let him go in and play with her as often as he wanted to. She cried often, just cried for no special reason when he was with her or after he'd gone, and the doctor when I told him said 'Good.' And it was.

It was a long time before she asked about the shop, but she often talked about Addy's four hundred pounds. It was odd about that. I'd given it up—sacrificed it, as I then thought— for the shop, and relinquished my cherished dreams of a trip to New York. But it had all been, as it were, an empty gesture. When Dottie asked for the money, and I gave it to her, neither of us had stopped to realize that Henry, with his inveterate providence and good sense, had long before taken the precaution of covering the premises with every known kind of insurance. The four hundred was used up in immediate costs, for Dottie got cracking the very next day at putting the shop back in order and we had very little in the kitty by then; but when the insurance people paid up, which they did quite quickly, Henry insisted that I should take it back. It was very ironic, because there was still time for me to go to New York for Addy's book, if I hurried; but by then Henry was already ill, Dottie working desperately, and just in case I had been in any sort of doubt or temptation (which I really wasn't) David developed something-or-other, I've forgotten what, and couldn't possibly have either come with me or been left behind. So there the £400 still was, sitting in my bank, and when I thought of it it was as if Addy's ghost was waiting for me to do something with it. I'd told Dottie long ago about Addy's ghost, and she had readily appreciated the non-serious, emotional side of it. The truly metaphysical side, the moments when I almost believed in Addy as a tangible presence, had merely embarrassed her, so I never mentioned it again.

Now in her sleep or in moments of drowsiness when her 'dope' as she called it was beginning to function, she would ramble on about 'Addy's four hundred' and ask me repeatedly what I was going to do with it, sometimes sounding as if it were a matter of urgent personal importance to herself that I should make a decision. Sometimes she would make little anxious jokes: 'Addy's waiting, isn't she? She's waiting for you to decide. You mustn't disappoint her.' And once she startled me by saying quite seriously, 'She hates money being left to rot.'

At last I said that I thought I'd better sink it in the shop after all—it had been very hard, during the ups and downs of my first months of serious involvement in the business, *not* to use it. But to my surprise. Dottie was quite vehement.

'No!' she said. 'Not the shop. The shop mustn't drink everything up. Addy likes the idea of New York.' She smiled. 'She said she always wanted to go there, didn't she?'

'Not to me.'

She looked at me oddly for a moment, and said, 'I thought you told me——' After a while she turned away her face, and reached for a cigarette. 'I'm sure it should be New York,' she said.

'But I don't even want to go to New York now.'

'Don't you?'

'No. The shop——'

'The shop, the shop! Can't you think of anything but the shop?'

'You couldn't, for ages.'

She didn't reply. 'Sublimation,' she said at last. 'Is it that for you too, I wonder, poor Jane?'

I hadn't told her a word about Toby; I hadn't mentioned him for many weeks. Yet at that moment I felt she knew that he was—'lost and gone forever', almost as much as Henry was for her.

Addy's book came out, finally, in the autumn of that year, and it got a very few, very wonderful notices in some obscure highbrow magazines. The *New York Times* Book Review gave it a glancing notice, the key-word in which was 'esoteric', which, Billie wrote to me, was the kiss of death of any hope of popular success. 'Not that I ever expected it from those epic-minded morons,' she concluded furiously. But Dottie, who had just read the book for the first time, simply said, 'Oh, never mind. It's far too good for me, and for most people. Popular successes are for craftsmen. Addy's not even an artist. I think perhaps she's a sort of genius, or a saint.' She kept the book beside her and read bits of it again and again. I did too.

The book itself was beautiful, a wonderfully simple cover in pale shiny sea-green and gold. I was sure Addy would have been pleased.

And so the winter set in again, and Mrs Griffiths, whose attendance had been spasmodic during the nicer weather, became steady again, an infinite help with the house-cleaning and fire-making and even cooking, which I had no time for any more. I had perforce to leave her alone with Dottie a good deal and I took her aside and urged her most strongly not to say anything that might upset or distress Dottie in any way —no gloomy stories or chalk-pit workers. 'Oh my dear, I know the poor thing's not well in her head,' she replied. 'Of course

I won't upset her. I only hope no one else'll mention Mr Stephens to her.' Mr Stephens had been taken to hospital and was in a geriatric ward. It was not this bare fact so much that Mrs Griffiths kindly wanted to protect Dottie from; it was the truly awful stories that Mrs Stephens was telling around the village about the way 'they' treated him there. She was afraid to complain too much, or have rows with the nurses, because the old man had whispered to her that they 'took it out' on the patients if their families complained. I saw Mrs Stephens myself very often—she was still living in the back of the burnt-out post office; she was dreadfully unhappy, and would have had Mr Stephens back again whatever the risk, but the doctors wouldn't allow it. 'The only times I can be peaceful within myself,' she once told me, 'is when I can make myself believe that he's wandering when he tells me these horrible things. They can't be true, oh, they can't, nobody could be so cruel! But then how could he imagine anything like that? Sometimes I think it's all a judgement on me for what I said to him, the night of the fire.' And her fingers would begin to snap for Muffer to come to her side and be stroked, while the tears ran down her cheeks—'I'm sorry, dear, I'm sorry, I'm sure I shouldn't cry, you've got your own worries and troubles, I know. . . .' Seeing her did me good in the dreadful way of putting my own petty despairs into perspective, for what she was going through literally seemed to me the worst thing in the world.

During the winter there was not so much trade in the shop, but more in London, and I had to travel up and down a good deal. The Galloping Maggot had finally gone home, so I used Dottie's car. I didn't have to serve in the boutique, just take the stuff up, arrange it, and have discussions with the sales staff and so on. I managed to conceal most of my total ignorance for the first little while, living, as it were, on the quality of the merchandise and Dottie's hints, which I threw out in a casual way to impress them all with my apparent business acumen and originality.

After a while I began to gain a little experience of my own. I never developed, and never will develop, anything approaching Dottie's flair; but a workaday ability to keep my head above water in the commercial millrace was quite an achievement for someone like me. And what was more important in a way, I began to enjoy it. The moment that that happened, everything became a little easier, even the erstwhile intolerable aches left over from Henry and Toby.

I nearly always tried to see John whenever I was in town, and several times we had a meal together. He was doing neither specially well nor badly; his life just seemed to jog on. He had managed to get a room to himself, mainly because his two unsavoury room-mates had gone their several ways and he had to come to an arrangement with his landlord to pay a bit extra to keep other tenants out. He had rearranged the room, which was now an enlarged version of his 'box' in Doris's house—all the walls were covered with a dense, vibrant montage of posters, bits of fabric, newspaper cuttings, pin-ups black and white, male and female—a sort of glorious indiscriminate paper love-in. I added several items to his collection, including some of our carrier bags and some tea-towels which were now one of our lines, plus remnants whenever I had them to spare, though I had most of them made into patchwork cushion-covers or toys. His furniture was mostly either wicker, or metal, except the bed-head, which was a vast baroque thing he had picked up in a junk-yard, all carved with broken birds and fruit and bells and painted a bright, shiny mixture of colours—it was very psychedelic, at a time when that word hadn't been thought of. In fact the whole room was a sort of 'happening'; one had to narrow one's eyes and one's sensibilities whenever one entered, or be dazzled and almost intoxicated with all that chaos of colour John himself began to dress in a very far-out way, in what I then thought of as Caribbean clothes—bright yellow slacks, pink or orange shirts, even coloured canvas shoes. The effect was startling, but, once one's eyes had accustomed themselves, funny and pleasing.

John's and my relationship never changed, never varied, and hasn't until this day. I look upon it now as the one steady, reliable thing in my life. (Other than David; and I can't, I dare not, really count him. More and more I'm convinced that it is fatal, almost wicked, to depend on one's children; it's bad enough that they depend on you.) I'm ashamed now to remember that at first I was embarrassed to have John come down to the cottage. He looked pretty outrageous even in

London, before it began to swing; imagine how he looked to an ultra-conservative country village. It was Dottie who finally insisted that I invite him, and furthermore, go up to town and fetch him. She needed to see him, she said, when I had described him and his abode to her. So I brought him, and in the event of course it was not embarrassing at all; true, every eye in the high-street turned as we walked or drove along it. I was less susceptible to public opinion than I had thought, and not merely didn't care, but rather revelled in it; and John simply didn't notice.

Dottie, when we arrived, was downstairs—very unusual for her, she spent most of the time in bed, or at least in her room; but she was dressed and lying on the sofa. The effort this must have cost her surprised me (all this for John?). She actually stood up when we came in, and shook hands with him and led him to a chair, and then I noticed she had prepared a drink for him and everything, it was really quite astonishing—I mean, she'd only seen him about twice before in her life, and here she was, receiving him according to the first of her proverbial guest-categories ('There are three kinds of guests, honoured, tolerated, and bloody nuisances'). They sat down together like old friends and began at once to talk about Dottie's state of health, a subject I had strictly forbidden him to touch on, but she started it.

'I've been ill,' she said without preamble.

'Not hard to see that,' he said. 'What the matter with you?'

'Didn't Jane tell you?'

'She tell me you had a nervous breakdown.' I sucked in my breath. To my knowledge, the words had never been spoken in Dottie's presence till then. 'But I dunno what it is,' he added.

'It's like—if all the strings on your guitar went pop at once.'

'Ah. No music after—uh?'

She shook her head. 'Only jangling and banging.'

'Sort of like being crazy?'

'Very like it.'

'My Mama went crazy,' said John matter-of-factly.

'Did they put her away?' I stiffened in my corner, because I thought I heard a thin, panicky note in Dottie's voice, but it may have been just the contrast with John, who had spoken entirely casually.

'No, and you know why? Because we never told anyone. We just kept her with us. She wasn't mad, you see, she was just crazy. Didn't want to hurt nobody. Wanted to be different people. So we let her be whoever she wanted, and we kinda—loved her, and after a bit . . . she came back. And nobody ever knew.'

'How long was she like that?'

He shrugged. Time never meant a thing to John. 'Dunno. A year—two years maybe. Yeh, it must've been two years, with the time it took her to come back. That took a long time, till she was really Mama.'

'It's funny,' said Dottie. 'Even when I was at my worst'—she glanced at me, and away again—'I never wanted to be anyone but me.'

'You got a different kind then, I guess,' said John placidly. His brilliant shirt stood out fantastically against the worn, darkened floral linen of Addy's old armchair, like a bird of paradise in an old apple tree. He settled his back more comfortably, took a big swig of his drink, and grinned at Dottie. 'Me, I kinda like crazy people. Now, you take Doris. She wasn't at *all* crazy. But Mavis was a little, with all those things she had in her room, and the cat and all that. And as much as she was crazy, I liked her. And Toby. That cat was real crazy—wasn't he, Janie? In them days when we was all together? That was a crazy time, and I was never so happy like them.' He shook his head, fondly and reminiscently.

'I wish I'd been with you in that house,' Dottie said suddenly.

'Yeh man, that was a time all right!' He smiled tenderly at me, and then jumped up. 'Hey though! Where is he—that baby you had in you belly, where's that crazy baby shared all them good times with us?'

When he saw David, he carried on as if he'd never seen anything like him in the whole of his life. He danced, he shouted, he capered and sang; he lay down on the floor and rolled about, just as he used to roll on my rug in the L-shaped room. David fell in love with him—all of him, his woolly head, his black shining face, his expanse of teeth, his pink palms, his

Caribbean clothes. We couldn't drag them apart. John had to carry David to bed at last, and I didn't even get a goodnight. I left them alone in David's room, John singing and playing the bongo drums on David's tummy, to his utterable enchantment.

I went down to Dottie, who was lying on the sofa smoking and looking quietly at nothing as she often did. But she turned to me the moment I came in, and smiled one of her old, vivid smiles.

'What a wonderful, wonderful, wonderful person,' she said. Her voice, for the first time, sounded completely normal.

So Dottie got better. As John said, it took a long time till she was really Dottie. I helped, David helped, John helped, time helped—and in the end, she began to help herself, and at last one evening she came into the kitchen, put on an apron briskly and said, 'I'm making supper tonight, you must be whacked.' I was; I'd been in town in the morning, and in the shop all afternoon. But still I was doubtful, and she saw it, and said, 'Look at me, and don't worry any more. I'm cured.'

'Still. Take it easy.'

'I don't want to. When I was well, I never took it easy. If I take it easy now, I won't feel I'm well. And I've got to feel I'm well. One can't be a nervous wreck forever.' We looked at each other, she with an odd shyness which I had never seen in her before, and I searchingly, trying to see if this long-dreamt-of recovery was real or only a phase of the illness. And then suddenly we were hugging each other in the rather embarrassed, awkward way of women. 'All right then,' I said. 'The steak's in the fridge.'

'Have we any champagne?'

'No, sorry. I didn't have notice you were going to be cured today.'

'In that case, I'll stay crazy until opening time tomorrow.' We both laughed; I felt a surge of wild relief. At last, at last she was better! And hot on the heels of that unselfish thought, came the selfish one—at last I'm not entirely alone!

During that meal, which was a celebration even without the champagne, we talked as we had never talked before about the shop. I say never before, because in the early days it was all one sided, Dottie had all the enthusiasm, all the ideas; I was simply a sounding-board. Then, when in recent months I had desperately wanted to talk to *her*, she hadn't been there properly. Now at last some of her interest revived, we could begin to exchange true—and literal—shop-talk. I had so much to tell her; once I started, I couldn't stop. I put her to sleep eventually, poor girl. And after she'd gone to bed, and I was still lying awake, feeling terribly excited and stimulated, I had a wonderful vision of what was ahead for us—the first really cheerful, hopeful thoughts I had entertained for longer than I could clearly remember. Dottie and I would be real partners now; I had served my apprenticeship and could work with her on an even footing. The business now mattered to me as much as to her, and I knew almost as much about it. There seemed no reason at all why we shouldn't make a real success of it between us. And as for our mutual personal problem—to wit, men—in that elevated moment of anticipated happiness, there was no room for doubts. My old conviction returned to me full force—once one achieves self-reliance, once one has overcome the *need* for men, that's when they come, usually in droves.

I laughed into my pillow, fell asleep and dreamed of David, grown tall and handsome, making love to me . . . horrors! But I woke the next morning laughing because it was so obvious and Freudian, and I felt so happy suddenly, I felt that I, too, had been cured. . . .

This lovely feeling went on for several days—a week. I shared everything with Dottie, every titbit, every tiny incident to do with the shop, all the stored-up bits of gossip about the various suppliers' personal lives—I never seemed to stop talking, and Dottie listened, as I had once listened. . . . Our roles were completely and exactly reversed. Dottie was now the stay-at-home partner, cooking the meals, looking after the baby, taking phone-calls (we had a phone in the cottage now) and occasionally going to see people, though she said she didn't feel very good at that yet and I didn't encourage it. And I was the active one, rushing hither and yon all day and bringing my work home with me at night. I was only waiting for the day when she would volunteer to come with me to the shop, I could hardly wait to show her all I had done there, and for the delight of seeing her properly back in harness. I felt certain that as soon as she stepped inside the doors, her old passionate involvement would grip her again and she would instantly begin to flash round the place in her old way, upbraiding me for missing possibilities, re-arranging everything, asking all the questions that she still hadn't, somehow, asked. . . . Only when she did all this, would I be convinced that 'Mama had come back.'

After about a fortnight, I could stand it no longer.

'Today you're coming with me to the shop,' I said one morning over the usual hasty breakfast.

She stopped eating and looked at her plate for a moment, and I felt a physical qualm of uneasiness amounting to fear; not mine, but hers. Then she looked up with a quick smile and said, 'All right. It's time, isn't it?'

She was perfectly silent during the drive. I thought, she's worried about the changes, about what I'll have done to it. I rattled on, 'Look, love, don't be afraid to tell me where I've gone wrong. I've learnt a lot, but I'll never have your touch. You'll probably have to set the whole display to rights. I won't mind—honestly.' She didn't respond, and somehow my heart sank.

When we got to the shop, I didn't open up at once; we stood in front of the window, gazing in at the window-dressing, or rather she gazed at it and I gazed at her, trying to gauge her reaction. Her face was bleak; nothing came alive in it, neither satisfaction nor annoyance, and no excitement either, not a flicker.

'What do you think?' I asked at last, with forced cheerfulness. 'Not bad for a beginner? But you must re-do it.' She turned away from the window abruptly. 'Let's go in, it's cold out here,' she said, with a little shiver.

I unlocked the door and there was a whole silly shambles about who should go in first. I felt my nerves getting more and more on edge. Finally I walked in past her, and she followed slowly, looking round. 'Just wander round, get the feel of it again,' I urged her. She moved round indeed, but with a timid air, and when she touched things it was tentatively, without a trace of her old authority, rather like the sort of customer who has to buy a present for someone and hasn't a clue what to get. After a bit she turned to me and said, with a little sharpness, 'Please don't stand there looking at me. It makes me nervous.' I at once went into the back and busied myself there; I unpacked some new stuff, and when I had it dusted —and, incidentally, had made some coffee—I called her in.

'Dottie! Come through and see something.'

When she began to walk through, I realized suddenly that I hadn't heard a sound from her, not a footstep, since I left her; it was rather uncanny, as if she hadn't moved at all. Her face looked a bit white as she came in, and she didn't look at me directly.

'Look!' I said.

She approached the table slowly and picked up one of the pieces. It was the latest of Ron's things, now rapidly developing into one of our most exciting lines.

'I didn't tell you because I wanted to surprise you,' I said. 'But Ron's stuff is among the most successful at Heal's—they're crazy about him. He's quit his job in the factory and gone into this full-time—spent his savings in his own little foundry. I went up to see him not long ago. I so agree with you about him. He told me his wife nearly ran away from him when he left his steady job, but she's dead proud of him now he's doing so well—he's selling stuff privately too, and beginning to get overseas orders.' Dottie still said nothing, but stood turning the smooth glass round and round in her hands. 'You did that,' I said quietly. 'You brought him out and made him an artist. You've done that to quite a lot of people. Aren't you pleased with yourself? Don't you feel satisfied?'

Suddenly I saw that she was crying. 'My God, what's the matter?' I asked in dismay.

'I don't—feel—anything,' she managed to say, with great difficulty. 'That's all. Even about this—even this. Nothing, Jane. Just—sad, sad, sad.' She put the glass piece down and turned away, holding her face in her hands. I went to her and held her. 'It's gone,' she sobbed. 'That lovely excitement, that purpose and direction—I remember it, but now it's all left me. I've gone cold on it. I've even lost that! Oh God, I'm so lonely!'

I forget now which of us made the suggestion. Perhaps neither of us had to actually say it. It was hanging in the air between us for a long time, anyway, before it was mentioned. And then, suddenly, we were talking about it, and Dottie was showing animation for the first time in many long, weary, empty winter weeks.

'But it's your money,' she kept saying. 'Addy left it to you. How could I take it?' And yet, she spoke without conviction, for the sake of form, and I knew even then that she would take it; it was as if she had received some sanction which I knew nothing about. Because when I finally said, 'I'm sure this is what Addy would want,' she fell silent and looked at me gratefully, as if she had been waiting for me to understand something.

I was much more concerned about how she would manage over there on her own. Once I wouldn't have thought twice about it; I might rather have worried about how New York would stand up to her impact. Now she was undeniably changed; she was weaker, less sure of herself.

'What will you do over there?'

'I can't tell you yet. But something will present itself.' There was a graininess in her voice that reassured me a little. It was important that she felt a strong urge to go; it was the lack of strong urges in her life that had been, for these past weeks, the principle cause of her underlying fear and inability to come to grips with anything.

I watched her preparations to leave with a heart of solid lead. Glad though I had to be that she had found something she really wanted to do, I could not help crying inwardly after the hopes I had had for her partnership, companionship and help; nor could I completely withstand the terror of being left all on my own to run the business without her. I didn't in the least see how I could; I would have to find someone else; but at the moment, the mere thought of doing that was as untenable as the thought of re-marriage is to a widow at the funeral.

And ironically, it was only now that I suddenly saw Dottie doing all the things I had hoped for as far as the shop was concerned. Gradually roused from her lethargy by the notion, and then the definite prospect, of going to New York, she began one day to reorganize everything; she rearranged the displays from top to bottom, saying as she moved about in her old decisive way, 'Do forgive me, Jane; it's not that yours aren't wonderful; but they're *yours*, and if I'm ever going to get work in New York I have to be able to show people something that's *mine*.'

What she was doing, then, was setting things up for professional photographs; and when these were taken, she put her hands on her hips and said, 'There! Now let's put it all back the way it was.'

'No! Are you crazy?' I asked. 'It's ten times better like this.'

'Look, Jane,' she said quietly. ' "Us and Them" is yours now. It's all yours. You can do it, I know you can. Only you must do it in your own way, not by copying me.' And she forced me to let her put it all back. And that was the last time she ever set foot in the shop.

She left a week later. She went by boat, the cheapest way possible, in order to save money to live on when she got there. She travelled on an immigrant's visa so that she could get work. That was the only reason, she said. 'Good lord, can you see me turning into an American?' I couldn't, but if I had been there with her these five years, I would have been able to watch the process; in two more months she is taking out citizenship papers.

To be brief, then: in American parlance, she made it, and made it good. One might have expected it to be tough at first; but she never looked back. The first week, she got a job in the best shop in town, as a salesgirl in the department which sold English porcelain—it was her accent, she said, which got her the job; but it was her acumen and flair which kept it for her and got her promoted to head of the department inside of a year. Her salary was fabulous by our standards, but the cost of living was enough to devour it all—or would have been; but something happened which meant that most of her income went straight into savings.

I still have the letter she wrote me when it started—it arrived about eight months after she left England.

'I've met someone,' she wrote, 'whom it seems a good idea for me to live with. We've been sleeping together on and off for quite a while now, and he's keen that we should set up house together on—well, I was going to say on a permanent basis, but nothing's ever that, especially not in New York. Why not marry him, did I hear you ask? Well, it's odd about that. First of all, it's decidedly odd that such an *apparently* nice bit of Adam's-flesh is not married already (he *was*, of course; every man in America who isn't a raving queer or a monster—and plenty who are—have been married sometime). So one can't avoid suspecting a few unpleasant revelations sooner or later. And it's even odder that he should, as a matter of fact, actually have asked me. But the oddest thing of all, I suppose, is that I've refused for the paradoxical reason that I seem to be too old-fashioned in my outlook to get married to a man who tried to persuade me to it by remarking, "What are you worrying about? If it doesn't work out, we can easily get divorced." No, don't be put off him by that, or I'll be sorry I mentioned it. He's very sweet, very male (I think, though one's becoming desperately wary—the heartier they look, the softer can often be the marshmallow centre of their Mom-complexes) and very, very attractive. And there's another thing. Living alone for a woman in this city is just sheer hell, if only because of the others who are doing it. They are the unhappiest, sickest sisterhood in the whole world. . . . And then there are the wolves that prey on them—on *us*. Oh yes, yes, there are wolves in England, too. The difference is that over there, they at least have the grace to pretend that you'd be doing *them* a favour. Here, they make it thoroughly clear that they regard it as the other way round. I've never had this feeling of needing to—well, in the old novels they used to call it "placing oneself under a man's protection." In order to achieve this nowadays you have to place yourself under *him* as well, which in the present instance, I must admit, is not the worst part of the bargain. And who knows? One day I might lose my conviction of the impermanence of relationships, and he might lose faith in the all-curing cheap panacea of divorce. . . . Till then, we will each have someone to come home to. My God, aren't I picking up American! Soon you'll hear me drawling (or drooling) about Mrs Wagner's pies and those that pray together stay together.'

My first reaction to this letter was, that it was a vindication of Henry and his rigorous refusal to make love to Dottie. I had thought until then that he had been wrong; especially when I saw, after his death, that Dottie could hardly have been more deeply involved either way than she was, nor could her reaction to his death have been more violent. Yet the relative speed of her recovery—well under a year—proved to me, knowing her as well as I did, that Henry had been right after all.

Bill turned out to be more than a passing refuge. Their relationship developed as these things ought to, slowly and steadily, and now I'm convinced from her more recent letters that they will get married one of these days; 'I can't go on all my life being satisfied with godmotherhood-by-remote-control.'

As for her professional life, it is blooming. About two years ago she and Bill, who is a designer and graphic artist, pooled their joint financial resources and 'leaked', as she put it, 'drop by drop into the interior decorating business.' First a poorish friend's old house; then a richer friend's new house; then the flat of someone who wasn't a friend but had seen one of the other interiors they'd done. Then it snowballed; they had to take on an office, an assistant; in no time at all, Dottie was flying round as of old, making her proverbial 'contacts' over an ever-growing area which, when I last heard, stretched from Buffalo to Martha's Vineyard. 'It's a somewhat larger beat than Surrey,' she remarked dryly. 'At this rate I'll soon need my own aeroplane.' It would never surprise me to hear she'd got one.

And a few months ago, she mailed me a cheque for the exact equivalent of four hundred pounds. . . .

As for myself, I've managed. More than that it would be difficult to claim. David is six, and sturdy, and sweet, and sound as a bell—so far. The shop is a going concern; it is still partly thanks to Dottie, whose long arm appears from time to time in the form of imported handicrafts from places like Nantucket—all a little weird; wall-hangings made of string, table-tops of concrete with the bottoms of bottles embedded in it, or strange musical toys called 'whimmy-diddles' which make marvellous conversation-pieces but which nobody can play. They add an exotic note to the displays, but they sell better in London, where people's tastes are more eccentric and less practical. Another way Dottie still participates is by sending me rich and glamorous transatlantic customers. Many's the travellers' cheque that has dropped into the till from some bejewelled hand, into which, earlier, Dottie had pressed one of our flamboyant cards, with which I keep her well-supplied. 'I forget where we picked this up, but whoever gave it to us was most insistent that we should pay you a visit. . . .' And Jo and I exchange knowing smiles.

Ah yes—Jo. Well, Jo is my partner. After Ted died, which he did about a year and a half after Henry, Jo, who had always kept in touch, but sporadically, because of Ted's long illness, simply arrived one day with her station-wagon loaded with stuff and Amanda bound into the front seat with a safety belt. Jo looked older, and richer, and at the same time, softer. 'Ted's dead,' she said shortly, and turned her eyes away. 'No, don't say anything. Lots of people thought I married him for this moment. . . . He's dead, and Amanda and I are on our tod and we can't stick it, either of us. We miss him so *bloody* much, it's unbelievable. . . . Can we stay with you for a bit? Amanda can muck in with David, I've brought her a bed, and I'm prepared to sleep on the floor.'

Real desperation had broken up all her smooth, well-groomed, self-contained lines. I wasn't such a stranger to her feelings and situation that I could fail to make her welcome. Amanda 'mucked in' admirably; she's a bit older than David, but at three that really didn't count for much, and she was just what he needed. The very day after they arrived, we began to make plans. The kids would go off to the local play-school; I'd been meaning to send David, but he hadn't seemed keen. However, Amanda had been going for half a year, and soon convinced him that life without a play-school was unthinkable. Jo came down to the shop, moved her hands and eyes lovingly all over everything, and then said, 'Why don't I be your assistant?'

I stared at her. It seemed too good to be true! This chic, effectual creature, so alive, so attractive, was the next-best thing to Dottie that I could conceive of. 'If you have any doubts about meaning that,' I said cautiously, 'you'd better take it back, before I chain you up.'

Within a few months, it was all fixed and working like a charm. She was too wise to settle down in the cottage, although

244

it was perfectly pleasant and workable while it lasted, and we were both so damned lonely at the time that I was tempted to implore her to stay on. But she bought a house not far away; we did it up between us and she and Amanda moved into it. We saw each other daily, and the kids became—and have remained—great friends. They are currently engaged to be married, and are planning a wedding trip to Africa in David's toy helicopter to bring back animals, including two mature alligators ('to eat people with') and a boa-constrictor.

After a year, when I saw that she was serious and not merely seeking a temporary palliative, I asked Jo to go into partnership. Since then money has more or less ceased to be a worry, as far as the shop is concerned, and we've been able to expand. When Mr Stephens died, Mrs Stephens went into an old people's home, and the shattered remains of the post office came on the market. Jo went out one morning and bought it—just like that. She actually came home at lunchtime with a bag of groceries, from which she took various things, saying as she did so, 'Here's the peanut butter, and the jam, and the sponge, and the bacon, oh, and I've bought the post office too.'

I jibbered a bit at first, I didn't see how we could handle anything as big as the shop would now be; but it was a variation on Parkinson's Law; as soon as we'd moved into it we started wondering where the hell we'd squeezed everything in before.

Of course it all took time; the whole front had to be rebuilt and combined with our building. It was another year before the new frontage was ready, with a fanlight door in the middle, the 'Us' on the left, the 'Them' on the right, and the 'and' curving round the top of the fanlight. I took endless colour slides of it to send to Dottie, and she wrote back saying, 'I can't say much except smarm. The fact is, I'm nearly sick with something that feels very like jealousy. But good luck to you both. . . . Don't forget I started it.'

One of the ambiguous beauties of half-combining my family with Jo's is that both are fatherless. In many ways, of course, at least one man about the place could be a boon to us both, and we have often discussed the desirability of one of us marrying someone whom both of us could exploit, not sexually of course, but as a general injector of masculinity into the children's surroundings. But no such person has appeared, though Jo has had several near-misses and even I have had a few offers—three to be exact—one David hated, and one Jo hated, and the third the others quite took to, but *I* couldn't stand him, so that was that.

But in actual fact, it has helped with David—the fact of Amanda not having a father either. It definitely postponed the dreaded hour when he asked the inevitable question, to an age where it was *somewhat* easier to give him an explanation which held water with him and was not too far removed from the truth. It came up at last when he was going on four, and had seriously begun visiting round among the other children at his kindergarten. It came out quite straight, just the way I'd spent four years imagining it, and I had my answer ready:

'Why haven't I got a daddy?'

'You have one.'

'Where is he?'

'He lives a long way away.'

'Why? Why isn't he with us?'

'Because he and Mummy aren't married.'

He didn't understand this, but accepted it for a while, though he asked the same series of questions several more times later. Then came:

'What does my daddy look like?'

I had a picture of Terry when we were in a play together, long ago, and I showed him that. Terry looked very nice in it, tall and thin and handsome in his 'gorgeous juve' make-up; the weak mouth and hands didn't show. David spent a long time looking at it; my heart bled, but I stood it because I knew it was just, and in any case only the very beginning.

'Is he good?' he asked then.

'Yes, I think so.'

Later: 'Will I see him ever?'

'Perhaps.'

'Where is he?'

'Far away.'

'Why does he never come?'

'He's very busy. Maybe he'll come one day.' What would he think if he knew I had put Terry off coming, right at the start—that Terry didn't even know our address? He might think that was the worst part of what I had done. Terry couldn't reach us even if he wanted to.

It was when David had asked, in that same plaintive voice, 'Why does he never come?' for about the sixth time, that I began to realize, belatedly, that Terry would have to come. I wouldn't have believed that all the pathetic little questions in the world could have brought me to think such a thing, but one cannot conceive in advance of what it does to one's personal inclinations and resolutions to have one's child ask that kind of question in that kind of voice.

'Amm's daddy's dead, isn't he?'

'Yes.'

'Is my daddy dead?'

'No, I think he's in Paris.'

'Paris is far away, isn't it?'

'Pretty far.'

'In the distance?'

'Yes.'

'But it's not as far as being dead?'

'No.'

'Will Amm see her daddy one day?'

'No, darling.'

'But I will, won't I?'

'Maybe. I can't promise.'

I knew nothing about Terry's life. It was five years since I had heard anything of him. I put off any decision about contacting him for the very reasonable reason that I didn't know how to. But in the end, the questions, gentle, repetitive, persistent, grew too much for me. I rang up his old office, to ask—just to enquire. I didn't give a name. He'd left that firm, and moved to another. I put off ringing them for another couple of weeks, and then I had to try again.

'Does Terence Boyden work there?'

'One moment please.'

A click, a pause: then, incredibly, shockingly, Terry's voice: 'Hallo?'

It was too easy. Too sudden. I nearly hung up. I sat like a fool for moments with him saying 'Hallo? Hallo?' Then I said:

'Hallo, Terry. It's Jane.'

It was now his turn to retreat into shaken silence.

'I've been—half expecting you to call. How is he?'

'Very well. He wants to see you.'

'I'll come. Don't worry. You can't imagine. . . .'

'It's all right, there's no raging hurry——'

'Isn't there? I'll be down tomorrow evening.'

'The week-end's time enough.'

'Don't you want me to come?'

I had to be honest. 'It's David who wants it, not me.'

He was hurt, I could tell; the little-boyishness was still there, unattractive in a grown man, yet affecting.

'Well. . . . I'll come whenever you tell me.'

'Come Saturday. That'll give me time to prepare him.' And myself, I thought.

He suddenly said, 'By the way, I'm married.'

'Oh?' It was no sort of shock or surprise, at first I couldn't see how it could matter. 'Well, so long as you don't bring her. That would be a bit too much to explain.'

'To her, too,' he said, with a little unexpected dryness in his voice.

'Doesn't she know?'

'No, she damn well doesn't.'

This was an appalling complication.

'Listen, Terry. Maybe you'd better not. David can get along without seeing you. You're liable to get into very hot water if you don't watch out.'

'Oh, rubbish. One afternoon——'

'If that's all it's going to be, *much* better not to come at all.'

'Were you thinking I was going to come regularly?'

I paused to think. 'I'm not sure . . . perhaps. The where's-daddy-why-doesn't-he-ever-come bit wore me down at last past the point of coherent thought. But I honestly think it would be stupid for you just to appear once and vanish into the haze again forever.'

'But I want to see him! He's mine!'

A bright, shiny, noisy alarm bell started clanging insistently in my brain.

'Haven't you any children of your own?'

'What does that mean, of my own? David's my own, isn't he?'

248

It was on the tip of my tongue to retort, 'No he bloody well is not!' but that might have confused him. 'I meant—with your wife.'

'No. She can't have any.' He gave a dry laugh. 'Do you know, I had to go through all those hideously humiliating tests because she wouldn't credit otherwise that it wasn't my fault? And all the time I was aching to tell her I had a son, but I couldn't, of course.'

'Why of course? It was all long before you met her, presumably.'

There was a pause, and then he said shortly, 'It wouldn't have mattered with her, if it had all been before she was *born*.' Whereupon, needless to say, I realized he didn't love her and that this marriage, like his first, had been a mistake; I realized, too, that there might be another reason why he had been waiting, half-dreading, half-hoping, but always dreaming that I might contact him—and fill up empty spaces in his life.

Fatal. Fatal. No.

'Terry. I'm sorry, I've changed my mind. I——' I half-choked on the pompous lie—'I don't want to endanger your marriage.'

'Don't you worry about *that*.'

'Well, I do worry about it. And I don't want to get mixed up in anything. I—I don't want David to get mixed up either, any more than he has to be. It's better for him to—lack a father, than to have one who—flits.' I felt his hurt like a living wave humming along the wires, but I had to be ruthless. 'I'm sorry, love.'

He sensed I was about to hang up, without giving him my address, and he suddenly shouted 'Jane! Jane!' down the phone at me like a drowner. 'It's not fair! I always wanted to be his father, but you never gave me a chance——' I knew that if I gave him even a minute longer, a minute in which to plead, I would weaken, if only because once, long, long ago, long before David was conceived, I loved him. So I put down the phone.

That's all, about Terry. Except that I live in dread of the day when he'll inevitably walk into Heal's and see me there, or deliberately run me to earth. I am as sure as it's possible to be, that he'll turn up one day. Now I stop to reason it out, nothing except a happy marriage and a family could have completely insured me against him. *His* marriage, I mean; but I suppose if *I* were safely immured behind the barrier of wedlock, I would feel much less vulnerable.

I wish and wish that I had never phoned him, never brought David and me back into the forefront of his mind. The danger to David is considerable. And yet . . . one day when he's older, *he* may seek Terry out. But in the meantime . . . I don't know. I just don't know. The more I watch him, the more I gain confidence as a mother, the more I realize that I am, at my very best, exactly half of what he needs. Sometimes I watch him playing with Amanda; he is quieter and gentler than she is, shares more easily, hits back less readily; and I feel proud of him; but then I wonder whether that is normal for a boy, whether he oughtn't to be more aggressive, noisier. . . . He is very affectionate; he comes to me and climbs on my knee or straight up my legs into my arms for a kiss, and I hold him tight and cuddle him, and then suddenly I put him down. Because I'm not sure, even about that. And surely my very uncertainty, my underlying doubts, whether they're psychologically justified or not, about my ordinary instincts towards him as his mother—surely they must in themselves affect him? One should be confident all the time that one is doing the right thing, and I *would* be, if only the masculine element was there as a counterbalance.

Whenever a man comes along, any man, even the new postman, who is youngish and tall, David runs to him—he used to throw his arms round every man he saw, when he was about three, until he saw it embarrassed them; now he just stands and stares, as if they exuded some aura he needed to be in. Twice I have seriously contemplated making a dead set for men-friends just in order to secure a father for David. Each time I was lucky; they did something or other that put me off them so entirely that I ceased to be able to contemplate living with them, even for David's sake—I might do it for him, even so, if only I thought I was capable of hiding my own irritation or unhappiness. But in any case it's no easy matter to find a man who is willing to father another man's son. If only John were . . . ! Oh well. If only he were normal, and more mature,

and better educated, and had other work—and were white.
. . . Just the same, he's the nearest thing to a father-figure in
David's life, and David's heedlessness of his colour or any
other thing about him has led me to reassess my own ideas.
These biases are obviously not born in us; David recognizes
him instinctively for what he is, a thoroughly good man. Oh,
rarity! Good (as Dottie said) from side to side, right through
the middle.

That's nearly all. How inconclusive it all seems! Stories
shouldn't end in the middle, but the middle is where I am—
the middle of my life (I'm thirty-four). Let me finish off with
a word about Toby. So few marriages really work these days
that it needn't surprise anyone to hear of two failed ones inside
a couple of pages. This time it's sadder because of their
children. Whistler got pregnant, according to Billie's sardonic
account, the minute Toby hung his trousers over the bedrail.
It was a girl and they called her Rachel, and then two years
later they had another girl called Carissa, which I believe is
the name of a shrub in Hebrew. Billie relayed this information
dryly, but with ill-concealed anxiety. Toby and Whistler, it
seemed, were getting caught up in Zionism. 'It's all my fault,
I had to go and force her to join the Youth Movement. . . . I
thought it might do as a framework, instead of a religion . . .
idiot that I was. But how could I guess it would take hold of
her like this? Most kids grow out of it, like Scouts and Guides.
. . . Christ! What *shall* I do if they want to emigrate to Israel?
Surely he won't be such a damn fool—what do you think,
Jane?' She always talks as if I know him better than anyone,
even though I haven't seen him for all these years. I said I had
no idea, he'd certainly never mentioned Israel to me, in fact
at that time he'd hardly seemed to think about being a Jew
in any way. 'Oh, how he's changed;' Billie said—with what
seemed to me an ironic note of disapproval. 'He's Jewish to
his backbone these days. Do you know, I believe they light
candles on Eve of Sabbath? Not when I come, of course; they
don't want to shock me with all that rubbish; but for the
children.' I was surprised she thought it rubbish; after all,
the big synagogue wedding. . . . And she wouldn't have
wanted Melissa to marry a non-Jew, would she? She wagged
her head from side to side in an unconsciously typical move-

ment. 'Oh well of course . . . that's the point where all us Jews get pretty Jewish, I suppose. But there's no need to carry it to extremes!'

And then she began to report quarrels, and once Whistler came running home with an infant daughter under each arm and stayed for a week. Toby, who was in the middle of a novel at the time, failed to come and demand their return, so in the end she went back by herself.

Since then they have been muddling along somehow, but Billie, who's at her wits' end about the situation, has recently begun saying that as it's sure to end in the divorce courts anyway, then the sooner the better, 'before Melissa conceives again during one of their innumerable reconciliations.' She admitted to me once—she'd taken me out to dinner and accidentally got a bit tight, most unusual for her—that it's mostly Whistler's fault. 'Madness to get married at that age! I was wrong, I should have encouraged them to have an affair and find out by living together that she was far, far too young and selfish and volatile to be a good wife yet. She could have been, would have been—but later, later. What a tragedy, Jane! That's what it seems to me. A tragedy.'

And Toby? Well, she says he's a wonderful father, but not such a wonderful husband. The writing obsesses him more and more. His first was good, but nothing special in the way of a popular success. The second was better, but somehow didn't get the right reviews. Then came the third, born, I could see, of his disappointment in his marriage; and did I, in that one, discover parts of myself—broken up, dispersed, reassembled as all-but-recognizable fragments of two different characters, but there? He even quoted me a couple of times. The funny, disturbing, wickedly demoralizing thing was, that both the women that had bits of me in them were very important in the life of the hero, and the hero was Toby all right, my Toby, overlaid and disguised and changed, but nonetheless the Toby I knew and remembered. . . . And that book was a best-seller.

I *don't* love him any more. I *don't* hope and dream that one day he will come to me. He is not, any longer, the father I would want for David—a man with his affections divided: how could he love my child as much as his own? But when I read that third novel I felt a clutching at the heart, that what-would-have-happened-if? feeling that is perhaps the saddest thing in the world. Toby wasn't ready for marriage either, five years ago. No doubt it wouldn't have worked any better with me. . . . He writes so maturely now; that flippant joyous putting-of-the-finger on things has jelled into wisdom and insight, even into himself. (How that book must have hurt Whistler if she understood it! She has failed him worse than I did.)

I do yearn for him a little, still. . . . Zionism and all. . . . Of course I'd be no use to him there. Oh, rubbish, what am I talking about him for? I only meant to tell what had happened to him, and here I've dropped back five, no, six years. . . . It's Billie's fault, really. She said straight out the other day that he should have married me and not Melissa. And then, damn her eyes, she had to add: 'I think he thinks so, too.'

I sat there in her office, struck dumb, not knowing what to say or think. I remember thinking, if she doesn't go on and tell me what she meant, I'll never know another moment's quiet —but I could not, for my own sake I dared not, ask the question that would have brought out the elaboration. She was sitting there like a bright-eyed, rather wicked bird, the tip of her long little-fingernail between her teeth, her eyes fixed on me, waiting . . . and I didn't ask, and she didn't go on, so now I'll never know what he said to her, if anything. . . . Or if it was just one of her bits of feminine naughtiness, dropped like a stone into a pool to stir up the water-beetles and watch the ripples she's caused.

I see I've got nowhere as a person. I haven't changed (does anyone, ever?) and I haven't even grown up in the sense that I most wanted to, of becoming strong and independent. What play or book was it, in which one spinster says wistfully to another: 'Tell me—when did you give up hope?' Jo and I use this as a catch-line every time a man leaves our lives— somehow in a perverted way it cheers us up, if only because each of us has said it about the same number of times to the other. I would like to give up hope, I'm sure all my relation-ships would be quite different if I could; just settle for being *one*, instead of this haunting feeling of being half of some double animal, the absent other half of which one keeps feeling for at one's side. And how often is Dottie's backward shadow upon me! More now than ever, seeing that it is over David too.

Was I wrong to have him? I've even asked myself that. Life is tough and getting tougher, I mean harder to succeed in without the negative virtue of impenetrable toughness, and I see no signs of this in David . . . which is probably my fault.

In one of his last letters before his quiet, unobtrusive death, Father remarked: 'Don't make the error of bringing David up to be too sensitive and gentle. *Let* him stamp on caterpillars and play with toy tommy-guns and bash other children and kill little furry things with a catapult. Ah, don't look so horrified, my darling. He's a male, and that's our world; he must train for it, or he will shrivel up inside himself and die at the things he'll have to see and do later if he wants to survive.'

Darling Father. He knew what he was talking about. He once told me that when he was in the trenches in the First War, he felt sick every time one of his pals killed a rat, although he loathed the things. The other, greater horrors, the human deaths, he could never talk about. . . . His vulnerability punished him all his life.

But I swear I don't know how to blunt that quality in David which I love so much. The trouble is, I simply can't *want* to. . . . Whenever I read that letter of Father's, I can only think desperately to myself: 'He was right about so much. But about this, he's got to be wrong.'